Copyright © Ted O'Connell 2020
All rights reserved. No part of this book may be reproduced or transmitted in any form or by
any means electronic or mechanical including photocopying recording or any information
storage and retrieval system without permission in writing from the Publisher.

Library of Congress Cataloging-in-Publication Data

Names: O'Connell, Ted, 1968- author.
Title: K : a novel / Ted O'Connell.
Description: Santa Fe, NM : SFWP, [2020] | Summary: "Professor Francis
   Kauffman has unwittingly landed himself in prison where he's faced with
   an insurmountable task: execute a fellow inmate. Charged with igniting a
   political insurrection among his students at a university in Beijing,
   Kauffman is sent to the notorious Kun Chong Prison, where his existence
   grows stranger by the hour as he struggles with the weight of his
   imprisonment and his incurable need to write about it in a place where
   art is forbidden, and the inmates must act as executioners. As cultures
   clash in his filthy, crowded cell, it soon becomes clear that he's
   destined for a labor camp…or worse. At turns surreal and brutally
   honest, this literary thriller spans continents as Kauffman reflects on
   the turbulent family history that brought him to China, where he leads a
   solitary, expat life of soulless insurance jobs and all-night writing
   binges, only to wind up fighting a battle for his life inside the walls
   of Kun Chong"— Provided by publisher.
Identifiers: LCCN 2019023440 (print) | LCCN 2019023441 (ebook) | ISBN
   9781733777735 (trade paperback) | ISBN 9781733777742 (ebook)
Subjects: GSAFD: Suspense fiction.
Classification: LCC PS3615.C5838 K3 2020 (print) | LCC PS3615.C5838
   (ebook) | DDC 813/.6—dc23
LC record available at https://lccn.loc.gov/2019023440
LC ebook record available at https://lccn.loc.gov/2019023441

Published by SFWP
369 Montezuma Ave. #350
Santa Fe, NM 87501
(505) 428-9045
www.sfwp.com

For the strong women

Julie
Amelia
Ellen
Madeleine

"For I was indeed stolen out of the land of the Hebrews; and here also I have done nothing that they should put me in the dungeon."

—Genesis 40

"Our prisons are different than prisons in the past—each prison is actually a school, but also a factory or a farm."

—Mao Zedong

The Burden

I don't know why we don't eat with the other prisoners on the first floor. The guards carry our food upstairs using an old metal burden with four shelves to a side. The load is rather heavy, and there's a servile look to this method of bringing prisoners food, and lots of it. Apparently we are supposed to suffer but not starve. No doubt we are being fattened up for some kind of labor assignment in one of the far-flung provinces of the West, but nobody knows for sure. None of the men in my cell has lived here longer than three months, which suggests our stay at Kun Chong is only temporary.

Be that as it may, why shouldn't a prisoner be the one hunched under the burden, struggling up the stairs? The guards never show an ounce of shame in their labor. They grunt a little, sigh as they shrug off the yoke, but they don't complain. No one ever thanks them. Food is not that heavy, but the trays are industrial-grade stainless steel and the chains connecting one shelf to another are made of burly iron links.

I would like to ask the guards how much the burden weighs, or see if they'd let me give it a try, but I haven't spoken a word of Chinese since arriving here a month ago. From the first, I pretended not to know Chinese. I don't know exactly why I chose not to speak. The answer may be deeper than I know, some brainstem itch or a childhood memory involving a cruel babysitter or a scary cartoon. On the November day that I arrived from the adjudication center, battered and wasted after twenty-six hours of interrogation, I was in no mood to talk to anybody in any language. Talking, after all, had got me into trouble. And it goes without saying that torture, while it can make a man say almost anything in the heat of the moment, can make a man dead quiet in the aftermath.

I now live with seven other men in a large cell with a common toilet and a vile wash basin. Our room is four-by-six meters with a single high window looking east toward the yard, two identical locked doors facing north and south, and a wide sliding gate at the entrance. Bunk beds occupy the corner spots, and a large wooden table stands in the center of the room. There are two radiators that run full blast, and when it gets too hot we adjust the temperature by climbing onto the wash basin and sliding the window open a few inches, which is a tricky move considering the bars. This helps somewhat with the stench of prisoners. Every day we smell bile, shit, tooth decay, and a fetor like rotten onions from our armpits, the rank hint of semen in our loins, fungus from our toes. Even our ears stink. When we do shower, about once a week, the soap is a raspberry sherbet-colored block that smells like the renderings of a diesel tractor.

But today it is raining and the breeze coursing through the propped-open window seems fresh compared to the smog of Beijing. I sit in a wooden chair to the left of the entrance, looking out through the bars into the corridor, listening to the cold hiss of the radiators. This is how I do my writing. No pen. No brush. No ink stone. Only memory. I start each session by murmuring from the first line to the most recent line, every word I have composed in the best order, with revisions, until I'm positive I'll lose nothing. I must have it all down without mistakes before adding another line or two, sometimes an entire page on a good day. Two pages is the most I've done in one sitting, but that was a week ago in one of those bouts of ecstasy that any artist experiences from time to time.

Other than a tits and pussy drawing etched into the underside of the sink, I haven't come across any art made by prisoners or guards—

for we are permitted no art at Kun Chong. No writing, no drawing, no films, no poetry, and no music other than officially-sanctioned propaganda. If a guy starts humming a pop song, he gets poked in the ribs with a bamboo goad.

But I don't mean to sound like some uppity Westerner badmouthing the Chinese, as I love the Chinese. Most of them. As a foreigner in this country, getting your blood drawn at the clinic or buying a subway pass, you come to realize that every cold exchange is not for lack of love. Life is a machine and this particular machine has 1.5 billion parts. The people mean no disrespect, and I feel the same toward my jailers. They cut my hair with dull scissors. They jab my scalp looking for lice. They set food trays on the table with an animal clank. I could speak Chinese with them, but I don't.

The rain softens. I hear a factory going in the distance. I hear the women playing featherball next door and now the guards scolding them for yelping after a good play. The female inmates are under strict orders to speak softly and not excite the men, and by the timbre of their voices it seems the guards have draped some weighty fabric across their bars. The women live to the north in a room that we assume is the same size and configuration as ours; the guards live to the south in a room that was once the institutional library, and all rooms are connected by doors that are locked. Women and books: farther because they are closer. I shut my eyes and listen to the radiator and the muffled punting of the featherball as I attempt to work out a long, concise sentence that explains our sleeping arrangement.

We have four mattresses to eight men, which means we alternate nights sleeping on the floor and in a bed. I've heard men complain that it wasn't always this way. Before I arrived, an inmate would get two consecutive nights in a bed every twelve days, and while the second night on a cot must have seemed luxurious, something can be said for the simplicity of the new rotation. A guy never wakes up wondering, "Was that my first night in bed, or the second?"

Sometimes I feel guilty for not talking to the other guys, like I've lost faith in humanity, but I'm not the pessimist everyone thinks I am. I love people. I hate some. I am tempted every day to join the conversation. The men talk about duck blood soup and medicine wine, about which herbs improve circulation, how to tell whether or not a restaurant is using recycled cooking oil. I would like to ask them about folk remedies for my cough. There are days when it would be nice to put in my two cents about Party corruption, or weigh in on that story of the famous doctor from Tsing Hua University, discoverer of the bird flu vaccine, who at age sixty was forced to retire in accordance with Chinese law and after publicly upbraiding the archaic policy was sentenced to two years of forced labor. Would we ever see him at Kun Chong, the famous Bird Doctor?

I miss giving a full-throated laugh to a joke, though I don't really like jokes. I miss saying, "That would be like playing a lute to a cow" in a strong Hunan accent, if only to show off my Chinese like I used to do on campus, and before that, at the office on Jinrong Street. As it is, when one of my cellmates says something funny I have to play the role of the guy who laughs at a joke he doesn't understand.

One of these days I'll shake hands with a man and say, "I am Francis Kauffman: teacher, writer, former policy analyst for the China Life and Casualty Company. I come from Berlin, I come from Chicago."

My cellmates think I meditate. They don't know that I am writing to the *dop, dop, dop* of water leaking from the ceiling pipe. Today is the first day of rain in a long time, and the air outside smells as if snow is on the way. I close my eyes and move through language like a ship through ice floes, with that kind of resolve and fear. One of the men shouts, "Snow! We have snow! Look, snow!" and the others rush to the window and tug at his pant leg, trying to bring him off the sink so they can have a look. Standing on the sink is the only way we can access the high window that looks out into the yard. Here stands the incomparable Fang Feng, former investment big shot and tennis champion. He insists on being called by his last name, like some international pop star or frat boy. Fang looks like the kind of Han Chinese you see on subway videos in advertisements for "All Mine Cologne" or "Sexy Chocolate." Angular jaw. Handsome. The kind of mean eyes that women can't help falling for.

His Nikes put little gray tread marks on the porcelain. He reaches up and shimmies loose a four-inch piece of hardware from the window. The metal is rusted and flat, with three holes. He laughs and we all laugh because it is so easy to find weapons in this place.

I know almost nothing about prisons in other parts of the world, but I would hazard that here at Kun Chong we have comparatively more opportunities to fashion the tools of our demise. It's as though the invisible hand of Confucius will keep us in line, or it's just another example of the lax attitude toward safety in this country, as with seatbelts, stray electrical wires, smoking, and "tofu construction" in earthquake-prone cities. We eat with green plastic chopsticks. Hard plastic. It would be easy to file them to a deadly point. As for our metal food trays, they would never be allowed in an Illinois penitentiary. In Joliet they probably serve food on flimsy rubber trays made of some polymer that is safe even for toddlers. Here, the trays are heavy enough to inflict a fatal head injury. I don't know how I could make a dagger out of a food tray, but I suspect I've only been here long enough to touch the tip of my creativity. Not that I would ever kill anyone. It is only this wicked environment that puts my imagination to work making weapons from everyday objects like bedsprings or the cord that runs along the edge of our mattresses. Our faucet stem, loose as it is, could be ripped out of the sink in a moment by any man of above-average rage.

After Fang hops down from the sink, a few other prisoners take turns climbing up and looking out the window. Snowflakes swing down. I don't need to see the landing of the flakes to know how they kiss the ground and dissolve into nothing.

"I should have never looked," says Wu Kaiming, clambering down from the sink, skinny arms and all.

"Punished by your own desire," says Brother Gao. "At least that's what the Buddha would say."

Fang motions with the piece of metal as though to stab himself in his own modest Buddha belly.

I smell pork fat and rice and that aggravating peppercorn that makes my mouth numb—though I shouldn't complain. Prisoners elsewhere in the world sup on wormy milk, moldy bread, or nothing at all. They pay for it with their very own livers and kidneys. Bone marrow if the match is right. Our leaders know us. They know we must be well nourished to be good workers, and though no word has come regarding our future, it is hard to imagine we won't be put to work.

Between the bars, gazing at an oblique angle down the hall, I see a guard's boots tapping to the rhythm of his lunch. His leg twitches as he eats. Some men never lose this tic. It starts in the primary school years, the knee bobbing, whether you grew up rich or poor, gentile or Jew, capitalist roader or communist liberator, a spark in your nervous system. I hear the ticking of his chopsticks against the metal tray. He gets the same food as us, the only difference being that he can go for seconds. I know I should be hungry, but today I don't have much appetite.

I sit and listen to one of my cellmates snoring, another smoking, two playing cards, another pulling the top off his cricket cage with the faintest clang, another shaking the *Kun Chong Daily*, and another silent as a gecko. This last man, tan with a twisted face and dirty fingernails, seems to have done something very bad, surely a murder or rape. The men treat him as an animal, and I don't mean a pet. He is more like the pig grazing in the garbage dump. The rat in the alley. I would rather be a pet than this man. He has beautiful hair in spite of his unpleasant face and gnarled hands. He must be in his late thirties or forties, it really is hard to tell with some of these laborers. They always look older. His hair is pretty enough for a fashion magazine, thick as a marten's pelt, shiny like coffee beans.

In my darker moments, I look at his eyes—the right pupil is enlarged from some injury—and wonder if he is really much different than an animal. Because he is the only one besides me who does not read the propaganda books piled on the crate, we assume he cannot read. Let's say he has an IQ of 70. Through no fault of his own, his abstract reasoning is limited. Nor can he truly enjoy fine art. Would it be a sin to say the man is more animal than me? This is the kind of comment that could get me fired from any number of jobs in civil society, not to mention putting off friends of all stripes. What I mean to say is that if I'm perfectly honest, I can admit that Xu Xuo seems less than human. The blank look in the eyes. He seems to think of nothing. He lies on his cot staring at the ceiling, waiting to be nothing. He is sentenced to death for a crime so terrible as to be unknown in our circle.

I once took part in a psychology study where I was asked to view a series of faces belonging to people of various ages, races, and walks of life, all dressed the same. The male subjects had the same dull haircut, the females the same bob. Our task was to look at each headshot for three seconds and guess the individual's education level. I can't remember the purpose of the study, or maybe I was never told. At any rate, the researcher later told me it was "creepy" that I was the only respondent to identify all of the subjects' education levels correctly. I wasn't the only teacher in the bunch, either, as she had controlled for this.

And what of Xu Xuo?

I have seen his brown uncircumcised penis at the toilet. I have seen the birthmark on his backside. As a naked man he is not bad looking. He has smoother skin and less body hair than me. It is the animal dumbness with which he eats his food and puffs his pillow that gets to me, the way he crouches on the ground and does nothing. In another life, if I were not in prison, maybe I'd be kind to him if for no other reason than to cool my guilt. But here, I don't care. The other day when Xu Xuo made one of his dog-like gestures to Wu Kaiming, wanting to have a look at the cricket in the clay pot, Wu Kaiming, who is not a mean man, said, "Don't even look at that cricket. You shouldn't even be allowed to hear his song at night."

"You're a dead man," said Fang. "You can't hear anything in death."

I could have smiled at Xu Xuo to lighten the mood, but I didn't. I don't. The lifespan of a cricket is only sixty days, which expressed as a fraction with a numerator of $60d$ and a denominator of eternity (e) is no time at all. Consider then the man who lives sixty years. The man who lives $\frac{60y}{e}$ contributes little more to the universe than this cricket, whether or not he has studied Archimedes, Flaubert, or the Torah. I don't have any illusions about my time here. I only went into teaching so I could have time to write and because I hated office work, not because I believed in the fundamental goodness of knowledge. If I believed in the fundamental goodness of knowledge, that would mean I believed educated people were better people. Nor did I enter the profession, as my students often supposed, to make life easier for them. Or to make them rich. Even the fortunate sons and daughters of civil servants won't get through life without smelling other people's shit.

My cellmates have agreed that everyone should try and do his business between 8:30 and 9 in the morning. In this way, rather than getting bombed intermittently throughout the day, we undergo a blitzkrieg of foul odors for about forty minutes. Sometimes a man can barely make it to the appointed hour. Other times, he gives what he can and lives the rest of the day half-satisfied. The men encourage one another to eat as much fiber as possible, and if one man admits that rice stops him up, he is told to avoid rice.

"The problem is, I love rice," says Yu, just as the guards are bringing our food.

"Drink lots of water."

"Then I won't sleep through the night."

"This is prison. Who sleeps through the night?"

"I do, sometimes."

"And what about Brother Gao?" says Kuku, the college kid. "He can sleep with a rat crawling on his face."

"Don't remind me," says Brother Gao. "You'll ruin it for me. I'll start worrying at night." Gao is a little brown man with limpid eyes and twisty ears that sit low on his head, making him look like a cuddly monkey.

"It's worse to think about women. Sometimes I think about them and barely sleep a wink."

"What does the American think?"

"He's not American. I think he's from Europe."

"…think about what?"

"You speak a little English. Go ahead and ask him."

"About what?"

"Ask him if he thinks about women."

"If I ask him that, he'll wonder if I think he's a fag. I don't want to bring it up. Let's just pretend we're all straight, even you."

The other men laugh.

"I think he's not gay. But he's only very strange."

"If you ask me, I think he can understand every word we say. I think he speaks Chinese."

Down the corridor, the guard is singing a pop song. For a measure or two, I'm really not aware if he is singing in Chinese or English. The wind scrapes against the building. Yellow dust sweeps through the bars. We can hear the white noise of an auger or conveyer belt on the other side of the prison complex.

"The Europeans can suck my mother's cunt. We Chinese invented gun powder. The compass. The rudder. We invented paper and the printing press. What did the Europeans invent?"

"The plague."

The men wait for me to flinch, to speak. I keep my eyes closed as though locked in meditation. A guard staggers into the room and sets down the burden. I come to the table and we all eat together in one sloppy rectangle, our necks bending low to our troughs, chopsticks ticking, lips smacking. I'm clumsy with my chopsticks on purpose, dropping gristle and rice like a dumb foreigner. After lunch, the men get out their mahjong pieces and start a game, using the board they have etched into the concrete floor. Xu Xuo shuffles over to have a look at the game, then turns away like a sniffing boar.

Sometimes I feel sick for my thoughts. If I happen to learn that Xu Xuo has raped four girls, would I still feel guilty for looking into his eyes and seeing less "there" than when I look into the tawny eyes of a gorilla? We have all, I assume, experienced that moment of rapture at the zoo when we make eye contact with a primate and feel the presence of God. It's like crossing some spiritual divide between the human and animal worlds. But to cross the divide going the other way, to see the animal in the human, is reprehensible. Xu is a common surname, held by a Ming dynasty scholar, a famous painter, and a Taiwanese popstar named Barbie. His given name, Xuo, is nothing I've heard before and even the native speakers are confused by it. In lighter moments I call him Barbie Shoes. In darker moments I want the guards to haul him away and carry out his sentence, put his eyes into another world so I don't have to see them in mine.

And here comes the chubby guard right on cue.

He hands a slip of paper to Wu Kaiming (the cricket man) who reads it, his face registering dread or sadness, something too heavy to speak. He wants somebody else to read it to the group, so he turns to Brother Gao. Just as Gao is springing up from his crouch, Fang snatches the paper for himself. He climbs up to the sink, his Nikes straddling the grubby porcelain sides, standing not as before with his back to us, but facing us, looking down on us. The effect is like those extreme low-angle shots in early German films. He reads the note silently, grabs a shock of hair, and says, "Fuck!"—sneering at the dead man on the cot.

Xu Xuo is biting his thumbnail.

"What does it say?" says Brother Gao.

"It says we are responsible for carrying out Xu Xuo's sentence. Us. The inmates. We have to do it."

Red Flower

I should explain how I ended up teaching English to unlikely counter-revolutionaries. Let me be clear that I came to the university because I wanted a life of writing and thinking—not so I could become a radical professor. Anyone in a free society can read about that little bump in Chinese history when the Painted Sky Nuclear Power Plant leaked radiation and three banks failed in the same week, "The Big Meltdown" as it came to be known, with its spate of protests and peasant insurrections and WikiLeaks and magisterial suicides—followed by the so-called "Red Flower Revolution" that never amounted to more than a sloppy social media campaign to bind factory workers, Tibetans, Uyghurs, students, coal miners, and middle-class investors in a common cause. A CNN cameraman got killed when a tear gas canister slammed into his head. Seven protesters got trampled to death in Beijing, including a thirteen-year-old boy.

The government flinched but kept a firm hand on the rudder. The middle-class types angry about losing their retirement accounts were allowed to "stroll" in the streets until they got bored, whereas ethnic rabble rousers out West got crushed with bloody swiftness. A very unlucky number of activists and lawyers (44) got detained/beaten/spirited away. A boy from Peking University got sentenced to four years of forced labor for wearing a t-shirt emblazoned with "Charter 20." One hundred Scientologists got locked up for meeting in public.

A journalist who called for the reunification of the two Koreas won himself a meeting with the secret police. A poet here, a painter there. A mill worker. The stories are nothing new. The blackmailing of a prominent United States senator to grease the extradition of dissident rocker Billy Bao Chun hardly surprised anyone.

But I'm getting ahead of myself, as all of this happened after I was taken from the university. I only want to point out that my shining young business majors were never going to be among the dissidents. They were bright square students of e-commerce and finance. They had scored in the top five percent on their national examination, or they had been given a leg-up by virtue of their ethnic group, and had come to Capital City University to make their parents proud and eventually land a good job. They wanted to be part of a system, not against it, and the shortest path to a BMW was not by marching in the streets for displaced peasants or abused factory workers.

My students just wanted to get good grades and adopt silly English names like Panda, Vanilla, Coco, and Gingerella. I tried to keep a straight face when they introduced themselves as "Joker" or "Lioness." In a moment of teaching passion, I would skate across the dusty floor of Room 201 and come to a stop right before a pretty girl wearing fuzzy pink earmuffs, and say, "Enid, what do you think?" The floors in the School of International Business were slippery, bare concrete like the floor of this prison. Each classroom had a front and a rear door leading to the hall, but invariably one of the doors was overlaid with a kind of cage bolted to the jamb. The exterior windows had bars, that was nothing new for China, but even the high interior window was barred. The thick gray paint called to mind the subways of my childhood.

This was the oldest university in China. Many of the buildings had outdated lighting, scarred blackboards, and sibilating heating systems. In winter, most students kept their coats on. The huge campus had been cut in two in the middle of last century when the ring road system was designed, and as a result you now had an east campus and a west campus. A giant six-lane road with an overpass cut through the university so that students rushing to class with their greasy *bings* had to walk under a grimy underpass. They would dodge underground for a time, then bop back up to a sunlit world of flower beds, rock gardens, sculptures, obligatory plaques to the obligatory dead, drooping pine trees, and prolific poplars that were showered every fall with a salty-smelling pesticide.

The trees, the trees! Cap U boasted some of the finest arbors in the city. Yes, their leaves were eternally covered in smut, but they were living trees all the same. There was so much concrete, steel, and glass everywhere that it was easy to forget nature, and after a long day in the city running errands, say, renewing my passport or pricing fake Turkish rugs at the silk market, it always felt soothing to walk among the foliage back to my apartment. I never learned the names of those pine trees with the floppy tops and rangy limbs with short clusters of needles, but they were the stuff of watercolor paintings and the best Chinese poetry.

On a snowy day, I could look out from the fourth floor of the Foreign Experts Building and gaze at a copse of white-coated beauties in the courtyard, their dark-green color almost black against the white building across the courtyard. In summer, especially when the weather got hot, I would walk up to a tree, tear off a cone, and let the sticky stuff linger on my fingers because it reminded me of my childhood in Germany before we moved to Chicago.

In prison, you can't get close to a tree. The only sap on your fingers is of dubious origin.

On campus, students could buy necessities at jam-packed little grocery stores or use *ba ba*'s credit card to purchase an iPhone at the licensed university Apple store. They could eat on the cheap at an outdoor food stand, or use their campus card at the student canteen. Of course there were walls surrounding both campuses and at each gate young guards in ill-fitting uniforms stood waiting for their moment.

They didn't do much, mostly checked parking passes and waved cars through the checkpoint, but one day they would get their chance: today ogling girls in mini-skirts, tomorrow chasing a dissident through the alley.

There was everywhere in China, but especially at universities, this contrast of the old and the new. You would sit in a state-of-the-art lecture hall enjoying the most synesthetic presentation imaginable on the South-to-North Water Diversion Project or the Eternal Rainbow Power Plant, which aimed to be the ultimate recycler of plutonium waste, and afterward take a leak in the foulest of bathrooms, where you'd turn with cold dripping hands for a towel or an electric dryer only to find wires poking out of a hole in the wall. Mocking you. A student who had scored a zillion points on the *gaokao* and who could write circles around most British or American students in English lived in a roach-infested dorm room no better than army barracks. On the tiled campus roads, where no rules safeguarded the rights of pedestrians, Lexus SUVs would overtake tricycles pedaled by toothless men hauling cabbages to university kitchens. Every student had an Apple laptop or a comparable knock-off. At one school within the university, students were encouraged to explore the far reaches of cyberspace with every gadget conceivable; at another school, computers were banned in the freshman dorms. When it was time to spray the trees with pesticides—and when wasn't a good time?—a tanker would come through blaring the first few bars of "Happy Birthday" as a warning to all campus residents to close all windows, close all windows, while men wearing coolie hats and cloth masks trained their hoses on the trees, water gushing to the birthday music—but never the second part of "Happy Birthday" where the melody leaps an octave, which made the chiming so much like those feeble ice cream trucks in America that could never quite finish a tune.

We seemed to be sampling some kind of Mao-era austerity, with the bars everywhere, the chipped blackboards, and the grubby strings that we pulled to switch on the lights. The cold concrete floors seemed totally incongruous with the students' iPhones and sparkly boots. The blue hum of the overhead projectors and the futuristic chimes of the Zuckerberg computers reminded me that in spite of the backward ideas that had circulated in these rooms in generations past, we were moving forward. Yes, it would take time. But the room would get renovated, the blackboards replaced by whiteboards, the students' odd little iPads replaced by woRens, and in a few years my kids with the funny English names would be the pistons of the world's most explosive economy.

One spring day at the end of the term, I shut off the lights and paused to reflect on the year's teaching and as I felt my gut working on lunch I swore I could feel the ghosts of the Great Leap Forward and the Cultural Revolution. Probably what I felt was no more real than what a tourist feels standing in a yard at Dachau or a slave-trading plaza in South Carolina—a bogus sense of terror—but who's to say what emotions are real or fake? When I mentioned this haunted feeling to a few of my students, the girls giggled, and when I tried to explain further what I meant, they said flatly, "It's just a classroom. They're all boring like this. It isn't like in your country. Where are you from, Mr. Kauffman?"

"Chicago and Berlin. Why is there a cage over the rear door of our classroom?"

"If there is a door, it is meant to be locked."

"But this is not a door, this is a cage."

"We don't know," they said, shouldering their bags and strutting down the hallway on their high heels. In their wake, I could smell jasmine perfume and the eggy street food they'd had for breakfast.

I suppose to them the bars had become invisible. And if one of the students had awoken one morning with the goal of ridding the school of all penal motifs, she would have had a tough time finding who was in charge to remove them. The bureaucratic structure at the university was maddening. I worked under the umbrella of The Language Institute but had an office in the School for the Enhancement of English Acumen but delivered my classes in the School of International Business; and when a decision needed to be made as to some English prerequisite or supply request, I often didn't know who my boss was. I answered to three different deans with the surnames Wang, Wong, and Chong. One dean was the academic dean, the other was the Party dean, and the scope of their duties was only vaguely understood.

No matter. I was there to teach. I had given up a fancy office building and a high salary to exercise my mind.

In a country where Tibet was not discussed in groups larger than five and "June 4" got sandblasted off the walls of cyberspace, I was assigned, in addition to my duties as a writing instructor, a class called Debate and Critical Thinking. My course convener, a small brilliant man with salt-and-pepper hair and a face that looked like it would never wrinkle, encouraged me to exercise the students' critical thinking skills. Professor Bao had a son who spoke fluent German and was studying dark matter at Leiden University. Bao was no dummy himself. He could explain the difference between transitive and intransitive verbs with examples in three languages, or yammer about predicate nominatives while swiping his card in the cafeteria line. Over lunch at the faculty canteen, our subsidized meals costing about three dollars, Bao would shovel pork and rice into his mouth (with the same green chopsticks we prisoners now use) and rail at the generic quality of his students' reasoning.

"Ask the class to write a response to any question, and you will get about three answers. Maybe a little variation, but not much. Eight students will say x; eight students will say the opposite of x; and eight students will say y."

He had a habit of making a loud ticking noise with his chopsticks. He would pause mid-speech, clack his sticks, and tell me the stupid things his students had said that morning.

" 'It is high time the Chinese government take action to stop vehemently the westernization of Chinese traditional culture.' These students are among the brightest in the country. They scored very high on the *gaokao* in order to be placed in this university."

Bao, in spite of his brilliance, had trouble making the "th" sound. Had he taken my course as a young man, I would have gotten him to say "there" instead of "zere" and "healthy" instead of "helssy" but in the end I preferred that he sounded exactly like himself and not some TV weatherman from Ohio.

"Or take ziss one," he said. "When I ask my students about what should be done about the Mai Tian Food Company putting toxic elements in their flour, they can only say the government should do a better job enforcing the law. But if I say, we do not have a body of laws, we only have men who carry out the law, the students insist that we have laws. In countless cases I give them, they think they have a constitution that protects them. Do you know why the university forces them to take thirty-seven hours of compulsory classes a week? So they have no time to think. They are so busy thinking, they have no time to think!"

In my three years at Cap U, we had thus far debated whether or not to ban smoking in restaurants, whether to allow gay marriage, to raise tax rates on the wealthy, and the extent to which business and ethics were compatible. I had asked students to consider whether the ambitious schedule at the School of International Business encouraged competent students but did not cultivate creative thinkers. As I had run out of topics, I asked Professor Bao if it would be all right to let the students debate the one child policy, the Facebook policy, the five religions policy. He said I had nothing to worry about. I was a foreigner.

So I went into the classroom the following semester and asked the students to argue whether the government should tear down the firewall, whether the one child policy while beneficial from a sustainability perspective was anathema to human rights. "A-N-A-T-H-E-M-A," I said. "Put it on your list for next week's quiz." We had spirited discussions about *guanxi*. I taught them the words "pernicious" and "sedition" and directed little skits that had the slapstick quality of Yiddish theater.

Let me say that I did not have a class of natural-born revolutionaries in any of the sections I taught. About half the students believed that censorship of the internet was necessary to maintain social harmony. Other students believed that not owning private property, even if it meant that a peasant could be kicked off his land at any time, was good for the country as a whole. There were students who were angry about corruption and smart enough only to criticize the latest convicted official that the government wanted us to roundly condemn. And there were some quiet students who knew what was what, knew the extent of the latest purges, but they entertained no illusions about changing the system. One girl named Candy simply decided to leap from her fifth-floor dorm room on a rainy Tuesday morning in March. They covered her with a pink quilt. Some of her classmates placed yellow flowers by the metal grate where she had landed. Twenty-four hours later the flowers were gone and after three days of sadness things got back to normal. Students were thereafter instructed not to take the English moniker "Candy."

I fed them questions that were safe—"Should the university put a halt to mandatory military training for sophomores?"—but edgy enough to make for good discussion. I asked them to debate whether the double major in English and business was too ambitious, too stressful, less likely to produce innovative thinkers.

When did I cross the line?

In my fourth year I started sending students online news articles that were blocked in mainland China, say, a story about peasants in Anhui province getting bumped off their land with paltry compensation, while a Party official received a fat kickback from developers. Nothing new there. Some of my students were curious about international perspectives, so I'd send them an article or two, and they'd reply, "This is so inspiring. Thank you for the articles! I definitely will take it into account."

Then there was an earthquake in Guiyang province and as with previous quakes, the autopsy of the buildings revealed more tofu construction. Another journalist was silenced. Another got roughed up and all I did was cut and paste a story from *The Australian* called "Another Quake, Another Coverup" and send it to a few students. I had a VPN. I could sit in my room in the Foreign Experts Building and read one version of what was going on in China. Maybe it wasn't the perfect truth, but it wasn't a lie of silence or censorship. The Western media were slanted in their own way, terribly anti-China in many respects—and yet it was worth pointing out to students that while the headline in the *San Francisco Chronicle* read "Seven Killed in Chinese Coal Mine," the *China Daily* headline read "Two Workers Rescued After Mine Collapse." Who wasn't telling the truth?

The first articles I sent were hardly radical. I didn't understand why the government was blocking them. A Costa Coffee company was denied a business permit because the proposed site sat too close to the Temple of Heaven, but the Chinese-owned Mr. Li's fast food chain wound up in the same retail space. The daughter of a party secretary got busted for cocaine possession. Another party official got caught with his virtual pants down when it was discovered he had 113 pornographic videos downloaded to his government computer. A Guangdong deputy minister admitted to lavishing luxury gifts on twenty-five mistresses so he was duly purged. The first public execution in fifty years took place in the western province of Xinjiang. An outspoken cancer researcher died mysteriously from complications due to acute radiation exposure. An online peer-to-peer investment company known as Wise Uncle got caught running a 7.2 billion dollar Ponzi scheme. One after another I cut, pasted, clicked, sometimes without bothering to check the source. As time went on and students started getting more information from microblogs, I was often the last one to know about a particular news story. Landslide hazard on Rain Mountain? What hazard? And what about the story of the elementary school principal who put rat poison in a second grader's yogurt? Was it true?

Perhaps I was too curious. Had I stuck to the insurance business rather than the dark matter of storytelling, I would have lived a typical expat life of shopping at Jenny Lou's on Saturdays and visiting a prostitute once a year. More to the point, I would have never landed in Kun Chong had I not met Vesuvius and Queena.

For three years I had a special student-teacher relationship with these girls, the kind of bond that only comes along once or twice in a teaching career. Education at its best has this kind of reciprocity, love, and abiding respect. Though I first came across them in my Business English class three years before my arrest, I got to know them best in the worker's canteen on the east campus of the university. Every Tuesday night, I would sit at a table for a few hours, and students who wanted help with their English could bring me an essay, a poem, a speech, and in turn they would help me with my Chinese. Some nights I would get twelve students, some nights only four, but for two years firm I could always count on my two girls, that is, until their senior year when they became occupied with job applications and handsome underground poets. But I'm getting ahead of myself.

Vesuvius was from a village in Guangdong province. Her parents ran a small hardware store on the outskirts of a factory town. She was a pretty girl, not stunning in the way of some Cap City students who could make you stop chewing your food, but beautiful in the way of the spirit. She was no alabaster Han Chinese; she was a brown ethnic with apple cheeks and brilliant white teeth. When you see a photograph of a ruddy Hopi woman with high cheekbones and almond eyes and you think, *She looks Asian, the land bridge hypothesis must be true!* you are looking at Vesuvius.

When I asked how she had picked her name, she said in a thick accent, "I choose it because I like volcano!" She was smart. She had the kind of mind that could overcome inferior schooling and poor nutrition and was precisely the sort of person my father would have pointed to as evidence of self-determination and the pointlessness of social engineering. When she came to the university, she had trouble making the "n" sound. The "m" sound came out instead so that in certain combinations where the "n" sound was prominent, "name" would sound like "maim," and "never" like "mever," and so on.

She had two brothers, one of whom was in the military and had been forced to put down a peasant protest in Sichuan province in spite of his sympathy with the *laobaixing*, or common people. Their homes were going to be razed to make room for a highway, and the soldier boys went into town with clubs and mace and helmets, and who knows what they did? Vesuvius had no idea if her brother had shot a man or merely pushed back the crowd with a baton. She told me the story with a sigh, with her pretty blinking eyes and that searching look of trying to find the right words in English.

I remember chewing a wood ear mushroom and leaning in close to her words, which smelled of tooth decay. The Youth League was adjourning their meeting at a round table in the corner, stuffing iPads into sparkling bags and inserting ear buds, jangling keys to their fancy cars. All the boys were over six-feet tall, all of the girls lithe. I said, "Has your brother questioned anything?"

"It's not a big deal. I think it happens a lot."

What she knew was that 500 peasants had marched through the main street of the village banging pots and drums, some of them carrying gasoline bombs and firecrackers, and that once the bulldozers ceased dozing and the tear gas went fluttering, the clan dispersed. It's easy to imagine the tangle of bicycles and three-wheeled scooters, the useless swinging of gardening tools.

I tried to search the incident on the internet but nothing came up. Then, one night at a hutong party near the tea market, I met a self-proclaimed political poet who brought me outside to smoke a cigarette and tell me what he knew of the deaths at Zhong Mountain. Fifteen people shot. Twenty injured and thirty detained, many of them beaten in captivity. One guy got run over by a bulldozer. As in most hutongs, the walls were a hue of gray that appears blue in the frail light. Perhaps it was the wine or the sweep of fog in the night, but I remember that fluid, Picasso blue as one remembers the taste of blood on the tongue.

The poet's name was Woody, or Wu Di, and like me he was a big fan of Neruda, Plath, and Milosz—and we both agreed that the name Cseslaw sounded a bit like the Chinese word for "toilet." As he fiddled with a cigarette lighter he told me again, perhaps too freely, that he was an activist. (The shrewd reader will question, earlier than I did, what kind of Chinese man introduces himself as a "political poet" to a perfect stranger?) I asked him how he managed to burrow his way through this land of censors and philistines, to say nothing of the secret police.

"I'm not even using any social networking. It's too easy for the government to track us these days. So we're using poems. They are short, they rhyme, everybody can remember them, but they contains the truth. It is our wish that nothing gets lost. I mean, of the truth. People had better know what happened in essence."

He took a drag from his Baisha and looked up at a persimmon tree set against the starless sky. "Can you follow a poem in Chinese?" he said.

I nodded and listened to the lyrics. He recited them again and by the third time I could say the poem out loud.

"*Hen hao*," he said, *Very good*. "Most people need to hear it four times. Many of us believe that on upwards of two million Chinese know this poem. They know what happened at Zhong Mountain."

"My student Vesuvius doesn't know. Her brother was one of the soldiers. It wasn't reported in the foreign press, and he didn't tell her what really happened."

"Fuck the foreign press. Vesuvius will know this poem. But she and everyone else must promise not to write it down. I don't know why I trust you, but I do. You seem old, as if you have lived longer than your years. You must be a good teacher. You have a good memory, and your Chinese is excellent. How did you get so good? Most big-noses are hopeless when it comes to learning our language."

"I came here as an exchange student a long time ago. All I did was study Chinese and flirt with girls. I sort of got addicted to both."

A worry cut across his face. He took a drag from his cigarette as though trying to suck something out of nothing. I now felt the dull pain of cold in my fingers and toes, the first tremors of shivering. I have never cared for cigarettes but I have long been jealous of smokers on very cold nights, the warm glow of the ember, the rush of smoke into lungs.

"What's the matter?" I said in Chinese.

He tossed the cigarette in the naked dirt at the base of the persimmon tree and smiled with his bucked teeth. Tobacco stained. He had long greasy hair that fell to the collar of his leather jacket. "How do you know I'm not on the side of the government? An infiltrator?"

"You're too smart," I said.

"But they too have intelligent people on their side."

"How do you know I'm not an infiltrator?"

"Because you look scared."

"I'm only cold. Can I have a cigarette to warm my chest? I don't have good lungs. I shouldn't smoke, but I'm very cold."

He tapped out his last Baisha and gave it to me.

It was one o'clock in the morning. An old man came along pushing a black bicycle down the alley. The wind shifted and I got a gust of sewer gas that was as much rotten cabbage as shit. I lit the cigarette and tried not to gag.

"In any case," he said, "I've got to get out to the countryside. I'm wasting my time with these city people, especially the college students. You get two or three really passionate ones, but in the end, no critical mass. We'll see what happens when the economy collapses. The corporate debt is a serious problem."

"I'm afraid some people agree with you," I said. "All these companies are leveraging an awful lot. But there are others who say it's good that the government is finally willing to let a few companies fail. In this way, one could make the argument that the Chinese system is becoming more natural. And maybe in the long run that's a good thing."

"But the corruption is only getting worse."

He then recited another poem about peasants losing their lands to a coal-fired power plant and another lyric about dead pigs floating down the village river. A fetid sound.

"You think poetry can save the world?" I said.

"Maybe not, but it might at least save poetry."

His poetry was a tad tendentious for me but there was also a power that I envied.

He said, "Do you have any students I can use?"

"Me? Not at all. I only teach English to business majors. They're all gunning for office jobs so they can read stock reports and trade commodities and drive Mercedes SUVs."

"There must be a few angry ones, or desperate ones. Tell me about your students."

Queena reminded me of Anne Frank. Those shadowy eyes, the pointed chin, the puerile lips, the little cogs turning behind the face. As for the iconic photos of our most famous girl in hiding, I remember gazing at them as a boy and wishing Anne were prettier. Even then I knew it was a shameful and stupid thought, but I couldn't help feeling sorry for her, that she wasn't better looking. I couldn't help wanting to fall in love with her and feeling that my failure to get the hots for Anne was somehow a failure to love the humanity we were all instructed to love. She was just a dull girl. (Needless to say, my guilt over these feelings got doubled by the fact that my father was a Jew—technically a survivor, having escaped the Nazis as an embryo—and my mother was a Catholic.) In any case, Queena had the same kind of lean face and intense eyes, always a colorful barrette sweeping her hair to one side. She probably weighed ninety-eight pounds. Her pronunciation was on the mushy side, but she was advanced enough that she could help Vesuvius say "eminent domain" and "enemy."

When I met Queena she had a fish bone stuck in her throat. After sitting in class for fifty minutes, thinking it would be impolite to interrupt the professor on the first day, she approached me at the break and asked if she could visit the campus doctor. She pointed to her throat. She placed her dainty little hand on her neck and said, "I can feel it right here. It is wery uncomfortable when I swallow."

"Go, go, go. Get yourself to the clinic."

"It's not a big problem, but I sink I should go to the doctor. My roommate will bring the notes to me."

When I last saw her, she was slumped over my dining room table, bawling through a story she didn't want to tell. But this came much later. Before she ever set foot in my apartment, there were evenings in the bustling canteen when Queena and Vesuvius came to meet the strange English teacher with the burgundy tie. Our discussions on grammar invariably moved elsewhere. They asked about my love life and my impressions of China. I asked about their families. As it happened, Queena's father had been forced to abandon the family hotel in their hometown to make room for the same highway that displaced the peasants who rallied and lost against Vesuvius' brother. Queena's hometown was a good 500 kilometers north of the peasant riot, but it was the same four-lane highway, and her father gave up without a fight.

"Was he angry?" I said. "Did they compensate him for the loss of his business?"

"Only so little. He was angry at first. Then he accepts it."

"And the hotel?"

"It is totally gone. I went to the compulsory military training after the freshman year, maybe three weeks, and when I came home it was only a hill of rocks and dust."

"Rubble," I said. "Do you know this word?"

"No."

"It's a good word," I said. "Usually for bad things. When a building collapses or is blown up, we say it is 'reduced to rubble.' That terrorist attack in Shanghai when the museum came down, that building was reduced to rubble."

"Rubble," she said, which sounded like "row bell."

"Rub-ul," I said.

"I think I understand."

"Weduced to rubble," said Vesuvius.

"Reduced to rubble," said Queena.

I tried to excite them about the coincidence that the same highway had intersected both their lives, that the forces of the universe had touched their families and brought them together as roommates. They only giggled. I then said something sappy I would later regret: "Don't you see? We're all connected. We can't just look at some peasant uprising as something apart from our own lives."

The lights dimmed in the canteen. Only a handful of students remained, poring over foreign-language texts, murmuring passages in Albanian, Finnish, English, German. This was a famous language school. The Chinese were making sure they would have graduates who could speak the mother tongue of every economically-relevant country on the planet. Workers banged food trays against garbage bins, wiped tables with dingy rags. I could hear the harsh chatter among the foodservice workers in the kitchen.

"But the highway didn't affect me," said Vesuvius. "Only my brother."

"Only my brother," I said. "You are Chinese. You're Confucian. You're collectivist. Didn't Mao Zedong say 'I have witnessed the energy of the masses. On this foundation no task is impossible'?"

Vesuvius giggled, "Yes, but I think he would want the masses to stay on the side of the highway and witness the big destruction vehicles coming through."

"Get out of the way all together!" said Queena, leaning into Vesuvius and going pink with laughter.

"Actually," said Vesuvius, "I don't think it is so bad for the government to have this power. Sometimes it is bad, but sometimes it is good. For example, when the peasants are making unsanitary conditions, it is easy to remove them. It is better for more people."

I asked Queena where her parents used to live and where they live now.

"We before lived in the hotel. In back."

"And when you returned from your military training?"

"My parents were living in one of those little blue houses. I don't know how you call them. It is the same as the workers living in, the construction workers. But it is only temporary."

"The word you want here is *temporary housing.*"

"All of my things were in storage. My mother was cooking on the ground on a little stove. But it was okay. My father had a little money and he wasn't going to stay angry forever. The highway is good for the economic development of the country."

"What does your mother do for a living?"

"She was an accountant. But in the last two years, she only stayed home to make sure I did my homework. They are thinking about starting their own business now. They hope the new highway will give them a good opportunity for profit."

That night, I walked past the construction site of a new thirty-story building on campus, all wrapped in green mesh. Dark clouds had rolled in from the west. I could see welding flashes like tiny bursts of lightning inside the building. I could hear the grind of saws and the thunk of nail guns, workers calling to each other across future walls and empty floors. I went to bed and dreamt of a worker screaming in agony after a beam fell on his legs.

Like anybody else I could feel hazy compassion for the working man, but it wasn't like I was fomenting unrest via my students. I was too busy writing stories about Jewish boys getting seduced by housemaids and the students were too busy organizing fruit carving contests or reciting Kennedy's *Ich Ein Berliner* speech. By the time I got to campus, more than two years had passed since the so-called Peasant Martyrs fell to government forces in the South, ten years since the Jasmine Revolution, and more than three decades since the Tank Man stood his ground on Tiananmen. To these kids, 1989 was ancient history. Me? I was only a boy on a plane to America on the night of June 4, 1989, when the soldiers opened fire and tank drivers crushed the students' bicycles, crushing the heart of the revolution.

I think of the soldiers who fired bullets into the bodies of the innocent. I think of them often, wishing I could meet these aging men in prison where they belong. It's never too late for justice. Maybe the whole system can be flipped, like those slivers of magnetite in the ocean floor that reverse poles every few millennia, and the bad men will be put in jail and the righteous set free. I suppose I sound religious about now. My cellmate's cricket died last night. I had begun to depend on its chirping to help me sleep. One of the men ate the cricket and smiled, saying it was very crunchy.

A Beautiful, Impossible Place

I hear a factory over the wall. I can taste the sour air of manufacturing. Word has it the new arm of the prison is being built entirely out of recycled materials mined from the world's thickest landfills. Old ironing boards, bicycles, plastic bags, and bottles are being melted down and reformed into studs, joists, beams. This explains why we receive meals with "all five colors," because eventually we will be put to use building the prison complex to make room for all the dissidents, rapists, money launderers, and one or two scapegoated Party officials. We are building our end to the west.

I know something about labor camps, where the guilty labor alongside the innocent in garment factories, steel mills, rendering plants, and garbage dumps. I hope naively for a milder form of re-education, perhaps in a tea field or a rice farm. I could stand to wear a coolie hat and trudge through muddy water under the open sun, dragging a leveling tool across the paddy. I would chew tea leaves as I worked. Or let me plant ten thousand trees on the steppes of Outer Mongolia to slow the desertification of the Middle Kingdom.

Instead, they seem to want to kill us with boredom. Or anguish. That we have been assigned the task of administering the supreme penalty to Xu Xuo is old news, but the warden's envoy has not furnished us with any guidelines either in the ways of mercy or efficacy. Not a single restriction or explicit direction has been handed down. We've been given no tools and little inspiration for the job. There is only the sense that if things don't end badly for Xu Xuo within a reasonable time period, they will end badly for us. The guards have placed their bets and the odds are on Fang Feng, who happens to be at the infirmary this afternoon getting a tooth pulled.

Wu Kaiming sits on the edge of a low bunk, crouching over his clay cricket cage as if a new insect might spontaneously appear. The mattress above him sags from the weight of Brother Gao, who lies on his back gazing at the ceiling.

Both men agree that Fang Feng, who is generally mean and selfish, hasn't lost much sleep over the problem of Xu Xuo, and this is proven in real time by the way Fang slumbers on his back for six-hour blocks. Fang is the second-best sleeper in the room, Wu Kaiming being the real baby of the group. His snoring has a whistling quality that sounds almost happy. This leads Gao to the conclusion that our punishments are not equal, in spite of the fact that punishment parity seems to be a goal of the system. The slogan "JUSTICE THE SAME FOR EVERY MAN" is painted in bright red characters above the door leading out to the yard. None of us have studied the prison theory propaganda, but their treatment of us suggests some effort to punish every many equally (Xu Xuo excepted). We piss into the same squat toilet laid in the floor like a grave. We shave with the same razor, sleep in each other's beds, eat the same food, suffer the same horrible smells, drink the same metallic water, choke on the same carp bones, and play by the same rules. The lice enjoy all our heads alike. Obviously, total equality of punishment is unattainable, since each man is his own person with his own idiosyncrasies and dislikes. No one would argue, for example, that Jack, the loudest snorer, suffers as we do in the night, but then you can say that Wu Kaiming, who grew up in construction zones and can slumber through anything, has it easier than Jack. Clearly the ban on writing harms me the most. But maybe each one of us has something of our favorite self taken away: Xu Xuo can't drive a cab; Fang can't gamble in Macau; Wu Kaiming can't play his *erhu*; Brother Gao can't hike Yellow Mountain; Jack can't drink white liquor; Mr. Yu can't play tennis; Kuku can't hold hands with a pretty girl on campus.

If I had my way I would be listening to Dexter Gordon on a fine stereo, lying on my back on a couch in a brownstone in Chicago on a summer day, with children of all races playing by a gushing fire hydrant across the street. It seems now like an impossible place. I don't believe that people in America will get me there. Still, I entertain fantasies that my mother, father, and sister have sold the lake house to pay for a posse of lawyers, senators, and human rights activists to get me out of this prison, and briefly goes the fantasy the way of the next burp.

We eat mounds of rice. We have enough fatty pork and gristly chicken for brain energy, stringy pak choi for digestion. I chew my food to the smallest bits to make things easier on my GI tract. Obviously they are trying to build us up for something. As much as I would like to stick to my vegetarian diet, I fear that our days of eating well will end soon, so I eat meat. To have ample food and no sexual distractions, no music or theater taking me away from my work is not such a bad thing, and I do find on good days that I can still call up words with relative ease. In my mind I write, "Suffocation would be easiest," and already the sentence is perfect.

Don't Set Yourself on Fire

The first word that I had gone too far with my students came from Dean Chong Liu Chong. Dean Chong was one of my favorite people in all of China, who in spite of his Party affiliation—he seemed to be a vice something—never made me feel anything but comfortable. He had an artistic temperament that I could relate to. He wore his silver hair long, curling just above the collar of a dark blazer, and he walked on a bad hip that he had injured on a fishing boat in Alaska. If I saw him on the street and didn't know better, I would have taken him for an architect, an artist, or the owner of a hip coffee house rather than an enrolled member of the CPC. By law, he should have been retired as he was past sixty, but apparently he had connections.

He enjoyed taking the foreign professors out for long dinners where he ordered donkey meat and entertained us with stories of his younger days in Iraq. During the war with Iran, when much of the Iraqi labor force was busy wasting itself in the sand in that eight-year slog, China sent workers to keep factories running, and it was Chong's job to act as a liaison. He could speak English, Arabic, French, and for all I knew, Russian and Persian as well. He was a brilliant man. He was funny. He ate every meal as though celebrating the birth of a future village hero. As he poured more Yanjing lager into our little beer glasses, he'd tell us about how the Chinese workers helped the Iraqis do some fishing on the Tigris River—"You know the Tigris? It is an ancient river. Then you know the river I am talking about, yes!"—and when a turtle got caught in the net, the Chinese would ask if they could eat the turtle. The Iraqis gave them the turtles for free at first, until they realized they could make a profit.

At this point in the story Chong would knock his beer cup on the glass tabletop and guffaw. If Chong laughed and you didn't, either you had recently received word of a friend's suicide or you had undergone electroshock therapy. Chong had a way of bringing a story to a climax, releasing the wolves of laughter, and then ramping things up again. Typically his turtle story was followed by the donkey story.

"We Chinese, we love donkey. It's much more tender than beef."

(Sometimes when I am here in my cell chewing on a leathery chunk of beef, favoring my left molars, I hear Chong saying, "Much more tender than beef.")

"There were a lot of donkeys roaming the countryside in Iraq. They belonged to no one. The guys I was with, they asked some of the locals, 'Do you mind if we slaughter this donkey?' No problem. And then again in the next town, they went to the villagers: 'Do you mind if we slaughter this donkey?' No problem." Chong made a slashing motion across his neck. "It was tough work to prepare these animals." He wrestled with the imaginary animal right there in the restaurant, as the serving plates revolved on the spinning round table. He grew so animated that his face turned red and his glasses slipped off his nose. He had quite fashionable hair, this man in his sixties, and a mind that seemed to work frustratingly fast, as though his tongue and hands couldn't keep up with the lightning speed of his neurons. Whereas bushy eyebrows made some men seem grizzly and decaying, on Chong they looked handsome, calling to mind the two inky horns at the top of the Chinese character meaning "half," literally two foot prints above the character for "criminal," which, like many composite characters made no sense at all.

"We had only a few dull knives. Not enough refrigeration space or freezer. In any case, when the locals started noticing their donkeys disappearing from the roadsides, instead of thanking us for getting rid of the traffic nuisance, they started charging us for the donkeys as well. Nothing is free! Everything has a price!"

The day I got called into his office, it was clear we would not be discussing the edible animals of Mesopotamia. He closed the door and indicated a blue couch along the wall. The latch clicked two beats later, as though by some ghostly force. The office was mostly white-on-gray, dusty, piled high with papers and books. On his computer screen, a very agitating gargoyle with booming female breasts flapped its wings on a pop-up screen. Considering that he was the top-ranking dean of the School for the Enhancement of English Acumen, it seemed strange that his office was no better than mine. A faint whiff of urine wafted from the bathroom two doors down. The paint was peeling on the wall behind the radiator. The building had once served as a dormitory for faculty members, back in the days when professors got paid only a notch above clerical workers. I couldn't go anywhere in that country without being reminded of the past, even as so much of the past had been bulldozed and high-rised.

I knew I was in trouble. I knew exactly why. I hated the little kid feeling of being in trouble, of pretending you knew nothing of the charges, of banking on the one percent chance that you had been called into The Authority's office for some surprise reason, something possibly good.

"I think I know why I'm here," I said, taking off my pollution mask. "Am I teaching the students too much? I mean, is the material too sensitive?"

"Please," he said. "Please," smiling big, like it was time for another donkey story. He indicated the blue couch again. Apparently I hadn't sat down, nor had I taken off my scarf. I was holding my leather valise with a death grip. My looking like a businessman in China was not an act. Almost a decade at the offices of China Casualty had got me in the habit, and once I became part of academia I found that dressing well brought me respect. While many of the foreign professors dressed like students and probably wanted to be students, if not sleep with them, I occasionally wore silk vests and tie clips. Every night I polished the incessant Beijing dust off my shoes. Perhaps I was overcompensating for my thin frame and boyish face. That afternoon, lowering my haunches to the blue couch, I felt like a little freshman in big trouble.

"We are terminating your contract," he said. "Your resident status will be revoked. You have one week to leave the country."

I said nothing.

Why did I have such a hard egg in my throat? I had nothing to lose. This was not my country. I sometimes hated the place, I missed my sister and my mother, my best friend Mac, and yet I didn't want to leave China. It wasn't only my affection for the students, my naïve sense of liberty and justice; this was personal. After eight years at the insurance company in which I had dreaded nearly every minute of office life, never having enough time to write, always giving my best energy to an entity that relied on the fear of death for survival, I had finally found a job I liked. A vocation to go alongside my writing. In the main, I found that I was at last useful. I was inspiring students to think. Looking back on it now, I cannot believe it took me that long to find out what I wanted to do with myself. Eight years! I had wasted eight years toiling for a joint venture that had changed from a reliable Life and Casualty firm to a big-balled holding company that dipped its wick in all manner of luxury hotels and golf courses on five continents, which relied on whorish monetary policy, endemic corruption, and capitalist zeal for survival—to say nothing of their reckless faith that asset prices would never fall—and I wasn't about to go back.

Nor did I want to return to the States, where I faced the prospect of working in the insurance industry again, possibly getting a position in the leftover subsidiary of the company my father had run to bankruptcy, or looking for adjunct work at any number of Midwestern community colleges named after presidents or streets, where the work was honorable but the pay disgraceful. Here in China I enjoyed free housing, great food, female adulation, and considerable status as a foreign expert. As a point of fact, the words "special" and "expert" were part of my official title.

"Thank you," I said to my dean.

"For what?"

"For not punishing me."

"I'm firing you, I have no choice, and you don't view this as punishment?"

"There is a small chance I have been misunderstood."

I then adopted a stiff, formal tone that I must have felt helped my cause. "If I may say a few words in my defense, I feel that I've become an asset to your university. I would like to say, Dean Chong, that I feel it would have been fair to warn me off certain taboo subjects. I have not been given clear guidelines nor a chance to make any mid-course corrections. I can change. If you want me to make the students write about smoking bans, that's what I'll do. The last thing I want is to cause trouble. I'm thinking of the students. Ask them. I've tried to be useful. The evaluations are good."

"In fact they are excellent," said Chong. "Some of the best in our department. But this isn't the issue, no, unfortunately this is not the issue. Tell me exactly what you have been teaching them."

I started with the tame ones, *Should the university ban freshmen from having personal computers? Should the curfew in the dorms be lifted?* and moved methodically toward the more sensitive material until I arrived at last to Monday's question: *Is corruption in the Communist Party a product of feudal China or Mao's regime?* (admittedly a clumsily-worded query as well as a logical trap for students, any of whom with half a brain had written that corruption was due to a constellation of factors)—but I had been late to class and had come up with the prompt on the way to the building, with the cars and scooters snapping at my heels and the incessant *gong, ging* of construction making me nervous.

"I know," he said, his anger rising. He glanced out the window, where I could see yellow autumn trees, a roofline, and distant skyscrapers all shrouded in a haze of pollution. Muted colors. By comparison, Chong's skin looked red as a fisherman's. In fact, he had worked on a salmon boat in Alaska. He had been all over the world in his sixty-some years, a man who seemed to have lived nine lives. He reached over to his mouse on the desk and clicked away the booby gargoyle, deleted a cartoon character with Betty Boop eyes, then exterminated a half-naked girl sprawled across the sudsy hood of a BMW.

Then came an image of a Shanghai hedge fund manager staring catatonically into a computer monitor. The caption read something that I took to mean, *Hard Landing?* The economic meltdown would not be marked as in years past by frantic traders on the floor of the stock exchange but with the dreadful hum of computer algorithms.

"The economic news is not good," said Chong, clicking away the report. "Hopefully, it is only a correction."

A page of Chinese prose appeared on the screen. "This is an essay written by one of your students. You can understand the Chinese, yes?"

I nodded.

There is a quality to Chinese that must be described here. To the non-native speaker, the language can sound combative, uneasy, sharp-edged. Even after ten years in this country, sometimes it still sounded like arguing to me. What Dean Chong read was pure manifesto. Logical, elegantly composed and powerful, it wasn't merely a youthful rant. The words were arrow-sharp and cunning. In Chinese they sounded dangerous not for their anger but for their incisiveness and youthful purity. I'm speaking now of that keen sense of justice that children have, which we all lose by degrees as we grow older and more a part of society. This student clearly loved his country, and why I assumed "he" has no explanation other than my way of hearing the tone. He started with a fair enough statement that contemporary China for all its economic advances and rapid development lacked an ethos that was attractive to the rest of the world. "We" were soft on soft power. "We" lacked a compelling adventure narrative akin to the Gold Mountain. "We may sell everything under the sun and even get rich, but we will never be the envy of the world. No one will want to be like us in the ways that matter…"

This opening salvo seemed to be the complete essay, and though it was well-written (you could hear things tonally that the student probably couldn't produce in English) the ideas weren't anything I hadn't heard. In class, students seemed free enough to voice these concerns to the extent that there was the illusion of free speech. Students could lament the westernization of China, experience the catharsis of a minor diatribe, and get back to their friends' text messages. In some ways, criticizing modern greedy China was to give a nod to harmony, was to give a nod to Confucian order, was to give a nod to the central authority of the CPC.

Chong's voice grew louder as he reached the turning point of my student's essay. Who was the writer? Han Duo? Or the boy from Class #8 who called himself Derrick?

"China is like the world's whore," went the essay. "The whole world abuses our labor (that is the body) for their own orgasmic pleasure (which is the hedonism of material goods) and this relationship among the nations is purely physical. In other words, no other country wants to marry us. They only want to use us physically. It is no wonder, given the history of polygamy in feudal China, which lamentably is rearing its head yet again in the guise of our current Party officials…"

Chong's voice now sounded like he was the man giving the speech. Droplets of spit landed on the monitor, glowing in that prismatic way of water charged with electricity. By contrast, his hands lay calmly in his lap. He had delicate, narrow hands (just like my cellmate, Wu, now zipping his fly) that seemed too small for his bulky fisherman frame.

The essay took a feminist turn and I doubted Han Duo was up to the task. Among the papers in my valise at that moment were two compositions, bloody with red ink, by one Ting Ting and another Sunny, whose compositions were similar in spirit though not as bold. I doubted those girls could have turned Monday's prompt into the felonious dissertation on Chong's computer. The writer went into scandalous detail about the Yunnan Party official who had broken Bo Xi Lai's record of one hundred mistresses, then on to four more party officials who had allegedly had affairs. As though trying to get himself in trouble, the student quoted Ai Wei Wei's last words before his disappearance: "The college kids and the intellectuals are somewhat useless. All they have are smartphones. But the peasants have flints. And gasoline." Of course it all made sense, it made wicked sense, but instead of hearing the genius of the words, the effect was something else.

I began to experience a sinking feeling that I had incited one of my students to commit academic suicide. What would their parents think of me, after they had spent so much labor and love and money on their one child? All those Saturday tutoring sessions, the hours upon hours of preparation for the national exam so their son or daughter could leave the sewer-smelling village and join the new elite at a top university—all so some uppity language teacher could push the pupil over a cliff. I felt like a murderer.

It occurred to me that this was precisely why Dean Chong seemed angry with me. His knee bumped up and down like that of the prison guard at mealtime. The dean had a daughter of his own at UCLA. He knew what it meant to bet all your chips on one child. Intellectually, he probably agreed with everything in the composition. Why was it that his own daughter could get on an airplane and within thirty seconds of takeoff say whatever she wanted—"The First Lady is a whore! China is a whore! I'm a whore because my mother is a whore and so is the Virgin Mary!"—and yet she could not come to one of our classrooms wearing a T-shirt that said "35 May"?

I hated this world sometimes. I wanted to get up and leave it.

Then came the telltale final paragraph. In naked disobedience of my directive to put the main claim at the end of the introductory paragraph, Vesuvius waited until the final paragraph to cry that free speech and only free speech could save China from totalitarianism, that every person under thirty who did not have a child should rally at Tiananmen square on 35 May and demand democratic reforms. Vesuvius had the rhetorical habit of saving her best point until the end, and after fighting her on this for several weeks and realizing I had become the sort of teacher I hated—the one who pounds the life out of young writers—I let her have her way.

Just as I was convinced beyond any doubt that Vesuvius was the author, the essay went into a third movement that seemed entirely like someone else's writing.

"There are not enough jail cells to hold us all," she wrote. "Only in this way, with full transparency and freedom of the press, will the backdoor dealings and favoritism come to an end. Only in this way can we become not only more attractive to the world than the Gold Mountain but alas better than the United States, for we can achieve true equality of socialism with Chinese characteristics. We don't have to be like America. We don't want to be like America. We are China. We have our own Chinese Dream, and it is not the dream of a handful of overstuffed civil servants."

Hands shaking, I opened my valise and rifled through the papers as though searching for evidence that my lessons had nothing to do with this self-immolating composition. I heard a toilet flush down the hall and now the hawking sound of a man spitting.

"This student hasn't taken a class from me in over two years," I said in Chinese, which is how the conversation continued.

"She wrote to the prompt that you gave your students on Monday."

"She wrote this in two days?"

Here I was aided by a bit of Chinese grammar. In spoken Chinese "he" and "she" sound exactly the same. The only difference shows up in the written character. Had we been speaking English, I would have given away that I knew the student was a female.

"The students talk," he said. "I suspect he is one of your followers, and he has a younger friend in your Monday class who tells him what you are telling them."

"It was a dumb prompt. I was late to class. As is well known to all, I'm rarely late to class, Dean Chong, but that morning I spilled coffee on my trousers and had to run back to the apartment and change, way up to the fourth floor, and as a result I was disgustingly late to class and ill-prepared, and for that I apologize."

"Do you have any idea of the consequences? They can take you away for a long time and put you in a labor camp. A foreigner would likely only get sent home, but you never know..." Here his voice trailed off. "The conditions in those places are very bad, very unsafe. It isn't like they will torture you or anything like this, not as long as you respect their authority, but in the event of an accident or illness, you could die, Francis."

"Are you sure that's it? Can you talk to somebody? You have a good position, you know people."

"This is why I'm angry with you. I won't have my position for long if my foreign instructors are viewed as troublemakers."

"Can't you explain that this student hasn't been enrolled in my class for two years? Tell them I'm sorry and stupid. Tell them I'm very naïve."

"That would load all the blame on this...what's his name?"

I hesitated.

"For the safety of the student, Francis, you must tell me his name."

"Gong Honghua."

"A girl!"

"She's like a niece to me. I feel terrible. No, you should do everything in your power to protect the student. I'll go to a labor camp if it means protecting Honghua."

I used her Chinese name, Red Flower, for reasons that were not entirely clear, perhaps an effort to put distance between me and the real person I knew as Vesuvius.

"She posted it on the internet," said Chong. "For all I know she may be already in custody."

He took off his glasses and wiped the moisture from his eyes. Then he turned his venom on me again, lips glistening with spit. "Don't you understand the shit you have created? She is her father's daughter. Your actions could get her to a labor camp! But I don't know. We took the essay down immediately. For all I know she's in her dorm room studying right now. My daughter, when she was in high school, she liked to study on her belly, with the book spread out on the bed. It always looked so uncomfortable to me."

"I'm sorry," I said.

He took off his glasses and rubbed his eyes. "I have run this exchange program for twelve years. You are the only foreigner who has really given it his all to learn Chinese. Your Chinese, in fact, is the best of any foreigner I've ever met. It would be such a shame to waste it."

I should have resigned. But for some reason I set my valise on my lap and said, "I would like to stay. For the students. I promise not to cause any trouble."

"They will ask this girl where she got her ideas. They'll ask where she learned to write like this, who filled her head with counter-revolutionary thought."

"She'll protect me."

"She probably will."

"I don't mean that as a good thing."

"She hasn't been your student for a long time, but you still meet together in the workers' canteen, yes?"

"Not this semester, no. I mean, we've seen each other on campus, we've chatted."

"How long have you chatted?"

"I don't know. With her and the other one, Queena, it's easy to talk for a long time without watching the time. Both girls have family problems, they're homesick, nervous about life after graduation, and as such they seek advice from professors."

"Any money? Have you give them any money?"

"None. Their families have had a really rough time, some of it, frankly speaking, caused by corrupt party officials."

"Their situation is not unique."

He leaned back in his chair and for a long time said nothing. I had never seen Chong so silent. He stared at the monitor and watched another popup screen float into being: cartoon sea creatures swimming in a fantastic aquarium setting with a spider's web in the center. The big yellow fish were not hammerhead sharks exactly but suggestive of hammerheads. Chong wasn't using the screen simply as a void to stare into. His mind was working. He let out a little laugh and said, "This is my favorite one. Do you know why I like this crazy stuff? My daughter is studying computer graphics under the tutelage of a famous professor, a genius, only twenty-nine years old and already a full professor at UCLA. That man designed this. The fact that he is a genius and has chosen to produce this with his mind, I cannot tell you if I respect it or not. But this is what my child wants to study. It's her life."

He clicked away the ocean and stared at the prose, which by comparison looked cold and bureaucratic. "Your student is a good writer," he said. "She makes a lot of sense."

He reached over to his mouse, right-clicked twice, and deleted the composition. He emptied his trash bin and said, "I'm not under any illusions. Her thoughts won't go away. You have a four o'clock class, Francis. "Critical Thinking and Debate," yes? If today is in fact Wednesday, that is where you should be. At least for the time being." He glanced over at the newspaper on his file cabinet and said, "Another billionaire in handcuffs. Look at that guy. Pretty soon there will be suicides. You watch. And who knows?" he laughed. "If the economic trouble is severe, I may be coming to you for financial advice, Francis."

That afternoon, I was useless in the classroom. Cotton-mouthed. Simple words came out twisted. Every time I heard footfalls in the hallway, I expected a group of security thugs to storm the room and pin my arms behind my back. Standing near the window as I held forth on the Toulmin model of argumentation, I found myself contemplating my escape by leaping into the hedges two stories below. I'm the last man on earth to do anything so brave, but there's no accounting for fear. The chalk dust on my fingers felt new, the wooden sound of my voice foreign. I felt pressure behind my eyes, blood pooling in my ears.

The students, on the other hand, were living the life they had earned by performing well on the national exam. Some were slouched half asleep, some were looking down at their mobile phones, either to scan a microblog or check the spelling of "hurriedly." Most of them kept their fall coats on, as the day was blustery and we hadn't entered the heating season (that appointed day in mid-November when the heating systems fire up in every building in the city, no matter the weather). Their desks were strewn with notebooks, thermoses of hot water, electronic dictionaries, furry pencil cases, and greasy plastic bags containing half-eaten street food. They had leopard-patterned glasses cases and neon holders for their Apple devices. At least three students were reading textbooks for other classes. My students were eighty percent female. They all had beautiful lips.

I had planned to begin the lesson by discussing whether universities should abolish the compulsory military training for undergraduates. In the past, this topic had produced colorful recollections of five a.m. wakeup calls, gummy *mantou* for breakfast, beds made "as firm and square as tofu," faint-inducing sunshine, afternoon watermelons, and the dull evening lectures on Mao Zedong thought.

But I scrapped that lesson plan in favor of debating taxation on stock dividends. Predictably, 1.5 students found the topic riveting. They wanted to talk about what was happening in the banking sector, but I steered clear of any controversy. "Mr. Kauffman, do you think this is the hard landing that Professor Wu predicted? He had said it would be similar to the Great Depression in 1929 in America. This is what Professor Wu said. Too much loose credit. Too many stinky loans in the banks."

The students knew my past. They knew I had worked with one of the big SOEs and had an MBA. I deflected the question by saying that it was necessary and healthy in a free market system for a certain number of businesses to fail and it was probably a good sign that the Chinese government wasn't saving every sinking ship. A necessary evil, I said. The inefficient firms get weeded out (thinking of my father and how he would have espoused such thinking before he became one of the weeds) while the efficient firms survive.

After I guided the class back to the lesson, they were attentive enough, lowering their mobile phones with quiet shame when I called on them. They spoke knowledgably about the latest trading scandal in the United States. They quoted Mark Zuckerberg on some ethical principle of stockholder versus stakeholder philosophy.

Then I suffered through one poor girl's speech about donating blood, and another speech about fame. This young lady with the cat-eye glasses wanted to prove that "a famous person must have worked hard to achieve their famous status."

I tried to take notes and evaluate their presentations, but my mind was nowhere and everywhere. I felt dizzy enough to lie down. My joints ached.

To be in this room at all, these girls had tested among the elite, and this is what they had to tell the world? In a country where Tibetan girls set themselves on fire in protest, where Catholic nuns were jailed for speaking out against the government, where thousands of new-age cultists were swept up in raids, where corrupt construction companies made school buildings that collapsed as though made of Popsicle sticks, where women were forced to abort their fetuses—these girls were discussing the merits of fame and the need to give blood.

When the second girl finished, I looked down and saw that my notes on her speech were unintelligible even to me. Words half-drawn. Fragments not related to the speech. For some reason I had written the phrases "trapped by the asbestos factory" and "Russia attacks Ukraine—boat ride in the afternoon." I had been thinking of an afternoon in Berlin on a boat on the River Spree, resting on my mother's breast and drifting with the current, watching the sky and bridges pass overhead. Chimes sounded in the hallway. The students gathered their things. Then the River Spree became the Chicago River and I felt confused and sad.

"What about next week, Francis?" said a girl named Luna, who had the silken skin of a nine-year-old. "What shall we study for next week? And why did we not discuss the military training this week. Many of us had prepared."

"Sorry about that. Forget about military training. Next week, we'll discuss e-commerce. I would like us to debate the virtues of an online business versus the brick wall."

"What?"

"I mean brick and mortar business."

After class I tried calling Queena but she didn't answer. I got halfway through a text message and, realizing the stupidity of the move, hit delete. I went outside and roamed campus, wearing my pollution mask like an outlaw, looking for my two favorite students. I went to the canteen, to the library, poked my head into the badminton gym. I checked the café by the business school, the little market by the old folks' apartment. Four or five times I passed in front of Queena's dorm, feeling like a felon, feeling the ghost of the girl who had jumped from the fifth floor window. Laundry hung in the windows. I saw near-sighted girls walking arm-in-arm to dinner. The Muslim girls cycled along the path wearing head scarfs and dresses over jeans. Two malnourished migrant workers trundled barrows loaded with thick wire, and nine workers in the rock garden raked poplar leaves.

A pimply security guard eyed me from his corner post, looking up momentarily from his handheld video game. His drab green uniform was ill-fitting, the buttons and lapels suggesting a bygone era. He was among the hundreds of thousands of young people in China who worked an extremely boring job. Once or twice he had chased a peeping tom from the girls' dormitory. Another time he had helped an old woman up from a fall off her bicycle, but that was all. Perhaps today would be his day to apprehend a dissident professor or give chase to a wide-hipped volcano named Vesuvius.

I had 140 students and as I roamed campus in the hazy twilight, many of them waved to me: "Hallo, Francis," "Hallo, Mr. Kauffman!" "*Chi le ma?*" Have you eaten yet?

"Have you seen Queena?" I said.

"Who?"

"Her Chinese name is Zhou Qian."

"No, I haven't seen her."

"Vesuvius? Her roommate?"

"I don't know this girl."

As I neared the Foreign Expert's Building, I saw Queena waiting for me under a dusty pine tree by the bicycle rack. She sat on a concrete bench with her knees touching and her back straight. She had been crying. I wanted to hug her in the way of a tender uncle, but instead I nodded toward an outdoor stage in the courtyard, far from any windows.

"Let's talk over there," I said, indicating the rostrum where I had never seen anyone perform. There were plum trees and persimmon trees nearby, a cement sculpture that looked like a stump of petrified wood. Queena wore a blue felt coat that was plain compared to the furry-hooded fashion statements preferred by her well-to-do classmates. Her hair was in a ponytail. She wore suede boots with poofy fur on the cuffs, like something Santa Claus would have left under the tree. I imagined her father spending the last of his hotel compensation on those cute boots, saying, "Try them on, daughter. Go on, try them on," and the girl bending to stuff her feet into the warm cocoons.

"The secret police took Vesuvius away," she said. "They didn't name the charges, but I know it's because of her essay. She was so stupid. She posted it on RenRen and people posted some of those things on their microblogs. The officials took her away this morning after breakfast in front of everyone. They drove onto campus in a green SUV. Three men were waiting for her outside the canteen, right where the construction is happening. They asked for her student ID booklet. She asked if she could go back into her dorm to get it and they said, 'We're not stupid.' A boy from our class was standing behind the green car. He was the one who pointed her out. Do you remember LeBron? He was the boy, it was this boy. When I got back to the room, everything was made upside down. My backpack was gone. They took my notebooks, even my textbooks they took."

The magpies in the persimmon tree made harsh calls that sounded like dry grain rattling in a bucket. In the distance I could hear the traffic on 2nd Ring Road and the gong sounds of construction near the west gate.

"Did they question you?"

"No, because I stayed behind the fence near the volleyball courts. I should have gone with her. I should have angered one of the men and made them take me. Instead, I stood at the corner of the fence and waited. What are they going to do to her?"

"They'll put the fear of God into her. Then she'll be back in a week studying consumer demand theory in the library."

"Vesuvius isn't afraid of God. You haven't seen us lately. You don't know how we had changed. We're not the freshman anymore. We're angry. My father, he acting very strange. He's depressed all the time. He won't leave the apartment after the business failed. After the hotel was torn down, my parents tried to sell cashmere, but they were up against competitors who put wool in there. He tried to explain to the buyers that the other peoples put wool in their cashmere, which is not one hundred percent. It was high time the buyers realized this. But they didn't cared. They just wanted him to lower his price. They just wanted to buy as much as possible at the lowest price. He had lost so much money. Now, he doesn't know what to do. He is borrowing from my uncle. He's lucky he has a brother. In my generation, who will help us when we get older and have troubles? Vesuvius has two brothers. I have nobody. My father, the last time I saw him, he seemed a little like crazy. He joined a Christian group. The same people who built those big boats one time to prepare for the end of the world. It is very strange. He drinks too much alcohol. He used to drink a little during festivals or in the busy times at the hotel. Now he drinks it every night. He kneels to a crossfix in the living room."

"Crucifix."

"And then he hides the crucifix in the ceiling. Because he's worried the government will arrest him for having this thing."

"They could. They've done it to others."

"I feel sorrow for my mother. She doesn't know what to do. She thinks he was stupid to sell cashmere. He should have stuck it to something he knows. Another hotel maybe. Or maybe he could have been a manager at the new hotel. Remember when it first happened and I wasn't so mad? I believed it was fate. Everyone must sacrifice for the good of the country, and it was simply our turn, our bad luck that the highway came through our property. This was before they built a new hotel, four stories higher, in the same spot as my father's. We found out it was a rich man who was friends with the local Party official. The official pays my father a pittance and he turns a big profit by selling it to his friend. Why wasn't my father given this opportunity?

Truly the road was widened, but mostly on the other side. There had been no need to tear down my father's building."

I told her about my visit with Dean Chong. It was unclear to me why I still had a job. Either my dean had only been trying to scare me or he was sticking his neck out for me because he liked me or needed the staffing. I told Queena to lay low. "What do you mean?" she said.

"*To lay low* is to stay out of trouble. Don't say anything you shouldn't say. Don't write about sensitive matters. Don't send me any text messages. Get your degree. You're only two semesters from graduation. Don't set yourself on fire."

Then she spoke in Chinese: "The self-immolation people, I don't understand them. They are very strange."

"Don't say or write anything political."

"How can you say this to me?" she said. "Vesuvius, all she did was write an essay. My father, all he did was put his hotel in the wrong spot and then try to sell cashmere. A few weeks ago, the government arrested four leaders from the Fu Long Gong and, according to rumors, they have been executed. Some people on the internet were very angry about this. Other people wrote on the blogs in English, 'Gong of Four' and 'Going, Going, Gong' to be funny, to call them this, which I don't think is funny."

She switched back to English. "People in my generation are laughing on RenRen with 'Ha! Ha! Ha!' but we wonder if it is really the government bloggers or just assholes. I hate some of these people. Maybe those Fu Long Gong are a little crazy, like my father's religion, but it's only their thoughts."

"The Fu Long Gong pretty much wants to take down the Communist Party," I said.

"The government thinks they can tell a person how to think. All Vesuvius did was think with words."

Her bottom lip quivered. She sat on the top step with her skinny legs stretched out, her body rigid with anger. I noticed a little whitehead in the crease of her nose and a tear pooling in the corner of her eye. I gave her a silk kerchief from my coat. I was the kind of man who always had a tissue or a kerchief ready for crying females. My Lulu had resented this because it made her feel like I was planning to make her cry. One of the magpies in the persimmon tree shook its tail feathers.

"If they can put Vesuvius in jail for writing a letter, they can do anything."

"But you know this, Queena. You grew up with this system. You're not saying anything you don't already know."

"It feels different now. If I throw some piece of trash on the floor, maybe they will arrest me."

"Vesuvius made some incendiary points. Please tell me you will keep your head down and study. Graduate. Then get a job and buy your parents a microwave."

"What difference does it make if I graduate? Why? So I can work for some company runned by the state? So I can make them all rich, the men who think they can control our lives?"

"They sort of can. They appear to be doing a bang-up job of controlling us."

"Are you scared?" she said.

"Yes."

"I thought you were brave. In class, at the canteen, you always made us feel like we could be brave just by thinking right. All those informations from the foreign press. I thought you were brave."

"I believe in fear. If fear makes you take some kind of action that others label as brave, fine. What do you want me to do? I'm a foreigner. I'm expendable."

"I thought you would help Vesuvius. Don't you know some international lawyers or journalists? We can make a big story of this."

"I don't know anyone."

"We have to do something."

"There's no 'we' about it. I already feel bad enough about Vesuvius. I filled your heads with all this dreamy human rights stuff, but look at the history of your country. They crush you, Queena. Even when you have a revolution, the hero of your revolution later turns around and crushes you. There's nothing you or I can do. I'm sorry. I feel terrible about Vesuvius. If her father ever met me, he'd have every right to punch me in the face."

"I'm very angry, Francis. You don't understand the deep underneath of my anger."

没有

My shoe is untied.

Fang tells me so in Chinese.

I almost take the bait and look down, but I'm saved by the guard shouting, "Grab your pillows and fall face to the floor! The chicks are coming, you fucking pigs! Fall to the floor or we'll burn your eyes out with a blow torch, you fucking pussies!" which I thickly pretend not to understand. Fang's breath is in my ear. Brother Gao tackles me from behind and covers my head with a pillow. Lying there with my nose pressed to a circle of spit, I can hear the patter of women's feet as they make their way down the corridor. I'm not convinced I have fully escaped Fang's interrogation, though for the time being I am safe.

Plow Buffalo or Jackass

Today the men are taking up the question of the prison's location. They have ruled out the western provinces, as our 7:30 sunrise seems too early for Yunnan, Qinghai, or Xinjiang. There is only one time zone in the Middle Kingdom. This means that people in the far western city of Kashgar eat breakfast at 10:30 a.m. and enjoy summer sunsets at midnight. I don't think we are out west, but then again, the warden could set the clocks to an hour of his choosing.

"It's not Sichuan province I can tell you that," says Brother Gao. "There isn't enough fog here, and our heating system is too good. Back home, in winter, everybody stands around wood fires because the houses have no heat."

Every man's former position in society colors his opinion. Xu Xuo, having been a taxi driver, doesn't say a thing because he only cares about location as it relates to a city. Brother Gao really wants to rule out Sichuan because he can't bear the thought of being near his family. Kuku, the college kid, jokes that he doesn't know anything that hasn't appeared on the *gaokao*. Fang, who must have scored very high on the *gaokao* in his day, tells us we are stupid for not considering the possibility that the prison has its own time zone or that the light flaring up behind the east wall every morning may be artificially produced. "This could be done rather easily with those thirty thousand-watt xenon search lights from the United States. That company who made them was going gangbusters until one of our Chinese firms stole the trade secret and undercut them." He wears chunky fashion glasses, and he styles his hair using spit and a dingy little mirror—waiting for his chance to be seen by one of the women.

Wu Kaiming, the cricket man, says the air tastes like burnt heroin. How does he know this? He used to buy heroin from an Englishman in Shanghai, which everyone except Xu Xuo finds historically hilarious. The bald man who calls himself Jack—after Jack Lord of *Hawaii Five-O*—thinks we are only miles from the famous Terra Cotta Warriors, and he cites as evidence the soft clay soil he noticed while digging a trench recently. He launches into a fresh retelling of the story we've all heard dozens of times, of the farmer in 1974 who was digging a well and doinked his shovel on the head of an ancient warrior. Yu, the man who claims he did nothing, thinks we are in Chairman Mao's home province of Hunan.

The guard with the lank greasy hair, who has said nothing for six hours, butts in to say with pride that he hails from Chairman Mao's hometown. He has seen the Chairman's yellow house. Nobody seems impressed. He drums his fingers on the desk, yawns, sniffs the air, and when his time is up retires to the guards' quarters next door.

The new guard on duty, the stocky one with the bags under his eyes, announces his arrival by hawking phlegm into a bucket, giving his adenoids a real workout. He's not satisfied with boredom. He smokes and smokes. He gets up frequently to fill his hot water bottle, frequently goes to the bathroom, frequently peeks into our cell and tells us to wipe up our spit or make our beds.

Yu manages to get on his good side by complimenting his brand of cigarettes and the shine of his shoes. The guard softens a bit and when Yu asks him to tell us what the guards' living quarters are like, there are answers. Turns out this guard is the type who can't stop talking.

We learn the layout of the room and what color the ping-pong table is, and so on, like a blind man asking for a description of his sanatorium. Each guard has private sleeping cubicles. Their space used to be the library, but now the shelves of books are arranged to section off individual rooms, much in same way that panels in modern offices give the illusion of privacy to workers—though in this case a guard can simply reach over and pull down an old edition of Li Bai's moon poetry. A flat screen TV sits on one stack of dusty books. According to our guard, the cubicles for the most senior guards have thick adobe walls made of plaster and old books, those old hardcover editions making excellent insulating material. Of course there are posters of NBA basketball players, women in bikinis, and portraits of the warden.

As the guard yammers on, I look up and see old shower pipes poking out of the wall. The shower heads are long gone and the pipes are gobbed with mortar. I am Jewish enough that I imagine how easy it would be to use the aging infrastructure to shoot nerve gas into our chamber.

"Why is there a door between our rooms?" Yu asks the guard.

"The guards used to have it good. We slept where the women lived now, and your room was a bathroom with private shower stalls and good mirrors for shaving. That's why you have that drain in the center of the room. On our side, people used to sit in the library and read, but of course the Cultural Revolution changed all that and I guess they never got back to using the place as a library. Who needs to read all that old stuff anyway? We can get what we need from the internet. And the volumes are so old, they have no purpose."

"So the doors used to connect all three rooms," says Yu, fingering his mustache. "And the men could pass freely from room to room?"

"What did I just tell you? It's not that complicated. There were no prisoners in this part of the compound, only guards. But what do I know? I'm only telling you what I've learned secondhand from talking to the old guards. Maybe I was a little boy when this place was in its heyday, when the guards had a much better life. Some guards had real power, real influence, and some were active members of the Party. To be a guard back then was a position of status. You would write home to your parents that you had reached the level of guard in a maximum-security institution that kept watch over the highest-profile criminals. I don't know about other prisons, but this was the case at Kun Chong. Hands down, without question, Kun Chong used to be the best prison in China. Two of the Gang of Four were held here, though there is some dispute over which two, with most agreeing that the Chairman's wife was not at Kun Chong. At any rate, you guys are lucky to be here and not some other joint. Life is good here compared to the Yellow River Complex. They'll take out your liver in the first week and give it to some high-level alcoholic official who needs a transplant."

Six of us nod in agreement that we are lucky. Yu, feeling emboldened by his good relations with the guard, asks this man if he has a key to the door that separates the guards from the prisoners.

"Why would I answer a question like that?" says the guard, and at once his shame is made obvious. He does not have a key and wishes he did.

Naturally, a discussion arises among the men as to whether the doors make us feel less or more imprisoned.

"No difference," says Fang. "It's a stupid question."

"But what if one day a door gets left unlocked?"

"No chance."

"Very little chance, a small percentage maybe, but you can only say 'no chance' in the case of a wall, which can't be opened without some serious demolition." (This is Yu speaking.)

"You're not being realistic, Yu. How'd you end up here anyway? What did you do?"

"I'm a criminal without a crime."

"You lie."

"I mean this in all seriousness. One day I was driving a nice car to work. Then I got put here. No charges."

"Just because you haven't been charged doesn't mean you're not guilty. You must have done something."

"I swear to the sky, I have done nothing wrong. Think what you will. I have done nothing wrong."

"But maybe you broke the law."

"He's a clever man. He sounds like a lawyer himself. Listen. He's making a distinction between morality and the law."

"You guys are terrible philosophers."

Brother Gao clears his throat. "It's true that a person can break a law without doing anything morally wrong, and it's also true that a person can break no laws and commit moral atrocities."

"Brilliant, Master Kong!" says Fang. "Such a genius! What were we talking about before? It was far more bearable listening to you guys talk your stupid talk about doors."

"What about the window? Way up there, does it make us feel better or worse?"

"I wish I had earplugs. I wish I was like that foreigner and couldn't understand shit."

I flinch. I think I flinch. It may only be a neural quiver just before actual motion begins, and somehow I manage to ride through that little gauntlet of silence without getting caught. Why don't I speak? When I was brought to Kun Chong, an all-day journey by blindfold, I kept getting switched from one handler to another. Perhaps there were twenty men who moved me from vessel to vessel, most of them speaking in broken English, *Left, right, stop. Go pee. Get in the car. Mind your head.* After not speaking Chinese for a few legs of the trip, I stopped all together, and each subsequent handler assumed I knew only as much Chinese as most Westerners, which is to say, almost none. Somehow, this seemed to give me an advantage, though I haven't felt it yet. Now I'm afraid to speak Chinese because if I started now I might seem like a liar or a spy.

Later in the evening the discussion turns to rumors of peasant uprisings and high official suicides, bloody battles in the streets, but no one knows a thing. It's all hearsay, and as soon as the guard overhears us, he orders us to change subjects. After some earnest shrugging, the men take up Wu Kaiming's proposal for rearranging the beds. Considering the doors are extremely unlikely to open either to women on one side or books on the other, to say nothing of a flat screen TV, Wu Kaiming proposes shoving the beds in front of the doors. Though it has mostly been conceded by voting members of the cell that these doors are no better than walls, and while it might seem logical not to waste the space of the doors, as soon as the matter of the bad *feng shui* is mentioned, the proposal goes down by a vote of 5-2 with one abstention by the foreigner. Even Xu Xuo has voted.

Darkness seeps into the prison. The air smells of dew. There must be trees and grass nearby. The sound of Fang brushing his teeth fills the void.

At just this moment, we can hear the women being herded up the concrete stairwell, coming back from the re-education room. A guard from below shouts "Females!" and our friendly guard, the resident Kun Chong historian, brandishes his bamboo goad and starts poking us in the ribs and genitals. "Down, you scumbags! Don't you even think of looking at the chicks. Get down, you sorry little fuckers. Don't stick your dick in the drain, Fang! I promise a dragon will bite it off if you stick your little wick in the hole. We'll castrate you. And don't think we don't mean it."

The guard is surely putting on a tough-guy act for his comrade, and yet another part of him seems to truly enjoy his obscenity and power.

We all know what to do. Faces down on the floor.

The shuffling feet kick up the dust and make me want to sneeze. We can hear girlish voices and at least believe we can smell their bodies. This is a particular kind of cruelty, to have books I cannot read behind one wall and women I cannot touch behind the other. I open my eye a crack and see Xu Xuo's thick, blackened thumbnail, a good seven millimeters long. I feel the goad in my spine and close my eyes again.

We have never seen the women's faces. Once, when we were marching to the re-education room, a guard forgot to pull the drape and we saw the women lying prone on the floor with pillows over their heads, their rumps lined up like cuts of meat. Most were lean as girls.

But now we lie in the dark under our own pillows, listening to their feet, their voices, hoping for the faintest scent of a woman—even as we know they stink like us. In time, the sound of shuffling and giggling and cursing guards dies down and the women settle in for the evening. A factory cranks up for the swing shift. No moon rises in the window. Time creeps and the movement of the women lingers like the feel of the sea in your legs after getting off a boat.

"Hey, Brother Gao, when was the last time you had sex?"

"I don't know. Seven months ago."

"Who with?"

"My wife, of course. How about you?"

"The last time I had sex," says Yu, "I was with a mistress."

"That's adultery," says Wu Kaiming. "I knew you weren't innocent."

"Adultery is not a crime."

"My father has a mistress," says Kuku. "Everybody knows it, even my mother, but we all pretend everything's normal." Kuku is a wiry kid with plump, wet lips and a flat forehead that looks as if it has been trained on a cradleboard. Melancholic. He doesn't smile unless it is impossible not to: if Fang is crouching on the floor and scratching himself like a monkey or Yu has made an amazing shot in flyswatter badminton. Kuku is from Shanghai. I gather his father is a mid-level employee for one of the telecom companies, not rich and not poor but apparently with access to technological gadgetry of spies.

How did Kuku wind up here? He was caught running a cheating ring for the *gaokao* entrance examination and sentenced to four years in prison, and when he gets out he won't be allowed to matriculate at any major university in China. Thousands of students cheat on the *gaokao*—my students have told me this. Every June, ten million kids sit for the two-day exam. It's the only way to get into university, the only criterion unless you happen to be a virtuoso pianist or a fish-like swimmer, in which case there's a place for you somewhere. Cheaters wear tiny ear pieces. Cheaters carry tiny cameras imbedded in their erasers, snap photos of tricky questions and relay them to gangs of cheaters in a room somewhere, who find the answers and whisper back to Cheater #1, who pretends to scratch his head so as to remember the name of General Zhang Fei's second son. Ah, there it is! Hummingbird stationery with iPods installed in the furrowed paper. Students with fake disabilities lugging crutches and bulky braces with cell phones installed, their fathers having bribed doctors to provide a note. Other students bribe teachers and proctors to give them the answers. Recently, female students have been instructed to not wear bras with metal supports so as not to set off metal detectors.

"The worst part," he says. "The chick isn't even pretty."

The kid's voice is flat, without a scratch of humor. He's a woeful boy with the willowy limbs and tender skin of a fourteen-year-old, though he's probably closer to twenty. Some say he was put with us because he had a high risk of getting raped if he were put with the harder criminals in the "Tea House."

"I was screwing my wife in the exact moment the Secret Police burst into my apartment," says Fang. "I'm not kidding. I was just about to come. You don't believe me? I'm telling the truth. It was around eight o'clock on a Friday night. Can you believe the timing?"

There is a sense in the room that some of the men might like to hear more details, but by and large this is not the raunchiest crowd I've been around. Fang offers no further details about his *coitus apprehendus*. In at least one respect I'm glad to be in this specialized division of a Chinese prison as opposed to an American prison: namely, that I don't have to listen to the men talk about masturbation or brag about the horrible pleasures they've spat upon women. Pornography, that great failure of the imagination, is nowhere to be found at Kun Chong. We each take care of our own needs quietly at night, and how each man handles his mess is his own business. There is only a little banter about "tying one off" or "hitting the salt mine."

Stuck in a roomful of men all day, with female inmates on the other side of the wall, sometimes I feel that the sight of a good-looking woman would cause internal bleeding. I fetishize bikini bottoms that I uncoiled around a girl's legs twenty-two years ago and wander in my thinking to a garbage dump where that bathing suit must still exist under a filthy heap. Perhaps these mind movies starring teenage girls make me a sort of pedophile. If at age thirty-nine I keep going back to the girls of my youth—none of them forgotten, ever—maybe I'm a disgusting creep.

If I started speaking with the men, if they asked about my experience with women, I would tell them about my Lulu, the Shanghai woman I dated for three years. I see her unzipping her leather boots in our room at the Peninsula Hotel. I smell the tang of her armpits after we make love and then I'm swept back twenty-three years to Felicia B. in the backseat of her father's VW, just a girl showing her woman-size breasts to a boy for the first time.

"How about you, Xuo?" says Fang. "When was the last time you got lucky?"

Xu Xuo is curled up with a pillow and blanket on the concrete floor next to Fang's bed. The blanket is turquoise blue with flower patterns, much too lovely for this place. Xuo punches the pillow and says, "I don't know."

"Of course you know. Unless you're like me and have women all the time. Don't tell me you can't remember the last time. Come on. Tell us."

"None of your business."

"Do you like children? Is that it? Answer the question, you half breed."

"I'm going to sleep."

Fang leaps out of bed, making the springs creak, and slides to a stop just short of the sliding door. He whistles for the guard and says, "Excuse me, guard. Can you come here, please? I really need your help."

The guard spits, then saunters over. Fang leans in close and asks in a confidential voice if Xu Xuo's sentence is for child rape. "I'm asking you because he hasn't denied the charges. I asked him directly, didn't I guys? I asked him point blank if he was put here for raping a little girl and he avoided the question."

Xu Xuo stands up. Terrible posture. He snaps at Fang, "Maybe you raped somebody!" This is the first time I've heard him raise his voice, or seen his bottom teeth when he talks. His receding gums suggest that he is older than I thought. In his mid-forties?

Fang asks the guard to find out the exact nature of Xu Xuo's crime. The guard says he'll see what he can do. "Most of us have no access to the files, but I have a buddy who works in the intake center. Maybe I'll ask him. What's it worth to you?"

"What can I give you? I'm a prisoner. I have no money. What? Should I give you my shoes? Okay, how about this? I have a Mercedes Fourmatic in a garage in Xi'an. How about I give you the building code and let you drive it for a few days?"

The other men *ooh* and *ahh* and suddenly the mood in the room eases.

"What if he keeps driving your car every day?" says Wu Kaiming. "How would you get him to stop?"

"It's okay," says the guard. "I don't know how to drive. And there has been widespread looting in Xi'an. One of the most popular items stolen from the wealthy has been luxury cars."

"Then I have nothing to give you. Can you please answer our question? We're dying to know. Since it's related to our responsibility."

"I understand," says the guard. "I'll try to find out what he did. But I can't promise anything."

Why is Xu Xuo still alive? He has been condemned to death in a land where the execution of justice is legendarily swift. Naturally, the men discuss the matter. Unnaturally, they hold the discussion in front of Xu Xuo, using the third person like he's not even there. One man speculates they are keeping him alive as a form of torture. Another says they plan to use his labor.

"But nobody is working."

"That's going to change. You can hear the factory over there, can't you? You've got ears, I think. They're just now making a plan for us."

There is talk of opportunities to sell our organs, and any day we expect to be briefed by the medical staff about our options.

"So they're keeping that man alive, spending money to feed him just so he can work?"

"Then he's no better than a plow buffalo or a jackass."

"And neither are you. It's the same for all of us."

"Welcome to Kun Chong."

A Slumber Party

One night, returning late from a lecture I hadn't wanted to give at the Steve Jobs Institute, two girls jumped me in the courtyard of the Foreign Experts Building. I had just wheeled my bicycle under the pavilion where four generations of bicycles were locked up. Annoyed that the automatic light hadn't flicked on to help me negotiate the lock, I was fumbling for the keyhole when two figures sprung out from behind the scooters. My heart gave a jolt. I let out a squeal and buried my head under my arms like some wintering bird. Where other men react with force, I cower.

"Francis! It's us."

"Who are you?"

"Queena. And this is my friend Snowy. We're locked out of our dorm."

"Why don't you go to the karaoke place like everybody else."

"We went to a meeting this evening. We met Billy Bao Chun in person. Only briefly because he had to leave, but it was really him. He came to lends his support to the Alliance, and he even gave one of his signed LPs to our leader. But it was all very fast and dangerous. He told us we'd better be smarter than the bastards. And then we were scared to take a cab from that place, so we took a bus and two subways and now we are locked out."

Billy Bao Chun was a pop star turned punk rocker who was

among the most tactical dissidents in China, a master at turning the government's own words against them. Handsome, if a little heavy, he had one of those voices that sounded melodic if he were only to read the phone book. He had become such an international star that it was hard for the Chinese to put him in jail. After all, he had written the hit song for Disney's *Confucius*, and his smoky voice could still be heard in shopping malls, restaurants, and shoe stores throughout The Middle Kingdom. These days, much of his music was banned, he had difficulty getting permits for his concerts, and cameras were mounted on power poles outside his swank Shanghai studio. All of the attention only made his triangular, goateed face all the more iconic.

As happened from time to time, students who came home after the 11 p.m. curfew got locked out. Boys would sometimes sleep outside with the cats. Girls could either wake up the dorm auntie—suffering scorn and points reduction—or hang out all night at KTV or a 24-hour KFC.

It was past midnight. In the five stories above me, four windows glowed. A Siamese cat slinked along the gray wall at the far end of the courtyard. I could hear the surfsound of 2nd Ring Road in the distance. The night was clear. I looked up and saw Venus nailed to the blue dome overhead.

By then, my eyes had come to terms with the darkness and I could make out Queena's face, her cheeks painted rosy from the cold. Her friend looked younger, with acne around the mouth and full lips, quiet eyes, and a fur cap with the red communist star front and center. Though I had poked fun at my students for missing irony from time to time, tonight it was my turn to be in the dark. I didn't know if the star was a joke or not.

"We need a place to stay," said Queena.

"Not here," I said. "Call somebody else."

"Just one night. We're locked out of the dorm."

"You'll have to wake up the auntie, then. I'm sorry."

"If we wake up the auntie, there is a record. You don't understand. If we never come home they assume we are in our beds, but if we wake up the auntie, the university has a record."

"What if there's a camera out here?" I said.

"There isn't. Not here."

Snowy jabbed Queena in the ribs and the girls giggled. Snowy said in Chinese, "Tell him about the men who chased us."

"How did you get in here?" I said. "Did you sign in with the lady in the foyer?"

Queena held up her forearm to show off the raspberry skid mark. "Over the wall," she said, indicating the wall to the west. Two cats yowled in the alley. "We'll scream if you don't let us in." She twitched a smile and I saw at once that all the goofing around in the night was cover for a more serious condition: the girls were frightened to the bone. It wasn't out of the ordinary for students to visit with professors in the Foreign Experts Building, whether to arrange some cultural event or celebrate Romanian independence or get some Chinese tutoring or brush up on one's Finnish. The Russian who lived below me was an ardent entertainer, too ugly to be suspected of impropriety. I often saw the shoes of his female guests outside the door: cartoonish sneakers and stiletto heels.

I really wanted to turn the girls back into the night—but, safe as Beijing was compared to most cities, I couldn't live with myself if something happened to them. I had already caused enough trouble for Queena. Six or seven hours and the girls would be gone.

With no good choice, I whisked the girls upstairs and gave them hot chocolate. Queena's friend took off her star hat, revealing fiercely straight bangs of a style that would always bring Asia to mind. Her alluring figure filled me with shame, and I looked away. They did not belong here. Queena tossed her blue felt coat on the easy chair like she'd come over a hundred times. She went to the window and took in the view of the dormitory across the courtyard, the grid of windows and bone-white tiles, the three large pine trees sagging with beauty.

With the windows open, the apartment smelled of smog and construction dust. A big building was going up on east campus and of late they seemed to be messing with the sewer system. Every time I came home the odor was a little different, and I was in the habit of linking the smell to various memories of the past. A bus stop in Prague. Midway Airport in Chicago. Mexico City. A coal-fired power plant outside Moscow. An alley in Bangkok.

Tonight I smelled Berlin, specifically *VobbeStrasse* where my father had brought me during one of our motherland trips to show me a stumbling stone in the sidewalk, brushing a sycamore leaf out of the way and pointing at the names, the dates, the Star of David imprinted on a brass plate set in concrete. "There, see? This is our name. This is the flat where your grandmother and grandfather lived, the Oma and Opa you never met."

I was fourteen at the time and bitter about being dragged halfway across the world to spend endless hours with my parents in beer gardens, when I should have been attending a theater camp at Northwestern, where I had been offered a chance to play Caliban. We had argued about my going on the trip. I'd lived in America for six years and was at the age where I didn't want any part of being German. I listened to Nirvana and used the word "like," like, all the time. I'd gotten past the middle school phase where dumbass, unironic kids called me Nazi because of my accent. Worse, I was old enough to start realizing I was originally a mistake, and Berlin was just rubbing it in. There's no shame like finding out you're the product of a hookup. Better to be Caliban, the offspring of the witch of Sycorax and the devil, than some wimpy kid who existed only because of a ripped condom.

"They took your Opa away and killed him, but your Oma escaped."

I knew the story. It was dramatic and sad, but I wasn't willing to give my father what he wanted. I knew my grandmother had been at the hospital getting a gynecological exam when the SS stormed the apartment and arrested her husband and parents. My unborn father was the acorn in her belly. His father was a stained-glass maker of some renown, who, according to family lore was fond of saying, "The morning hour has gold in its mouth." I had never heard this expression until my father said it that day, in halting German, *"Morgenstund hat Gold im Mund."*

It seemed an odd time to pass along this proverb, as I squatted down to read the letters stamped into the metal: "Here lived Amschel Kauffman, born 1910, deported 1938, killed at Sachsenhausen 1940."

Of that day, I only remember the stumbling stone itself and the scent in the air. I don't remember anything else. Surely, I would have gazed up at the flat. As a young man I was keenly aware of textures and shapes in the world around me, but for that day I've got nothing. I have no mental picture of the apartment, and yet I have a powerful memory of an unpleasant odor skulking from a nearby sewer, the wind shifting, and the fragrance of fresh bread wafting from a bakery around the corner. A sudden feeling of hunger. The German letters etched into the metal plate looked sturdy, eternal. I would like to report that in 1938 on that day of the raid, a heroically kind German nurse slipped my mother another woman's ID, but, as I eventually learned, the sorry truth is that my grandmother ended up with a gentile's ID due to a clerical error.

Thus my father and I were each mistakes: he the baby of an unwanted mother, I the baby of an unwanted pregnancy.

"What do you think?" he said.

Did the building have wrought iron bars? Flower boxes?

"I don't know," I said. "Looks like a normal apartment. How do they know this is even the right one?"

"You goddamn brat. I could punch you in the mouth."

骨头

"The foreign student dorm," said Queena, gazing at the white building across the courtyard. "It looks so far away."

"If that building catches fire, the students who are sleeping will die and the studiers will survive. It won't matter where a person is from or how much money their father makes. Only if they are sleeping or not. Terribly sad emails will go out to forty different countries in forty different languages, but they will all sound exactly the same."

"Teacher! Why do you think such monstrous thoughts?"

"I'm just trying to say how it's impressive that we have students from all around the world here. It's beautiful."

"But then you make it ugly."

"Art doesn't have to be beautiful."

"Should I close the window?"

"Aren't you hot? I have no choice but to keep the window open. I know I'm wasting a lot of energy and sucking in particulates, but what am I to do? They only have one setting. Hot. They say the fourth floor is like the tropics and the fifth floor is like a sauna."

I then noticed two pair of boxer shorts drying on the radiator beneath the window. "Let me get those," I said, shoving them into the nearby writing desk.

Queena's friend sat down in my chair and started playing with my favorite pen. I didn't like anyone holding my pen.

"This is Snowy," said Queena, introducing us again.

"Hello, Snowy," I said. "What is your real name? Your full name?"

"Li Xue."

"Pretty snow. Do you girls want something to eat? Are you hungry?"

"Where will we sleep?"

"There are two beds in there. One of them has clean sheets. I'll sleep on the floor in this room."

"It's only for one night," said Queena. "Snowy can go back in the morning, but I can't. I'm in trouble, Francis."

I was then informed that only Snowy would be going home in the morning, as the secret police had managed to snag Queena's purse. They had snatched it away in the NanLuo subway station moments before the doors closed. Those doors are ruthless, nothing at all like elevator doors, and in the struggle, she had let the purse go, knowing it would be better to give up her money, phone, and ID than her arm.

"There were two of them," she said. "They looked like businessman, which is why I didn't trust them. They were too neat for that time of night, for that subway line. They wanted to talk to me, and we started running down the steps, and they chased us just like in the movies. A train was coming the other way, it was coming, and some boys saw the businessmen harassing. So the boys got in the way. They were fighting, and the train was coming, and the men said, 'We're the police, get out of our way.'"

Snowy motioned as if the boys could have gotten tossed onto the tracks.

But the train stopped, and as Queena jumped into the car behind Snowy, one of the officials managed to reach past the boys and get the strap, and of course, the purse.

Now Queena, who had held it together to this point, was balling into her sleeve, saying in Chinese that she was stupid and ashamed, that the others would be furious with her because she had put contact information of Alliance committee members into her phone. She had a handwritten copy of at least part of the committee's platform, a little manifesto that was supposed to be memorized and not written down, and Queena, who didn't trust her memorization skills due to a scooter accident after high school, had copied them down outside the restaurant where the group had met, all of them upstairs in a bargain Sichuan restaurant with a large private room upstairs. She had just wanted a few days to learn the lyrics and intended to burn the paper, but now what?

I closed the window and pulled the drapes. I shut the kitchen door. I could smell the girls' shampoo, their skin, their youth, their fear.

"Can I use the bathroom?" said Snowy.

"Let me check it first," I said, not knowing what I was afraid of. In the bathroom I could smell cigarette smoke rising through the vents, and the odor angered me. I was angry with China for constructing such shitty buildings, angry at myself for choosing to live here, angry at the Korean below who smoked all hours of the day and night, angry at Queena for lying to me.

Fifteen minutes later, as though nothing had happened, the girls were in my bedroom giggling over an erotic magazine they had found in my drawer. They sat cross-legged on the guest bed, flipping the pages, laughing one moment, then discussing some woman's makeup the next. The magazine was quite old and, to these girls, ancient. For some reason, I could not give up this gallery of photos of a heartbreakingly beautiful Russian woman, eternally young, wrapped in various furs of lynx, mink, and fox. I had kept the magazine in its plastic sheath for fourteen years, longer than many marriages. The copy material was of very high quality. That it had traveled oceans without getting damaged or confiscated made me nervous that the girls would rip a page or leave a crease across one of the bodies.

Queena, her face no longer flush from crying, stood in the door holding a shoe horn. "What is this?"

"A shoe horn."

"What is it for?"

"Putting on shoes."

"Why do you need this to put on shoes?"

"I don't need it. I use it occasionally, for a certain pair of wingtips."

"He really likes bugs," said Snowy in Chinese, having found my cricket cages. She bent to coo at the little critters on the windowsill.

I had found myself in the middle of a slumber party. The young ladies were giggling. I happened to be interested in insects, crickets in particular. I had several preserved crickets in a cedar collection box. I also had a number of "Monkey Fur" folk art pieces by Chinese artisans, who had dressed crickets in fur and arranged them at gambling tables or rice fields, their spindly arms stretched out in motion—all inside a glass box about the size of the recipe box my mother used to keep in her kitchen cabinet. In the tiny entrance I had another collection of crickets in a multi-leveled cage that needed constant dusting. I had long been interested in insects, and ten years in China had given me an abundance of crickets, some the size of my pinky nail, others big as mice. Glistening, armored, with powerful, long legs.

"Stop looking through my things," I said. "It isn't polite."

"We want blankets."

It then occurred to me that the girls could have been spies charged with infiltrating my apartment and bringing back certain documents. I was convinced that smoking a cigarette with a "poet" had triggered the search. All I had were photos of a naked Russian girl, my father's shoehorn, and insects preserved in glass like Mao himself. If the Chinese wanted to comb through my writing notebooks, they might find plenty of strange material—say, "Kant Laughs Uncontrollably" wherein the revolutionary philosopher gets trapped in an arcade in Edmonton, Canada and actually likes it, or "North Song," which has nothing to do with China's forced sterilization program—and thus they would find nothing incriminating. Nothing about The Three T's: Tibet, Taiwan, or Tiananmen.

I gave the girls some blankets and brought them into the living room, where the thick ribs of the curtains hung across the window and a pall of Beijing dust lay on the desk. The clock read 1:15. I gave the girls hotel toothbrushes. I gave them clean t-shirts for pajamas and said good night. I clicked the door shut and spent the hollow hours staring at the ceiling, listening to my crickets and the far-off grind of construction. The girls never giggled again. The work crew never ceased, and at 5 a.m., just as I was feeling the tug of sleep, a loud clattering shook me awake—a steady drilling that sounded like the workers were grinding a hole into the hot center of the earth.

I went into the bedroom and woke Snowy. Knowing my students liked hot water in the morning, I set the teapot on the stove. I felt old and sick. The world outside was dark. Queena's friend shuffled into the tiny kitchen like a sleepy little girl, and the impulse to be a father felt deeply strong and I did not know this feeling was in me. I wanted Snowy to tell me that both her parents had died, aunts and uncles long gone, and would I be willing to adopt her? Would I? As the minutes ticked by and our intimacy increased, I missed my sister Rebekah achingly. Bekah had a pretty singing voice. Downy hair on her face. I wanted to plant one of those sloppy, sarcastic kisses on her cheek that she would wipe away, saying, "Eew, eew, eew, but I love you." I missed Rebekah's harp playing and the way she could disarm my father.

Snowy, sitting at the table, raised her arms to stretch. To my shame I realized that the shirt I had given her was too tight, one of Lulu's old shirts, and there was not much I could do but avert my gaze from the energetic boobs in my kitchen. I focused on a scratch in the tabletop. I didn't want to be where I was, and yet there was something special about the camaraderie of being awake with another person in the predawn. Snowy smiled when I gave her a glass of hot water and two wheat digestive crackers.

"I had better go before it gets light."

"I have coffee," I said. "You still have time. Don't worry. Would you like some eggs? A cup of coffee?"

"All my friends drink coffee. I can't stand it. My father is in the tea business."

"Do you dislike coffee for personal or political reasons?"

"How do you say? All of the above."

"All of the above," I repeated. Then I said in Chinese that I loved coffee but battled insomnia and should probably give it up.

"Your Chinese is very good," she said. "Most Westerners never get the tones right. Your tones are almost perfect. It's too bad you'll probably have to leave the country."

"When? Why?"

"It's just a feeling. Queena says you are a troublemaker."

"Is there something you know, something having to do with this group you're involved in, that you should tell me? Maybe I should leave. Maybe after the semester I should go back to America and be nobody special. Or go to Germany."

She broke her wheat cracker in half and sat there not eating it. She scratched at the acne near her mouth, and I realized my pillow case must have irritated her skin. Her look, the expression in her face was something I had seen before in other students, a kind of calm wisdom that belied her years. I may have been wrong, but it seemed a dangerous combination in this country, to be wise and angry and restless.

"This group is less popular than Queena thinks," she said. "They have some peasants, but not enough people who are The Desperates. The only people who will drive anything will be The Desperates. Right now, I think the group is much too fashionable. That's what I like about Billy Bao Chun and Li Wang. They are attractive to people, they have education, but they understand where the power is, in the masses, in the workers and the peasants. It only takes one spark. But I don't think Billy Bao is going to be around much longer. For all we know, he's being detained right now. How does this man get any sleep? How does he sleep knowing that one time the secret police could wake him up and take him away? Nothing will happen without the underclass. What is most needed is a single charismatic leader who can bridge this gap. But unfortunately anyone who fits this description will be taken away."

"You don't sound like a sophomore."

"I graduated two years ago. I only look young. My parents were very political in 1980s."

"This isn't like 1989. There's far too many foreign residents, and for that matter, far too few angry students. You have no critical mass. Most of these kids just want iPhones and Nike sneakers. They don't care about free speech. I mean, they give lip service to it, but asked to choose between a Lexus and free speech, nine out of ten will take the Lexus."

"I want both," she said.

The morning light was arriving. I had to get Snowy over the courtyard wall. What equipment did I have? A flimsy garbage can? My Italian bicycle? Snowy could lean it against the wall and put one foot on the main seat and another foot on the rear seat where Lulu used to ride. That had been the best way to get to Purple Bamboo Park, with Lulu riding sidesaddle in a short skirt and her arms wrapped around my ribs. There are many delights in this world, but not many compare to riding a lover on the back of a bicycle on a warm day in spring.

In the apartment, I showed Snowy how to lean the bicycle against the wall at just the right angle, and getting a little overzealous, I put my left foot in the V of the frame, my right knee on the rear seat, and up, until I was standing with both feet on two seats and my head grazing the ceiling.

Looking down, I said, "What do we do about Queena's parents?"

"I'll take care of it. Queena trusts me."

"Okay," I said, almost losing my balance. "That sounds good."

I got off the bike and went to the door, easing the lock open. I wheeled the bike into the hallway and watched Snowy carry it down the stairwell, her fuzzy hat with the red star disappearing from view. I waited by the kitchen window and watched her tramp through the weeds in the darkness, propping the bike solidly against the shadowless wall, then climbing up, over, losing the hat, waving goodbye.

Queena Moves In

Queena's stay in my apartment had now stretched to six weeks. At first, she insisted on sleeping on some cushions in the main room, but after a scare in which one of the *fu'wuyuans* entered without ringing the chime (Queena in the bathroom at the time) it seemed only safe to have us both sleep in the bedroom in the twin beds. The awkwardness of sleeping next to strangers never lasts as long as you think, and so was the case with Queena, as it had been with bunkmates in summer camps, sleeper cars, and dorm rooms. The girl spent a lot of time sleeping on her back in a strange position, with arms raised like she was the victim in a stick-em-up. She missed her stuffed Teddy so I bought her a Pleasant Goat.

Of course, she needed clean clothes, underwear, tampons.

As for buying underwear, I had two choices that would keep me from being noticed: I could go to a store called Blah, Blah, Bra in the shopping mall by my old office and pretend to pick out something romantic for a girlfriend, or I could go to the department store on Suzhou Street and buy a five-pack of youth undies for a daughter. I chose the latter, adding them to a mountain of groceries—including a fresh belt fish and a putrid globe of durian—to call less attention to the panties.

On days when I taught morning classes, I left the apartment before she awoke, and when I came back, she was often sitting cross-legged in one of our hideous wooden armchairs, my computer in her lap.

"Sorry, do you need the computer?"

The ladies in the lavender uniforms came once a week to clean the apartment while I was teaching. That left only one hiding place for Queena: inside her bed, that is, lying flat on her back in the large wooden box that served as a base for the mattress.

This apparatus needs some explaining, as I have never seen a bed like this anywhere in the world. No box spring or metal frame. The mattress rested on a thick piece of plywood over a wooden box. The plywood and mattress were very heavy, but thanks to some hydraulic rods inside the bed it was possible for a person of average strength to raise the mattress up and down like the hood of a car. Each time we closed the bed, bringing the heavy mattress to rest on its rectangular base, the energy would get stored in the hydraulic lift for the next time we needed it. In the open position, the mattress canted at a thirty-degree angle to form an open maw that made it easy to reach in and retrieve a manuscript or a pair of winter socks, or where a young fugitive could climb in without bumping her head.

We conducted training exercises. Pretending a visitor was on the way, I'd start singing a Taylor Swift song about ex-lovers and Queena would dive into the bed as fast as possible. I put a stop watch on her. Her best time was 3.4 seconds. She was very quiet. If we heard the cleaning ladies clamoring up the stairwell with their mops and buckets, in she went. If the door chime sounded, in she went. If there came a day when a pair of plainclothes cops trailed me up the stairs, my song would be Swift, conjuring the she-power of a culture far away.

Still, I was a wreck on Mondays, cleaning days, and found myself cutting classes short so I could rush home and see that everything was okay. To solve this problem I asked the lavender ladies to switch from Monday morning to Wednesday morning when I didn't have any classes, and during that time Queena would hide inside the bed. While the *fuwuyuan* mopped the floors and scrubbed the tub, I sat on the bed reading a book, smiling and saying, "*Xie xie,*" each time the lady passed by with her mop or broom. I was the mother bird guarding her eggs.

The box under the bed was roomy and Queena was a skinny thing. Most foreign experts stored suitcases, blankets, and boxes of Christmas cheer inside these beds. One morning after the cleaning lady had gone downstairs, Queena popped out of the other bed, not the one where I'd been sitting, and we had a good laugh.

At night I brought her bubble tea and bags of takeout from the various cheap restaurants around campus—pork in fish sauce, eggs and tomato, tofu swimming in black gravy—or I made her some of my own vegetarian dishes. Lentil soup, vegetable casserole. A few times she cooked me a meal, but she wasn't much of a cook because she had grown up doing so much school work.

"I don't know how to do anything but read, write, and add numbers," she said. "I barely know how to sew. I'm an average tennis player. I don't know how to knit or take care of animals. I cannot even keep a vegetable alive. So many of us are like this, and it's high time the Chinese schools changed this."

For exercise, Queena did *tai ji* in the living room, or danced to an aerobics program that aired on CCTV on Thursday nights. She only had one pair of pants, so I cut down a pair of my flannel pajamas for her and the draw string kept the baggy cutoffs from sliding off her tiny waist. She read a good number of my books and seemed especially fond of Dickens, Flannery O'Connor, and Flaubert's *Sentimental Education* (she had already read *Madame B*). She thought the scrivener Bartleby was a bit crazy. She was taken by Thoreau and seemed offended when I told her that Henry was not all he made himself out to be, that he had strolled into town most days to feast on his mother's cookies.

"But he spent a night in jail," she said. "If he wrote these things today in China, don't you think they would put him in jail?"

"You have a point there."

"He could say more in 1848 than I can say today."

"America has four percent of the world's population and twenty-five percent of the world's prison population. Land of the free. And the free speech you talk of, our courts equate money with speech."

One afternoon when I came home, Queena shrieked with delight because *The New York Times* had done a story on her underground group. *The Times* had interviewed key players in the Alliance and had referred to the imprisonment of a female college student that sounded a lot like Vesuvius.

"Read this part," she said. "It says students from several Chinese Universities are bonding togezer to form pro-democracy clubs using code names and VPNs."

"Toge*ther*. Get that tongue under the teeth."

"What do you think of this?"

"A handful of students do not a movement make. Remember, you're reading *The New York Times*. They love your dissidents, and while I won't say the writers exaggerate per se, what they choose to cover makes it seem like more is happening than, you know, reality."

"A boy got taken away because he had a t-shirt in the trunk of his car. It was in English. *CPC = Corruption, Power, Criminals.* He was sentenced to four years of forced labor."

"There are stupid college kids everywhere."

"The leader of our alliance—he is very handsome and a bit sexy— he says that they can't put one hundred thousand people in jail, if we all commit acts of resistance in simultaneously."

"Simultan*eity*. It's a tough word. Even for English speakers, it's a toughie. Look, I imagine the girls like your leader an awful lot. Does he like them back? I'm just saying, I know men. Even the well-meaning ones, it's hard not to be tempted by young females."

"He sleeps somewhere different every night."

"Please don't invite him over for dinner."

She asked me questions in the evenings that had nothing to do with social revolution. What was the difference between a confirmation and a bar mitzvah? What was my job like at the insurance company? Why did Europeans love scarfs so much? How come I wasn't married?

Late one night she insisted that I tell her about my girlfriend.

"It'll only make me feel lonely," I said.

"You're not lonely. I'm here to bother you every night. Was she Chinese?"

"Yes, she lived in Shanghai. It was an epistolary relationship, I mean, an email relationship. Very distant. I don't recommend it."

"Why did you come to China?"

"It's complicated."

"But why?"

"One answer is that I wanted to get away from my father. Another answer—the one that makes me appear more like a filial son—is that his company went bankrupt, and just when the old bird seemed ready to strangle himself, the feds let him keep a smidge of equity in his house and a JV worth nothing. The Chinese took it over, toxic assets and all, and as for me—"

"Your father must have been very rich!"

"He was. Then he wasn't."

"Both our fathers lost their lifelihood."

"The situations are hardly the same."

"You never tell me anything about your life, Francis. How did it happen with your father?"

"Oh God, Queena, that's a long story."

"Tell it to me, Uncle. You never know. If one of us gets taken away, we never see each other again, and we never tell each other our deep secrets."

"I don't want to know your secrets."

"At least tell me about the Chinese company. Did you make a lot of money? Was your firm as successful as BIG?"

"I'll tell you about the pit."

没有

Workers had started digging a huge pit on the lot next to our building, what looked to be the foundation for a new, greater building, if not an underground parking garage. It seemed unfair that a developer could buy the rights to that property (nobody "owned" land in China) and put up a building that would block our view of the amazing Great Future Building, which looked like a living Escher painting the way it seemed to defy gravity. The view from our offices was one of the best in the city, and on a clear day you could see the mountains in the distance. Here was the long boulevard streaming with traffic, here was a glinting mall with flying eaves, and in the middle of it all, as though a bomb had exploded, a pit of tawny soil. Machinery like so many toys digging into the past.

Sometimes when I was bored with work—and when wasn't I bored with work?—I'd stare out the window at the giant creatures clawing and scooping in their great sandbox, the hardhat men taking cigarette breaks, the dump trucks hauling loads of dirt. I could see the guts of the city, the huge concrete piles that held up the road and the buildings. There was a kind of voyeurism in seeing the foundation for the new building, as if anyone who knew a thing about construction could spot the obvious flaws and bring a lawsuit if only the legal system would allow it. The piles did not run that deep. They looked vulnerable to erosion and decay.

No one in the office knew what was being built. No one seemed annoyed that our nice view would be erased. All cities experienced this. Skyscrapers stood close together. The old ones got dwarfed by the news ones. Life went on. I started feeling that I alone was preoccupied by this pit. Some of my coworkers thought I was strange for caring so much, so I would shut up about the matter for a few months, as the hole got deeper and more organized. Then I couldn't help myself and I would ask again, getting no answer.

The only one who would know anything, I realized, was our chief executive. Although I called the firm "the insurance company," Mr. Li had transformed China Life and Casualty from a humdrum insurer into an audacious holding company with high-profile acquisitions of the NexCo Tower in Chicago (formerly the Hancock building), Hotel Ouis in Paris, Winchester's Online Auction in London, and dozens of premium golf courses around the world. The subsidiary of my father's insurance company had been purchased long before these mega-deals, snatched right out of the jaws of defeat. In fact my father had filed for Chapter 7 and was to have his beloved company slaughtered at market when the Chinese came knocking. Why they had chosen to rescue a joint venture whose stock price sat at four cents a share is still not clear to me, but to make a long story short, I was recruited to Beijing as part of the deal. You could say I volunteered. You could say my mother begged me to help preserve some vestige of Chicago Central Casualty and Life, overlooking the fact that I detested office work in general and the insurance business in particular.

Through a private investigator Mr. Li had learned that I had studied in Beijing as an exchange student eight years prior, earning an award for excellence in Chinese studies. They knew I had an MBA from Chicago and that I'd worked for my father's firm, doing everything from actuary to claims to sales, and thus I became a pawn in the negotiations overseen by our lawyer Mr. Mendelsohn, whom my father called Mr. 400 in honor of his hourly rate. A week shy of my thirtieth birthday, I left my father stewing in his zebra chair in the living room, with his bourbon, his fourth-place White Sox, and a crippling case of anhedonia—and moved to Beijing.

The Chinese were surprised when I insisted on maintaining a middle management position, where I could process data on the growth possibilities of liability insurance in the PRC, which figured to be a huge untapped reservoir, though the only reservoirs I was interested in tapping had to do with words and women. I seemed to do my best writing between 10 p.m. and 3 a.m. Not the best habit for an employee, I admit, but there was a Starbucks two floors below that kept me walking and caffeinated.

At any rate, I enjoyed a special relationship with our CEO, Mr. Li, who trusted me beyond logic. He desperately wanted his firm to behave more like a western company and was always pumping me for advice on how to spruce up our internet presence or how to expand our market share of life insurance policies. He liked to trot me out for big meetings, as I was good face for the company. The fact that he knew I was a writer was not a mark against me but rather fed the stereotype that Americans were the "creative ones" while Chinese employees could not think outside the box. If I gave an opinion, he affirmed my genius by caressing his handsome, aging face and murmuring, "Yes, yes." In spite of my special relationship with Mr. Li, I was very nervous about asking him about the pit.

He was an impressive man, with angular features and silver hair, large glasses that were out of fashion and therefore gave him a kind of brainy credibility. He was one of those leaders who could spend two minutes with a stranger and make him feel like the most important person in the room. I should note here that in spite of my lack of passion for the job, I was a good employee. I was repeatedly recommended for promotions, which I turned down and kept secret from Lulu, who would have liked nothing better than to date an executive in a successful firm. Mr. Li was well aware of my positive performance evaluations.

Every time I saw him coming, say, at a Christmas Party or a Spring Festival gathering, I braced myself for his unctuous manner, and every time I came away smitten. Because of his limited English, he tended to repeat the same lines: "How is your father?" and "You are a hard worker, very hard worker" and "I must apologize for the bad air."

I would reply in Chinese and we'd have some good conversations about Chinese architecture, Mexican silver, or Italian olive oil. He proclaimed himself an Epicurean and wanted nothing less than the best things of the world. I believed him when he said he wasn't like the younger generations drowning to death in their stuff. "I don't want many thingsuh. I want ze best thingsuh," he once said in English, before elaborating in Chinese: "I want the best towels, the best candles, the best lighting. You know who makes the best yogurt? Bulgaria. You know who makes the best salt? Israel. The best coffee comes from Africa, or even better but too expensive is the coffee from Bali. There is a cat that shits out the beans, already processed with some enzyme that makes the coffee very smooth." He would smile, showing his dingy teeth, and say, "These days in China we can get almost anything. In fact, we and the Russians are responsible for driving up the prices of the top-rated wines. Now, put this in perspective, Francis. Keep in mind that my parents were taken away to work on a reform-through-labor farm, leaving me to be raised by my grandparents. I had one toy. It was a rubber duck. I bit the nose off."

One afternoon I found myself standing behind Mr. Li in the queue at Starbucks. He was chatting up the barista, saying he wanted his cappuccino to have foam like the beard of Santa Claus. He paid for my black coffee and explained that he liked to come down here to stretch his legs and gaze out the window. He had spent the previous week in Paris on business and wasn't yet back to his old self.

"I should probably do *tai ji*," he said in Chinese. "But caffeine works faster. I hope you don't mind my standing. I'm not in the mood to sit. Some of the greatest thinkers in history did their best work standing up, you know, Benjamin Franklin, Leonardo Da Vinci, Laozi if we consider walking as a form of standing. You don't mind?"

"Not at all," I said, and the two of us stood at the window watching the workers in the pit. A giant forklift was moving down an earthen rampart with a bundle of rebar dangling from its tines. It looked like a dangerous maneuver, all that weight slung forward, and I almost wanted the machine to tumble head over heels just so I could see Mr. Li's reaction. I wanted a truer picture of the man, to know what he thought about the project below. I couldn't imagine him losing control, but there had to be some circumstances that would unhinge him.

"He must be a skilled driver," I said.

"Yes."

"The progress seems pretty good."

"Too slow," he said, his lips thin. "We need to get more bodies down there. I'm in no mood to talk about it. You and I, we feel the same about it, no?"

"Of course."

"We need more bodies down there. How can we expect to boost our GDP without enough workers?"

And that seemed to be all. Mr. Li's cup was empty. I still had coffee left.

Seeming to focus on a group of workers standing behind a welder, he shook his head and said, "Look at those guys. Standing around." He tapped out the last of his foam and said, "Back to work. Be sure to say hello to your father. You can tell him about the project if you like, but my advice is to wait. I suppose you may have turned to him for advice on the matter, but if you don't mind keeping it a secret a while, you know, until we jump some hurdles, maybe that would be best."

I meant to ask him what project he was talking about, but before I knew it he was on his way back to his office.

The number of workers increased wildly after that day. Things began to look a little disorganized down there, but then again, an anthill looks pell-mell to the untrained eye.

One day I saw a worker slip in the mud and fall under the tracks of a bulldozer. His legs looked very soft, as if they could transmit no experience of pain. He must have cried out to the world, but I couldn't hear him over the jetting sound of the espresso machine. The yellow bulldozer rolled along unaware of the injured man, and another vehicle came along a few minutes later and scooped up the injured worker in a front bucket. The man did not writhe in pain or reach for his legs.

His white helmet rolled down a rocky embankment and two workers ran to retrieve it as two others ran to comfort him. They wore the same white helmets and blue jumpsuits. It was a dreary, rainy day, and the smog hung thickly over the city. I could not see the mountains or the Olympic rings on that day.

The workers trotted alongside the bucket of the steadily moving backhoe. The vehicle had to go down a steep grade first before hitting a rampart that would take them up and out of the pit, and in this way it seemed reasonable to raise the bucket, which is precisely what happened, only the workers wanted to stay with their friend, so they clung to the bucket, adding more weight to the front. These were scrawny men, most of them no more than seventy kilos, which seemed like nothing for a big Sany loader—but the driver panicked. He sounded the horn and motioned for the workers to let go. Two men had managed to climb into the bucket with the injured man. Two were hanging from the lip, and one was trotting along through the mud as the machine ambled into a depression. He still had a cigarette in his mouth. He was one of the brown immigrants from the sticks. He had a rugged, photogenic face.

I heard chatter from the coffee bar and another whoosh of steam coming from the espresso machine. Two women in business suits were discussing their sons' onerous homework schedules and the number of hours each boy spent studying for the *gaokao*.

No one but me seemed to be aware of the spectacle in the pit, and as I looked around at the other buildings around the square, I wondered how many eyes were taking in the scene. What were the chances that only I, six poor workers, and two drivers had witnessed the accident? Eventually, my foot soldier with the cigarette in his mouth scampered out of the way and the two hangers-on let go and dropped.

Halfway through my story, Queena started dozing off, her eyes fluttering and her head bobbing forward as if trying to get through class after an

MSG-laden lunch. She didn't seem much interested in my painstaking description. I stopped talking. The sudden quiet awoke her, and in this way she was like my father, who would snap awake from the deepest, snoring slumber the moment I attempted to turn off his TV at 2 a.m. in the green-carpeted landscape of that bedroom overlooking Chestnut Drive. He would choke on his breath and say, "Hey, leave that on!" as if anger at his son was his go-to emotion, and dutifully, I'd click back to whatever thriller was on HBO at the moment.

Queena said, "I'm listening. Keep going."

But I heard my neighbors tromping up the stairs after a night of drinking, most likely the Slovenian woman and her beau, so I put my finger to my lips, "Shh," and Queena swallowed. When we heard the door shut upstairs, I resumed my story. Queena yawned and said, "That is so sad about the worker."

As the backhoe was making its way out of the pit, I turned to the people in the seating area, hoping to catch somebody's eye and share the awe. This Starbucks was a marquis store on the expansive second level, with a gorgeous glass staircase spiraling up from ground level, a chandelier, a purling fountain, and cobalt walls decorated with modern art. The women kept talking about their sons. A few people were fingering their iPads. One man was watching a movie on his laptop, ear buds poking out of his head like electrodes.

I tried calling Lulu but had no service. This had never happened in this spot and I saw across 2nd Ring Road, atop the National Television Broadcast Building, a copse of radar dishes and antennae that looked capable of communicating with an alien force. I felt panic in my heart. I took a step toward the baristas, as if anybody in a uniform could help.

A young security guard paced the landing above the spiral stairwell, his hands on his thick belt. Too many times I'd found these guards to be friendly but useless, so I rushed into the elevator and pressed "68," the top floor where the executive offices were, knowing Mr. Li was in today because an email had informed us (in a somewhat bragging tone) that he would be meeting with the Minister of Commerce in the afternoon. And truth be told, I had been looking out the window at the time of the accident because I was hoping to see a motorcade of black Audis with red flags whipping in the wind. I found beauty in those formations, however sinister they seemed.

But the elevator would not go to the sixty-eighth floor, or the seventh, or the first. After pressing all buttons, only the square for the sixth floor lit up. So I went back to my office and told my coworkers Cindy Wu and Cheng Si what I had seen in the pit. Cindy was a leggy girl with a black bob. Cheng was a jock who was into Teslas he couldn't yet afford. They both struck tragic expressions and said, "How terrible!" and "Construction is dangerous." Cindy, who was beautiful except for a giant mole on her neck about the size of a June bug, relayed a story of workers who had fallen nineteen stories to their death in an elevator at a construction site in Chongqing. Cheng, who was busy tapping out a text message, managed to talk at the same time, ruefully sharing his own story about a welder from his hometown who had died on the job. "Half those guys are blind by the time they get old," he said, moving his thumbs.

"I think I should tell somebody," I said.

"Yes, I think it is right to tell someone," said Cindy. "But he won't get much, especially if he's an immigrant worker. At least they should pay his hospital bills for a limited time."

"There's always weather you can't predict in advance," said Cheng. "Without accidents, none of us would have a job." And then realizing how callous he sounded, now finished with his text, he said, "What I mean to say is, there's a purpose to our work in the casualty sector."

"In fact, he's lucky this happened in this day and age," said Cindy. "In years past, they would have forgot about him totally. That is to say, much needs to be improved to the system, but the government is making strides."

"One hopes so," said Cheng. He was shaking his cell phone like a bartender making a martini, or a gambler with a cup of dice.

"What are you doing?" Cindy asked.

"I'm trying to get in touch with a girl from my hometown. A total stranger. It's a kind of microblog. If I shake, and she is shaking at the same time, maybe we can meet for lunch."

"What if she's not pretty?"

"Then I keep walking. The restaurant is surrounded by glass, so all I have to do is keep an eye out for the woman keeping an eye out for me. If she's a dog, I don't enter."

"That's mean."

"She's a total stranger. She can't be emotionally harmed."

"But she's from your hometown. Maybe she spent forty *kuai* on a cab to get there."

"No. The point is, you only respond to someone shaking her phone in the same vicinity." Then he broke into English, "It's no harm, no foul."

"I don't understand," said Cindy.

"*No harm, no foul* is a basketball term from the NBA."

"I'm going back to work. I have to print these things and get a bunch of signatures from a bunch of men."

"Well, you look good today. Especially here," he said, cupping his hands under his breasts. "I'm sure you'll have very good luck getting their signatures."

"Go shake your phone, mister."

Then he looked down at his phone with a sour expression and said, "Shit. No service. That never happens here."

I went to the window and looked out at the yellow pit. A cement truck was pouring sludge into a black hole the diameter of a village well. The backhoe was gone. The workers had been replaced by other workers. The yellow bulldozer kept moving. Nothing looked unusual.

The next day I got a call from Mr. Li's assistant asking would I be available to speak with Mr. Li on my private mobile phone, and would it be too much to ask me to be somewhere other than my office at the time of the call, which should occur in about two minutes? Sally's voice was beautiful as ever, especially the vowels, so round and buttery, that I wanted to keep her on the line, but I was too confused to say anything further.

I left the office. I went from a warm-carpeted hallway into a cold stairwell, closing the door just as my little turd of a phone started chirping. Was it more polite to say, "Hello?" and pretend I didn't know it was Mr. Li calling, or was it more polite to say, "I'm right here, Mr. Li." Both seemed awkward for their own reasons and as I huddled in the cold cement stairwell staring up at the blinking light of a smoke detector, I found myself unable to speak after pressing "Receive Call."

Mr. Li's reedy voice, full of enthusiasm, said, "Francis? *Wei? Ni hao*, Francis?"

"I'm here," I said. "I think I lost service for a minute. Good afternoon, Mr. Li."

"You may call me Shen Pi."

"I'll keep that in mind, yes."

"I have great news. The investors, at least the ones we were counting on, have all signed on. And the regulators have approved the tax abatement." He then said in English after I failed to respond. "Slam dunk!"

"Slam dunk," I repeated.

"This news is better than expected. You will see a nice bump in your salary. By today in fact, by 5:30 or so. Be sure to stop by the seventh floor and sign the paperwork. We don't want Uncle Li in trouble, now do we? I know we are far from finished with the project, especially one of such eminent magnitude, but we must pay ourselves, no? What many people fail to understand about our system is that I am an employee, not unlike you. I may be the chief executive officer, but I'm not an emperor! I answer to the board of directors and the stockholders. I must perform according to their high expectations or I'm gone. They'll have my head on a platter. But as I was saying, the salary increase has been enthusiastically approved by the board. As for your duties, you'll have a few more responsibilities, but they are nothing you can't handle."

I felt a strangling sensation at the neck, knowing I would have less time for writing. I didn't care how much money they gave me. Bumping my hours up by ten percent would send me over the tipping point into despair. The stench of the emails. The morning meetings. The horror of those sixty-five-page Market Analysis PDFs. I thought of the famous lines I'd memorized in Chinese class from *Du Fu*: "I am about to scream madly in the office/Especially when they bring more papers to pile higher on my desk." I quietly coached myself to be strong enough to say no.

"You don't have to do much more than what you're already doing. We like having you where you are—not too high, not too low, right where nobody can find you. You're not like your father in this respect. You are definitely not the nail that sticks up."

He was laughing heartily over my phone, his powerful little voice echoing in the stairwell. He kept talking, leaving the little "ehn" at the end of his sentences that was common among working class people. He was a sweet man in this way, who meant no disrespect by saying that I was unnoticeable. He thought it was a fine quality. I was not arrogant like so many foreign businessmen.

"I like you, Francis. To be honest, when we first met I thought you were a little strange, like your mind was off thinking about dirty things. But now I have come to respect your unassuming nature. I see that you're funnier than most people give you credit for. It pleases me to deliver this good news. And by the way, I would like you to teach me English once a week. This would not be part of your obligation as an employee. I will pay you separately at far better than the going rate."

I heard footsteps below. I imagined a troop of stocking-capped workers hauling some long, thick electrical cord to install on the roof. In China it seemed that workers were everywhere, like Oompa Loompas always in motion. But then I recognized the footfalls as high heels, and once I heard the steel door slam shut, I brought to Mr. Li's attention my concern for the fallen worker in the pit. I described what I'd seen the day before, the man slipping under the tracks, the front loader scooping up the man, and other workers climbing into the raised scoop or hanging by their fingertips. Mr. Li listened for a good while.

"I know," he said. "A tragedy. I have sent some officials down there to give extra safety training courses to the workers. I will do everything in my power to ensure the safety of our men. Of course, when you consider the scope of the project and the quality of workers these days, some incidents are bound to happen. Nonetheless, we don't want another such occurrence."

"What happened to the man?"

"We are taking care of him. We're fixing him up with one of the best prosthetic legs from Germany. You know that Olympic runner a while back with the prosthetic legs? There's hope for people."

"You mean the guy who murdered his girlfriend? Never mind. I'm only wondering, is this worker being covered by the subcontractors? Us? The People's Net? I can't imagine anyone covering a worker at that level. Those prosthetics, and he may need two from what I saw, wouldn't they cost over a hundred thousand yuan?"

"It's complicated. He doesn't work for us directly. But thank you for asking. I must not be late for my next meeting. Without investors, the world would grind to a halt!"

After the call, I went back to my office and stood at the window looking down at the pit. I seemed to hear my coworkers whispering, "He's at it again," but it may only have been my imagination. My right ear was throbbing from the conversation in the stairwell and I had hardly slept the night before, owing to a volley of emails with Lulu.

I had sent her one of my stories, a new one dedicated to her that I thought was pretty great, and after a week she still hadn't read the piece. Her job was killing her. She was still in her twenties and expected to work seven days a week, 9 a.m. to 10 p.m. All she did was complain about how boring it was to be an auditor for a large company, acting as though someone had put a hatchet to her head and said, "This is your career. Do it now or I'll make your skull bleed!" She complained that her managers were uptight. Then she got mad at me for correcting her grammar, this, after she had expressly asked me to correct her English whenever possible.

The day was clear and bright with a brilliant sky and the mountains in perfect view, the blue sky showing through the Olympic rings. Smoke chuffed from the exhaust pipes of the construction vehicles. The cement truck had moved on to another hole, filling the column with cement for the next pile. The workers went about their tasks, slicing bars of steel with white fire, gouging the soil with scoops, waving drivers into their lanes, piling rubble in wheelbarrows. I did not see the white chubby man or the brown man with the widow's peak or the man with the cigarette. I did not see any of the workers who had trudged through my memory before.

By the time I finished my story, which truly had no end, it was one o'clock in the morning and I was so sleepy I almost didn't notice Queena standing at my book case. She was admiring a portrait of my sister. Bekah wore a sardonic expression that seemed to suggest the stupidity of portraiture, and the inability to ever know how the mere presence of her photograph could make me feel so deeply lonesome. Her face a little soft from a year of dormitory food, her eyes dark and hard like my father's— she had done her hair in little ringlets for the portrait.

"She looks like you," said Queena. "She's very pretty. Did she work for your father's company as well?"

"Not in a million years," I said. "She's a lot younger than me. Too young to work for the family firm, thank God. And anyway, she's brave enough to say no to my father. She wants to build latrines in Africa with no profit motive whatsoever, and she is utterly unafraid to tell my father so. She is a kinder person than ninety-nine percent of humanity."

"Why are you so afraid of your father?"

"Oh God, Queena, that's a long story. Time for bed."

A Visit from the Warden

Today we are taken down the hall to the re-education room to watch a movie. We all get very excited. This would seem to be our treat for Chinese New Year. Even if it turns out to be the most barefaced propaganda, there's entertainment in that. If it's one of those Chinese VXX movies, the bulging comic book breasts will be welcome as there is comedy in those violent sorcerers and ninja stars, deadly spider silk and poisonous goo issuing from the mouths of she-men. We'll all be entertained in some way.

The room is cold and ageless as our cell, and here again I can't tell if the building is fifteen or a hundred years old. There's a high window covered with a green blanket to keep out the light, a wooden lectern on a concrete stage, and a much-divoted blackboard. I have been here before, it seems, and now I realize that the room is all but a replica of Room 201 in the business school at Cap City University, exactly the same but with bricks filling two of the windows. What are the chances that the same architect has designed both buildings? I think of Mr. Li, who loves architecture, and wonder if he would be ashamed of the dull design, if he is such an Epicurean that he cares about the aesthetics of prisons.

In spite of the room's austerity, the audio-visual equipment is state of the art. Bose speakers hang on the walls. A screen drops slowly from the ceiling with a pleasant hum. A blue light glares from the eye of an overhead projector and I find myself admiring the dust motes suspended in the funnel of light. Dim room. Eager voices of men with schoolboy energy. Something new is happening.

I don't care if they show us terrifying scenes of severed limbs, a health bureau film on head lice, or a soap opera. My writing hasn't been going well in recent days. My thoughts keep breaking off, and the men, being restless, awaiting our eventual call to labor, have become obstreperous. A wicked cold is making the rounds through the cell block, leading to an increase in spitting. Rumors persist that a man from the "Tea House" was given an injection, moments before execution, to preserve his kidneys and save the life of some high official's son. Maybe what I need now is some headless entertainment. If they show us a film on Maoist thought, even a reasonable attempt at convincing us that order and harmony demand sacrifice, I'll take it. I'm tired of my own mind. I'm sick and tired of my cellmate's banter, which in recent days has turned more pornographic.

Two special guards wearing bulletproof vests and helmets enter the film room. One guy carries a machine gun, the other a strangely-curved billy club. They check for bombs and weapons, asking us to stand and raise our arms, spread our legs, frisking the guys up front before making their way to Xu Xuo and me in the back row. I often end up paired with Xu Xuo because neither one of us talks.

Outside in the yard, prisoners from another division are doing calisthenics. Farther off, the sound of fireworks smacks the air. The guards check the cubbies under the desks (where my students used to stash their cell phones and greasy bags of street food). They order us to drop our trousers, and the taller guard, the one with the funny billy club, snaps on latex gloves and begins checking between our cheeks. His friend stands with a machine gun pointed at the ground, and after the last man is checked the duo files stern-faced out of the room. It's hard to know if their expressions are baleful or bored. I've seen more animated tollbooth workers.

Five minutes later they return with the warden. How do I know he is the warden? Because he receives no introduction.

"I do not think you are animals," he says, taking his place at the lectern. "A zoo is for animals. You are men and you deserve to live as men of this nation or any other nation, with your free will and your desires and your convictions. If you have made grievous errors against society or mankind at large, there is ever the chance for atonement in your time at Kun Chong, even and especially if it means changing your mindset through labor. I want to personally apologize for the delay in your work assignment. I know many of you are eager to get to work, to atone, or at minimum to have some of your curiosity answered—but above all to start chipping away at the great work of restitution. The sooner you begin laboring, the closer you are to release."

The warden has a large square head and crescent eyebrows, hair dyed jet black and slicked down with pomade. Pushing seventy, he wears silver bifocals. His face is unblemished and he looks like a good candidate for an electric shaver commercial. What mostly shows his age are his long teeth and the loose skin at the neck, just above his firmly-knotted tie. He speaks with a thick Beijing accent, where Ns turn to Rs, so that *guan*, "closed," sounds like *guar*, and *hou*, "later," sounds like *huar*.

He apologizes yet again for the delay in our work assignments, blaming bureaucracy, oversight, parts not shipped on time, parts shipped too early, misplaced documents, delays in approvals of particular petitions which, when laid in the hands of mid-level staffers—for there's never a delay when the head official himself gets hold of the reins—seem to hover in limbo for lengthy periods. "Add to this, the naïve view within certain quarters of the government that the *laojiao* system should be scrapped altogether and you have a recipe for paralysis. Indeed, there are so-called reformers who want to do away with a system that has not only undeniably helped build modern China as we know it, and which still plays a vital role in state harmony, but more importantly where you're concerned, a system that has given untold men and women honest opportunities to contribute to something larger than the self. No doubt, abuses occurred in the past, before the time of Deng Xiaoping. Perhaps you have heard the stories of cannibalized workers and over-zealous organ harvesting— but as they say the best time to plant a tree was twenty years ago. The second best time is now. I rue the day that our penal system resembles that of the United States, where prisoners rot away the hours with no purpose whatsoever and as a consequence use all their pent-up energy toward violent ends."

He waves his hand as though at rotten meat. "Bureaucratic paralysis!"

I pretend not to understand a word.

He rambles like any minister of Government X and I gradually find myself dozing off, vaguely aware of my surroundings and fairly able to avoid resting my head on Xu Xuo's shoulder. This would be to rest one's head on death row. It is said the human head weighs eight pounds, but in this dark warm room with the hum of the projector and the cadence of a lackluster orator, the bowling ball on my shoulders feels like a sixteen-pound Brunswick.

When I hear my name, *Laoshi* Kauffman, Teacher Kauffman, I snap awake and look at the warden.

He smiles. "One does not expect a teacher to be such a poor, sleepy student."

At these words, a jolt of adrenaline hits my heart and I'm immediately on edge, pulse thudding in my neck, eyes dilating, sweat gathering at the fingertips. Because the warden is an educated man and I am an educated man, I take his challenge as a badge of honor in spite of the panic flaming through my body. I feel a certain pride in being the one man the warden has chosen to address and I sit up straight, ready for the next volley.

"The teacher is going to stop his lying and speak some Chinese for us."

A conspiratorial murmur passes through the room.

"He is going to stop pretending he doesn't understand our language and make his self-criticism in perfect *pu tong hua*."

The other prisoners look at me: some with anger, some with bemusement.

"Back to the old days," says the warden, "when a man could give a self-criticism and feel better afterwards. Nonetheless, you are lucky the Cultural Revolution is long gone and we are back in the habit of respecting our teachers once more. If it were 1972 right now, look out! We'd put a dunce cap on your head and hurl eggs at your ribs. But fortunately we're more purposeful at Kun Chong."

He steps away from the lectern and walks through the dusty column of light, his shirt flashing white as a priest's collar on Holy Thursday. "It has been a long time since you have held court in a classroom, Master Kauffman. I'm sure you'll feel right at home. Teach. Teach. What is that American expression? *Those who can, teach.* I'm fond of that expression, having served as a provincial secretary of education myself many years ago." He then says in English, "I studied in the United States for two years, in Greencastle, Indiana."

I have no strategy in mind as I march to the head of the class. When I grip the sides of the lectern and gaze out at the shadowy faces of prisoners and guards and the blue light aimed at me, I try to sound professional. I want to ride the formality established by the warden so that maybe I can appeal to the higher nature of the men.

"Dear colleagues," I begin. "Thank you for giving me a moment of your time this afternoon. Thank you for allowing me to explain my circumstances and to reflect on our time together. As the warden has stated, it is true that I speak Chinese. It is true that I have followed your conversations with great fascination and sympathy, albeit in a furtive manner. Let me explain why to this point I have kept this a secret."

The faces of the men—I can't tell if they are shocked or angry. Some twitch and whisper, while others hang their mouths open. Their ruddy mugs seem flat and far away, like the blotches of a crowd in a theater on an anxious winter night.

I pause for a moment, shocked by the fluidity of my Chinese, no doubt a result of hours of listening to my cellmates. It helps that I'm aping the bureaucratic style of my warden, which in its formality lacks the challenging idioms of street speech. "I had no ambitions to spy on you or uncover secrets. I work for nobody in my homeland, if it can even be said that I have a homeland. I was born in Berlin, Germany, and moved to Chicago at the age of eight by force of my father, who had bounced back and forth between Germany and America because he had married a German girl that he had impregnated out of wedlock when she was twenty-five, and he forty."

I falter and gather my thoughts. It would be a tricky-enough story to tell in English. In Chinese I have to figure out a way to make the chronology clear—that my father had come to Berlin as a tourist, in a manner of speaking, on a sort of pilgrimage to the city where his parents had lived before his father and grandparents (but not his mother) had been taken away to a "work camp" run by the Nazis. Who does this? Who goes back to Berlin to pay homage to fallen ancestors only to knock up a Catholic girl he met in a disco? I am struggling with how to begin this next chapter. "We were Jews—"

"But what is your crime?" says Fang.

"I stand accused of inciting two university students to protest, of harboring a counter-revolutionary in my apartment, and contributing to the instability of society. I have also been accused of an inappropriate sexual encounter with one of my students. I am accused of aiding and abetting the foundation of shell companies and bogus joint ventures, as well as two counts of money laundering, insofar as I had been asked to spirit money out of the country for a man who had already divested the maximum amount under Chinese law."

Here, a clot forms in my throat, not so much from the mention of money laundering but for the sting of the phrase "sexual encounter."

My chest heaves. I feel a nasty cough coming on. Somehow, I manage to relax my throat and continue, and as I hold forth in the lecturing style that I am sure my warden desires, I seem to be aware of my hung jury. Three men acquit me, three men despise me, and one man is impossible to read. Brother Gao and Kuku are on my side, which is hardly surprising. Wu Kaiming can be talked into anything. Jack, Fang, and Yu are against me. Xu Xuo looks on in that lizard-like way he has of regarding an empty desert. His hair has grown over the ears and looks pretty as a girl's, moist and shiny. Among my greatest fears—along with losing the capacity to write, being rejected by my father, unable to love a woman, losing my sister—is that my fate would one day rest on a single juror of limited mental capacity.

The warden nods, directing me to continue.

"When I came to this prison I was honestly afraid, and as is well-known to all, some traumatized children go through periods of silence so as to let their psychological wounds heal. I am not a child, but the instinct not to speak came upon me in the same way. I was dumbstruck. Speaking too much had got me into trouble, so it seemed a dangerous thing to speak at all."

What I say, of course, is mostly shit and the men can smell it. How can I explain that I was scared of them, that my sense of fear and betrayal on that cold November morning was so great that I mistrusted their kind in a way that can arguably be described as racist? I was rejecting their language and their companionship.

Still, there is pleasure in giving a lecture, in hearing my own voice and being listened to. I take up the old joy of university teaching, of the blooming energy of youth that can make a middle-aged professor feel young. I continue with my speech, waxing nostalgically of humorous Kun Chong moments I have witnessed and could have taken part in had I only opened my mouth. I close by stating that I look forward to their companionship, come what may. Never in my life have I given a more florid lecture.

The warden and the men clap, some vigorously and others not. A hand goes up in the middle of the room, underneath the blue light of the projector. Fang is a smartass, but he is well-educated. He has a squeaky voice and his words carry well. He is not my friend; he will never be my friend. I dislike him in the way that school kids dislike each other, not for any good reason but for his confident good looks and arrogant eyes, for the way he taps out his penis after urinating, the imperious way he puffs his pillow at night, the manner in which he assumes leadership of the cell, ordering men to do this or that. *Don't throw your nail parings on the floor. Don't take a shit in the middle of the night. Don't be so chummy with the guards. Don't say anything bad about the Party or you'll get us in trouble.*

He is the detested student I can't ignore, the one I must call on because it is my professional obligation. "Fang, you have a question?"

"You only said you were accused of your crimes. You haven't said whether you committed them."

I would have been happier had he rambled on in his typical, bombastic way, which might have called attention to his own motives. But no. The brevity of his question stones me. In the hazy glare, I focus on three pairs of legs in the front row, disembodied, slippered, a tapping foot, a quiet knee. The legs of the men look inconsequential, crushable, waiting calmly for the answer to a reasonable question. I have to satisfy the warden somehow. He is no dimwit. If I signal even the slightest retraction of my self-criticism, he'll have me hauled off to the Tea House.

"I am guilty as charged. I have done exactly everything for which I am accused."

"Even the sexual conduct?" said Fang. "You had sex with one of your students?"

I can't answer. If I tell the truth, I might seem to accuse the warden of lying.

Vesuvius would spit on the man and get herself bound in fisticuffs. Bartleby would prefer not to answer. Jesus Christ would find some clever way to turn Fang's words back on himself. Abraham would invent the perfect lie on the spot, claiming God had ordained him unto intercourse. David would sling a satchel of rocks. But I am phlegmatic.

"Answer the question!" Fang shouts.

If this exchange had taken place in our cell, one of the men would have told Fang to back off. But here and now on movie night, with the warden standing off to the side in a calm, dark state of neutrality, the men stay quiet. Fang is basically in the middle of the room, third row, at a desk between Brother Gao and Yu, and given the small stature of his companions, he rises like a pinnacle in the dark. I hear the distant wheezing of the industrial complex. I feel a cool draft from the window behind me, the one covered with cloth.

"Yes," I say. "I had an affair with one of my students."

"How old was she?"

"Twenty-one."

"How did you take her? Did you give her a good grade in exchange for her pussy? Did you slip something into her drink? Did you rip her clothes off and force your Jew dick inside her? Did you spray your filth all over her virginal body?"

"Why do you hate me?" I say.

"It is practically rape, you know, to keep a girl sequestered in your apartment and force her to commit sex acts in exchange for protection."

"You have something against me."

"You come over here to our country, you and all these arrogant foreigners, and you stir up trouble. Trouble against the Party and trouble against the People. You are the enemy. You are an enemy to me and an enemy to the people of China. Clearly you are an enemy to the girls in your class."

"Are you trying to impress the warden?"

Here the warden steps in, glancing at his chunky Rolex and saying, "We have an important video production to view. In a few days, we will be leaving Kun Chong for another place where you won't simply wile away your time in a rectangular cell. As I mentioned at the outset, we want to offer you the opportunity for re-education. Out in the open air, men like you may find a common goal through labor. Those of you who have lived the easy life for too long will embody the righteous life of peasants and workers."

Something here makes Brother Gao flinch, something he doesn't like. He tugs at his ears.

"And in this way you will gain a new measure of humility and harmony with the Republic and your countrymen. Some of you are going to work in the vineyards for the Greatwall Wine company, and some of you will work in the plastics mine."

Here again I feel like a schoolboy, murmuring to myself, *Please send Fang to the plastics mine and me to the vineyard…Please send Fang to the plastics mine and me to the vineyard, please, oh God, please.*

Because I am still at the lectern and the warden is to my left against the wall, it seems as though I am endorsing the warden's every word. I have an instinct to nod as though I'm at some conference on linguistics. I want to step down, but that would be an affront to the leader, so I wait. A breeze slips through the fabric behind me, grazing my neck. I shiver against the chill. Because I am slight, when I shiver I really shake.

"Excuse me?" says the warden, a little perturbed. "You have something to add?"

I grin at the warden (or the warden's shadow, I can barely see him for the blinding blue light) and say, "I'm cold. When I'm cold, it is my reflex to shiver."

"You don't really know what it means to suffer, do you?" he says.

"I do."

"Your hands are lily white."

"His hands are filthy with rape!" says Fang.

The warden says, "That's enough, Mr. Feng. You are the prisoner, is that clear? It is not your job to interrogate prisoners at Kun Chong, much as I appreciate your sentiments."

"I do know what it means to suffer," I say.

I am willing to admit to a sex act that never happened, but I am not willing to bend on this philosophical point. I cannot explain myself. I don't make any sense.

The warden laughs and says in English, "Roll the film!" as though we are living in a different time and place where movies do in fact "roll" twenty-four frames per second, when mustard gas prowls the fields of battle and syphilis whispers from chancre sores and women give their woks to the Great Leap Forward and laborers at Dachau mix crumbling mortar for the crematorium and black boys hang from magnolia trees in Mississippi—someplace long ago and not in a room with a screen showing a nervous little arrow scurrying from window to window, from "project library" to "show iMovie."

The warden gives me a look indicating I should return to my seat. The two helmeted guards carry an orange easy chair in for the warden. He sinks into the seat and crosses one leg over the other. As I make my way back to my desk, I catch a nasty whiff of body odor from one of the inmates. Over the next quarter hour, two prisoners from other cell blocks make confessions, one for selling poached African ivory, the other for feeding a donkey to a tiger at the Chongqing Zoo. A regular guard comes in, yoked with a burden, and serves us pork buns, chicken feet, and tea that tastes like soil.

We are shown a gruesome montage from dozens of prison movies in which a man makes a run for freedom only to be shot, usually in the back. There are clips from Chinese Revolution films, Holocaust films, World War II films, cowboy movies, and scenes from Mexican Narco flicks. Some fugitives get their toes chopped off. Some get hanged from oak trees. Some drown in burly rivers. No man ever escapes.

Movie Nights

When I was in high school, I used to sneak out at night and ride cabs through the worst neighborhoods I could find, east into Englewood and Fuller Park, through Blue Island or Back of the Yards, scribbling in a notebook the whole way. I'd find an all-night diner in Hyde Park and pretend to be an edgy college kid writing his masterwork. I felt more like myself as a pretender than when I was doing normal high school stuff. Though I'd spent half my life in America, at school I was pretty much always "the German kid" with the hard-to-lose accent and the adult clothes—not cool enough to go out drinking with the popular kids, uninterested in drugs, terrified by what I wanted to do to girls, but totally turned on by Chicago at night. Sure, I was an elitist kid engaged in nothing more than slumming, and not much of my writing was honest, suffering stuff, but I managed to impress my teachers. At least my sketches had voyeuristic appeal. I got very good at describing scenes and found years later that my best lines came when I was half asleep and not trying too hard.

On more than one occasion I came home at two or three in the morning to the sounds of some violent movie my father had fallen asleep to—machine guns and mortar fire—and rather than sneak past his room, I'd creep in and switch off the TV.

Which never failed to wake him.

"Don't turn that off!" he'd snort as if fully awake. "I'm watching that."

Sometimes I'd sit on the carpet at the foot of his bed, watching the Nazis blow away the French, the Americans blow away the Japs, or Clint Eastwood digging his way out of Alcatraz. After risking my hide on the south side of Chicago (I mostly encountered harmless drunks or strung-out prostitutes who giggled at me, once an actual pimp named Trigger) I just wanted to be with my father. Even a fat snoring old Jewish man who peddled insurance and wore white golf shoes, because he was large and my father, could make me feel safe. As much as anything, I liked how the nervous, flickering television cast grotesque shadows on the wall.

I can't tell you if these nights happened twice or six times. My memory is shaky on this account. I know there were a few nights where he gradually awakened and we talked about the filmmaking or the actors' real lives (Did I know that Charles Bronson was part Indian?) or some episode in history pertaining to what we were watching. He knew a lot about the Vichy Government, about Patton in Africa, about the science of rifling. His mind was far more encyclopedic than mine, his recall much sharper. But I could feel more. I could weep over a sepia-toned scene of a little French boy tucking a note into his satchel. My old man could name the architectural style of the chateau in the background.

I loved the smell of the new carpeting and sometimes I'd fall asleep on the floor by his bed like a boy half my age, as if back in Berlin. In the mornings, he'd pretend like nothing happened. I'm not sure whether I liked this treatment. In some ways it was fun to keep our movie time secret. In other ways it made me feel like he was ashamed of something, as if real connection between us was an embarrassing mistake he wanted to forget.

"I'm a terrible Jew," he'd say, stirring his coffee with a strip of bacon. "I eat bacon. I drink Irish Whiskey, and I use a microwave on Saturdays."

I remember him hitting grounders to me at a park by the lake, commanding me to take off my glove and field them bare-handed if I wanted to develop soft hands. My palms just got bruised. I had grown up in Berlin exposed to *fußball*, tennis, and swimming. I was relatively new to baseball. Finally he said, "The hell with it. I think you'd rather study clover in right field than play shortstop, am I right? Hey, no sweat. At least we know what we're dealing with here. Smart kids like you usually end up outperforming the jocks anyway."

All fathers are contradictions. Mine could recite soliloquies from Hamlet, but in daily life he talked like a butcher. He knew curveballs. He knew Billie Holliday. He knew the grid of Chicago streets like a cop. He knew how to make Béchamel. He could move a lawnmower out of his path with one arm, but he didn't know how to start the thing. He was smart enough for an Ivy league school but had worked as a cabbie to put himself through state schools, which is a lot more than I could say for myself.

When I was in college, I remember my father claiming the Chinese would rule our asses and if I wanted to take the globalized future by the balls, I ought to learn Chinese. He was serious. He asked if I had any interest in signing up for the *Be in Beijing!* program and I jumped at the chance. A few days before I left for China in my junior year, which technically lay within the time period when my father still worried I was gay, he came into my bedroom and slipped me box of rubbers.

"Good luck with the Chinese gals," he said. "You don't want to risk using any cheapo latex."

He wore a Burberry raincoat that flapped in the *woosh* from the heating vent. With his seven o'clock shadow and his black hair tousled by the walk home from the train station, he might have looked like a flasher if not for the shiny, tasseled loafers. His feet were shockingly small for a big man. "I'm sure it won't be Berlin in the '80s," he said, "but you never know."

"Don't worry, Dad. I like girls."

"It's okay if you don't. Better if you do."

"Then it's not okay, if you put it that way."

"I should have named you Frank."

"You've told me that about twenty-three times."

"By rights you should be a Catholic kid. If it was the other way around, if Mom was Jewish—"

"I know, Dad."

"Do you believe in God, Frank?"

"Don't call me that."

"Do you believe in God?"

"The answer to the question doesn't interest me."

He sat on the bed beside my folded clothes and looked out the dark window at an elm tree moving in the wind. "You don't even like me, do you?"

"You're asking me about God."

"It interests me. That's why I'm asking."

"Of course I like you. You're my father. But I don't care about God, like, whether I believe in him or not. The answer doesn't matter to me."

"Well, He may not have invented AIDS—that was some monkey in Africa—but He didn't stop it either. Be careful, son."

After two semesters, I was hooked on the expat life in China. I convinced my father to let me stay for a summer intensive course. I went back after senior year and traveled through Mongolia, Tibet, and the steamy South. I saw the golden eagle hunters on the steppe, the gumdrop mountains of Guilin, the bonfires on the streets of Sichuan—all of which convinced me I wanted to do something besides work for my father's ho-hum insurance firm. When I got back to the States, I mustered all the intestinal fortitude of an origami crane and enrolled in an MBA program. Just as my father wanted. And this generous man, who could have handled the tuition easily, forced me to work for his company for three years in all departments to pay him back for a degree I never wanted in the first place. It was like being an ROTC recruit; I had to pay my dues to the Fatherland before I could do what I wanted, which was study comparative literature at U of C, which I finally got to do after my three-year sentence was up, resenting the old man every time I walked past the mossy hall where Milton Friedman had lectured.

Why do boys want to please fathers they might detest?

I once showed him a very good story called "The Possum and the Jew," which I had published at age twenty-five in one of the best lit journals in the country. The editor, who had discovered the likes of Cole Drinkwater and Sharya LaFontaine, had written that my story was "gloriously weird and fiercely wrought," and further, "At your age I'm almost worried this is one of those brilliant accidents, sort of like the band that never tops their first album. It's that good." I had spent countless hours revising this two thousand-word blessing. My father skimmed it in five minutes in the kitchen, murmured, "That's real cute," and tore open a bill from the landscapers. I was furious. I wanted to go upstairs and set fire to his entire closet of suits and neckties.

Instead, I said nothing.

As I got older, I discovered I could both please him and enjoy his company by talking stocks. We'd sit on the portico at sunset, drinking Old Fashioneds and nibbling on watercress sandwiches, discussing how world trends would favor this or that company. He had a feminine jaw like mine, though he outweighed me by seventy pounds. He had the lips of a woman and the knuckles of a catcher. His belly protruded hard like a muscle.

He once claimed that a few of my stock tips had netted him a quarter of a million dollars, but I think he just wanted to make me feel good. He appreciated my opinions on peak oil, peak water, and what the impending food bubble meant for grain futures. I might have warned him about the mortgage-backed securities crisis if I hadn't turned my attention to studying Poe and Jameson and Goethe. I might have kept my antennae on the goings-on of the market instead of reading Susan Sontag.

Which brings me to the recession, famine, feast, failure, and a few fatal fiduciary *faux pas* by my father, and finally to the old man pacing the living room, rattling ice cubes in a cocktail glass as if to cool his boiling blood: "Bah! They accuse me of weak liability structures, when we were just being nice. Try to treat people decent, you get screwed. It's the dandies who couldn't pay their mortgages that shtupped us, and the bankers in love with all this subprime crap—believe me, I've read what the smarty-pants wrote in *The Wall Street Journal*—and these government clowns put all the blame on us. We're not half as toxic as BIG, but we're not too big to fail. Hey Francis! You're a writer. I bet you love their euphemisms: 'Risky financial maneuvering,' 'Poor liquidity management.' Have I made fun of that one already? Or how about this?"

He picked up a sheaf of papers and, peering through his reading glasses, mocked the commentary from Standard & Poor's: "The financial position of Chicago Central Casualty and Life has become untenable."

He had gotten into mortgage insurance at exactly the wrong time in human history. He had leveraged an awful lot of money to grow the firm.

He looked down at some documents on the table in the foyer, no doubt a letter from a creditor, and muttered, "Goddamn Shylock."

It wasn't all my father's fault. There was that pesky recession. There was the internet itself. When evidence of his company's financial stress leaked into cyberspace, this triggered a sort of "run on the bank" in which thousands of policy holders took their money and fled. Without proper liquidity, when accidents happened and liabilities came due, Chicago Central didn't have the funds to cover what any faithful insurer promised to cover. This broke my father's heart. He had gone into the insurance business for the right reasons. When he first began selling insurance for Mr. Pinker door-to-door in the Polish neighborhoods in Chicago, in the German neighborhoods, in the Czech district—his first job after college and the only business he would ever be in—he had truly believed in selling security, piece of mind, *responsibility*. Now he felt like a crook and a liar.

In a bizarre way, in a cruel way, in a shameful way, I enjoyed watching him go down. He was vulnerable. I was now the virile one.

How could this feel good? Where is the satisfaction in watching your father suffer? He let his guard down. He let me in on things. Because I had an MBA, because I was now an adult, he confided in me, or at least vented.

One afternoon I was in our musty basement with our incontinent dog Chuckles, looking for a writing notebook in one of the boxes, when he came down through a shaft of light, feet heavy on the steps. I was already annoyed that I couldn't find the notebook that I was sure contained a brilliant fragment about a whippet and I just wanted to be left alone. I had recently received a thirteenth rejection on my octopus story (a modular piece with eight sections!) and was hoping the lost whippet story could salvage a year of failure.

I could hear my sister upstairs plucking a few notes on her harp, warming up. I always looked forward to those few minutes at the beginning of her sessions, when she was just screwing around, playing like a summer bird. But Otto Kauffman was crushing the bird with his heels, the way he came down the stairs. Nearing seventy, he was still a big guy, but the shape of a feeble old man was beginning to emerge. Knobby elbows. A humped back. He held a cocktail glass in one hand and a pack of Marlboros in the other. He wore a button-down sweater and hound's tooth pants. He sneered at the dog and tapped the Marlboro pack until a clean white cancer stick slid out.

"Smokie treat," he said.

"I thought you were quitting."

"Hey Francis—"

"Could you not smoke down here?"

"What do you call a guy who promises to pay for a broken vase if the vase gets knocked over by a cat, a guy who pockets money every week just in case your heirloom gets toppled?"

Was this a riddle? I looked up from my boxes and said I didn't know.

"What do you call a person who doesn't pay up?"

I didn't answer.

"A shyster, an asshole, is what."

"That's one way to look at it."

"Sometimes I feel like Richard Nixon, who, by the way wasn't such a bad guy. 'I am not a crook.' I think he really believed that. But what about me, Francis? Am I a crook? Is your old man a crook?"

"Of course not," I said, believing it, but afraid to say he'd made some really dumb financial moves. I reminded him that the mortgage bundlers were the crooks. The homeowner who bought too much house was to blame. The men behind the oh-so-clever financial instruments were to blame. I didn't want to talk about his particular failure. I just wanted to find that peach-colored writing notebook, grab a few kitchen things for my new apartment, and go. The air smelled faintly of ethylene from a clutch of old apples sitting in a silver bowl on a card table. I was dreading the infusion of cigarette smoke.

The sound of my sister's harp grew louder. She was only fourteen but already quite good. She was going over a difficult baroque passage again and again, annoying herself, then seeming to get it, then losing the thread. The notes traveled into the dim basement and I happened to notice the sunlight shifting into one of the window wells, illuminating the cobwebs. Just under the window, an antique chandelier slumped in an easy chair that had been shredded by our cat and relegated to the basement. My father had plans to rewire the chandelier, polish the glass, and hang it in the foyer.

"How bad is it?" I said.

"I feel like a criminal," he said.

"You're not a criminal. What you're feeling, Dad, it's a universal, existential condition. Original sin isn't just a Judeo-Christian concept. The feeling that we are born criminals, born condemned, is—"

"Are you trying to shrink me? My own son? Don't shrink me, Francis. Leave that crap for your literature papers. Tell me what your MBA profs would say about me. Honestly."

"I couldn't say."

"Thou liest. What would they say about me? Surely they would have some way of making me an example of what *not* to do. They're professors, right? Professors love anecdotes. Mine always had anecdotal diarrhea. What would they shit out their arses when it came to The Tragedy of Otto Kauffman and Chicago Central Casualty and Life?"

He drained his drink and was on to the ice cubes.

"I suppose they would say you didn't diversify enough. Credit default swaps not such a great idea. I suppose they would say trafficking in derivatives was a bit zealous, for an insurance firm, I mean."

"But words! What dirty words would they come up with? Give me some fucking metaphors. *Trafficking* I like. Goddamnit, you're a word guy. They have names for chumps like me. Give me a nasty word."

"Victim of—"

"No!" he said, hurling his cocktail glass into the chandelier. He had been a third basemen in college and still had a great arm. To my surprise, the chandelier absorbed the force of the glass like a Frisbee golf goal, the crystal shaking, tinkling, then going silent in the easy chair. The sound of the harp kept coming. The cocktail glass never shattered, almost as if to prove my father's impotence.

"Make up a story that tells the fucking truth!"

That got me mad. "You wouldn't read it anyway, Dad. When was the last time you read a book that wasn't some dumb crime novel? An actual work of literature? Nobody reads anymore. And the people who have the most power in this country read the least. It's a real fucking problem."

"Wah, wah, wah. I read your story."

"You said it was *cute*."

"It didn't make any fucking sense. No sense at all. Who in their right mind would get off his bicycle to pick up a dead possum and start talking to it? You're lucky I said it was cute. You're lucky I didn't tell you what I really thought."

"That proves your impotence!" I said.

"What?"

"Nothing."

"That doesn't make any sense either. Quit trying to be weird and just give me a good, raw story that feels like an ax to the heart, like you're chipping ice to get to some fucking water. Simple. Cold."

I gazed into the window well at the metal grate and remembered playing jail with my cousin.

"I am not a victim," he said, his brow knitted in admiration of the chandelier. "I am a reckless, capital loser. You know what I did? I didn't say shit, in fact I looked the other way when Harry was marking our investments as *non-performing* when we all knew they were *default*. Liar, liar. Pants on fire. Me and Harry—a couple of real honest Abrahams." He lit a cigarette and said, "I'll probably get lung cancer on top of it all. I'll be diagnosed with Stage IV cancer and my insurer won't be able to cover the medical bills."

He blew out the match and tossed it in one of the elaborate pedestal ash trays that until recently had stood in our living room. We were surely the only family on Chestnut Drive who still owned ashtrays that existed as full-blown pieces of furniture. Rebekah had insisted we get rid of them, and of course he had listened to her.

"I could have been more conservative with our investments, Francis. My advice is: Don't get greedy."

He then noticed the dog squatting to shit in the corner. He picked up a rotten apple from the silver bowl, reared back, and let fly for Chuckles, missing her by an inch and leaving a brown splotch on the back wall.

"Goddamn apples," he said.

His second pitch hit her squarely in the ribs. She yelped, then scampered away with shit hanging off her tail.

Rebekah stopped playing the harp. She came downstairs in a yellow sundress and comforted the dog, a sort of genuflecting that spoke of purity and control. She reminded me of a character in a Chekhov story. She rubbed Chuckles under the chin and looked up my father. "Stop it, Dad. You're being violent."

"Derivatives," he said. "Now that's a violent word."

He sat on the edge of an old couch and put his hand over his face. "I'm sorry, honey. Go ahead and play your harp. I'll be a good listener. Play something in D."

Only Rebekah could spin him like this, and when she did it, I felt both admiration and jealousy.

"D-minor," he said. "I wasn't very nice to your brother."

You can't say it isn't sad when a rich man loses his fortune. You can say he deserved it. You can say he was greedy. You can say that his suffering pales in comparison to a boy eating dirt in Sudan, a girl getting abducted by the Boko Haram, an Appalachian grandmother getting her mountain blown to smithereens by Massey Energy, a prisoner getting his toenails yanked out, but you can't say it isn't sad. The life went out of my father. He couldn't sleep. He almost never left the house. He drank too much. Forgot to shave. Turned pale. Lost all capacity for pleasure. No golf, no strawberry shortcake, no ninth-inning home run by the White Sox could cheer him up. He claimed that food had no taste. He put on weight nonetheless.

My mother held out hope for a Swiss bank account, a tax shelter in the Cayman Islands, but my father was too old-school for that. He lost his fucking shirt. Filing for bankruptcy was now the only hope if not a means of buying time, a chance to cut costs, scramble for some capital, and possibly wait for the market to correct. Could it happen? A late inning rally?

On a miserable day of miserable weather in a miserable season, he filed for Chapter 7 and was to have his beloved company put to final rest when we got the call from Mr. Li's translator. Somebody actually wanted to take the subsidiary, a joint-venture with a Chinese firm that had never really taken off. The Chinese were willing to pay enough to cover some of the fines my father had incurred and to leave him—via many long conversations with insurance regulators—fifteen percent equity in his house and not much else. He had no IRA, as everything had been tied up in the company. His unsecured debt, totaling thirteen billion dollars, got wiped away like mud on a windshield.

One bright morning, a snappy-looking Mexican boy from the car dealership came and took my father's Boxster away. I remember my old man pushing the curtain aside, peering out at the icy driveway and saying, "He barely looks old enough to drive."

For a few days my father seemed relieved, and during the proceedings he'd put me on the line to speak with the beautiful-sounding translator, insisting that I show off my Chinese, which was a little rusty at that point. I couldn't quite follow what she said in Chinese, only sense that her voice was lovely in any language. There was something about a visit, and I said yes. Further emails suggested that I might want to join the firm in Beijing.

Initially, my working for the firm sounded like a piece of friendly social banter. Later it became clear it was mandatory, and here was the rub: The difference between the high-context Chinese style of communication and the direct, American way. I said as much to my father and he said, "Well, their way is annoying. If you want something, just say so. I don't know how Goldy-Sachs puts up with it. Well, okay, I do know. I know exactly why."

He made the money sign with his fingers and I resisted the urge to tell him he looked like a character from *Grease*.

Later, we gathered in the living room to suss out the terms of the deal. A large yellow envelope emblazoned with red Chinese characters had arrived by certified mail and my father tore open the contents with a stiletto that he claimed had belonged to an officer in Mussolini's army. My mother wore a purple track suit that made her look like the host of a children's TV show. Papa Otto poured the contents onto the coffee table. Every document was clearly printed in English and Chinese on that long A6 Chinese paper. Every document had an elegant red chop at the end.

"Can you read this stuff?" said my father.

"Some of it. I'm much better at speaking."

"Which character means *bankrupt*? Which one means *loser*?"

"Stop it, Otto," said my mother. "You stop it. You stop feeling sorry for yourself."

When she was angry at him, her Berlin accent got a little thicker.

Outside, it was February in Chicago. Rain pelted the driveway in a manner that surely portended black ice, as today was thirty-four degrees and too weepy to snow. I watched my mother watch the rain. With her smooth skin and golden hair dyed by an expensive salon, my mother had always looked younger than my father. Today she looked half his age.

"Honey," she said. "We should not have the lawyers look at these?"

"Me first," he said. "I'm tired of people telling Otto what to do. I used to tell Otto what to do."

I looked around the living room and realized for the first time how dated the place looked. It didn't look like a rich family's house anymore. The low ceiling, the sunken living room with its white plush carpet and leather couches, the zebra-hide pillows. The mantel was so dusty I wondered if we could still afford our cleaning ladies.

My father put on his reading glasses and for the better part of an hour sat grunting at the terms of the deal, the language of lawyers. Times like these, he still had some Yiddish in him and the ancient curses were joined by thrusts of sarcasm that made him sound like Joe Baseball Fan:

"Yeah, right."

"Puh."

"Come on."

A plane passed overhead. A crow squawked in the yard.

"Goddamnit. Francis, I hope you don't write like this, do you? You should be a law professor. Teach these clowns how to write."

Getting bailed out by the Chinese made him feel ashamed. His friends would call him a sellout, un-American. But in the end, he had no choice.

My father assumed I would go to China or work on a transition team in Chicago for the sake of the family, for my sister, for their retirement. After all, they had clothed me and fed me, and if I'd heard my father say it once, I'd heard it fourteen times: "If you don't feed babies, they die. They die if you don't feed them." I'm not sure why he insisted on the second part. In any case it was a fundamentally unfair thing to say. By this sort of thinking, I could never repay my parents. No child could. The notion of working for the subsidiary in Chicago, doing more than my summer intern work, terrified me. I felt sick to my stomach at the prospect of walking the same halls as my father. I hedged, said nothing, was too spineless to say I wanted to be a writer.

Yes, I had recently won a fiction contest that netted me all of two thousand dollars, but it was a laughable amount of money by business standards. To abandon the family firm and eke out a living as a writer seemed treasonous. I should have felt liberated. I should have observed coolly that Chicago Casualty was dead, the king was dying, and I had no better plan than to hit the road like some modern-day Kerouac, if only I had the taste for alcohol. I should have listened to that Rhodes scholar Dr. Kristofferson, who defined freedom by loss. No. I didn't even have the guts to bring it up as a joke, that I would have preferred teaching English at a community college for pennies an hour, or failing that, waiting tables at night and writing mornings. I had been waiting to see what would happen to the company. I was secretly hoping that bankruptcy would hit us like a piano from a fourth floor window. I wanted to erase all prospects of following in my father's footsteps. Actual poverty sounded appealing.

I was ready to let my father's happiness burn so I could be happy. *Too bad, so sad, you had a good run, Dad. You lived a good portion of your life as a rich man. Get over it. Retire. Collect social security.* He was sixty-nine at the time. The end for him should have been the beginning for me.

It didn't help matters that my sister was "super-excited" about starting at a private high school known for its stellar Arts and Enrichment program. Either I could work for the firm in China and make enough money to send her to an institution that had dedicated practice rooms for harpists, or we could let her go to Jordan High, where kids were getting shot. My father had thrown in the towel. He could not set foot in the old building on Adams and Wacker. My mother and I were tasked with cleaning out his office.

My father, whispering from his sick bed one morning (for he had thrown out his back and got shingles in the same week) directed me in a low voice to destroy a cache of dirty magazines he'd hidden behind a row of bygone actuary reports in his office.

The avocado-green carpet in my parents' bedroom looked very dated. What had seemed a cozy lawn on those 2 a.m. movie nights now seemed a disgusting trap for dust mites. There was a vial of Vicodin on the nightstand and beside that a *Car & Driver* magazine with a red sports car on the cover. My father, Mr. Bigshot Otto Kauffman, eyed his son with a look that said, *Heh, heh, who doesn't keep a little porn?* before casually adding that I mustn't let mother find "the other stuff, heh, heh, just toys and whatnot." How to describe his look of embarrassment? His hangdog eyes and furrowed skin? Put it this way: I have lived in prison and not seen so heavy a pall of shame on any man's face.

My Meaningless Name

We wait for our work assignments. For six days we do nothing but wait, having been told that our assignment will be handed down after the new year festivities. Kun Chong is short-staffed, as the more senior guards have gone home to visit their families. The junior guards are left behind to drink white liquor and set off fireworks in the yard. They toss bombs in toilets, which creates a horrible, volleying echo that hurts our ears. The ringing settles in and invades our sleep. During the day, in the quiet, what else is there to do but sit in my writing chair and gaze out through the bars?

The main gate of our cell, which slides beautifully on greased wheels, opens to a pointless view of a bulletin board on a cinderblock wall. But down the corridor to the left is a large open stairwell with a butterfly-shaped portal that can only be seen at an oblique angle. If I sit to the right of the gate and very close to the bars, I can look across the hall through the stairwell and, threading my gaze through the portal, see the top portion of a persimmon tree above the prison wall. The distance seems about thirty meters. The wonderful thing about a persimmon tree is that even in the leafless winter the tree holds its fruit for a long time. These persimmons are like simmering planets in a dying universe. Their drab orange might be my favorite color. The view through the portal is the closest thing to a work of art at Kun Chong and for this reason I fear the warden will order the tree chopped down. The magpies sit on branches and preen themselves.

I sit here imagining the birds as the fruit and the fruit as the birds, the persimmons flying away on flapping leaves and the birds splatting sweet juices on the ground, and maybe someone is calling me, one of the guards or Brother Gao (the only prisoner who talks to me these days) calling *Ni hao* to get my attention.

"The food has arrived."

I answer in Chinese. I turn to see our tavern table set with eight metal trays, a tin can in the center with green chopsticks sprouting from the soulless dark.

Before we eat, I ask the guard to let me try out the burden. I feel loose and free now that I can communicate in the language of the prison, putting things exactly as I like. "Why don't you let me have a try? I'm the prisoner, not you. I'm the one who just made my self-criticism and therefore deserves to be punished for my lies. I am a liar and a criminal."

My fellow inmates, now excited, implore the guard to let me try. "Let him do it, let him do it, fun, it'll be fun."

I am long and skinny. After two months in prison with modest exercise, I stoop to bring the burden's pole to a balanced position across my shoulders, a stinging pain starting at the base of my neck. The thing shouldn't be so heavy without food. I walk around the room and the men egg me on.

A woman calls from next door, "What's going on over there? Where's our food?"

"No talking to the men," says the guard. "Shut up." Then he puts away his sour expression and becomes one of us again, laughing easy and fanning me with his awful breath. He takes the burden from me and shows the correct posture. He massages my shoulders and tells me to relax. He speaks in Chinese and I am happy to respond. I duck under the yoke and with my legs take on the weight again. As I plod in circles around the dinner table, the men clap and sing an old work ballad about carrying a great, big bucket from the well and asking the heavens to please let it leak, sky, please lighten the load.

"It isn't heavy enough," says one man. "Put the food back on the trays."

"No," says another. "I'm not risking my dinner. He can't be trusted with our food."

"What can we put on the trays?"

"We own nothing. We're prisoners."

"Our shoes are too light."

"Our clothes are too light."

"Pillows?"

"Ack! You stupid egg."

The men ask the guard to bring something weighty from the commons, but he refuses on security grounds. He is the guard with the limp greasy hair and the handsome teeth, a burn scar on the back of his hand that looks like the split top on a loaf of bread. "I'm not permitted to bring foreign objects into the prisoners' quarters. This is your game."

"Two men," says Yu. "We'll choose the two lightest guys to lie on their bellies on the bottom rungs."

This suggestion earns a great hurrah and within seconds the two lightest men are picked out: Wu Kaiming and Brother Gao. Gao has the quality (there is one in every group) of being liked by everyone, hated by no one, not even by the hateful. He has a soft cartoon face with large round eyes and a modest chin that does not make him look weak so much as merry. He looks like a boy. Wu Kaiming is taller but rail-thin, with spidery fingers like mine and a chest that caves inward. As he plops down on the tray opposite Brother Gao, I swear he's going to crack a rib.

Having been a swimmer, I don't lack core strength, but even light men are heavy in pairs, nor is there anything especially intelligent about the design of the burden that could lighten my load. I tell one man to scoot forward a few centimeters and both men to spread their palms on the floor and give me their weight gradually. I am sweating now but laughing, full of incredible joy and pain. Snot trickles from my nose, and one of the men wipes away the dribble with his bare hand.

I am up now, bearing the weight of three men on two narrow feet. I have never done anything heroic in my life. I have never won a swimming meet or a wrestling match, and only once took first prize in a writing contest. As an exchange student, I won top honors for my Chinese, but I have never won an award for strength or brutality. Financially, I have made over a million dollars, but this is a victory I don't care to win, and in any case, a million dollars pales in comparison to my father's best years; and it may be my spite for him as much as the loving cheers of my comrades that allows me to go three times around the room with two men prone like flying supermen on metal shelves. My father will always be a brawny man, three times stronger than me even in old age, his iron grip powerful till the day he dies. Though I was a good swimmer as a young man, in the pool locker room I hated getting undressed in front of him, and to this day I am scared to death of standing naked before men, though women have told me I have a handsome body.

"One more time!" cries Fang, and I almost believe he means to encourage me rather than poke fun at me.

I finally set down the load and shrug off the burden. I massage the bony knobs at the base of my neck and shake the fatigue out of my shoulders. I have won. The guard with the greasy hair inspects my reddened palms. He asks for my name and I tell him my meaningless dictionary name, Kaofuman.

"Ka-Fu-Men," he says.

"Kao-Fu-Man," I correct him.

"No," he insists, "Kafumen," changing the tone on *fu* so my new name contains "good fortune."

The men clap me on the back and give me a place at the head of the table, indicating the food tray as though it's a setting of fine China at the Westin Hotel. I see elegantly-curled rinds of pork, pearly rice, and dainty krill among the spinach. Wu Kaiming is laughing so hard, tears darken his shirt like rain drops. Yu's eyes are damp with laughter. Merry faces all around. As far as I know, there is no phrase that singularly means "laughing while in prison," but we could use one. The gut-wrenching salvation of laughing in jail cannot be compared to any other joy. The impassive neurons fire the same as for pain and pleasure. I'll never again feel such fun, precisely because I am a prisoner among prisoners. No laughter will ever again be so painfully perfect.

With my chopsticks, I snatch my food piece by elegant piece, bringing the gristle to my mouth, the rice to my tongue. I pretend to wipe my mouth with a white cloth napkin. Fang jokes that I must be at Lost Heaven, his favorite restaurant in Beijing.

The party ends the moment one of the special guards in blue, clad in his bulletproof vest and helmet, posts our work assignments on the bulletin board across the corridor. The paper says we should not expect to head off to work any time soon, though it is still advised that we increase our calorie intake and eat nutritionally. They have listed our numbers and names, including a different Chinese version of my name, "*Ke Fu Men*," which could be translated as "To Subdue Buddha at the Gate."

Ke = subdue, overthrow

Fu = Buddha, merciful person

Men = door or gate

Snakeskin Body

To this point, Queena had not left the apartment in twenty-five days. The arrangement was getting on my nerves. If the company of students in my teaching life made me feel young, the presence of a student in my apartment had the opposite effect: I felt old and revolting. My bad breath, my hemorrhoids, thinning hair, nose hairs, my latest chest cold with its detestable phlegm. It got to be so much work to make myself presentable. But this girl of twenty-one, roughly half my age, could go for days without a shower, splash water on her face, and look refreshed. Because we did not eat fish, her mouth did not smell of fish. Because she ate meager portions of food, the bathroom after her flush smelled no worse than mushrooms or moldy grass clippings, childlike, as of a nursery school—while I dropped bombs that made me want to escape this place. The only thing that kept me sane was swimming laps in the campus pool, which Dean Chong had told me was fed with deep fossil water treated with soft salts rather than chlorine.

I didn't feel old in the classroom. I moved well and spoke with a strong voice. I looked young for thirty-nine and felt spry when I skidded to a stop on the dusty floor to make some dramatic point, or when I climbed onto a desk to illustrate the objective narrative point of view. But at home with my young companion, growing old felt like a moral deficiency. I was disgusted with myself in spite of the fact that I was doing a good thing for a deserving soul.

She asked to use my razor to shave her armpits. I said no problem. She asked me to remove a particle of Beijing smog from her eye, so I sat her on the kitchen counter and with exceeding care ran a cotton swab under her eyelid. I helped her with her "homework," this being the scholarly work she had assigned herself to pass the time. I tried to explain why one of the major Chinese banks was in need of a bailout and what it meant to the world economy that the Russian president had been assassinated by a computer. I put her in charge of feeding my crickets.

What I mean to express, if it is not already clear by now, is that I felt a certain fatherly tenderness toward Queena. For one, her father was falling apart and she needed support. I had tried keeping my distance, but the girl wouldn't allow it. There she was at my doorstep like some infant left in a basket. I took Queena in. I fed her and clothed her. When the lens of her glasses fell out, I snapped it back into place.

For all the warmth I felt, her presence also reminded me how far I was from ever becoming a father, how terribly I had failed in my relationships with women. I could hardly expect to carry on the family name if I couldn't love somebody. What did I have to show for myself after almost four decades of existence? I had my weird stories. I had my students. Four crickets in a fancy bamboo cage. Did I even want children? Lulu wasn't going to be much help. In one of her longer emails she wrote that raising children was overrated, "but I would never say this out loud in China, at least not to some peoples. They would say I am a witch. So I only say this to you and some friends."

I shared this information with Queena and she spent four hours writing an essay about how the modern Chinese woman *really* feels about children. Queena scarcely knew a thing about motherhood, and yet that was the sweet diligence of Queena and why she had been such a good student. She had a high tolerance for her own bullshit, as all good university students must. She said she wanted to write a book like me and I somehow had the guts to tell her I had not in fact published a book.

She looked up from my writing desk with a puzzled expression. "You haven't written a book?"

"I think we are witnessing a microevolution of the Chinese species," I said, changing the subject. She was wearing my brown slippers, much too large for her feet. I didn't want to take them from her; I wanted to sew a pink bear on the tops. "The need to do homework seems to be in your constitution."

Another puzzled look and I realized she thought I was speaking of the Constitution of the PRC. I explained the difference, but she looked offended. I noticed then a colony of pimples on her forehead and very greasy hair. She wore jeans and a well-worn turquoise blouse, which had a blotch of crusted soup on the cuff. She hadn't showered in days and wasn't sleeping well at night. Behind her, the curtains were drawn and a sandstorm was batting at the windows. Millions of specs from the hopeless Gobi Desert had made their way to die in Beijing, like sperm issued from a lonely man into some lavatorial abyss. I counted twelve days since we'd looked out the window.

She looked around at my bare walls, my books stacked on the ground, my plastic plants.

"I'm bored," she said. "I miss my friends. I miss the dorm. I do not like sleeping in the same room with my teacher."

"*As* my teacher. Don't say *with* my teacher."

"I hate it zat I can't look out the window. I want to go to a restaurant like a normal girl. I want to post a message on Weibo. I want to go shopping with my friends."

All of this she said as if blaming me for her situation. More to the point, she used the tone of an ungrateful brat.

"What do you want me to do?" I said. "I didn't make the rules of your country. I didn't invite you into my apartment."

And here she looked down like any shameful daughter. I expected an apology and an end to the battle. Instead, she turned over my insect collection and stormed past me into the bedroom. She slammed the door so hard the knob fell off, clattering to the floor. Anyone living in an adjacent apartment would know that two people were having an argument. The Englishman next door stopped playing his *sanxian*. I hadn't even been aware of the music. He practiced so often. The German upstairs seemed to be in the shower. I could hear water whooshing down the drain, down through the pipe in the wall.

Of course she began crying, and when I went in to check on her I didn't see her anywhere. She had climbed inside her bed to have her cry. Either she wanted to be darkly alone or feared getting caught, perhaps both. Her bed was made neatly according to our house rule, the plain white comforter suggesting the industrial look of a hospital.

I didn't know what to do, so I stood still for a time. Through the walls I heard the *sanxian* again, the throaty twang of three strings singing into a hollow body with a snakeskin top. The high and low notes had cat and dog-like qualities. The slides up the neck made pleasant little squeaks and if I could identify one area of his playing that had improved it was that slide technique.

The girl was crying.

The ancient music was playing.

Traffic bleat in the distance.

A worker hammered at metal.

Old ladies chatted in the courtyard, smacking their bare arms to bring blood to the extremities, paying no mind to the sand storm.

The German who lived above me flushed his toilet again.

I leaned down to the bed, close enough that I could see the coarse grid of the cotton weave. I said, "Queena, I'm sorry. I didn't know you felt this way."

This triggered another spate of crying.

I sat on the other bed and waited.

"Why don't you take a bath?" I said. "The water will make you feel good."

"You're the teacher," she said through the box. "I'll do whatever you say."

"None of that. It's good for you to express yourself."

"I'm embarrassed. I'm very bad. I'm a bad girl. I'm an in-grateful guest."

I held back the urge to say "*un*grateful." This was a curse, to be a petty teacher. It was something about myself I detested as much as the smell of my own shit.

"Queena!" I said too loud. "Come out of that box right now!"

The Englishman stopped playing his instrument and the lingering note, poorly struck, sounded like the moan from a palsy in a wheelchair. Just then a high-pitched whirring started from the construction zone, maybe a cutting wheel or a high-tech saw. I had no idea what it was but I hated the rising Doppler effect, so much like a subway train speeding past your station, the arrival, the assault on the ears, and the fading departure.

The mattress popped up with a hydraulic hiss and Queena sat up, looking somewhat refreshed in spite of her red eyes. Just as she was climbing out of her box, we heard a knock at the door. Queena fell back and I let the mattress down with a wooden clap.

I opened the door to find Dean Chong standing on my welcome mat, wearing a dark overcoat and holding a purple gym bag. Grit from the sandstorm clung to his hair and the shoulders of his felt coat. A whiff of alcohol came off his body. He had the look of a man who had put in a long day but still had a few more meetings, his silver hair tucked behind his ears.

"May I come in? For a chat?"

I hesitated. The only answer should have been yes. He was a Party member who had saved my ass. I heard a knocking through the wall and for a moment thought it was Queena moving in her box. Then I realized it was only the Englishman next door, setting his instrument against the wall. I stepped back and said, "Yes, of course. Yes, though I have a Skype call soon. My father. I'm Skyping with my father."

"Yes, of course. Your father had a very rough financial time, yes?"

"Yes."

"Very unfortunate. Very sad. Very sad to see a good man go down."

"Yes, come in."

(I admit that I'm narrating this scene like a freshman creative writing student, in the abject realistic style of listing every gesture and inane grunt in the social ritual. But that is exactly how the exchange went.)

"Would you like some tea?" I said.

"Ah yes, I would like some tea. Only if you have the time, Francis. I'm sure your father needs you."

"There's always time for tea," I said. "In China."

Chuckle, chuckle. "Uh-huh-uh, yes, there is always time for tea in China."

"Welcome to China," I exclaimed.

"May I have a seat?" he replied politely.

"Yes, of course. Sit anywhere you like, but watch out for crickets. Some of them have been escaping of late. Have you been to the gym?"

He set down his purple bag and took a seat in Queena's chair, smiled, then looked at the goldenrod curtains blocking the window. We agreed to speak in English. He started in about the financial news coming from the BBC and how he was privy to some alarming information from an old university chum who held a high position at the Industrial & Commercial Bank of China, who warned of a total meltdown of the economy and who lamented but understood the national policy of only allowing Chinese citizens to invest a maximum of 350,000 yuan per year overseas, which, of course did not seem to affect The Elite who could take advantage of all manner of loopholes and shell companies and Party connections, to say nothing of the American habit of setting up secret offshore companies in Panama or Seychelles (laughing now, gazing suspiciously at the curtained window) and saying, "Yes, yes, it does not look good for men like us with our modest university salaries," and then he went on to explain the Chinese pension system—and if I struggled to catch his drift because he rambled, I struggled even more due to the sounds coming from the bedroom, a *thunking* that I was sure had to be the Englishman next door but might have been Queena trying to get out of her hiding place, thinking I'd forgotten her. I made a point to laugh with added volume at certain things Dean Chong said, though it wasn't easy. There was nothing funny about the financial collapse he foretold.

"Be that as it may," he said, "I did not come here to tell you about my financial anxieties. I'm sure you have worries of your own, albeit you have been shrewd enough not to put too much of your money in the Chinese banks. My advice to you is to put your money elsewhere. You don't have restrictions like I do. You have much more freedom, Francis. Much more freedom. Least of which, you don't have to worry about a daughter, as I do. No, I merely came to chat about next year's schedule. In addition to Business English, we would like you to teach one course on international relations."

"I can do that," I said, failing to point out that I lacked the qualifications.

He sipped his tea and crossed his legs. "You have no children, is that right?"

"No children," I said. "But I'm more or less supporting my sister right now. And my parents."

"The university tuition is very expensive for Mei Mei. If the worst happens, I shall have to bring her home. She will be at a disadvantage. But what can one do?"

He drained his tea cup and stood. Then he reached over and pumped my hand with a very Western handshake, the kind I had witnessed from Chinese businessman who knew they were in a weak position. He was trying too hard, but for what?

He said goodbye and walked out the door.

It wasn't until his footsteps clacked out of earshot that I noticed his purple gym bag in the corner beside my umbrella. I shouted his name down the stairwell and shouted again, then hushed, now understanding. I wouldn't open the bag and count the money until Queena was asleep. Tomorrow, I would walk to one of the local banks and make my first modest deposit. A few days later, I would find a different bank.

Fang in Love

One night we discover that Fang has fallen in love with a woman next door. In the deep well of night, when all our dreams are strangest, Wu Kaiming snaps on the light to reveal Fang curled up at the base of the "woman door," struggling to put himself together. He is wearing one shoe. Without going into detail, suffice to say he has found a way to pleasure himself and shoot physical proof of his love under the one-centimeter gap at the base of the door. I can smell it from my bed, the odor like melted brie.

Strands of black hair cling to Fang's face and neck. These are no tiny locks for a lover to stash in a velvet box or slip into a book. These are thick shocks yanked painfully from her scalp to prove her love to a man she has never fully seen.

Fang sits with his back against the wall, confessing every detail to his fellow inmates. The guard is asleep and Xu Xuo is asleep. Jack sits at the table with his hands folded, firing questions at our stunt lover. Fang confesses to writing love letters, scrimshaw style, on the sole of his Nike shoe.

The next morning Fang tries to act like all is normal. He drinks his congee like the rest of us and does push-ups alongside my bed, pull-ups from the bars of the high window.

When Jack asks him what he was up to last night, Fang surprises us by saying he's in love. He seems happy to report this.

"Who is she?"

Fang does one more pull-up and lets himself down, shaking out his arms, rubbing his calloused hands. He seems like a totally different guy, reasonable, smart, thawed by love. "I'm not going to tell you her name, but she's amazing. It's incredible that you can fall in love with someone's voice and her mind. Physically, I have only seen her eyes and her hair."

"Which means as far as anybody knows, she looks like ninety-nine percent of the women in China."

"You're wrong about that. Haven't you ever looked at someone's eyes up close? Nobody's are the same. Hers are like kaleidoscopes."

When I think of Fang in love, I remind myself that Adolf Hitler and Mao Zedong also experienced true love. President Vladimir Putin many times. Nero, not so much.

"Listen to you," says Wu Kaiming. "You sound like a mystical poet. How have you seen her eyes?"

"Through the cracks," he says, pointing to the door with its louvered top half. "I pry the gap open with these nail clippers, just a little, and I can see her eyes quite well."

"But it's dark at night except for the hallway light."

"That way is south," he points. "The women have the moon passing across their sky and if it's full between the hour of three and four in the morning, the light shines right through their window, right against the door. I'm telling you, I've seen her eyes at night. Why would I lie about this? And now that everybody knows our secret, I intend to see her eyes in the daytime too."

"Sounds good," says Wu Kaiming. "Did you use the nail clippers to carve the note into your shoes?"

"No. I used one of the lenses from my glasses. I crushed it with my heel and made several nice shards. They make good cutting tools."

"And then you look through the slit and study her kaleidoscopes with one good eye?"

He nods, and now I notice how he's squinting. I imagine he'll have headaches soon.

In the days after Fang announces he is in love, our little nation state experiences an era of harmony. Fang stops being so sarcastic. He stops making dagger motions at Xu Xuo. He volunteers to sleep on the floor every night, so that every now and again one of us gets to spend two nights in a row in a bed. We experience fewer rat dreams, which Wu Kaiming claims he has remedied by sleeping on the table top. Declaring it not so bad, he has also managed to convince Brother Gao to give it a try. When we play "dare or dare" (essentially "truth or dare" without the lies) Fang no longer calls for tricks involving the toilet. In fact, he shows a rather creative mind.

Eat a bowl of noodles without chopsticks. Ask the guard for an extra roll of toilet paper, then fart when he gives it to you. Drink a cup of tea while standing on your head. Make soup broth shoot out of your eye sockets.

He arranges competitions where men have to transfer water from one bowl across the room to the other, carrying liquid in their mouths. In another, we have to push a dust bunny across a finish line using only our noses. We stack our mattresses in the middle of the room and hold high jump competitions. If the guards get on our case, Fang charms them.

Then one night he says, sounding like any Shanghai husband, "We've decided to start trying for a child."

"Under the door?" says Brother Gao.

There is no other way to say it: His eyes twinkle, and this twinkling is mirrored by the joy on Fang's masculine, sculpted face. He answers only by smiling in that particular male way of preening himself after a sexual conquest.

"What if she turns out to be less attractive than you think?"

"She's not," says Fang, a little irked, showing his old self again.

"But, under the door, do you think it can really work?" says Jack. His bald head is getting paler with winter.

"What about the temperature of your seeds?" says Kaiming. "I hear those little critters die as soon as they hit air."

"What do you think?" Fang says to me.

Do I hate Fang? Does the answer matter? I have an interest in him not hating me. I should say what Fang wants to hear, but as always I have real trouble not being frank. "You can do it," I say. "But it's dangerous."

There is silence after I've said what everybody knows.

Fang turns to the toilet and unzips his fly. "The hell with you guys." He has not turned his anger directly on me but at the logic. Get a woman pregnant in this place and you could be in real trouble. Fang sits on the bed opposite his lover's wall, eyes fixed on the metal door, having trouble focusing because of that missing lens. He takes off his glasses and sets them on the mattress. "So maybe they force her to have an abortion," he says. "Happens all the time."

"I don't mean to be a busybody," says Brother Gao, "but aren't you married? Don't you have a wife out there?"

"Nobody's married in here. Nobody has a degree or a position, nobody owns shit. Whatever you were before Kun Chong, you are something different now. Fuck, Brother Gao, sometimes I wonder how you can be so fucking stupid for a smart guy. Can anybody argue with me? Even you, Big Shot?" he says, jerking his head toward me, his mean blood pulsing again. "Never mind. I'll have a good time trying."

The guard comes in just then to collect our food trays. He slides a rubber trash bin through the entrance. We knock our trays against the side, spilling slop over slop, the women's food already dumped. Brother Gao holds up Fang's tray of unfinished food but Fang waves him off.

"I want to stay hungry," he says.

I notice once again that our guard has no weapon, not even a can of pepper spray or a nightstick. When he bends under the burden to haul our dinner trays away (his friend has already started down the stairwell with the women's trays balanced like Lady Justice) I say, "How come they don't make one of us take the trays down the stairs? Do they really think we'll escape?"

"No, they're not worried about that."

"But it seems strange to me, you doing that heavy work while we sit up here licking our chops after a meal. I wouldn't mind doing it. I used to love going for walks after meals. Tell me, why are the guards always doing this work?"

"We're prisoners, too," he says, before taking up the burden and leaving. Down the stairs and into the night.

The Oxford Definition of "Incendiary"

In the days before Queena left, I began to wonder if the man next door, the Englishman, knew I was hiding somebody. His playing turned louder and more aggressive. I could hear it plinking through the hallway, the notes scurrying high and low along a scale that did not seem from East or West but out of time and place altogether—a song of rising danger that was more accurate than any language.

"It makes me nervous," said Queena. "The way he plays lately."

"You hear it, too," I said, slicing off a piece of mango for the crickets.

The two of us sat facing the cricket cage—Queena with a canister of oatmeal in her lap, me with my mango—taking turns shoving food between the tiny bamboo bars. The cricket named Caliban hopped on the chunk before the cricket named Woolf.

"What are your classes like? Are the students mad at you? Do they think Vesuvius is stupid?"

"Everyone pretends nothing happened."

"Everyone?"

"Like everyone else in China," I said. "Perhaps two of my students want to change the world. The other 142 seem resigned to the system."

In the same class period in which one girl gave a speech mentioning that possibly more than 200 factory girls in Guangdong were systematically raped by their superiors, another girl came up to me after the bell to complain that the format I had set up for the midterm exam was unfair. Students were gathering their things. The frizzy-haired girl named Eartha was at the console trying to properly eject her thumb drive. The complaining girl, a certain Gloria who had the lips of a fashion model, had rushed to the front of the room to get my attention before the others. Gloria was the daughter of a comfortably-installed civil servant.

Eartha, meanwhile, had clicked a command that made her photos flash on the screen, and from my angle, gazing over Gloria's satin-black hair, I could see among the goofy poses of Eartha and her friends at an ice rink (wearing Teddy Bear hoods) several images of Tiananmen 1989.

The trampled bicycles smeared with blood, student bodies lined up in the basement of a hospital, the burned-out bus on Chang An Avenue. Tanks with obscene erections rolling across the square. The man in the white shirt, holding his plastic bag, facing the tank.

The remaining students stopped and stared. A tall handsome boy named Han Duo struck a somber look. Two girls dropped their bags on the table and giggled. Eartha tried to end the slideshow, but the recalcitrant computer kept flashing the images.

Eartha with her parents at a banquet. Eartha and her classmates standing in front of a platter of fish. Now back to the Teddy Bear hoods, now the bloody bicycles, the burned-out bus, now an anniversary vigil in Hong Kong.

Gloria, meanwhile, was explaining that if debate group D were allowed to listen to debate groups A, B, and C discuss the same topic, group D had an unfair advantage. This was unfair, as she was a member of group A. I asked her if she would be coming to me with this problem if she were a member of group D. She thought for a moment and smiled. "Of course not."

"Which means if you were a member of group D, you would consider it fair?"

"No, I would think it is an advantage for me, but I would not say anything."

She then told me a better way, her way, to organize the midterm debate, but I was distracted by what was happening in my room. Students from the next class were streaming in and noticing Eartha's slideshow. Some didn't care. They'd seen it all. They had a quiz to study for and quickly sat down and opened their economics textbook. But others murmured, pointed, shared what their parents had told them or not told them of the event.

I finally reached down and hit the power button on the CPU. I told Gloria I would take her thoughts into consideration. I told Eartha to take her thumb drive and get to class.

"But I think the photographs is on the hard drive," she said.

"I'll take care of it," I said.

The following week I got a "new student" named Li Cheng. Getting a new student mid-semester was not normal. At first Cheng blended in quietly, but after a week he began to get vocal about the rights of Tibetans and it seemed obvious that he was trying to find out which students were potential counter-revolutionaries. One boy, a pale Uyghur, took the bait, saying that his people had experienced some of the same intimidation tactics as the Tibetans. The girls mostly giggled because Li Cheng was so handsome, with his penetrating eyes and strong chin, his broad shoulders, thick hair, and plump lips. If you snapped a close-up of his mouth, you wouldn't be able to tell if he was a man or a woman.

Beautiful boy. Clumsy spy. I expected more from the CPC.

He said things like, "We should organize a protest on campus" to a dead silence.

He said, "Anyone who believes the government's version of the story is a fool. They're all a bunch of corrupt clowns."

But some of my students' fathers were civil servants and very nice men.

He said, "It is high time we take action to put power in the hands of the people. We mustn't be afraid."

"I'm afraid," said one of the students.

"Me, too," said another.

"Can we discuss something else?" said the class monitor.

Later, I told Eartha that I thought Li Cheng was an infiltrator sent on behalf of the government.

"Yes, of course," said Eartha. "We all know it. Zat's why he doesn't have a girlfriend. He is so handsome!"

As for his debate proposal sent to me via email—"I would like to discuss the need for increased activism among college students in Beijing"—I replied that he should pick a less incendiary topic and attached the OED definition of the word. Then I spent twice my usual time picking apart the logic of his manifesto.

"Look here," I said to Queena, rotating my laptop for her to see. "Look at this idiot's proposal for a paper." I was at my desk. She was in the easy chair playing a computerized chess game I'd bought her at a department store.

The Englishman plucked out a bluesy riff on his *sanxian*, then dribbled off into parts unknown, beautifully and without structure or time, now higher up the neck and more angry.

"I can't stand it," said Queena. "Tell him to stop."

"I like it," I said, taking a sip of my afternoon coffee. "He's playing what I feel. It is more accurate than language, Queena. These are not good times."

"Turn on the TV," she said.

First I had to find a new battery for the remote. Then I aimed the little bugger at the flat screen TV the university had provided me, and with Queena's guidance I found the state-run evening news. The first story reported on a famous Chinese NBA star donating millions of yuan to dig wells in Africa. Sandwiched between a feel-good story about the government's mission to plant a hundred thousand trees in the Gobi Desert and a snazzy montage of the luxury apartments inside the great Epicuria Tower came a ten-second news release about a sodium leak at Painted Sky Fast Reactor Nuclear Power Plant. The authorities "were in the process of controlling" the leak.

Then came a commercial for an anti-aging cream, then an ad for Nike sneakers, White Mountain tonic wine, and a cereal called Milk and Egg Stars. One after another, ads played for everything from headphones to steam cleaners. I hadn't watched much TV at all, and it struck me that ten minutes of solid commercials could hardly be a normal practice. How could the TV producers expect to hold an audience?

Now came the images of the meltdown at Painted Sky Fast Reactor Nuclear Power Plant: the workers in safety suits, the crush of vehicles leaving Jiasong City using all six lanes, the high-level official admitting that earlier reports of the leakage being under control were incorrect, the news anchors feigning journalistic neutrality. There came cartoonish diagrams of the reactor and fifteen-second explanations of extremely complex nuclear arcana, how molten sodium can burn hot enough to melt the armor around the reactor but that Painted Sky had been engineered for passive safety, which meant the chances of widespread radioactive contamination were highly unlikely but that indeed some radioactive contaminants had been wisely released in order to relieve pressure in the containment center to prevent an explosion.

"I think I should leave," said Queena. "I don't feel good. My luck is running out, so I must go. But I don't know where to go. My family, my relatives, that is the first place the police will look. And it wouldn't be fair to my friends, to put them at risk."

I took a sip of coffee. "You don't think I'm sticking out my neck for you?"

She lowered her eyes, ashamed. She looked worn down. One of her eyelids was sagging, lending a certain asymmetry to her face that shouldn't have been her due for another forty years. She pulled a flake of skin off her lower lip and said, "I only mean that as a foreigner you have more protection than a Chinese person. In China, they go after your whole family."

"Of course. I know this."

"I thought you would support me. I thought you were on my side."

"Don't play games with me."

"No, it's fine. I will leave. Soon."

"You can't leave until you have a plan."

The crickets started chirping, oddly, in the afternoon. The *sanxian* player hit the strings again.

身体

As we now know, the accident at Painted Sky turned out to be the worst nuclear disaster since Fukushima. The plant manager committed suicide. The story got out. People were incensed that the CPC actually thought they could cover up, of all things, a nuclear meltdown. People were informed, but only after twenty hours of trying to contain the sodium leak.

A Chinese member of the International Atomic Energy Agency was forced into exile following comments he made that were critical of the Party: "I have stood with my country for many years. I have been a faithful member of the Party, which has brought about great changes since the opening-up period began. Indeed, I have stood with my country when it was the target of bitter and often cruelly-biased international scorn; I have stood with my country as it witnessed a change in leadership four times. I have stood with my country in spite of its sometimes frustrating habit of giving preference to GDP over sustainability and public safety. However, now I must stand not for any Republic but for Humanity."

His speech was disseminated all over the country via social media, then promptly taken down, then re-posted in a code language, then taken down. Some parts were hard to forget and the people memorized them. The phrase "Stand for Humanity" became popular among the angry.

"At this time I hope to humbly speak not only to the elite who may have access to these words through various modes of technology. I most want to speak to the common man, the taxi driver, the peasant, the fisherman, the seamstress, and all the people kept in the shadows. Most of all, I wish to speak to the victims of the disaster. I have failed you. I could have done more to ensure your safety."

I began to make plans to leave the country. I searched for airline tickets at internet cafés, being sure not to use the computer in my apartment. I soon had to stop that practice, as it became clear that I was being followed by a plain clothes security officer. A man wearing a black baseball cap and black pollution mask appeared at the No. 8 bus stop one afternoon as I was on my way to the Golden Resources Mall. His costume seemed ridiculous. He was a twiggy man in his thirties, with sloping shoulders and a pigeon-toed gait. I saw him the next day, too, climbing into a black Jetta as I hailed a cab. He became my companion, his dark eyes tracking me from my apartment to the business school building, from the canteen to the drycleaners. He tended to stay a half block behind, unless I made for the subway, in which case he would hustle to catch the same train, always one car back. His black-themed costume seemed like something right out of a bad spy movie, that is, until I noticed the voluptuous bunny icon on his jacket above the word "Palyboy."

One cold day in November, a group of migrant construction workers were staging a protest by the east gate of campus. A worker had been injured from a fall, his ribs, leg and arm broken, and the manager for the construction company was refusing to pay the medical bills. I had heard about the incident from my students, and I was surprised to see organized resistance taking place on campus in the current climate. No students were picketing, as they had too much to lose and too much homework to do, but the wife of the worker was there with a hundred or so laborers outside the blue modular where the supervisor posted orders. Behind the modular stood the half-built Science and Math Center, shrouded in green mesh. I saw ruddy, toothless men from the countryside raising their mortar-crusted shovels at the sky. From what my students had told me, the university was staying out of the fray, as they had contracted the work out to a construction company.

I knew better than to show any interest in that scene, so I kept walking. One of my debate students tried to wave me down, thinking I would be interested in the drama, but I marched right past her. Indeed I looked very much the part of the apathetic Elite, with my Windsor knot and my long felt winter coat. I could feel the security officer on my heels, weaving through the students and protesters, keeping me in his sights.

A fair number of students now stood back at the edge of the tiled walk, hanging out under leafless trees to watch this livid woman, the wife of the victim, swing her arms and shout curses at the manager, as police officers wearing helmets attempted to tackle her. She was a wide woman in her late thirties, with curly hair cut short. She was dressed in the plain uniform of a menial job. I never saw the officers finish their job, as I kept my eyes on the stream of bicycles and sedans coming head-on, ever ready to knock me down. I wouldn't have been at all surprised to hear volleying blasts of tear gas canisters.

I saw in the reflection of a window my companion stopping to buy a hard-boiled egg from a vendor. A girl on a pink bicycle swerved to avoid me. A Lexus SUV passed inches from my toes, and for an instant I lost control of my bladder and felt a warm squirt of urine on my leg. I hadn't realized how badly I needed to go to the bathroom. My knees were shaking.

The next morning, my masked friend was waiting for me by the that same egg vendor. She was an older lady with a butch haircut who had probably spent her whole life brewing eggs in black tea. She had been there since the Cultural Revolution, same lady, same recipe. Steam twirled up from her tin kettle like white ghosts. I had seen this lady before, how she crouched on her haunches for hours at a time, never taking a rest in a chair. It was bitterly cold, the first real hard freeze of winter, and something about the crispness of the air emboldened me. I was also very hung over from a bottle of wine I had drained after putting Queena to bed.

I broke into a trot and waved to get the attention of the man in the black baseball cap and mask, a costume which again struck me as ridiculous. He was wearing the Palyboy jacket again. "Sir, I noticed you purchasing eggs from this old auntie yesterday. They must be good eggs. Can you tell me, are they good eggs? Should I buy a couple? As you know, I'm just a professor here. I don't make millions of yuan, that's for sure. I must be thrifty. What do you think, my friend?"

I wanted to hear his voice. He froze for an instant, said nothing.

The egg lady, standing up from her crouch, gave me a wide smile of crooked teeth. Her fingernails were filthy. She stirred her pot with a big spoon and the steam curled away into the Beijing air. My plainclothes cop looked at me with disdain, not appreciating my antics. It dawned on me that he probably made less money than me by an appreciable margin. A certain jaundice in the whites of his eyes suggested a hardscrabble life. This frightened me on the one hand, as I may have insulted his status, but relieved me on the other hand as it meant the authorities had assigned me a low-level agent. He wore beige slacks and cheap loafers. He had a sprinkling of acne on his wide forehead. He was only about 1.7 meters tall, with a large head and a weak chin.

"The eggs are fine," he seethed, turning away from me and heading down the street with his hands in his pockets.

Wise Uncle Ponzi

One cold bright morning as we are in the yard doing calisthenics, Jack asks Fang what he's done to deserve prison. The two men stand side by side in the front row along with Brother Gao, who looks like a little boy next to Fang. His ears sit low on his head. Kaiming, Kuku, and Mr. Yu occupy the middle row, while Xu Xuo and I form a back row of two. All of us are in the early warm-up stage, bending at the hip and rotating our torsos, our breath fogging the air. Frost coats the ground. A few birds chatter. In the distance we can see a factory pouring smoke into a clear blue sky.

Fang lunges forward on his left foot and holds the position for a time. "I ran an online investment firm with my father," he says.

"Which one?" says Jack.

"Wise Uncle Financial Services."

"You started Wise Uncle?"

"My father needed me for the technological knowhow. I'm very good with computers."

"But you ran a Ponzi scheme!"

"What is a Ponzi scheme?" says Kuku, lunging now on his right foot, back again.

"Don't they teach you anything in school?" says Jack.

"The boy cheated on the *gaokao*," says Yu. "That's why he's here. Therefore, he retains very little information from his education."

"Fundamentally, you take somebody's money to invest, but you don't really put it into a real company," says Jack. "You get more investors and use their money to pay returns to the first people, making it seem like their nest egg is growing."

"It was a bit more sophisticated than that," says Fang. "The problem is that my father and his old cronies put too much faith in their Party connections. They thought they could do whatever they wanted forever without getting caught, but I had ideas to make it sustainable. We could have kept it going if those old assholes would have listened to me. You have no idea how much money we amassed in one year."

"How much?"

"Nobody really knows. My point is that I could have kept it going."

Fang holds forth in a way we have rarely seen. The love drug has turned him into an investment analyst, albeit one without glasses. Rather than put up with monocular suffering, he has ditched the whole kit and caboodle. "We were a peer-to-peer lending platform. We could have kept going, I'm telling you. Initially, we just filled a void left by the state-run banks. You know how they are, they don't care to lend to the little guys, or to a student, or to some girl who wants to start a beauty business or whatever. We provided a service of linking investors with business entities. Some of the entities happened to be completely fake."

"Much more than some," said Yu. "I hear upwards of ninety-five percent were false companies."

"No," says Fang. "That's what Mr. Zhao said in his public confession. There were government officials who could have come out looking really bad in this case, especially members of the Propaganda Department, which let us advertise during the evening news. Therefore the authorities were hell-bent to extract from Mr. Zhao a very serious confession. Whatever. Maybe two-thirds of the entities were fake, and many of our financial instruments were bogus. We gave them fancy names that nobody could understand. If somebody asked too many questions, we put him in touch with one of our lawyers, who would explain that our financial products were trade secrets, the very reason for our extraordinary success."

"How can you not say this was a Ponzi scheme?" says Jack.

The pace of our exercise has picked up now and we are short of breath, more so the speaking ones.

"I never said it wasn't a Ponzi scheme. I'm saying it wasn't a dumb, simple Ponzi scheme as one of you characterized it. I'm saying I knew a way to keep it going. Our goal was to get an initial pool of investors and give them great returns of twelve percent or so, then tell them if they brought in their friends, we'd give them a kick-back. We sometimes told people that in order to earn maximum profit, they could not remove their money for a certain period of time, which gave us room to work."

"It's all Deng Xiaoping's fault," says Brother Gao. "If Deng had never taken us into the free market, you probably wouldn't be here."

"And I would have brown teeth, a stupid Flying Pigeon Bicycle, an ugly wife, and barely a pot to piss in. I'm telling you, I could have made it work."

"How?" says Kuku, who for once sounds smart. Just that simple question, the way he says it, sounds like he's already done the math, he, who has never heard of Charles Ponzi.

"This is a valid question," says Brother Gao.

"Let me finish!" says Fang. "Stop interrupting me! My answer to your dumb question is simple: Real estate."

Three of the men shake their heads, as though Fang is a lunatic. Even Kuku knows what happened to real estate values after the Meltdown.

Fang stops to catch his breath. "Deng Xiaoping said, *It is glorious for a few people to get rich first.*"

"That's not what he said," counters Jack. "He said, *Let some people get rich first.*"

"Patience! Listen. I don't mean investing in real estate only. I'm talking about how we did some shadow banking for the big developers. Some of those guys were so hungry, the banks weren't giving them enough capital. But we'd loan them money at a killer interest rate, maybe as high as twenty percent in some cases. Do the math. If we pay returns to our clients of nine percent, even twelve, we clear eight to eleven percent. That's how you keep it going. Nobody gets hurt."

"Perhaps in the final analysis, the free market economic system is much like gambling," says Brother Gao. "I suppose you didn't mean to harm anyone. You wanted to give the money back."

"Marx would spin in his grave," says Yu.

"Fuck," says Fang. "Do you think any of our leaders really believe in Marxist thought? But back to my point: Because we were in total control, there was no reason to continue giving returns of twelve percent. There's always going to be ups and downs in the stock market, right? We could just watch the news, wait for a down-tick, especially one that the *China Daily* made sound scary, and then adjust returns to three percent or something like that. The key was to get a big pile of cash up front, which we did. We were one of the biggest, if not *the* biggest online firms of the peer-to-peer model."

"I think it would have been very difficult to continue," says Brother Gao. "In light of what happened."

"That goes without saying," says Fang. He does another burpee and is barely out of breath. He looks healthy and handsome, which I'm ashamed to say makes him more likeable. His triceps twist like ropes. His complexion has the quality of a Roman statue, and now I'm like everybody else, choosing the quarterback or the CEO based on non-moral qualities. Or is it the fact that he is honest? He says, "Everybody got screwed. Of course, if the economy turns rotten, then the rot spreads. That's obvious."

"You're the only one here who's a worse cheater than me," says Kuku.

"But at least you didn't steal any money," says Jack, speaking directly to Kuku. "At least you charged clients for actual services rendered."

The guard with the nose like a mushroom orders us to run in place, so we run. Mr. Yu, who has never smoked a cigarette and has good wind, picks up the thread about Kuku's crime. "But if the kid helps one student cheat and prevents a better student from getting into a top university, the argument could be made that he is stealing future income from the more deserving student."

"Because he is stealing opportunity," says Gao.

"I got really rich," says Fang, turning the attention back to himself. "It was awesome for a while. I had plenty of girls. A Lamborghini Huracan. My wife was hot. I'm telling you, being rich is killer fun. I don't care what anybody says."

"I think there are two types of people," says Brother Gao. "Predators and prey. The habit of the predator is to attack the weak. This is why a cheetah selects the lame gazelle out of the herd. The cheetah has no interest in wasting energy on the alpha. I imagine there were a lot of novice investors attracted to your webpage, people who got caught in the national fever, even old ladies nearing retirement—"

"Shut up," says Fang. "I made my confession loud and clear. I said I got caught. I'm not trying to say I'm not guilty, unlike some people in this place." For a moment I think he's referring to me; then I get that he means Yu, the man who claims he did nothing.

"But now you're in love," says Gao. "If you never got caught, you would never have fallen in love with what's-her-name, the lady who pulls out her hair. You haven't told us her name. In any case, you're in love, which, no matter where you are in the world is the best possible state of being, those first weeks of being in love. There's nothing better. In fact, if I had a choice between experiencing the fullness of love—I mean right in the middle of the hot time—while in prison versus a terrible relationship out there in the free world—"

"Shut up." Fang cuts him off before he can elevate his philosophy.

"You're trying to cheer me up. That's one of my pet peeves, when people try to cheer me up. I hate that."

"But as for your earlier point," says Jack. "I really think it's reasonable that the man who did nothing, let's call him The Man Who Did Nothing"—(we all laugh except for Fang who starts into the jumping jacks with a sour expression)—"that he really has done nothing wrong. It's mathematically possible. It's not out of the realm of possibility. This is a Chinese prison, Fang."

"Fine. All I'm saying is, fine, so I made off with a lot of money, but it wasn't like everyone got ripped off. And there's no such thing as risk-free investing. Look: If we were dealing with some old granny who only had six thousand yuan, we didn't touch her assets. We mainly took advantage of people who had a lot of money to begin with."

I turn to Xu Xuo and say, "Maybe that makes it a worse offense. How do you know the person who puts in a million yuan isn't giving you their life savings?"

Xu Xuo nods, flapping his arms.

A beat later, Brother Gao makes the same exact point, and I'm not sure he hasn't overheard me, though a good three meters stands between us. "One could say that cheating the rich is equal to cheating the poor."

"Fine. I'm a criminal."

"A criminal in love," says Kaiming from the middle.

"All I'm saying is I netted a lot of money, but it's no worse than what hundreds of Party officials do every day, and I don't think it should be considered a capital offense."

Jack and Gao stop exercising. We all come to a rest. Fang has made this last point assuming we already knew.

"You're going to be executed?" says Jack, rubbing his bald pate, wiping off sweat.

"Supposedly my case is still working through the court system."

"But the conviction rate is eighty-five percent."

"Ninety-five percent," I say from the back. I can't help myself. Nor can I explain why my timing is so poor when it comes to conversations involving Fang Feng. No. I can explain it very well. I hate the man, whether he is in love or not, persecuted or not. Rationally I know it would be best to stay out of this bully's way, and I'm a reticent person by nature, but it seems I can't help putting my foot in my mouth. I can't decide if I'm being brave or petty, the worst side of my teaching self surfacing at the wrong time yet again. Maybe the knowledge that Fang will be put to death emboldens me.

If this were a prison movie, Fang would attack me with a hand-made weapon that appears magically from his pants waist. I feel a thrumming in my chest, the adrenaline ready to flood my extremities so I can outrun that capitalist wolf. He is a foul human being.

Instead, Fang says, "Francis has a point, but his numbers are off. The conviction rate is ninety-nine percent."

I fully expect Brother Gao to open his kind mouth and say that a man still has a one percent chance of living, but Gao never gets his chance. The two guards leading the calisthenics tell us to shut up and sing.

"It's time for the patriotic songs."

I expect the scratch of a needle on vinyl, followed by fuzzy marching bands bleating over ancient gray speakers mounted on one of the watch towers, but instead the sound is full and clear, as though transmitted by the finest audio equipment money can buy, seeming to come from everywhere and nowhere. It seems obvious now why Fang wants to give the world a baby, and by this I don't mean he has some holy impulse to produce life in spite of death. He is so full of hubris, he's willing to let a boy or girl grow up fatherless. He thinks he can live by his offspring.

Kuku is the only one not breathing hard, but he is visibly shaken by Fang's revelation. He belts out the tunes in earnest hope that the guards will notice his effort and make a glowing report to an important prefectural minister, who will commute his sentence. Fear shows nowhere else as in the eyes, and fear is what I see on Kuku's face, a nervous shifting of the gaze from place to place as though looking for high ground during a tsunami. The idea that a man can be put to death for almost anything has got to him, and he seems desperate to shake it off.

At a lull in the program, Kuku pretends to dribble a soccer ball across an imaginary field. Then, conjuring a tennis match, he swings his arm through the sad air. When the guard returns with our water, Kuku falls into rank in the back row next to me.

"You like sports," I say.

"Yes, very much," he says.

"Were you serious about it? Did you spend a lot of time running around?"

"I wasn't very good. I'm pretty much average at everything. I hated studying. Always the stupid *gaokao* hanging over our heads. I knew kids who studied for the test four hours a night, over and above their school work. I knew kids that studied ten hours a day on weekends. Me? I would leave the apartment and go find a basketball game or a football match."

Kuku in his blue tunic, with his spiky hair and soft skin, appears robust compared to us—but only because he is young. His muscles are not well developed. He is not tall or stout. I can't speak for his hand-eye coordination, as I have only seen him smack a wad of bandage with a flyswatter, but I bet he is average in that regard, too.

"And your father helped you?" I say.

"More than helped me!" he says, his chest inflated. "He insisted on it. I had no choice. He forced me to cheat. I tried to refuse, but he got angry and threatened to cut off all financial support for me if I didn't play his game."

"You're not a victim," says Brother Gao.

"We're all parasites," says Jack. "Parasites and cheaters. It's the only way to get ahead in this country. If you're a privileged parasite, they say you have *guanxi*. If you're a miserable parasite like one of us, they say you are a criminal who should eat congee every morning and live in a cell with your own shit."

"And no women," says Wu Kaiming.

"This is the military-style training I was supposed to do at university," says Kuku. "It would have been just like this but with girls."

"Wrong," says Fang. "They separate the girls from the boys. But you still have to sing these stupid songs."

Kuku starts singing. Halfway into "The East is Red," he launches a wad of spit cleanly over Yu's head onto the frozen puddle beneath the chin-up bar. I have a terrible imagination: I see spit and think of semen.

Blank Space

When I lived in Beijing, I liked that I could freely spit in public. I was prone to chest colds and tended to produce phlegm for weeks on end, so it was a nice freedom to rear back at any moment and hurl a salty capsule over an iron fence, or find a square of matted dirt around some poor tree on the sidewalk. All of us were constantly hacking our lungs into the cold world. But I didn't like spitting in front of Queena, so most nights I'd step out onto the balcony and let a good one fly into the bushes below. One evening while we were watching an awful Ming dynasty mini-series that was so bad it was almost good, I slipped out to the balcony and got a little dreamy.

Crisp winter night. Not much pollution. The indigo sky made the dorm across the courtyard seem especially white. I could feel the first symptoms of a cold, a swelling of the lymph nodes in my neck. I could hear Queena softly giggling at the nasally voice of the Vietnamese eunuch in the palace court. She seemed to be covering her mouth to stifle the laughter. Looking down, I saw old man Wang, our garbage collector, pedaling his tricycle to the dump. I saw an old lady walking briskly along the circular driveway, slapping her arms to aid circulation. I must have been thinking about my father or my octopus story or a lesson plan for class, because I stayed out there longer than usual, missing my sister, missing Lulu, wishing I could slice into a loaf of my mother's *stollen*. Had the temperature been four degrees lower, had the bitter cold sent me back into the apartment two minutes earlier, it might have been the end for Queena—for a black Audi happened to pull around the circular drive and stop at the entrance of the building. Two men in dark slacks got out. One of them was wearing an ear piece.

I started singing the first lines of "Blank Space" and turned inside.

Queena was already shuffling for the bedroom. We were so efficient, neither one of us whispered good luck or goodbye, but I remember her lustrous dark eyes and the way she seemed to know this was no false alarm. (I should mention that a week earlier we had improved her hiding spot, so that not only would she duck inside the bed but she would shimmy inside three mismatched cardboard boxes that we had glued together like the head, thorax, and abdomen of an insect. I called it "Queena's Carapace.") I skated around the apartment in my black wool socks, searching every tabletop, nook, and cranny for signs of a female fugitive. I slipped a hair tie into my pocket. I put away Queena's dinner bowl and left my own at the kitchen table. I removed towels from windows. I opened curtains. I was down on all fours reaching for a bra under the sofa when the knocking came hard and insistent.

Before I could answer, two members of the secret police barged into the apartment with a pair of housekeepers in tow: a woman named Fei Fei, who had heroically unclogged my toilet one Saturday, and the new girl, a slender thing who wore her hair in a ponytail. Next to the dark blazered policemen, the ladies looked cheerful in their lavender uniforms. The cops were middle-aged hacks with cheap shoes and unnaturally black hair. The taller of the two men had puffy eyes.

"You know these apartments better than anybody," he said to the housekeepers. "Let's see where he's hiding that girl. No bullshit. He's gonna get what's coming to him."

He then screamed, "Where is she?"

"I haven't seen this student in over a year," I said.

"Smart lip won't work with me, big-nose. You better feed me something solid or I'll feed you to the sharks."

And here is the trouble with art: It filters all experience so that I can hardly sense life in its pure form. Every scrap of paper blowing across pavement is art, every cluck of the bureaucrat's tongue, every note of the cuckoo bird, every duck carcass drying in the sun. Where there is art, there is criticism, and in the theater of my mind not even the most earnest eulogist escapes judgment.

To digress even a little more, I once attended a lecture by a great writer who explained the origin of one of his odder stories with the following anecdote. One afternoon he had been left alone at a friend's house in California when the friend burst in, pale as a corpse, having personally witnessed a bank holdup downtown, and as the story unfolded over the kitchen table it dawned on the writer that if he had been at the bank in the same position as his friend, he surely would have laughed uncontrollably at the canned dialogue of the masked bandits, who, according to the friend really did say, "Stick 'em up, Bub" and "One peep out of you, and the bullet hits the bone," which surely would have earned the writer a bullet in the ear the moment he cracked a smile—all due to his inability to separate art from life.

So there I was, standing in the cramped space between the bed and the closet, a uniformed woman to my left, listening to a man excrete dialogue straight out of a bad thug movie. "Fragrance clings to the hand that gives flowers," said the tall guy, to which his friend replied, "I smell a rat." Laughter gathered at the corners of my mouth and threatened to tear my face apart. I thought of the consequences, the seriousness of the matter, and tried to think of unlaughable things such as hair clogs in bath tubs, cat shit, babies born with clubbed feet, my father hitting me grounders, Queena hogtied to a chair, anything to keep from laughing. Looking back on it, I'm sure the anxiety of the situation fueled the impulse to laugh, which seemed stupid beyond logic.

"Tell me where the girl is hiding. We know she's in here."

Fei Fei pointed quietly at the base of the bed. "There is a storage area under the mattress."

"Then open it up!"

I supposed Queena was snug inside her cardboard carapace, protected by boxes that had shipped laundry detergent, rice wine, and a microwave. We had stuck them together with masking tape, and I was hoping our construction would hold.

Two women popped open bed #1 with a hydraulic hiss. I saw my suitcases, and extra pillow, a bag of summer clothes, and the erotic magazine. They opened the next bed to reveal three boxes, a wrinkled blanket, a box of tissues, a package of crackers, and the two thermoses, one for water and the other for urine—but the idiots did not see these items as part of a college girl's hideout. Perhaps the officers failed to see the crackers. I suppose it all came down to context. Because the first bed established the gestalt of "storage space," they saw the second bed in the same way, even as they were looking for evidence of a stowaway. A C note does not always sound the same; it depends on the notes above and below it, the chord that is being played at the time, and the chords occurring before and after the note is struck. Had the woman opened Queena's bed first, the men might have poked further and snagged their prize.

"Keep looking!" said the official.

The women scurried around the apartment, opening closets and poking at my clothes, peeking under my writing desk, checking under the kitchen sink. It didn't take long for the women to determine that the girl was not in the apartment. Queena's extra clothes were stashed above the ceiling panels in the bathroom. Barrettes had been banned. Her toothbrush was my extra one. There were no food wrappers that didn't look like mine. As for dirty laundry, we kept that in my guitar case, and after laundry was done, Queena absolutely had to dry her clothes over the stove. We kept tampons in the case for my fancy chopsticks.

I trailed after the housekeepers, putting things back in order. While the cops were in the kitchen looking for traces of a girl, I went into the bedroom to close the beds. And what did I see but the cardboard boxes torn open and the curtains luffing in the breeze from the open window. Cold air shot into the room. I closed the bed and just managed to slide the window shut when the cop with the puffy eyes ordered me into the main room.

"Get in here, you!"

I expected to be led away in handcuffs, but instead they shut me in the bathroom while they searched for evidence of a crime. Naturally, I sat on the toilet with the lid closed, wishing for a book. The air was stuffy, redolent of my afternoon relief. Noticing a long black hair clinging to my blue bath towel, I plucked the thing off and ate it. I wondered how Queena had managed to climb out of the window so quietly. I figured there was a fifty-fifty chance she or I had made some sloppy mistake that would get me locked up. I thought of these as my last moments as a free person. I looked up at the vent, wondering if I was skinny enough to crawl through the heating duct to some place of freedom.

The officers left. To this day, I don't know why they didn't take me with them, and no doubt it wouldn't have made any difference—but at the time I was only happy to be free. I was free to walk outside and buy a sweet potato from the man in the underpass. I was free to go to the swimming pool. I could have sat in the sculpture garden, gazing up at the pine trees like any free person, anywhere, at any point in history.

After I heard the Audi drive away, I eased open the bedroom window and looked for signs of Queena's escape. I could see her footprints on the dusty top of the air conditioning unit. From there, she would have hung down to the second-floor window ledge, clambered onto the next unit and repeated the stunt until she had landed in the bamboo. Looking down, I could see the path she had taken through the little forest.

I went back to the main room, hands shaking. The floor was grubby with the footprints of the intruders. I could smell their skin, their breath, the odor of their spicy food. The apartment was dead quiet. I mopped the floor and took a shower. I put on a robe, opened a bottle of wine, and sat listening to the magpies in the courtyard. I felt very lonely. The swollen lymph nodes suggested this cold would be a bad one. I dismissed it as hypochondria. I took some ibuprofen, drank the wine, and felt glad to be alone again, frankly relieved not to be responsible for Queena. And then came the fear that for all I knew she was now strapped to a chair in some bright interrogation room with no means of shielding her face from the enemy's syphilitic spit. I felt like a wicked man for sipping merlot, for enjoying the soft feel of the terrycloth robe on my naked body, for hearing the magpie cries as anything less than a lament.

It was then that I noticed my laptop was gone.

I was draining my glass when I saw the lonely power cord snaking across the desk. I stood up and looked for my passport. That too had been taken. Worse, they had taken one of my manuscripts, three notebooks, and two thumb drives, roughly the equivalent of ten years of creative work. My panic now seems naïve, like a freshman who feels his life is about to end because a crashed computer has wiped out his term paper. I thought nothing of real death. I should have feared for my life, for Queena's life, but I could only shout, "You fuckers! You motherfuckers! You didn't have to take my writing. You bureaucratic, weasel fuckers!"

I wanted a glass of milk. I wanted cool milk from my mother's fridge. Then I felt manly, as I hatched a plan to go to the United States Embassy and work out a reasoned diplomatic approach that would allow me to peacefully leave the country and get back my writing. I felt full of myself, knowing I had good friends like Dean Chong and Mr. Li who had Party connections. I was educated. I was special. I wasn't some recalcitrant tag artist flipping off the government. I was part of the business sector, where the real power in the world resided. I conjured a ridiculous fantasy of a bureaucrat handing me a cardboard box containing my laptop, the novel manuscript, and my passport stowed in a Ziploc bag, the case number properly marked with a bold Sharpie. The bureaucrat, a certain Todd with fourteen years of experience in the Foreign Service, would shrug and say that the men who came to my apartment were just some low-level goons who liked to scare Big Noses.

On the television, the miniseries played on with the volume muted. The Vietnamese eunuch was stealing a little bird from a tree in the garden and stuffing it into his pocket. As often happened with low-budget Chinese TV, every so often a cinematographer working his way up in the business captured a gorgeous scene. The lighting on the boy's face, the dappled pink of the cherry blossoms, and the cool jade horse set against a backdrop of stone—all of it was elegantly presented, as good as anything ever filmed. I was in another reverie, staring half-drunk into the ancient courtyard, watching a bird suffocate beautifully, when the screen flashed to a breaking news story of a Beijing skyscraper on fire.

What I saw was half surprise and half prophecy: the Epicuria Tower wrapped in flames and black smoke from head to toe. What was once a pit outside my office window had become a skyscraper and then a firework. I thought of 9/11. I thought of the Chicago fire. I thought of bodies burning. I worried deeply about my office mates next door. I expected to see people jumping out of windows, but for now the news anchor, who looked about seventeen, was lying to the public that all but ten people had been evacuated before the fire got out of control. That part of Beijing was generally windy. I had felt the gusts many mornings on my way to work, and now, on TV, I could see the black smoke getting tugged and wrung by the wind, while the world outside my window stood still as the scene in the Ming Palace gardens. It crossed my mind that everything was made up, that maybe this wasn't live footage at all but something that had burned yesterday.

Cut to a helicopter shot of the fire. Surrounding the burning tower were six-lane roads, exit ramps, railways, and giant digital billboards. The Beijing Future Building, which itself had caught fire fifteen years before, stood safely a few blocks to the west.

Selfishly, I realized that this would not be an opportune time to contact my old boss Mr. Li and ask him for favors. He had been so passionate about Epicuria, and now he probably felt terror-stricken, or worse, responsible for the fire.

No sooner had I processed these thoughts than the news channel switched to footage of a United States Naval fleet gathering off the coast of North Korea.

I couldn't take it all. I got up and turned off the TV.

Fortunately I had memorized my passport number. I put on comfortable clothes, strode over to the door, and found that it had been locked from the other side. I tugged at the lever. No release. Nor could I turn the hand lock. I pirouetted on my socks, turning now to my cell phone which sat on the cabinet ledge beside a receipt for a faulty BreatheSmart air purifier I had planned to return. I scrolled through my contacts looking for Mr. Li's private number, the one he had given me for his English lessons, but when I attempted to dial, the account was void. I tried using the apartment phone to call Dean Chong, but the line had been cut.

I prepared a backpack with water, pork buns, ibuprofen, toothbrush, razor, eight hundred yuan of my own cash, plus what was left of the money Chong had given me. I had friends in this city. I didn't know what the hell I was going to do, or if I'd ever reach the American embassy, but I had some vague notion that with no passport to book a hotel room, I might wind up on the street.

I sat on the bed and pulled the backpack to my chest, knowing I had better think everything through before climbing out the window. I was not very good at this sort of thing. Should I take an extra set of underwear? Long Johns? Should I prepare to spend the night outside in thirty-degree temperatures?

In the distance, I could hear a construction crew working, a scooter honking. I could feel the Epicuria Tower burning on the other side of the city. Thoughts flashed very quickly here: that I somehow knew it wasn't a terrorist attack, that it had to be a function of poor construction, that Beijing was not made of wood and could never burn like Chicago, that many stories of human folly had a Mrs. O'Leary's cow—a mythical cause that never existed and that was badly needed. And why did we need Mrs. O'Leary? For the same reason that the Germans needed the assassination of Herschel Grynzspan to justify Kristallnacht? No, these were not the same. And why was I thinking of the Night of Broken Glass now? Why?

I grabbed a pad of paper and a pen. My backpack bulged in a way that was very irritating. Thinking I could buy a new SIM card on the street, I stuffed my phone and charger into the zipper pocket. Then I said "fuck" for the third time that night, realizing the phone could be used as a tracking device. I said, "You cunts" out loud (a word I had seen hundreds of times but never spoken). I went to the kitchen and looked in the fridge. A block of cheese sat on the bottom rung, gathering mold. No brilliant ideas came to mind.

As if it mattered, I put on a starched white shirt and a tie, then remembered to shave. My hands shook so badly I cut myself and bled onto the shirt. I grabbed an identical shirt from my closet and tore off the plastic from the dry cleaners. I had some vague notion that looking dapper would help.

Then I had an idea to bring the phone and leave it in the back seat of a cab. The cunning gave me a boost of confidence. I climbed out of the window, stepped onto the air conditioning unit, hung down. I soon found myself on the second-floor balcony of the Korean's apartment. A shy man who lived with books and cigarettes, his living room was dark. The balcony was even filthier than mine, coated in a thick pall of dust. Down below, a car came around the circular driveway. I waited for it to pass, then stepped onto the window ledge, onto another air conditioning unit, hung down. Then I dropped into the bamboo thicket with a grunt, turning my ankle as I landed. Adrenaline sharpened my hearing and sense of smell. Cat urine. A Hebrew podcast. The smell of rice cooking. Energy coursing through my body.

I heard a Chinese woman say, "The fire is very terrible," and it seemed like I was born with the language. I could move through this country efficiently because I could speak, and that was surely an asset, but I would never be able to blend in.

I stepped out of the bamboo and was met immediately by my old friend in the black mask and baseball cap. All we lacked were dueling revolvers; such was the spacing and the pregnant pause of the moment. He stood across the driveway on stone steps beside a leafless jujube tree, his coat unzipped to reveal a pistol in his waist.

"Shall we go get some hard-boiled eggs?" he said.

"I am willing to leave the country."

"You should have done that a long time ago."

He barked a command into his wristwatch. A moment later a black sedan with government plates came plowing through the darkness.

Area 44

Today we are loaded onto a darkened bus and carried into the mountains. Sunlight seeps in around the edges of the boarded-up windows. After a time my eyes adjust and I can see whiskers on chins. I share a seat with a bald man who incessantly sucks the crud out of his fingernails. His breathing is raspy, as from damaged lungs, and his mouth gives off the odor of tooth rot. Graffiti are etched on the seats and paneling of the bus in brazen defiance of Kun Chong rules. All things considered, the men and I seem to be in pretty good shape. Nobody is crippled or visibly ill. The mere act of going somewhere is refreshing, even as we know it could lead to a worse place than prison.

As we wind down the backside of a mountain, the driver doesn't bother to downshift and with all that brake pumping there comes the smell of burning metal and oil. The blocked windows let in more light on my side of the bus, each slat of plywood glowing at the edges in pretty rectangles. We eat moldy dumplings and hard-boiled eggs. We piss and shit in a five-gallon bucket that gets passed up and down the aisle every two hours. In the beginning, the bus smells like every other bus, of brake fluid and warm rubber, and then the air gives way to an outhouse stench.

After a journey of ten or twelve hours, the plywood is removed, and we find ourselves in the middle of a shanty town on a vast landscape of garbage landfill. Flocks of birds hover here and there. Signs along the road mark the sector as "Area 44." Nobody cracks jokes about the unlucky numbers, *four, four, suh, suh,* which sound the same as "death, death." We pass through a slum of abandoned concrete buildings and terraced fields of vegetables intermixed with plots of trash. It is an everything world where an exurban ghetto morphs into a rural shanty town, then morphs back to a ghetto as we travel. A few men on the bus speculate about which city stands in the distance, but no one knows for sure. The road is lumpy and pocked. From my window I see tire shops, convenience stores, vacant storefronts, fruit stands, cigarette shops, and noodle joints. People live in cruddy, stained buildings. They poke fires in makeshift stoves. The workers walking past our bus with shovels on their shoulders sneer at us, or seem too tired for sneering. A woman stands with a red-coated baby in her arms. In the distance, farmers work the terraced fields among heaps of trash. Power lines cut across the sky. Haze blankets the horizon. Planes roam overhead, banking into turns and slipping behind far-off skyscrapers.

On a steep slope beside an abandoned three-story building, I see garbage strewn down the hill. Were this a still photograph, the stuff would appear in motion, cascading over a muddy cliff and pooling at the edge of the sidewalk.

Paths wind among the trash fields and rows of green vegetables. What looks like chaos is highly organized. Everyone knows who tends which section. The plots are not square and that is just how nature would have it, for she is never square. Always round. One man tends the leafy greens within his terrace walls. Trellises on the terrace below him. Turnips here, eggplant there, and nobody questions who owns the turnips. Do they share tools? Do they plant the same seeds? Squat over the same toilets?

A man stands on a cracked sidewalk staring at our bus. A cigarette hangs from his mouth. In his left hand he holds a hoe, standing on end. In his right hand he holds two more tools, a hatchet and a knife. The metal looks dull, the sky above him hazy. The birds whirl and swoop and peck. Nothing shines today. Something in the man's expression tells me the arrival of prison laborers is not good. The man looks up and watches a drone pass overhead and zip up over the trash hill.

One of our guards takes the microphone from the console and barks, "This is Area 44. You must now get off the bus. Don't talk to any of the local hicks."

We work for two months in the plastics mine. They march us every day into the great dumps among the villages and put us to work with rakes and picks. The thick dust is hard on my lungs, especially with the cheap mask they've given me, and soon I'm battling bronchitis and lethargy. Maybe it's pneumonia. As fate would have it, the prisoners from Kun Chong who've come to this wasteland are Fang, Xu Xuo, and Brother Gao. Rumor has it the other men from our cell are working in the wine country, as their offenses are less serious.

"I don't know why you're here," says Fang to Brother Gao. "You're a good man. You belong in the vineyard, not out here with us scoundrels."

I spend what leftover mental energy I have doing writing exercises, putting the landscape into words. The dump extends on through old villages and settlements, subsuming various burned-out buildings that may have been railway depots or fertilizer warehouses in days past. Houses not belonging to towns have been annexed by the dump. The original families are long-gone and a new wave of desperate people have moved into the glassless homes. In many cases, the old, tiled roofs with the flying eaves cannot be destroyed. Where every other part of a building is ruined, even the walls, the ancient roof remains.

Unlike Kun Chong, there are no female prisoners here. No one knows for sure, but there's speculation the women are housed in Area 43 or Area 45. But of course there are families living among us, and there have been rapes, of course, and of course there have been prisoners raped by prisoners and children of wives raped by prisoners.

Smog everywhere like Beijing on the worst days in January. Moth-gray haze cloaking the hills, buildings, and trees. There is one area of concrete slab that used to be an industrial zone. You can see the outlines of buildings and rooms laid out in rectangles on the slab, the trace remains of walls, the floor plan written in disaster on the ground. You can't tell if an earthquake, bomb, or wrecking ball has flattened this section of Area 44. Beyond the slab are walls and bushes, greedy vines, and twisted trees. Many of the walls separating the old neighborhoods are buried under debris, and above this mantle of earth new brick walls have been constructed.

Being new workers, we draw the night shift. We work from dusk till dawn on heaps of trash, trudging through the refuse with wicker baskets strapped to our backs, collecting cans and plastic bottles. The bottles get transferred from wicker baskets to fibrous sacs the size of small cars, which are then towed by men to the processing plant. Powerful floodlights bring a daytime glow to the rolling fields of garbage, as bright as any Friday night *fußball* game in Hamburg. Outfitted with reasonably good leather boots, we scramble over piles of soiled clothing, rotting lettuce, ruined sofas, watermelon rinds, paint buckets, and lump after lump of plastic bags. There is a kind of pleasure to this indiscriminate trampling over human history. For one: I haven't worn good footwear in months, and my boots fit like a charm.

We claw open plastic bags and gut them of anything worth making into something else, looking for shampoo bottles or soup cans. Iron and petroleum products are our specialty. The floodlights scare away most rats. We clamber over laundry machines and disemboweled chair cushions, heel down steep embankments of roof tiles. I suck asbestos from sheaves of splintered tiles as the excavator turns over the top layer, its great hydraulic arm swinging in the night.

We scoot out of the way of the shining blade of the crawler and its ever-rolling tracks. Fang hitches a ride on the back of the vehicle, and for an instant I see him as a boy and do not hate him. His shoulders are broad. The labor is making him stronger. Brother Gao wants to capture a rat for a pet—there is no shortage of materials to make a cage—but he is having terrible luck and insists he'll do better in daylight when he can catch them napping.

Xu Xuo works sluggishly as ever, prying open plastic bags with a chopstick.

"He's probably looking for little girlie underwear," says Fang, and my heart grows heavy as I think of the time I went to the department store to buy underthings for Queena.

"I hope the other men are enjoying their wine," says Brother Gao.

"They won't drink any wine," I say. "I'm sure they're doing the hardest work in the whole vineyard. Pruning is back-breaking work. Maybe they're worse off than us."

"What could be worse than this smell?" says Fang, sticking his nose into the air.

Rotting animal flesh. Rancid cooking oil. Fish fat, fermented bean paste, cabbage, mutton, chicken bones, paint thinner, and moldy carpet. Occasionally, a powerful waft like vinegar that isn't vinegar. Sometimes the stench is sweet, sometimes sour. Garbage can be very wet. Much of it is food, and the moisture oozes from the bottom of garbage hills and trickles down in milky-brown rivulets.

Here is a headless doll, there a legless chair. Thus far none of us has found the bodies of murdered husbands or wives, but we encounter all the things they would have hurled at each other. I see cracked teapots and worn shoes, rubber rafts and used condoms, bloody tampons and yellow roses that have lost only a few silk petals. I see pigs, cows, and children rooting through the garbage. The birds whirl and cry from above.

One night, a little girl with a wandering eye gives me a plastic NangFu Springs bottle, then trails me for half an hour, placing more plastic bottles into the basket on my back. I don't complain that she isn't sorting correctly. I look around for something to give her, maybe a doll or a pretty ribbon, and eventually I come up with a ticking watch. The time says 3:15 a.m., though it is closer to 10 p.m. The little girl wears baggy sweatpants with a blue dog on the right thigh. On her back she wears a beautiful, handmade wicker basket that could easily fetch three hundred dollars in a Soho antique shop. In one mittened hand she clutches a bag of pork buns. Her other hand is bare.

"Where are your parents?" I say.

She points to the mound of trash behind her.

"What is your name?"

"Lina."

I bend down, and suppressing a cough that wants to blast into the world, I say, "Lina, I speak four languages. Do you know that your name sounds beautiful in any language in the world?"

She smiles.

A few days later, now on the day shift, I draw work assignments that make it easy for Lina to tag along. She is very good at shooing cattle away from one pile or another, very unafraid to pit her forty-kilo frame against a horned steer and wave him away from a bag of stinking cabbage. She is a food collector. She follows the livestock. She keeps an eye on the pigs. I can't imagine that food is as light as the plastic bottles on my back, and yet she seems unfazed by the weight. I look for toys in the wreckage. We play badminton. One day when the foreman isn't watching, I build her a dollhouse out of scrap lumber. Nails are everywhere, and a piston from an old engine makes a good hammer.

She loves the house. She offers me dumplings and I refuse, saying I am vegetarian. She hardly understands the word, or my tone isn't right. I don't know where she's from, but it isn't Beijing.

One rainy day, not paying attention to how far we have wandered together, I spy a pink house beyond a copse of dingy trees. The day is foggy and wet. I can hear a creek skirting through the trash. This seems to be a border of some kind, though I don't see any signs. The pink house is a two-story thing that looks straight out of the Ozarks. I can imagine banjo music and the pleasant *pot...pot* of a gun range on a Saturday afternoon. All I hear is rushing water. Even if the water is full of toxic waste, it sounds as pretty as a mountain stream.

My reverie is broken when Lina smacks my arm with a plastic bottle. I look down and see her smiling red face, her brown-streaked teeth and inflamed gums, her precious little nose.

You are a darling little girl, I say in German, accepting her gift. I haven't spoken German in months, and the words come out like breath, easy as fog out of the woods. I have been trying for days to get her to stop giving me plastic bottles, knowing that it takes away from her job as a food collector, but she won't listen.

"Do you happen to know who lives in that pink house?" I ask, only because I am genuinely curious.

She shrugs, uninterested.

"Who lives in a pink house?" I say, changing the angle of the question a bit.

"Pink people," she says, laughing.

She has no idea of the poetic gift she has given me. No matter how sick, there are times when the mind overrides everything. I experience joy and then heartburn, congestion in the lungs. I have so much phlegm right now, it's hard to breathe. I cough bloody mucus into a kerchief and Lina doesn't flinch. She has seen everything disgusting, nothing of wealth, and her tolerance makes her a saint. If she died tomorrow—and there is no shortage of killers out here—she would float on as a saint. For once, the Catholic idea requiring a state of grace to reach heaven makes sense. Lina has a purity the rest of us lack. Her goodness, her willingness to give me plastic bottles and expect nothing in return puts her close to God.

I want to say, "I'm going to die," but I don't. I put my foot on a bag of clothes and the bag gives way. I falter and right myself and Lina giggles, and I continue clowning, flopping forward onto one cushy bag and another, coughing, spewing, laughing, smearing my chin with blood and mucus and the dirty milk of garbage, now tumbling seven feet down an embankment toward the creek. A cow drinking at the stream scuttles away with a snort. Lina giggles and giggles. Half the bottles have tumbled out of my basket. My young friend goes around collecting my collection.

"No!" I shout. "Don't touch them! I'm a sick man. I'm contagious. You mustn't touch anything I've touched."

The rage in my face does what it was meant to do. Men are made to scare children. My voice hasn't been this big in weeks.

"Don't cry," I say in a softer voice. "I'm sorry. I'm only protecting you. You mustn't touch my spit. My spit could kill you."

I take a seat at the edge of the trash heap and catch my breath, my legs splayed out like a rag doll. Lina sits on a rusted washing machine, nibbling one of her dumplings, kicking the panel with her sneakers. I wonder if this is the edge of the world. Could I wade across the creek, cut through the yard behind the pink house, and make it to the other side?

We sleep in a flimsy row hut with other prisoners from all around China. We four Kun Chong alums share a room with a single electric heater that gives off a toxic odor like melted plastic. The ceiling leaks. The mold in the ceiling tiles makes us all sneeze and itch. Every other morning in what amounts to our daily newspaper, we receive *The Labor Camp Report* under our door. The stories are always the same, or nearly so. There are mostly two kinds of information: (a) stories of men who have been shot while attempting to escape and (b) stories of men who have been injured on the job.

Running across the bottom of every page are the words, "SAFETY IS HEAVIER THAN TAI MOUNTAIN."

It is reported that a man sliced his hand open on a piece of glass, a man got his foot crushed under the tracks of the excavator, another broke his ribs from a fall, another got conked on the head with a shovel, while another got bitten by a dog. There is also good news of men who have been reformed though labor. They stand smiling in the sun with gigantic bags of plastic bottles ready for the recycling center.

We eat *mantou* in the morning and rice in the afternoon, occasionally with skewers of crispy pig or bony rib tips. They keep changing us back and forth from day shift to night shift, never with enough sleep in between. My toothache shakes. Phlegm thickens in my lungs. I finally get up the nerve to trudge over to one of the guards and tell him I'm sick, to which he responds, "Who isn't?"

"I need to go to the infirmary."

We are standing in the lee of the great excavator with its claw attachment. It scoops up a load of trash and swings it directly over our heads, sprinkling us with a granular rain that smells like fertilizer.

"What are your symptoms?"

"I'm very weak. Running a fever. I need some advanced medication for my chest."

"Okay, okay, I'll talk to the regiment leader."

"If I could work during the day consistently, instead of having my shift changed all the time, I might sleep better. I'll be a stronger worker this way. The other men are used to the night." I cough. "But I don't think I'll ever come around to it. I hardly sleep during the day, and I'm sure the lack of sleep is worsening my condition."

"You like to complain, don't you?"

"No, sir. I'm only describing my pain."

"I'll talk to the regiment leader."

Another load swings overhead, sprinkling us with asbestos dust again. I know the odor of asbestos, that burned rubber scent.

Out here in the dumps, sometimes prisoners fight with guards and even kill them. I don't know why the guards aren't armed, if they are guards. When a uniformed man is killed by a blow to the head with a brick, or smothered under a bag of rice, a new guard springs up in his place. Then after a few killings with no apparent effect, word spreads of the uselessness of killing, and the prisoners (who are also the workers) stop trying to kill the guards (who are also the workers).

But trash is colorful. In the heaps we see the entire spectrum of the world: buttery yellows, hot pink, rich scarlet, baby blue, taupe, cranberry, and emerald green. There are floral patterns and zigzags, flirtatious paisley and angry polka dots. Among the flywheels and rusty axles are tennis balls and red-feathered toys.

We spend the final week of our tour at a different mine a few kilometers to the north. We toil in the wake of the largest construction vehicles ever known: wheel loaders that stand two stories high, crawlers with blades as wide as a house, excavators that would dwarf any dinosaur. Somebody with clout has decided we should dig deeper, the idea being to go down thirty and forty years to a time when plastics and metal were thicker. The team leader announcing this plan—"We'll get fewer pieces but of higher-grade material"—does not himself seem convinced by the strategy. He has no choice but to repeat the words of his superiors.

Brother Gao says, "One generation is obsessed with steel, another with plastic."

But we aren't getting much good material. We find a lot of bicycle parts and almost no cars. I tell one of the guards that we are too deep, we've gone too far to a time when the developing nation wasn't producing a lot of waste. "The stuff's composting pretty well," I say.

"Shut up and work," he says. "You're only part of the plan. You don't get to make the plan. Maybe you're the god of some other universe, but here you're only one small insect."

I get back to work, and as I feel the guard retreating down the hill, I scan the heap for something useful, finding a toy airplane, some decent socks, and at last, a ballpoint pen. I slip the pen into the pocket of my work shirt, knowing already that if I hope to bring the thing back to Kun Chong, if I ever go back there, I'll have to carry it in my ass. This all but guarantees my writing will be full of shit. I think of my buddy Mac and miss him terribly, knowing he would find my joke hilarious.

The Falconer's Glove

After our tour is over, we are brought back to Kun Chong and reunited with our cellmates, who have returned from the vineyards with suntanned faces and black fingernails. We settle into our old routine, sleeping on the floor every other night, playing mahjong, eating chicken feet and pork belly. Then one night, just as life is starting to feel unchangeable again, Fang announces that his woman is pregnant. He has kissed her fingers under the door after receiving the news.

The next day Fang is taken away and castrated. He returns with his loins bandaged, his face blank and quiet. His glasses have gone by the wayside and his eyes have no desire to focus. Nobody says a word to him as he curls up on the bed against the wall: a caged animal whimpering like a man. Brother Gao doesn't bring him a cup of tea. Jack doesn't vow revenge. Xu Xuo stares at the ceiling. Our cell is quiet for a time. We can hear the magpies, the steady rumble of the factory, the asthmatic breathing of The Man Who Did Nothing, whose condition has worsened from the shower of pesticides in the vineyards.

Fang stays in that shriveled ball, crying for almost two hours. He wears baggy blue sweatpants to accommodate the bandage, and I can see white gauze poking out like the hem of a diaper. He is barefoot. He has beautiful feet, strong and sculpted like those of a tall Wisconsin woman I once had a crush on (I was fifteen, she was thirty-two). It doesn't matter that Fang has lost his glasses. He keeps his eyes closed.

As for the rest of us? Xu Xuo shuffles over to the toilet and pisses. Brother Gao slumps at the table, running his hand across the wooden top, which has been planed yet again to erase any carvings. Jack stands at the gate, holding the bars and gazing at the persimmon tree through the portal. Something has happened to Kuku. No one is talking, least of all the boy with the puerile lips. His hair has grown long now and he hasn't bathed in weeks. Nor has he eaten much of anything. He lies curled up on the top bunk in the corner, and my gut tells me he'll be allowed that spot for as many nights as he needs. Something happened in the vineyard. The kid is clearly shaken.

My condition improves, just from being out of the dust and by getting more sleep. Still I cough. I sit in my chair trying to write but can't hold much of anything in the mind. I feel guilty for hating Fang, but still I hate him, hating him all the more for making me feel guilty about my hatred, irritated that his situation interferes with my ability to work. What does it mean to hate another man? Is it to want him to die? To wish him pain? They aren't the same.

Baby-faced Gao is mustering a thin salt-and-pepper beard that makes him look scholarly or sick. He shuffles over to Fang's bed and takes a seat next to his whimpering brother, pats him on the shoulder in a way that Fang permits.

"Perhaps this means you're going to live," he says. "They wouldn't do this to a man bound for execution."

Fang closes his eyes tighter.

The chatter of the women on the other side of the wall is no different than before: the staccato of Chinese that never flows gentle on a foreign mind. They banter and complain as any other day. The din is the same until we hear a crazed scream explode next door, and the screaming warps into a howl and the howl into the shrieks of a woman gone mad.

It takes four guards to carry her out of the cell: three guys holding her limbs and one guy wearing a thick falconer's glove to throttle her neck and withstand her gnashing teeth. They've forgotten to pull the curtain, or left it open on purpose to show us Fang's sin. They drag her into the corridor, this writhing red human, much prettier than I would have thought, if anyone can be said to be pretty in her condition. She wears a red jumpsuit. She has high cheekbones and full lips and most surprisingly for a prisoner, a black pile of hair fastened into a bun.

Fang lifts his head and looks at his lover, his face twisted, eyes unable to focus without his glasses. You can feel the muscles working behind the eyes, trying to better see the woman he sees.

"I love you, Fang!" she says. "I love you!"

The woman looks to be twenty-seven? Twenty-eight?

The guards shove her face against the bars. One of them says, "If you men have never met a slut, here is your chance!" Her exquisite hand caught in the red grip of the guard calls to mind the worst sort of pornography.

The Lucky No. 8

I fell in love on a bus. My bus had pulled up alongside the No. 373, and to my left I saw a woman checking me out. Beautiful white face. Dark limpid eyes. Cornsilk hair. A quiet nose and a soft, downturning mouth.

We stared at each other like mother and child until her lips twitched into a wry smile in a glass box. I smiled in return. It is true that Chinese people will stare at you brazenly, but this was something else.

Her bus pulled ahead and came to a stop in the next block. As my bus continued on, I tried to look back to see if the woman in the white coat with the brown fur collar was getting off. Three more buses crowded my view and I had no idea if she was still on that bus or among the pedestrians. I was on a double-decker express bus, the No. 8, and had to go three more blocks before I could get off, my chest thrumming with adrenaline. Who cared that I would return to work late after lunch? That I had spent two hours in a café writing a fragment that was one-ten-thousandth as magical as her face in the window?

Out on the sidewalk in the smutty air, I resisted the urge to don my mask. I had thrust my hand in my coat pocket and was fingering the thing, the greasy felt. I was in love, and I thought, If I try to write this down it'll sound ridiculous. I'll have to make all the faces on the bus her face. I'll make the busses go in reverse, or I'll order the driver to order us to turn and sing "The East is Red" or else never get off the bus. The driver will clean the windshield with his saliva to give us a better view, throwing spit upon spit on the glass and using a rag to wipe circles on the city. Something must be done to express the inexpressible, to make "love at first sight" a terror rather than a cliché.

I walked south down Third Ring Road toward a construction crane in the distance, past vendors selling hard-boiled eggs and pirated movies. My mouth was dry not because I worried she would not be there but because I knew she would. I stopped and checked my face in the reflection of an old phone booth, picked a black sesame seed out of my front teeth. My white shirt was clean and starched. My tie knotted. My shoes felt slippery on the grimy pavement just as they had on my first morning in Beijing twenty years before. An old woman selling magazines, whose face stood out among hundreds of faces, looked straight into my eyes as if warning me.

I walked ahead to meet my lover.

I said, "Ni hao," and she said, "Ni hao."

After a long pause, I said, "I don't know what to do."

"Your tones are very good."

"In any language, I don't know what to do."

"You could ask me out for coffee?"

I looked around. I saw a block of apartments with bars on the windows and laundry shifting in the wind and mops slung over walls. I saw a row of tiny shops selling tobacco, hardware, badminton rackets, veggies, shoe repairs, propane.

"Around here?" I said. "The coffee is sure to be terrible. And I'd be late returning to work."

"But you got off the bus. Is this your stop?"

"No. I got off the bus to see you."

"And the office?"

"I wanted to see you again and talk to you. If I didn't get off the bus in this city of twenty-two million people, what are the chances I would ever see you again?"

"Bad chances."

She took a step back. She smiled but immediately turned it down a notch. I sounded like a predator, like I expected to check into a seedy hotel straightaway. She had a tiny perfect nose and dark, chocolate eyes. I took her to be about twenty-eight years old, though her skin could have belonged to a teenager. Felt coat. Hourglass figure. I couldn't tell if she was in fact this curvy or if it was the cut of her fashionable winter coat. In her hair she wore a silk bow the color of a Tiffany's box.

The thing I sensed from the beginning, that I conveniently ignored for more than a year, was my own quiet awareness that she was too philistine for me—not unintelligent, mind you, as I could tell she was smart by the end of that first coffee date—and that her good looks trumped everything. Beauty wins, most of the time. I knew right away that she wasn't dark enough or artistic enough for me, not German enough, not American enough, but I buried those concerns the moment she allowed me to study her perfect face in the window of a bus.

And knowing this, knowing her before I knew her, I answered her question on the pavement that day, "Where do you work?" in the way that sounded richest. Not, "I'm in insurance." Not, "I'm essentially an indentured employee in the insurance firm that my father founded and lost, but I'm aiming to leave as soon as possible." Not, "I'm a writer of underappreciated fiction who suffers office work only as a means to make money and support my family." I said, not lying, "I occupy a second-tier position at China Life and Casualty, which is a subsidiary of the Grand Palace Investment Group."

Her eyes got big, as though I had said something sexy. "I'm an auditor. I keep an eye on people like you. I think you are very handsome."

"I only wish our auditors had eyes like yours. It would make office life much more bearable."

This should have been her clue. This was her chance to swivel on her high heels and get on the next bus. She should have known that a man who hated office life was not her man. I wanted to reach out and stroke the fur collar of her coat, but just then a man with polio limped past, jerking his bad leg ever forward, and the elegance of the moment was lost. Just then something got stuck in my eye, some filthy spec of Beijing air, as happened from time to time, and knowing it was bad medical practice to itch the eye, I let the tears pool.

"You're crying," she said.

And I began to laugh, which increased the crying and flushed the particle. This was my single best "China moment" to that point in my expat experience. Already I was dreading that life would never again be this sweet, this intense. The physical proof of joy had come out of my eye and washed away the painful thing. The man with polio hobbled around the corner and out of view. Still laughing, wiping my eyes on my lapel, I said, "I don't know what to do."

"Don't you dare try to kiss me on the first date," she said, opening her mouth. "I'm a traditional Chinese girl. We make you wait."

How to explain those first three days of our relationship? She made me wait, alright, but only till Sunday. We met on a Thursday and went to dinner on Friday at a Persian restaurant in Sanlitun, walking the cold frigid night past Russian men looking for whores, kissing under the light of an iMac logo, and whispering goodnight in a cab outside her parents' dull apartment. Because she was in town for the weekend, staying with her parents (her aging father was a former nuclear physicist who had lost face in the Cultural Revolution, her mother a geneticist) we met the following day for tea, followed by three painful and blissful hours in a mall. We held hands. Her voice sounded like bubble tea. I would have walked anywhere with her. It was the stage in a relationship where I would have been happy to hike the fields of Chernobyl so long as I had Lulu at my side. We laughed at two mannequins near the exit of the mall, a headless man and headless woman, who had been arranged in a rather sexy embrace. She gave me a look that guaranteed we would have sex. Soon. Sometimes you just know. I told her I planned to book a room at the Grand Hyatt for Sunday evening, and when I asked if she wanted to join me, she said, "That would be naughty but perfect. We barely know each other."

"Maybe we are special."

"It would not be very Chinese of me, not in the traditional way. I'm scheduled to fly back to Shanghai on Sunday evening."

"Which means your parents won't know a thing."

"I will change my flight."

Flight requires more than liftoff. The problem was that after two hours of incomparable foreplay, just as we were launched in a position that would give us pleasure not only for eight seconds but for a host of recollections in the future, I caught a whiff of fecal smell from my crotch and lost the fire. I had a hemorrhoids issue that made my plumbing a bit leaky, the sort of thing that happens to anxious men approaching middle-age, and though the surgery was supposed to be simple, I had put it off, put it off, avoiding the Chinese surgeons. Just as Lulu was preening naked on the ivory sheets, as I was looking to the wall at an orange abstract painting to avoid getting a too-clinical look at her vagina, I caught a whiff of my own shit and sunk into shame. While her eyes were closed, her fake lashes scraping the pillow, her mind sinking deeper into the moment, I went soft. The suddenness with which this happened was itself impressive. How could so much rage drop so quickly?

"What?" she said in Chinese. "You don't have it?"

She sounded like a girl from the sticks, base in her need, her voice scratchy as a heroin addict's.

"What?" she said, now angry. "Shit!"

And thinking she meant the smell of me, I jumped away from the bed and locked myself in the bathroom.

Later, of course, she was tender and forgiving, the intelligent daughter of scientists, with her nifty explanations of my *condition* that she didn't call a condition, but rather, "A one-time thing, I'm sure."

"Yes," I said. "Never happened to me before. But it's not you. Probably, I'm just so attracted to you I get intimidated."

"Psychological and scientific reasons," she said. "There are both. Don't worry, Bunny. We'll try again sometime."

"Bunny?"

"You're my pet bunny, but next time my bunny will be hard as coal."

The next morning, at my office building, I saw from the coffee shop window a giant pile driver in the pit, slamming down, slamming down with perfect hydraulic force. It seemed the workers were readying a foundation for a skyscraper, and the way to anchor a tall building to the earth required drilling deep holes in the bedrock and sinking rods into the cavity. The sexual imagery wasn't lost on me. I had a literature degree after all. The memory of Lulu's nude pose excited me, and I let the feeling pass.

Beside the pile driver was a formation of cement bags stacked like a stronghold against mortar fire. There was a man wearing a red helmet and green greatcoat, talking on his cell phone. There was a patch of frozen ice. There was every few seconds a white flash from the welders at the base of the wall of the pit. There was an excavator. There was a loader.

The pit was three stories deep and as long as a soccer field. The excavation into the center of the city had exposed the piles and rebar of surrounding structures, the slabs of low-grade concrete that could look crumbly as a dry corn muffin. You could see the way things had begun but not really what was coming. You only knew that *now* was a pit inhabited by forty workers and eleven heavy machines. Cigarettes dangled from every man's mouth like a part of the uniform. The dirt was tawny, lifeless as the moon. The flashes of the welders flickered all day and night.

I turned away from the window and admired a photograph on the wall opposite the coffee bar, showing a close-up of a worker's hands thrust into a basket of red coffee beans. My phone buzzed and I got a text from Lulu. She wrote in English: "I want your hands on me again. I miss you so much. I safe back in Shanghai. Boring work. Miss you Frances!!!" The accompanying emoticons were four lumps of coal and two smiley faces, which I thought brilliant.

This was the first exchange in a long e-affair.

In the beginning, Lulu's frequent text messages annoyed me. She was nine years my junior and therefore belonged to a different technological generation, so it was expected of me to court her with my cell phone. After a couple of months I got into it. She bought me a fancy new phone that made it very easy to write love letters and other fragments with the new method, rather than my thumbs. Thus, given the chance to write something, I did. Some of the messages were lyrical. Others were banal. Something funny would happen, say, a woman would walk past me in a mall dressed as Minnie Mouse (not "like" Minnie Mouse) and with no one else to share my laughter, I would fire off a quick sketch to my lover. Not every communique was funny. When a street vendor threatened me with a cleaver, when the woman on a moped skidded on a patch of oil, when the police covered the student's suicide with a pink quilt in the rain, when the prostitute lifted her hem, I would render each tableau in clear, simple prose and send it to Lulu.

I received three or four messages a day, some with racy snapshots that, thank God, were never too clinical. All the same, I deleted every photo because I preferred the power of memory and because China itself made me paranoid. I didn't like reading her messages in my office, and I would have felt like a creep hiding out in a bathroom stall, so I usually did my reading and responding over coffee. The Starbucks was on the second floor of the building but because of the way the view dropped into the pit, it seemed to be much higher. There was a giant rotunda in the space and as you ascended the spiral staircase to reach the coffee shop, you could look up through a glass ceiling at the great sky and the long black face of the Palace Bank Tower. I never tired of this view, and for this reason, I always took the stairs and caught the elevator from L2 rather than from underground.

I liked the icy sheen of the polished granite floors and the silky feel of the gilded handrails, which I palmed lecherously even during flu season. I hated my job. I felt empty nine hours a day, but the aesthetics of office life were nothing to complain about, at least for ten minutes a day coming and going, longer if I lingered in the seating area by the Starbucks. This was one of those open storefronts in the transitional area between the offices and the shopping mall. This mall had an ice rink and a Fatburger, but my chief Mr. Li complained that it lacked the finest things. Many of the brands were second rate. The bakery was an abomination, serving up the worst kind of beauty without substance. Like me, Mr. Li was a sworn enemy of croissants made with margarine.

I wanted to quit. Every week I wanted to quit, but this became impossible once I got serious with Lulu, who had high hopes for me becoming a tycoon. She knew exactly what was happening in the insurance sector and the kind of insane growth that was possible in the most populous country in the world, where the life insurance penetration was less than five percent. Not only that, but there was chatter I might be put in charge of a team whose goal was to increase the sales of health and life policies to expats, another growing pool. She liked it when I sent her expensive gifts via express mail. I couldn't resist pleasing her in this way because the favors I would receive in our face-to-face meetings—all three of them—had value beyond money. Twice after lovemaking, I got up and wrote in the bathroom, nude on the toilet seat. Lulu didn't care for this. She thought I was not only strange and obsessed but emotionally impenetrable.

In the pit I saw large sections of sewer pipe. I saw men crouching close to one another to work out some engineering puzzle. I saw men pouring hot water out of thermoses. The workers lived on the northern bank of the pit in a three-story temporary housing structure, the ones with blue roofs that were everywhere in China.

Sometimes the men would drag things along the bottom of the pit using a hook at the end of a cable that went through an intelligent series of pulleys and booms. The workers mixed cement and dug holes. They sawed through concrete and inhaled the dust. When I was supposed to be firing off emails to the president of the Marine Insurance Alliance, when I was supposed to be shopping the mall for a gift for that special someone in the Party who could influence government rules for third party liability policies, or the banking oversight secretary who might vote for a change in accounting regulations favorable to our firm, instead I was gazing out the window at the dirty men.

They carried mortar bags on their shoulders. They pulled levers that set giant arms in motion, hydraulic and clawing. They wore camouflage pants. Red helmets. Yellow helmets. White helmets. The colors didn't seem to mean anything, but sometimes when all the hard hats were gathered together around a makeshift gambling table at the end of the day, the helmets looked like candy pieces.

Behind them in the near distance stood the spectacular Great Future Building, which was as much a sculpture as an edifice. It was shaped like the block letter of some new alphabet, similar to a three dimensional "A" without the crossbar. Sometimes I thought of it as a trapezoid, sometimes a tripod with an amputated leg. The building was a kind of arch, but it was twisted. As one leg of the arch ran up at an angle, it turned toward one direction, twisted, turned again, and ran down the other side to the ground. A great wicket of empty sky yawned in the middle.

The building defied visual logic like an Escher drawing, the way the horizontal arch thrust outward like a chin, suspended over the plaza far below. The building seemed impossible to describe. I would waste an hour of company time trying to put the building into words. I never seemed to get it right. Sometimes it seemed like an arch, sometimes a tower. There seemed to be no center of gravity save for the sky space in the center.

That I had drafted but not finished two novels, that my lover did not seem to care for my work, hovered at the edge of my consciousness always, though especially when I had trouble describing the odd, great tower. My inability to pin down this building stood for everything that wasn't happening in my life: my inability to quit my job or give myself to a woman, to craft the perfect story or to let go of the ones that were good enough to send out. So many projects left unfinished. I had built eighty-nine percent of a dozen great monuments.

I would turn off my phone and look outside at 2:13 p.m. and get a rush of inspiration, as if I had found the secret sequence of letters to finally build my beautiful edifice, and pretending to be writing a monthly report, I would start writing a sentence. Look at the building. Write another. Measure the angles with a protractor in my mind. I resorted to metaphors like "veins" and "sinew" to describe the steel runnels that ran down the black body of the building. I would call up Picasso, Gaudi, da Vinci by comparison, and after half an hour arrive no closer to a semblance of the tower. Much of the building was covered in diamond patterns from the crosshatching beams, but in the upper portion these beams spun off in curves, breaking the diamond pattern, creating open figures and arrows, a rhombus here, a spade there, a chaos of shapes. And in the foreground of the beautiful monument lay the yellow pit like an unfilled grave.

The Goad

Back at Kun Chong, Kuku makes the first killing attempt. He plunges the tip of a torn-off bedspring into his wrist and draws blood. A clumsy suicide attempt. Wu Kaiming and Jack wrestle the weapon away from Kuku before he can do any real damage, and the guards haul him off to the infirmary.

Jack holds the pigtail piece of bedspring up to the light and says, "How did he manage to yank this out of the mattress? Humpft. Looks like he sharpened the tip somehow with a file."

"He scraped it against the bricks," says Fang in a tired voice. "I heard him doing it."

"The vineyard was bad," says Jack.

The story goes that while Kuku was out there pruning vines and slinging manure, he managed to find out via Weibo that his girlfriend had taken up with another guy, and worse, had made damning comments about her "cheater" ex-boyfriend, worse, made fun of his small hands, ha, ha, ha! Wu Kaiming tried to tell Kuku that it must have been the government authorities who told her to say such things to make an example of him. How did Kuku manage to view Weibo while working in a field of vines? One of the guards had confiscated a phone from a new inmate and let Kuku have a look in exchange for a blow job, so says Wu Kaiming, who isn't given to lies. Thus the kid was shamed on many levels. He had to swallow a guard's semen just to get a snippet of his sweetie, only to find out he had been jilted.

I don't know how much I believe Wu Kaiming's story. Perhaps Kuku has been raped. Anything is possible. Perhaps Wu Kaiming is trying to protect his young friend. Sometimes a cover-up story morphs into something worse than the truth.

I don't want to write about Kuku's suicide attempt. I feel some obligation to tell his story, as if there is some fusty teacher hovering over my shoulder, saying, "You should write about that." A pimply guard stands in the hallway ready to poke me with a bamboo goad every time I look like I'm writing. How the hell is he supposed to determine this? Now I can't even write from memory, much less the pen that I smuggled in my ass and stowed in the P-trap beneath our sink. I had high hopes for that pen. And now?

The goader is the smallest of all the guards, a pale man with large glasses and square bangs. His hair is like a doll's hair, a kind of black helmet. I'm guessing he's about thirty years old: old enough to occupy an important position in the prison, young enough to have that low hairline. He has tremendous powers of concentration, the way he sits at his wooden desk and detects my murmuring truths in real time. He is not a peon. As it seems to me, he has a higher rank than the other guards, judging by the way he snaps at them and makes them walk under the goad when they pass. Interestingly, only one of the guards chooses to pass under the bar limbo style.

What really interests me here, which is later confirmed by Brother Gao, Jack, and ultimately even Fang—who despite his terrible spirit can be trusted in matters of pure reason—is the relationship between height and rank among the guards. Inversely, as it would seem, the tallest guards have the least power, while the shortest guards have the most. This suggests that the task of keeping me from writing must be an administrative priority.

"We know what you're doing," says the short guard, "and we can't allow it."

"But you let me speak. Anybody here can speak. You're saying I can verbalize my thoughts, but I can't do any so-called writing, not even in my head?"

"We know what you're doing."

"How do you know I'm not just daydreaming?"

"The way your lips move. It is so obvious what you're doing. Personally, I don't care one bit. Go ahead and play lute to a cow for all I care. But it's written in the old prison documents—I have seen them in their glass vaults—that no prisoner at Kun Chong is permitted the luxury of literary expression. This is meant to safeguard us against subversion and unclean thoughts. Even as a guard, I cannot write anything for fear that it would be passed to another man, or a woman, and possibly spread like a virus. They view our writing like venereal disease. And to tell the truth, I would like to write a book someday. I have ideas. But all that will have to wait until I leave Kun Chong."

He goads me with the bamboo stick every time he thinks a metaphor slips into my mind, and amazingly, he's right about half the time. I try to explain that metaphors are everywhere, that really all language is metaphor, but I sound pretentious. He pokes me again. This is what ribs are for, to protect our lungs from primitive armies. Maybe it's just as well. One of us has been castrated. Another is a dead man walking. Another has tried to kill himself. Next to this suffering, writing can seem stupid and elitist, and besides, I'd probably try miserably to tell Kuku's story with a hideous possum as my main character.

Through the wall, on the woman's side, a bowl falls on concrete. A tin bowl. There's no mistaking that sound. I sit in my chair by the barred window, half aware of the goad aimed at my ribs. One of our men is snoring. The white noise of the factory plays in the distance. The moment I compose a sentence about duck carcasses drying in the sun, I feel a jab to my side. A sharp pain.

"Hey, man," I say. "That's just how I think."

The thrust of the goad reminds me of that famous Slovak phrase without vowels, "*Strc prst skrz krk,*" which means "Stick your finger through your throat."

Wu Kaiming shuffles back from the toilet and climbs into bed. When he gives the comforter a shake, Kuku's weapon bounces to the floor, a sad coil, rusty with blood. The guard doesn't object when Jack snatches up the thing for his own.

Xu Xuo flinches.

"Sooner rather than later," says Jack, tucking the weapon into his waistband. He goes to the sink and takes up the razor and soap and shaves his head so that he has no more middle-aged crown. His pate is naked and pale as the underbelly of a fish. "We're just postponing the inevitable. The longer we put it off, the harder it gets."

"I have a question" says Yu. "Is it possible that one of us is better suited to the job, since, if he ever were to get out of here, he would be protected by international law?"

"No," I say, shaking my head. "No such thing exists."

Do we all feel the same? Do we all feel an equal weight on our heads? I suppose that each one of us has imagined stabbing him in the gut or binding his feet for the hanging. We are all so dirty and tired and depressed, killing this man now seems more possible than ever. Prisoners will do anything to change the status quo, no matter if it leads to worse feelings. Just change something. Just kill. Do away. Erase. Burn it down. Blow it up. Anything but the present state of affairs. Murder makes sense. I'm not saying we crave blood while he sits on the bed blinking at the wall, his long lashes dutifully blinking, blinking away the dust motes. I'm saying if it happens, it happens.

Xu Xuo stands up from the bed and goes to the wash basin, takes up the razor and shaves his neck. He is telling us that he intends to live long enough that it makes sense to shave; otherwise he might wind up with a beard, possibly a long beard if we can't get our act together. He uses water and soap like everybody else, working the foul-smelling red bar into a pink lather. He peers into the little square of alloyed metal on the wall, which serves as our mirror. Unlike in other countries, where metal would be etched with graffiti and lewd drawings, here the surface is clean and reflective. Xu Xuo works the razor over the chin, the cheeks, and now the pallet above the lip. He scrapes at the hair in his ears. He hocks a wad of spit into the drain and I think of my darling pen, desecrated again.

We still don't know the exact nature of his crime. As much as we doubt the Kun Chong Department of Reform, to say nothing of their Information and Communications Office, we can't help feeling they've got it right when it comes to Xu Xuo. No word from on high, no last-minute DNA evidence could change our minds. Fang inveighs against Xu Xuo's "taste for little girls" or his "evil little dick" (it isn't little) and we prisoners go along supposing he is a rapist or pedophile. People can be forgiven for some offenses, but not these, and it's a fact of life that in some instances you're a sinner for all time, whether you atone or not. You are an adulterer. You are a killer. A thief. A plagiarist. You may be forgiven, you may yet do good, but you are defined forever by what you did. Wu Kaiming is an addict. Kuku is a cheater. Fang is a swindler. I am a failure. Gao? Nobody knows what Gao did to wind up in this place.

Rumors have spread that Xu Xuo has AIDS.

"He gave it to his wife, he gave it to his baby."

"If he bleeds, get away."

Xu Xuo listens like an animal. His ears flinch. In his reptilian reticence, in not denying any of the accusations, he seems to accept the charges. Or he rises above our petty talk and frees himself from earthly guilt. But if you ask me, he doesn't have the mettle. Just how transcendent can a compulsive nose picker be? I am too chicken to ask what he did. Or maybe I'm afraid of the answer, but why? Let's say his only crime is that he defaced that portrait of Chairman Mao that hangs on the Tiananmen tower? No. Xu Xuo has been given the supreme penalty and I happen to know that anyone who defaces the Mao portrait will get between sixteen and twenty years (notwithstanding that a backup portrait weighing 1.5 tons can be hauled out of the vault and hung in less than an hour). If Xu Xuo is indeed the worst brand of criminal, then why not let Jack have at it?

One night after the guard has put away his goad and the men are asleep, I can hear Brother Gao stirring on his tabletop bed.

"Maybe the world doesn't need him," I say. "Maybe it's all right to kill him. It could be considered an act of mercy."

There are times when I am speaking Chinese that I feel like an actor, when the words coming out of my mouth aren't from me but from a character. It's part of getting the tones right. But that night, my words sound like me. It is Francis, I, me speaking my own language. Perhaps in my drowsy state, I speak from somewhere deeper in myself, maybe even deeper than one man, from some memory stored in our DNA.

"That's one way to see it," says Brother Gao. "We all want something simple, and that's a big problem with people. Big problem."

"I don't think it's simple at all. I'm saying I don't feel good about killing him, but maybe it won't really matter to the world."

I feel myself waking up a bit, a thrumming from inside my chest. I roll over and look at Gao, who lies on his back with his knees raised, staring at the ceiling. In the gauzy light from the corridor I can make out the boyish sculpt of his brow and nose, his lips moving. Here at Kun Chong we are never allowed the luxury (or fear) of sleeping in total darkness.

Gao says that as soon as you justify one killing, even on the basis of mercy, you open up the possibility of further interpretations and rationalizations and that people in general and the Chinese in particular are terrible line judges. "They either don't know where the line is or they move the line to suit their own ends," he says.

"Or they claim the line doesn't exist."

"No. They always draw the line and say, 'Look! There it is,' and maybe it wasn't there yesterday, or maybe it has just appeared five minutes before, but now it is drawn on the official paper. You're not thinking clearly. You're trying to entertain me."

"But look at it this way," I say. "If a large statue fell from a high wall and killed you or Xu Xuo, say both of you were standing side-by-side, I think most people would agree that the world would miss you more than him."

"Are you more valuable to the world than Xu Xuo?"

I hesitate, not because I have any doubts but because I feel socially obligated, even in the hole of night in a half-lit prison, to think before I speak. "Yes, my life is more valuable than his."

"Do you have children?"

"No."

"Do you regularly perform charity? Is your job a helping kind of work?"

"Somewhat."

"You know almost nothing about Xu Xuo. Only that he is strange. How do you know he's not an excellent poet?"

"Trust me. He's no poet."

"And even if he was an excellent poet, why should that make his life more valuable than a mason's? Just because you write books, that doesn't make you better than the rest of us who don't do that sort of thing."

"I've never published a book."

"But you haven't addressed the essence of my question."

"Fine, so, if someone makes good art, sure, yes, I think that makes them more valuable than someone who does nothing, or someone who steals or kills."

"You don't even know what Xu Xuo did."

"How do you know I don't know?"

"Nobody does. The guy doesn't talk. The guards only speak the language of rumors. Nobody knows."

"But there's an aura of guilt around the guy. I mean, he doesn't even defend himself. You have to admit that he seems like a creep, a real dirty criminal."

"Our senses are only good for smelling shit."

"Precisely."

"I'm not agreeing with you."

"But you are."

I am bothered and elated by Gao's undressing of my philosophy, his weakening of my argument. It has been some time since I've enjoyed any intellectual sparring. Brother Gao is the only man in the prison that I love. I hate Fang. I would kill Xu Xuo, though I don't hate him. I like Jack and Wu Kaiming. I pity Kuku and in spite of his suicide attempt and his likeness to my students find it difficult to feel any kinship toward him, partly because I can't stand students who cheat and partly because I can't stand students who care too much about test scores. Brother Gao is the only one I love. I'm bothered that he thinks I'm full of it.

"Look," he says. "The moment you say this man's life is worth more than that man's—you can justify anything. The peasants can do with poisoned drinking water and mercury in their meat because their lives are worth less. A vegetable seller sprays formaldehyde on his cabbages. China has no soul."

"I'm not saying the peasants' lives are worth less. I would never say that. But I get your drift."

Lying on my back, I raise my knees to match Brother Gao's posture, the two of us like devotees in the same house of worship. A bloodless religion? Does such a thing exist? Some days I feel so full of rage and hatred for this injustice, for this fucked up world, I want to hurt somebody. Gao and I don't belong here, and someone should have to answer for it. But whom can I hurt, hate, blame, or kill? Blaming the Chinese or the Government makes as much sense as blaming God.

Xu Xuo lies curled up on the floor with his back to us, facing the black space under the bed. His snoring is regular and deep, though it is only a matter of time before he'll stir and twitch like every man on death row. His blanket is the only one with tassels which, in a prison like this, is some extravagance.

"I don't hate him," I say. "But I think I want somebody to kill him."

"You're a writer. How can you say this? You're in the business of making products of the spirit. That's totally incongruous with the ways of a writer."

"William S. Burroughs shot his girlfriend in the face playing a parlor trick. Norman Mailer, another American writer, stabbed his wife with a pen knife. He also mentored a murderer who became a writer, who got out of prison and became a murderer again. Hitler wrote *Mein Kampf* in prison, and your Mao, he was an excellent writer. Would you like some more examples?"

"No," he said, changing positions. "You've made your point. I want you to tell me one of your stories."

"I used to love reading to people at parties, especially when my friend Mac was there."

"Do you write anything funny?"

"I think so. I think a lot of my stuff's funny, but people who don't know me don't always hear it. People who love me—they have no trouble getting the humor in my stories. But to be honest, it isn't necessarily the kind of stuff the Chinese find wildly humorous."

"Don't stereotype us. Trust me. Speak."

I tell him a story. Brother Gao is half the time in stitches on the table. It isn't easy. I am translating on the fly one of my shorter works, a rather bizarre and cruel story called "Mrs. O'Leary's Cow," wherein the Irish lady's clumsy Jersey winds up being responsible for the death of Christ, the pollution of the Ganges, and the dropping of a nuclear bomb on the babies of Pyongyang. I wrote it before the United States retaliation. How it still seems funny now is beyond me.

Brother Gao likes my cow story very much. Xu Xuo snores. The factory in the distance keeps chuffing. From the end of the dim corridor comes the sound of a guard playing a handheld video game.

I ask Gao to return the favor. Tell me a story.

"Shit," he sighs. "I guess I'll tell you what I did to wind up here."

He had been a rather lucky farmer. He had more land than most farmers, owing to some long-ago connections and administrative errors; and because people in the village liked him and respected his family, no one expressed any jealousy over his double happiness. "Only a joke," he says. "I didn't have twice as much land as the next guy, but pretty close."

He also had two children, a son and a daughter, which to his way of thinking was just as it should be. "I'm not one of these Confucians who insist on sons as if it's a right from Heaven. Sure, I wanted a boy to carry on the family name, but I didn't really care. Truth be told, I also wanted a girl."

His wife was pretty. Even her teeth were good, which was saying a lot for a village where starch-loving people ran around with broken smiles. He even had a good education in spite of growing up during the Cultural Revolution. He had an "uncle," not his real uncle, a professor from Mei Hua University who wound up performing his re-education in one of the rice paddies bordering Gao's. The professor taught him about Western philosophy, Socrates, Epicurus, Kant, Montaigne, Thoreau, and Eastern thinkers like Confucius, Laozi, and the Buddha. He took young Gao to the carvings at Dazu. He recited the poems of Du Fu but told the boy it was mostly ancient propaganda, so don't listen too closely, don't get caught up in that shit of believing everything ancestral is good. Brother Gao grew up knowing that Socrates and Jefferson owned slaves and that Chairman Mao had mistresses. Other kids in the village only knew that Mao was a brilliant military strategist who kept one hundred blossoming flowers in his head and liked to swim in ice-cold rivers.

Gao, groping at the corner of the table, manages to find his glasses and puts them on.

"In many ways I lived the Chinese Dream," he says. "I got a university education, learned French pretty well, then returned to my village to grow rice. My children were beautiful. Perfect. I mean, they misbehaved from time to time, acted selfish and undisciplined, but they were good learners and had handsome bodies. Good kids. My son could do backflips and he was an excellent reader. His attention span, his ability to sit in the light of a window and stay with a book for hours at a time, it was amazing. But he loved to play football, too, and had very lively feet."

Here his throat tightens and his words lose their balance. The pain is coming back. The moment of placid reflection over an evening rice paddy is over.

"Then my son was killed. It was a freak accident. Nobody's fault. Horsing around with his friends, he decided to walk along the top of a wall in the village. He was walking up there doing I-don't-know-what, I wasn't there, but he fell and hit his head on a drill press. The blow knocked him out. He never woke up."

Brother Gao takes off his glasses with one hand and covers his watery eyes with the other. He turns away from me and pulls his knees to his chest.

"And then, to have my daughter raped four years later by a pair of thugs who wanted to make her into a prostitute, my daughter, who was not a racy girl and who came from a good family. What evil and utter lack of reason made them think they could press my Lin Lin into prostitution? We caught them, that was no problem. Two men. The people of the village wanted to kill these guys and the plan was made to use a flatbed truck as the gallows and hang them from a big ficus tree. Step on the gas and, wham, they're dead. And what did I do? Stupid Gao? I put a stop to it. I had seen so much useless killing in our country. But still the thirst for blood was strong, and when I saw my daughter's tear-stained face in the light of the same window where my son used to read his books, I wanted to thrust a dagger into their throats and twist it. But I wanted to be good. I suppose it was really vain after all. Shit. I wanted to be some kind of hero. The Great Honorable Gao. Of course I didn't think these things directly, I only wanted to throw the men into the reservoir with truck wheels tied to their feet—but I felt some calling to something higher. I felt it in the earth, for example, in the dew on the leaves, and in the way the sky moved, even in the wheelbarrow and our little goat. I'm not trying to sound like an overflowing poet. I'm only trying to be accurate.

"So I spared the men their lives. I did not expect them to thank me or beg forgiveness. I had no use for lies. Give them justice. I wanted justice. Well, both of them had *guanxi*. I suspect they were in a crime ring that had dealings with some corrupt officials, and they had some information on the judge or his cronies. So what was their sentence? Two years in prison for raping a thirteen-year-old girl. It was insane. My wife threatened to kill the judge, to slit his throat. I told her I would handle it, and the following day I borrowed a car and drove to the district headquarters in the neighboring town. When I arrived, I didn't even have to do any explaining. A guard with white gloves stepped out of his post and said, 'Are you here to attend the Responsiveness to the People Forum?'

"I didn't know what he was talking about, but I played along. He was a young man with very large glasses and a crisp hat. His uniform was new. In any case, he said, 'As you are probably aware, the Party, starting from the highest official down through every minister, vice minister, and prefectural subordinate is dedicated to transparency and a vigorous fight against corruption as well as a promise to safeguard the People's rights without compromising social harmony.' He had memorized this speech, and just when I thought his straw-stuffed brain couldn't hold any more information, he kept going. He was like a stupid talking robot. 'At the heart of the Governmental Responsiveness to the People Program is a healthy exchange between the people and the officials and back to the people in a robust circular movement with the aim of fostering the greatest success possible of socialism with Chinese characteristics. In a word, your government wants to hear from you. We only ask that before taking your turn that you make an oath pledging your devotion to the People's Republic, divulge any vested interests pertaining to the matters at hand, and third, limit your comments to three minutes.'

"I asked when the forum would begin. He said one quarter of an hour, and in no time I was standing in the middle of a crowded room, behind a table only slightly larger than the one I'm lying on right now. The mayor walked in with members of the village committee, one rather important sub-prefectural minister, and, as fate would have it, the judge who had ruled in my daughter's case. The judge wasn't supposed to be part of the forum; he just liked to rub elbows with important people like the minister. Anyway, the ruling officials took their seats behind one of those elevated tables with the red curtains in front. The sub-prefectural minister gave a pretty speech full of lies, and then each committee member blabbered on for a few minutes, while the judge sat off to the side gazing into his cell phone. He was a bald man with blotches on his head, a rooster's skin neck, and heavy bags under his eyes. A real old-guard type, not one of these spiffy Beijingers who can talk about reform and make you believe it; and I knew as if I had been given access to top-secret files that he'd been given his post without having to earn it, probably without a university degree, at least not from a top school, and I knew that he was only listening to the complaints of the people because it would make him look good in front of the minister. He probably knew no more of the law than the dumb guard at the compound gate.

"After a few citizens gave their piece of mind on clean drinking water, better health centers, and the need for jobs, it was my turn. One of the guards handed me the microphone. I switched off the power and set it on the table and it rolled almost over the edge. I didn't care if it broke like a duck egg. I wanted to make a personal impression on these people. I'm not a big man, but I have a booming speaking voice when I need it. On the walls there were red banners hanging, one that said, I think, 'YOUR LOCAL LEADERS WANT TO KNOW YOU BETTER.' And the other one was something like, 'THE GOVERNMENT LISTENS.'

"As I recall, there were large bouquets on either side of the table, the kind of flowers that are impossible to identify as real or fake unless you're close enough to give them a good sniff. In fact, I had prepared a very logical speech that relied on Maoist thought and Confucian values to convince the judge that he surely must have made an error in judgment, some miscalculation of the law, you know, like a mistake in arithmetic, or perhaps a simple misunderstanding of the particulars of the case, and my little speech would amount to a true account of reason that no one could turn against—but I was nervous. Truth be told, I was too slow in getting to my point. The three minutes were up before I could really get to the heart of the matter.

"The judge ordered the security personnel to take me away. Of course I was frustrated, but mainly it was the cold, hateful way the judge looked at me—yes, I had humiliated him in front of a crowd— that made me lose my mind. I swore him up and down. I told him he would live in hell. He threatened to charge me with disturbing social order and exerting a negative impact on society. I repeated that my daughter, a girl of thirteen, had been raped, and I reminded the judge that the men had squirted their filth inside her, spoiling her forever. He said he didn't need a review on the legal definition of rape; the men were currently in prison.

"'But what about her future?' I said. 'Nobody in the village will want to marry Gao Lin Lin. She'll be treated like a criminal. Those men will be free in two years, when my daughter is fifteen, and do you think they'll no longer want to rape her then? Do you have a daughter, Mr. Long? Would you like these men to rape her?'"

"What were you charged with?" I say.

"I told you. Disturbing social order and exerting a negative impact on society."

"And they brought you here for that?"

By now, Brother Gao's rising voice has roused some of the men. I haven't realized until now that Gao was pounding the table. Xu Xuo, Jack, and Fang have probably been awake for at least the last part of the confession.

Brother Gao says, "In any case, I was put in the local jail for a few days, then released. But a week later some thugs came to my house and beat me with bicycle tires, which they had made into a kind of rubber whip that was very tough, heavy as a snake, and very painful, leaving me no choice but to fight back. What did I have? I grabbed a vegetable knife. It was the only thing around. Not even sharp. You could hardly stab someone with it. How was I supposed to murder somebody with this little knife?"

"Do you wish you would have let the townspeople handle the rapists?" I say.

"Of course," says Fang from the floor, his voice reedy and confident. "Haven't you been listening?"

I'm not interested in Fang's opinion. I keep waiting for the absence of testosterone to change Fang into a gentle man, but that hasn't happened yet, if it ever will. I'm startled by his voice and sad that the intimacy with Brother Gao is broken. After steeling myself to ignore Fang, I say to my friend on the table, "Do you wish they would have hanged the rapists?"

"Of course," says Brother Gao.

"I thought you were smart," Fang says to me. "You are now revealing yourself to be otherwise."

Ignoring him, I say to my friend, "But you just minutes ago made a case, essentially made the case, even if you didn't mean it, against capital punishment."

"In theory. I do believe what I said a moment ago, as a principle, but the real world is different. I'm not saying the men weren't acting like beasts. Just because we are peasants, there's no virtue in that. Some of the men among us are terrible, as is obvious. The intrinsic morality of the peasants was one of Mao's great lies, precisely because it sounded so righteous. Even I used to believe it."

Even more surprising than Fang's interruption, I now see that Xu Xuo has turned around and propped his head on his elbow. The tassels of his blanket lay across his cheek, and his eyes from this distance look like two wet prunes. He reaches under his pillow for his matches and lights a cigarette and then he lounges there watching us with something like studiousness. His face is now the face of a thinking man and I wonder if he is a night owl who has always preferred to work the small hours when the traffic isn't bad, who feels most alive from midnight to six.

Fang says, "Those who walk outside the village walls have no desire to return."

But the proper understanding of this proverb is lost on me.

"It's no good," says Brother Gao. "It's just the kind of simplistic thinking I warned about before—man's biggest problem—but killing happens. Something gets into us that's more powerful than human reason, and it happens."

At that moment, Xu Xuo takes a long drag on his cigarette. Though I hate the smell, hate even the dumb panda on the package, I enjoy watching the tip of his cigarette glowing orange, expanding the way an interesting question opens the mind. I begin to wonder, as I will a dozen times from now on, if I have completely misjudged this man. The truth is that I know nothing of the guy, nothing, and I have essentially trusted the judgment against him and the rationale to throw him in prison and sentence him to death. I have chosen to trust a legal system whose reputation for fairness is suspect to say the least. I admit to myself that the concept of "innocent until proven guilty" is not in our DNA. Here in prison, the epistemological questions become more disgusting than that fancy word *epistemology* suggests. I can't possibly know what Xu Xuo did, I'll never know, and I cannot justify his murder. On a rational level, I try to tell myself to give him a fair shake. I close my eyes and spell E-P-I-S-T-E-M-O-L-O-G-Y, a word I did not fully understand until well past the age of thirty, and ask myself how we can justify any belief. The *feeling* that Xu Xuo is a dirty human is so much stronger than any knowledge; it trumps everything. Somehow I know he is bad, and the feeling is akin to the way music can sometimes be more truthful and expressive than words. I mutter in my mind the dictionary definition I looked up in a newsstand dictionary in the San Francisco airport the day I left the States: "The investigation of justified belief versus opinion." As soon as the definition arrives complete in my mind, I'm hit with a shot to the ribs. The goad strikes me higher than usual this time, in the chest area, reminding me of the phlegm gathering there, the reason I cough.

Brother Gao giggles. Xu Xuo looks across the room at Fang, who now sits cross-legged with his back against the door.

For the first time in weeks, Xu Xuo says something: "I would rather die in a fight than at the execution wall."

The Tower of Babble

For the banquet Mr. Li had reserved a private room at One Hundred Blooming Flowers, a restaurant built on the stunning grounds of a Qing Dynasty summer retreat. According to my boss, the guests would include not only the board members and our entire exec team but at least four high-ranking Party officials, including the Insurance Commissioner, the Vice Minister of Transportation, and the Commerce Secretary himself, who was rumored to be in line for a Politburo Standing Committee appointment.

I should mention that Mr. Li, intent on improving his English, had insisted that we speak less Chinese so that he could get more practice using the most useful language in the world. In fact, I had been tutoring him a couple hours a week in the only place where he wasn't embarrassed: stark naked in the sauna of the fitness center at the Golden Sky Hotel. For a man his age, he was in excellent shape and I could see why he felt comfortable in the nude, whereas I was skinny, with an abundance of hair and freckles, a caved-in chest, and a penis that while not small was nothing to brag about.

We had been working on complex sentences involving the conditional tense, often in the context of business dealings that involved four or five things falling into place before a deal could go forth. Mostly our sentences were hypothetical. I did not generally like to talk about work matters and was much happier using sentences about his bicycle trips in Ireland and his wife's fetish for Waterford Crystal. But to get back to the story: Mr. Li had in fact informed me about the banquet. He had informed me three or four times, but the chief had a curious habit of mentioning something important repeatedly in small amounts, without going into any depth.

"You will come to the banquet on next Thursday and take a speech."

And, "Globalized cuisine for the speech. You drink-uh some tea before, okay Francis-uh?"

And, "Take the speech at the banquet. It will be good."

How I failed to understand him could be studied as much by the psychoanalyst as the linguist. Surely a language teacher like me should have understood that when Mr. Li said, "Take a speech," he meant that I would give a speech.

Forty minutes before the banquet, as I was shutting down my computer in the office, waiting for a little pinwheel to stop spinning so I could depart in a relaxed state of mind, knowing my computer was not sick, in that moment Mr. Li strolled into my office in a taupe suit. There was a buttery yellow rose pinned to his lapel along with a Chinese flag pin. He took from his pocket a little plexiglass box containing another yellow rose.

"You always wear dark suit," he said. "Not hopeful. Flower is hopeful."

"Yes, sir," I said. I wasn't trying to sound sycophantic. I really just saw an opportunity to use a common English phrase in context. I had a class to teach that night and had been thinking about the lesson. I was new to teaching and full of ideas, enjoying the part-time gig more than my dull office work. Probably I was wasting much of my creative energy that should have gone into writing; probably I was finding ways to avoid writing, but I liked the classroom and the students. I desperately needed fewer hours at the office, and I had been planning for weeks to ask Mr. Li in the sauna if I could take a pay cut and work four days a week instead of six.

As I was fiddling with the pin mechanism of my little Chinese flag, Mr. Li said, "You say thank you for the promotion. You thank them. Especially the Party officials. They not direct, but indirect. Your promotion. You thank them."

From his breast pocket he took out a Tibaldi pen and wrote my new salary on a sticky note. The amount was obscene. I felt a crushing sense of disappointment in my chest. I did not want one more ounce of responsibility, no matter how much money they gave me.

I was thirty-seven and had written only two stories that I considered great, and by great I mean they could tear you away from a lover, make you cry out loud, or make you so ashamed of yourself that you could hardly sleep at night—yet you liked the feeling, the ecstasy of having read great literature, *because* it made you ashamed, *because* it kept you awake at night, and like some naughty drug you couldn't resist going back to it. And if you didn't have it, you would feel dead inside or terribly sick. A burning building could not tear you away from the story. Two great stories, then. One of them had appeared in a famous American magazine, the other in a less heralded European publication whose editor, a certain Mr. Wulff, I much admired.

To make matters worse, my buddy Mac was scheduled to visit from the States in two months. Mac was a college roommate of mine from my undergrad years at U of C—smarter than me in myriad ways, a better reader and a fine jazz musician to boot. He was not only my best friend but an indispensable critic of my work, and to this end we had made plans to have a series of face-to-face meetings in Beijing in order to share our latest projects—which meant I had a deadline. Which meant I wanted less office work, not more.

Mr. Li twisted his pen closed and slid it back into its snobby little sheath. He smiled at me with something like fatherly love, as though I had really earned my position, as though I had finally achieved my ultimate goal, all of us together moving forward in China's great rise.

His tan skin looked as soft as a persimmon and the whisker dots on his chin had the look of ultimate refinement.

Not only did I not want the promotion, but I felt that the new salary was a kind of bribe to stay quiet about not only the injured workers but also the serious lack of follow-through on hundreds (if not thousands) of claims. I could plainly see that while the company was adding new policies at a decent clip, we weren't providing the kind of customer service that would promote long-term growth. I would have expected our complaint department to be overwhelmed, but we didn't even have a complaint department. I had very little to do with Accounting, even less so the investment side of things, but it seemed to me that we were taking on too much risk, buying too many companies, leveraging too much.

A week earlier, as I was riding the elevator down to the end of the day, I overheard an accountant from a consulting firm (who didn't know I understood Chinese) tell his sidekick that China Life and Casualty had become "a fucking ATM for investors." The whole system was floating on debt. The state's monetary policy was incredibly loose. Credit was too greasy. Everybody seemed to harbor a faith in the ever-expanding value of assets, whose perpetual motion was as irreversible as the inflating universe. As far as I knew, nobody at the company had done a risk assessment on what would happen if there was a run on our company, that is, if our policy holders pulled their names out of the hat all at once. Some would pay penalties, but many had stuck in long enough now that I doubt we could survive such an event and I wasn't about to give myself extra work to crunch the numbers. As for the injured workers, I could not get them out of my mind: the soft folding of that guy's legs, the other men hanging onto the lip of the shovel like refugees clinging to a helicopter, or sinners in some Italian painting trying to catch a ride out of hell.

"I'm supposed to give a speech?" I said.

Mr. Li smiled. "How many times I tell you? You take a speech today."

"*Give* a speech," I said. "We can say *give* a speech or *make* a speech. You would only use the verb 'take' with the preposition 'in' as in 'take in,' meaning to sit passively and watch a speech. I'm going to *take in* a speech, I'm going to *take in* a play."

Of course my lesson went on way too long. I was stalling for time.

"Let's go," he said.

In the elevator, with the aid of the mirrored walls, he pointed to my ears and said, "You have ears look like the former President Obama."

"I get that a lot," I said. "But he was never so nervous to give a speech. Are you sure I can't simply *take in* a speech?"

"You give a speech, you make a speech. You make a great *I Have a Dream* speech."

The dynastic prince's summer retreat was a beauty to behold, but I was too nervous to appreciate the tiled pagoda or the red beams painted with all manner of ancient motifs: the carp, the lotus, the cherry blossom, and the maiden. I had been in the country long enough that I was numb to the beauty of ancient things and I stepped over the high threshold of the door without a thought. As Mr. Li and I strolled the garden paths among mirrored ponds and draping willows, we were met by boys and girls dressed in Qing Dynasty costumes, yellow and blue like dandelion and corn flower, the youth bowing so dramatically it felt like a kowtow. The girls had white porcelain faces done up with fierce eyeliner and smoky blue eye-shadow.

Mr. Li ignored them and led me into a windowless room with a large round table in the center and a podium in the corner. The Lucite podium was an anachronism among the *mise-en-scène* of scrimshaw wainscoting of scaly dragons, flowering lotus, leaping goldfish, and tranquil tea houses. On one wall hung a giant calligraphic painting of ancient Chinese characters that neither I nor the powerful men (and one woman) now taking their seats at the table could decipher. Here an ink print of a foggy mountain. There a watercolor of cherry blossoms beside a wheelbarrow. This was China. No windows to or from any other world.

I saw many substantial watches of gold. I saw men lighting cigarettes and costumed girls pouring *baijiu* from clear flasks. Every five minutes, another gentleman found another reason to say *gan bei*, dry cup, and we would knock down a splash of burning white alcohol. There was wine, too, and good wine. The Vice Minister Miss Xia sipped only a little. She was a tall, nervous-looking woman with short hair and bone-white skin almost without wrinkles. She wore a mannish blue business suit.

Thinking our waitresses were incredibly tall, I looked down and noticed that the servers were standing on wooden-block shoes almost four inches high. Bizarrely came the fleeting thought that my grandfather, the one killed at Sachsenhausen, had worn wooden shoes in camp. How did I even know this? I sneaked a peek at one girl's hip and another girl's carmined lips. I admired their silk dresses and said to myself, *Where have I seen this particular blue? It is the cotton candy of America.* She poured me some more *baijiu* and moved on to the next man.

Around the table revolved a dizzying array of dishes. Crisp vegetables in a Day-Glo yellow sauce. Chunks of diced beef with red chilies and garlic. A long yellow fish stewing in a brown liquid. Gelatinous cubes of duck blood.

The meal progressed from finely-sliced donkey meat and other traditional Chinese dishes to Russian caviar and salmon with hollandaise. Mr. Li spent ten minutes describing every item on the menu: pears from England, fish from the Copper River in Alaska, dates from Israel, ginger from Vietnam, saffron from Spain, and wine from the greatest vineyard in China made by Chinese vintners who had apprenticed with the French. A great applause went up with this final declaration. More wine was poured by our lovely young ladies. All of the men around the table wore gleaming cufflinks. With the exception of Mr. Li, whose gray hair had a fashionable hue, all of the grandees sported jet-black hair dyed in accordance with Party protocol (so it seemed).

As I enjoyed the cabernet and felt myself wishing I was on a slow boat to France, I looked around at the men with their slick hair, handsome faces, and nearly identical manner and costume, and began to feel a little punchy. Sometimes you find yourself in a place and wonder, *How did I get here?* and the only answer is to laugh. Every smile had the same broad twist. Every hand wiped the mouth in exactly the same way. Any man who heard a good joke reared back like every other man. Miss Xia laughed at jokes she didn't think funny.

In the center of the table stood a giant plant arrangement that included spindly things from Madagascar, orchids from Thailand, and hard shrubs from the steppes of Russia. The wine glasses were Italian. The Waterford goblets felt so heavy it was rather easy to take a controlled drink even in my state of anxiety.

To my left, a man with chubby cheeks and thickly-parted hair gave his opinion that the name "Epicuria" was no good. "Too hard for Chinese people to pronounce," he said. "We need another name."

"People can use the Chinese translation," said a tall man to his left.

"The translation is terrible."

"No," said Mr. Li. "We want to speak one language." I could sense him wanting to explain the Tower of Babel story, then sounding out his audience and thinking better of it.

The CIO of Palace Investment Company, the chunkiest member of the group, gave a short speech thanking the dignitaries for their vision and dedication to the project, and above all to the development of China. He pointed out correctly that China had done a great service to the world economy by acting as a stabilizing force in the face of the economic tempests in Europe and the United States.

Then came the CEO of Sino Steel, who was very old and quite enamored of his years working as a minister in the previous administration, which clearly explained how he had managed to get past the mandatory retirement age of sixty. He explained that he was a graduate of Tsing Hua University in engineering and that he had total confidence in the pre-fab, modular construction of the tower. "Very safe," he said. "Very efficient."

"Only seven months!" said Mr. Li.

"It can be done!" said Mr. Prefab Steel.

Then it was the Secretary of Commerce, who started his speech by drawing comparisons between the Tower of Babel and the Great Wall of China, which offered plenty of confusion, as I couldn't see how The Wall had attempted to reach God or permitted all people to speak to one another. The long stony spine in the mountains was built to keep away the voices of Mongols, no?

And yet, one couldn't help liking these people. They were charming and intelligent. They knew the history of both the East and the West in ways that put foreigners to shame. Sure, they were dyed red in the silk of the Party, but with this central power they had a vision that extended for thirty years or longer, here, now, in this age when the Western world was poisoning itself with short-termism and the tyranny of the quarterly report. There was something to admire in their ability to gaze far out at the horizon and command swift changes to the Now. They could move boldly and without obstruction, and if that meant deracinating a few million peasants, it also meant they had the power to order up a national healthcare plan in a jiffy. They could build high-speed trains without having to slog through a hyper-democratic bidding processes or union demands.

They could build a new Tower of Babel, where all people would find in the Middle Kingdom, at the center of the world that everyone spoke the same language of money.

Mr. Li was back at the podium now, ready to introduce the architect of the world's finest shopping center, which was not as the Americans say, a "mall," but a tower, which would not be called the Tower of Babel by anyone other than a few insiders. For others it would be known as "Epicuria."

I saw one man lower his mouth to his plate and take up a flake of salmon in his silver chopsticks. This was the Secretary of Commerce, a thick man with a heavy brow and bold eyebrows. He looked familiar and I wondered if I had seen him on television cutting some ribbon with the chancellor of Germany. No. He had my father's face with Asian characteristics. There was that bullish resolve in his features, as though emotions were controlled by muscles rather than nerves. He bent to slurp some noodles from a small bowl and this is where the elegance left him. All Chinese men bend low to slurp noodles in exactly this way. The magistrate at the banquet looks the same as the steel worker at lunch.

The girls came around and poured the next bottle of red for the evening, using white cloth napkins to catch dribbles of eight hundred yuan "Chairman's Reserve" as though wiping an imperial baby's mouth. This was the legendary 2013 Reserve, which, perhaps because it came on the heels of several drinks, tasted even better than the first bottle. Oaky and addictive.

Mr. Li was headed back to the table to give way to the architect when he stopped in his tracks. He had forgotten something. He chimed his wine glass to quiet everyone and announce that he had forgotten to introduce our foreign friend, who was destined to play an integral role in the project as our Western emissary, a kind of ambassador, if you will, who would like to express his gratitude for his advancement.

What could I say? What's more, why was I put in the prestigious position of penultimate speaker? It hardly mattered that Mr. Li had forgotten about me. The result was uncontestable. The social tradition of ramping up from least important to most important speaker was imbedded in all men in all societies. In spite of the mistake, I was now granted a ridiculous degree of importance. Perhaps, owing to his mistake and the awkwardness of my position (in time and place) this is why Mr. Li shot me a laser stare that told me not to go to the podium.

But I was already on my way with a full glass of wine, newly poured by a lovely girl with fetching, hairy forearms, and I was emboldened by the absurdity of the situation. If one minute ago I had been quaking in my loafers at having to speak to these men, I now had nothing to fear.

Mr. Li, standing by the entrance (the door now swinging open to reveal the *maître d'* bowing to a gorgeous young woman in a fur coat, backed by the kaleidoscopic frenzy of nighttime traffic), gave a nervous smile. Laughing, he said, "He wants evidently to use the podium like the rest of us."

I started my speech by saying that soon after I arrived in China I witnessed the Grand Party Congress of the Communist Party of China and that unlike most Westerners who regarded the proceedings dispassionately, I was moved by the event. Sensing immediately that the men were impressed with my Chinese, I knew I had them. A foreigner, while a stranger and an alien, an outsider and invader, was also somebody special. A Westerner who could speak good Chinese held esteem.

I found myself speaking the language of ready-packaged platitudes. With another part of my brain I was able to observe my surroundings with the extra-sensitive antennae of a writer in a groove. I noticed the glint of expensive cufflinks. I smelled the rich fat of grilled salmon. I saw ancient wheelbarrows leaning against the Great Wall. I saw a white orchid bobbing in the draft of a closing door, and the movement of the orchid sounded like the giggling of the woman in the fur coat in the adjacent room. A girl pouring wine leaned forward with a straight back. Her dress shined like water. I heard the ticking of chopsticks and the ting of glasses. The servers asked "Do you want more tea?" in dulcet voices. How could anyone say no?

I was in the "Honor thy Father" part of my speech, where I explained how my pregnant grandmother had escaped the Nazis and fled to Canada, delivered a baby boy, married an American meat wholesaler and moved to Chicago, where the son Otto excelled in school and sports and thereafter sold insurance door-to-door before starting his own firm, which grew in value to two billion dollars before—and here I faltered, having no choice but to use the Chinese word for "bankruptcy," *po chan*, having no euphemism—before being partially rescued by Mr. Li and the shrewd investors at Palace (now discovering that my failure to find a euphemism played rather well as I had made the Chinese look heroic). It's hard to say the word *po chan* without sounding nasty and shameful. I made it ever-clear that my father and I were grateful, that in spite of my father's reactionary nature, I, we had no problems with socialism with Chinese characteristics—the dark chapters in Chinese history caused by totalitarianism and the iniquity of Man himself, not Marxism *per se.*

I stated clearly that my family had suffered. And the more details I offered of my father's suffering—long ago losing his biological father to a machine gun at Sachsenhausen, his stepfather to leukemia, putting himself through college by selling insurance door-to-door, telling the inspirational story of the saving grace of insurance to every Pole and German on the south side of Chicago (me joking that my old man's personal story gave him the moral capital to win any argument), and many years later the tragedy of his beloved firm going *po chan* at the behest of the mortgage-backed securities crisis and how his company alone was the only major insurance firm to sink in that swamp because a certain somebody hadn't diversified investments, which in the end left him neutered, a White Sox fan, forbidden from holding the reins of Chicago Central Casualty and Life—the more vigorously the men nodded.

I was on my way to explaining that my father, Otto Kauffman, was both admiring and envious of China's rise, when something unhinged me.

The Secretary of Commerce, in order to catch his sneeze, had reached into his breast pocket and pulled out a Winnie the Pooh handkerchief made of the finest silk. The chubby, happy bear and his jar of honey, his pink companion, were unmistakable.

The men clearly thought I had lost my mind. I was laughing uncontrollably to the point of tears. My ribs hurt. My voice went high and fluttering, all apparently because I thought sneezing was funny. I finished my speech, snotting the rest of the way, and in the end, a performance that might have earned me a hearty reception was met with tepid applause.

The Secretary was not amused. Face stony. Sensing the awkwardness of the moment, Mr. Li shouted "*Gan bei!*" and raised a tiny cup of liquor.

The architect took his turn at the podium, explaining his tower with the aid of a drop-down screen, three-dimensional models marched in by handsome graduate assistants from the Architectural Institute, and one of the new Sense Impression machines using music and fragrance. I smelled fine tobacco, fresh raspberries, French perfume, Mexican leather, sage, lavender, and jasmine tea. The architect explained the engineering principles inherent to the building. There would be state-of-the-art seismic engineering capable of withstanding a quake ten times the magnitude of the greatest tremors ever recorded. No terrorist bomb or flaming airplane could set this building on fire because the sprinkler system would spew fire retardant. (Someday, a thousand miles from the banquet chamber, Fang the prisoner would inform me that the special sprinkler system had been eliminated shortly before construction as it was deemed too costly.) The elevators would be the fastest ever, though you would only feel a pleasant floating sensation. And all of this could be completed in seven to nine months because the prefab modules would be manufactured off site by six thousand workers and constructed on site by fewer than three thousand workers.

Whenever Mr. Li felt the architect getting too technical, he chimed in with a joke or a platitude. The basic idea was to house all the world's finest things in one tower. Every employee would speak English, and a sizable number of employees would be fluent in Russian, Japanese, and Arabic. There would be a store called "These are a Few of My Favorite Things." There would be luxury condos on floors ten through sixty-six. The insurance offices would occupy the crown of the building.

"*Gan bei!*" shouted one man and then another. The men did not have great teeth, but their manners shined and their gold watches anchored them to success. These were not ideal times to launch a mega-project of luxury condos, and people say China is a faithless country? Mr. Li had convinced the men to convince themselves that the ebbing economy would flow again, and when it did, Epicuria would catch the crest of the wave.

卡夫卡

When the banquet was over and I had taken my share of excellent wine, I went back to my seventeenth floor apartment on Deng Xiaoping Avenue and wrote a long email to Lulu, detailing the absurdity of my circumstance and my untimely explosion of laughter, how the men thought I was crazy, how I planned to tender my resignation to Mr. Li. I would cash out my dividends and go to Bali and write full-time in a hut on the beach. I didn't tell Lulu how much money they were giving me. I would never tell her. Clever girl that she was, she would have identified it as hush money, something I was too naïve or unwilling to catch earlier. I felt solvent but unclean. I was tired of being put-upon by a neutered father, a troubled mother, and my sweet, sweet sister.

The traffic flowed on the avenue. In the window I could see the gibbous moon: no more than a fuzzy orb in the smog. I tried to do some writing but was too shot by the wine. I put my head on my notebook and fell asleep. Woke up at dawn with spit on the page like a wet dream. Outside, the smog was so thick I could not see the sun or the skyscrapers in the east.

Emails from America had accumulated in the night: one from an admiring literary agent who had read my work in *The Generator* and wanted to know if I had a novel in the works; one from an etymological society where I was a member; two from investment firms; and three from online companies confirming payment for my mother's plastic surgery, a ridiculous cable TV bill, and some back taxes on the lake house in Wisconsin. Before I could read them all, a new message came in from the mega-bank processing the mortgage on my parents' house. Due to reassessment, I would now pay $4,432 a month, up two hundred dollars. I thanked the gods that the old house was on the tacky side of mid-century modern, with a feeble kitchen and outdated bathrooms. Otherwise I'd be on the hook for six thousand a month.

There was a message from my sister, saying that dad was acting "really weird" and linking me to the tuition page of her private university, letting me know it was totally cool if it would be better for her to transfer to a state school and not have to pay such "crazy-ridiculous" tuition for an education, totally cool, really, but letting me know too that her harp professor was "amazing" and her service project in Cuba was only possible through Smithfield University's program and how she was part of Phi Theta Kappa and had managed to hold a 3.7 average in spite of her organic chemistry class from hell, etc.

Rebekah was happy. At the bottom of my screen in the little snow globe, I spied her freckled cheeks and intense, old-world eyes and thought she looked more beautiful and safe than she'd ever been before. I had taught her how to ride a bicycle. I had driven her all over the city for concerts and plays. Years later, when she suffered a serious rock climbing accident, I flew back from China to visit her in the hospital (one of only three repatriations in that eight-year period). Rebekah was a badass, a more gifted writer than me, a far better musician, a master of emotional intelligence, and she deserved to graduate from a badass school, even if the institution formerly known as Duke had made its fortune from the mass slaughter of unholy swine.

I closed the email server and looked out at the gauzy morning cityscape. The windows in the tall buildings were yellow, gray, or black. I told myself I would stay at the firm for one more year, no longer.

Always Can Feel Free
and Happy Through Writing

How Epicuria rose and fell is a short story. In the months following my dinner with the dignitaries, the tower grew skyward at a dizzying pace, each prefabricated module stacked one upon the other every week until the tower stood sixty-six stories high.

That took only three months. Then they got to work on the interior, which involved world-record quantities of gold paint and Siberian marble. There was a lot of slate and some very expensive barn siding from Normandy for the wine shop. The *China Daily* ran a few stories questioning the safety of the structure, in particular its readiness for a fire, but as with most columns of this nature, one architect's critical opinion got balanced with a second architect's blessing. Public debate in Chinese media was almost always an act of theater. To most readers, there didn't seem to be anything real to worry about. But the economy was cooling fast and pre-orders for the condominiums came in at a trickle, at which point prospective buyers started to bargain hard. Units started going at thirty percent below market value. Mr. Li put on weight but kept the faith. He decided to fill the place at any cost. "I will not build a ghost tower," he said. "My investors will be angry, but if the place is empty, they will run. How could this happen in a tier-one city?" he said. "No one saw this coming."

Which wasn't true. Even my officemates Sally and Cheng played the "I told you so" game, Cheng smiling big when he showed me the lease agreement for his condo. "A steal of the century," he said.

"They were hoping to charge twice that much," said Sally.

When the year was up, almost to the day I gave my speech at the banquet, I tendered my resignation. Mr. Li tried to talk me out of it, but he didn't try all that hard. I sensed that he was rather looking forward to not having to pay my salary. He insisted on paying me a nominal fee for consulting work, knowing he would turn to me for advice from time to time. When I tried to cut ties with the company completely, he whispered that he wanted me to stay part of his family, his tone so deadly serious I thought I might wind up in trouble if I went against him.

I quickly landed a full-time position at Cap City University and was told I could move into the faculty housing as soon as a unit became available. To disentangle myself from the firm, I signed a ridiculous number of documents in Chinese, all of them printed on that long A6 paper with the red company chop at the bottom of each document. As long as the company's seal was stamped on each doc, I was good. I didn't hire a lawyer to vet the exit paperwork. I couldn't get out of there soon enough. I signed six or seven papers, said my goodbyes to the sales team and the actuaries, and walked out of China Life and Casualty a free man.

Ah, the release.

For three days I did nothing but ride buses through the city, getting off where I pleased, strolling through strange neighborhoods in the south district, jotting down images of interesting scenes, hiding out in fish restaurants and writing until my hand hurt. Here was a mother stopping to unbutton her toddler's pants so he could pee on the sidewalk. Here was a street artist blowing glass. Here was a girl in a coolie hat fishing from a stone bridge over a stinking canal. Here was a lotus flower blooming in the warm September rain. I observed the city with a keenness that felt like my first days in country almost twenty years before, a kind of extra-sensory trance that was part of being any kind of artist. I felt like a traveler again.

A week later, having paid a steep fine to get out of my Sanlitun apartment lease, I moved into the Foreign Experts Building on the campus of Cap City U. I would pay no rent and eat on the cheap. I would teach and prep about twenty hours a week. It may be hard for those with MBA degrees to place such a high value on time, but for those who want to be writers or painters or musicians, nothing is more precious. I rattled off a quick note to my buddy back in the States:

Mac, I'm free.

Finally quit the insurance company.

Teaching load is only 10 hrs. a week. I showed them my two degrees and all my office experience and bargained hard and got a good gig. Praise Moses. I now have no excuses.

I miss you, my friend. To this day, I have still not had a truer friend, and maybe that's my problem, but I guess it's a bit late in life to fix stuff like that. Ah' well, all I care about is writing. I don't care if people hate me. As long as I don't have to sell insurance policies any longer...if I have time to write, I'll never be completely miserable! As for women, I probably still haven't gotten over my ability to want them and inability to love them, and the ratio between these two still remains unremedied, immature, sob, sob, sob.

I donated to charity a colorful variety of ties, tailored shirts, and at least two hound's tooth sport coats—keeping one dark coat, four white shirts, and some dark pants. I wore the same crimson tie to class every day. I was through with trying to impress people on the outside. I wanted to turn inward to my art with animal ferocity and approach teaching with the purity of a priest. I had nothing to lose. I took a three hundred-eighty percent pay cut. Lulu outwardly expressed support for my decision, but her text messages were slower in coming, sloppily written, then tepid, then short, then unwritten.

My one lingering concern, more like a crushing guilt, was the welfare of my family. I could not sleep at night unless my sister and mother—and to some extent my father—were taken care of. I sometimes thought of my old man back in Green Heights, slumped in his chair in front of the television, cursing the inanity of the newscasters, as though his depression were somehow my fault. What more was I supposed to do? And yet, one could never really get square with one's father. How could I ever repay the one who had given me life? *Babies die if you don't feed them; if you don't feed babies, they die.* Maybe he wasn't a stellar father, but he'd kept me from drowning in a kiddie pool. The time I got lost at Comiskey Park, he found me during the seventh inning stretch. When a math teacher boxed me on the ears, he stormed into the school and made that arithmetician quake in his loafers. And a dozen years before that, when it would have been easy to blow off the German girl, he had come back to Berlin to claim me as his spit and blood, his flesh and image.

I cashed out nine hundred shares of Palace Investment (well before they sunk) and set up a trust fund for my sister's education, arranging an extra forty thousand for her graduate studies. I put my mother in charge of an expense account. I paid off their SUV. I took out a fifteen-year term life insurance policy for my mother and father. I stupidly agreed to pay $14,000 for my father to belong to the golf club in hopes that he would get some exercise.

But the old bird up and got cancer.

About a week after classes started, I got an email from my mother saying that various biopsies, x-rays, and bone scans had determined that my father had prostate cancer, stage IIB, T2c. Not the earliest, not the latest. Surgery a must. Radiation a possibility. A prostate gland was about the size of a walnut shell, and the tumor was larger than the nut.

At his age and in that part of the body, cancer was a slow-growing sin. "Very treatable," my mother had written, quoting her husband.

I replied with a sympathetic email asking if I should come home. When a son asks if he should come home, it means he doesn't want to come home.

Father requested that I not so much as mention the word "cancer" in my next email. Next email? When was the last time I had emailed my dad? I typed "Otto Kauffman" into the search box and saw that I had last contacted him almost two years ago, only to tell him where he could find my golf clubs, which he had wanted to lend to a friend, whom my mother had probably recruited to cheer up my father. It made me angry and sad that I had paid $14,000 to the River Oaks Golf Club.

After a time, I closed my laptop and got out one of my Chinese notebooks. I loved my Chinese notebooks more than any writing paraphernalia on earth and had always done my best work in longhand at night. I'll admit to picking certain notebooks with coquettish designs and florid colors. Each notebook had a personality and it was handy to be able to distinguish one notebook from another, to find them under my bed years later and know that I had written this or that piece in such-and-such notebook. The unique design of each journal told me who I was at certain points in my life. Some of them had amusing slogans on the front, like, "Motivate Higher Office Efficiency/Spend Your Time and Energy Criticizing" or "For Work or Life, Always Can Feel Free and Happy Through Writing." A brand-new journal with clean pages got me very excited, and it's no exaggeration to say that sometimes opening a writing notebook gave me an erection.

Not so that night. I opened a new notebook the color of turquoise and tried to write what I knew of my father's story. I had written plenty of good fiction with monstrous, verminous fathers—rendered them not without truth—but I had never written the straight facts. Didn't I owe it to him, to cancer, to Jews, to write his history? I knew that he was about forty and already a successful entrepreneur when he took a trip to Berlin to locate the flat where his parents had lived during the War, to see the stumbling stone in the sidewalk that reminded Germans that the home had been occupied by the Kauffman family from 1925-1942, that Amschel died at Sachsenhausen in 1940.

Over the years my father had paid out conflicting details about how his father had perished—he was shot by a guard, he was gassed—and as with most family lore you couldn't tell if the story changed because of embellishment, censorship, or the shape of memory. I got bits from my father and pieces from my mother. I knew with some degree of certainty that Amschel Kauffman had worked as a glassmaker at Sachsenhausen, as the villa once occupied by the Kommandant had stained-glass windows fashioned in my grandfather's signature style.

It was a hell of a story, and yet I didn't feel any pull as I penned one tired line after another. What was my problem? The material alone should have set me ablaze. A good muse could make me forget time, forget a painful knee or indigestion, make me forget that I had to pee. But that night in Beijing, with the distant blare of a Chinese radio and the acrid smell of someone cooking onions below, I slogged from one word to the next. I couldn't find any groove.

I never asked my father how he was able to find the Berlin flat in the first place. Back in those days he must have gone to a library, carrying his mother's passport and a crackled photo of Jewish refugees huddled on a passenger steamer—or maybe a volunteer from the Holocaust museum had taken him on a tour of West Berlin. And what did he do? After two days of sick-hearted mourning, he went to an underground club, met a buxom West Berlin girl named Brigitte, and knocked her up.

He found out via telephone, in a phone booth in fact, three months after the deed. The voice on the line was my mother, and I was the source of her tears. By the standards of men (a low bar to be sure) my father did a heroic thing in that (a) he believed the German girl's claim that he had been her only lover and (b) he flew back to Berlin to claim responsibility for his orgasm. In 1979, my mother was a fetching woman of twenty-five, with caramel hair and dark eyes and olive skin, more Italian-looking than German. There was nothing of the ballerina in her; she was all round womanness. Her father was a junior executive in the growing telecom industry, her mother a stay-at-home mom. Brigitte had been a good kid, not a rebel at all, but West Berlin at the time made it so easy to go wild at night. As my mother put it, "Nobody ever told you to go home," and apparently the night she met my father, feeling her oats at twenty-five, she did not go home.

He wanted to marry this beautiful Brigitte and take her to Chicago. She liked the idea of going to the States, but her parents would have none of it, not least of all marriage, the fact of his Jewishness making things worse, not because they were anti-Semitic but just the opposite. They were the kind of Berliners who felt such profound guilt for the Holocaust that they couldn't abide having a son-in-law who would constantly remind them of it, just by his Old Testament eyes.

Long story short, my father refused to leave Germany for a time. I suppose he figured that to return to the place where the Nazis had systematically torn families asunder and then to participate in the fracturing of a family, well, that struck him as the wrong thing to do. He couldn't do it. I am told that for a year or so he worked as a middleman on the black market, trafficking in blue jeans, lipstick, and LPs (by bands he didn't like) and eventually earning the respect of my mother's parents—but I've often questioned the truth of this account, wondered whether he had it in him. I know he was there. It's just hard to imagine Otto K. existing in that ecosystem of all-night rages, cocaine, and strobing punk parties. The man I knew was an inveterate rule follower. He was all about assessing risk and planning for it, not daring to spirit riveted jeans over borders. (Then again, he had certainly taken financial risks at the end.) This I know for sure: What he saw of the communist state turned him forever into a zealot of the free market, steering him well to the right in all things economic and most things social. He also never wore blue jeans for the rest of his life.

While I was a baby in Berlin, suckling Mama's breast during boat trips on the River Spree, Otto was living in the shadows of the split city, while his half-brother back home in Chicago managed the affairs of their small but growing insurance company. When the black market life got a little sketchy, he went back to the States to make some real money. I don't have any sense of an emotional bond with him during that period. I only remember him as a visitor to our flat once or twice a year. He'd bring me Nikes and Tetris, sleep in Mama's room, gargle loudly after brushing his teeth with bubblegum-flavored Colgate (which he had brought for me and which I detested).

Later, when his half-brother died in a car accident, my father asked the in-laws if he could bring Brigitte and me to the United States for good. It was 1989. Nobody but a genius could have imagined that five months later the wall would come down.

I remember my mother coming into the bedroom to tell me the news. I was dreamily studying a sparrow on the windowsill and was annoyed when her interruption made the bird fly off. When she told me we were going to America, I thought she was talking about an amusement park. But here's the thing: I hadn't seen any pictures of an amusement park called "AMERIKA." When she explained that we were going across the ocean to live in a city called Chicago in *Die Vereinigten Staaten*, I was very sad. I wanted to catch the sparrow and stuff him in my suitcase. We boarded a Pan Am 747 and tried to sleep. I remember blue seats and red seats and a vague scent of vomit. Turbulence over Nova Scotia. Black people. Fat policemen. Kentucky Fried Chicken. An ocean called Lake Michigan.

Fast forward three decades to that night in Beijing, all I could make of my father was a dead sparrow crammed into a clarinet case. I was a sucky nonfiction writer. I had to kill the bird to birth the story. The only way I was ever going to fill every page of that turquoise notebook was to make up stuff, to bend reality and dream oddly.

I looked out the window of my apartment and saw a full moon in a blue Beijing sky. A red light winked from a distant communications tower. The moon appeared blurry through my overworked eyes. My father didn't want me to think of his cancer, so I didn't. He wanted me to think of his father, Amschel, the imprisoned one, and I couldn't. Amschel was a master of stained glass. I was too tired to write anything worth a damn and decided to hit the sack. I would start in the morning with the soft feathers of a stiff sparrow.

依然

I once boasted to my buddy Mac that I wouldn't mind spending time in jail because I'd have loads of time to read and write. The State would feed and clothe me and I would pour all my energy into art. No wasted energy on music, sex, restaurants, theater, and the like. I would not flinch from my target.

"You have no idea what you're talking about," he said. "From your perspective, that's heaven. But prison is hell. Try writing the morning after getting raped by some goon. Imagine not even being able to sit on your own ass. You think they'd give you a word processor and an expansive library? Do you think you'd be able to order Virginia Woolf through interlibrary loan? Or Borges? You'd be lucky to get Harry Potter."

没有完成

Mac still has a thumb drive with a handful of my stories and one of my failed novels, probably the least failing of the three. He's the only one who has this stuff. I don't even have what he has. You'd think that from where I sit right now, on a paint bucket in Area 44 in full view of a dog fucking another dog, with the rancid smoke of burning garbage curling into the air, I would be grateful to Mac—and maybe he was right about the worth of "The Jew and the Possum" and the one novel—but I'm still mad at him for not letting me, the guy who wrote the stuff, destroy every last word. I'd like to report that acute suffering at Area 44 has given me new perspective on all the writing I did. But no. The wickedness here makes art seem pointless and stupid.

Late one night on a community golf course in Chicago, drunk and despairing at my lack of success, I tried to toss the thumb drive into the canal that ran along the seventh fairway. As noted earlier, I lacked my father's throwing arm, and in any case a thumb drive is too light to travel very far. That little piece of intellectual property sailed over the fence and skittered down the embankment.

"Damn you!" said Mac, running after it. Both of us were skinny and un-athletic, Mac even wussier than me, so of course he went under the fence rather than over. "Shit!" he said, tearing his shirt. "Shit," he said again, as he scrambled through the prickly ash and buckthorn. He turned his phone to flashlight mode and swung the beam left and right. He was dressed well, in a hipster shirt with little skulls on the lapel and snug black pants. We had attended a reading that night by Alice Munro, and the little old lady had emotionally eviscerated us all to the extent that I felt like a literary twerp. My stories were witty puzzles next to hers. Mac was a Lit Crit guy with a tenure-track position at Loyola, so he didn't have to worry about his own shortcomings in quite the same way. His specialty was the shortcomings of others.

"You'll thank me some day," he called into the night.

"No, I won't," I slurred. I was already sick from the wine. I stood up to imbibe the fresh air, to walk this thing off. "Everything on that thumb drive is shit," I yelled. The water in the canal gave off a fetid sewer odor. It made no sound. I could only hear traffic in the distance, a plane on approach to Midway Airport, and Mac kicking around in the wild Chicago scrub.

"So far I've found one condom and two beer cans," he said.

"Take 'em and let's get the bejesus outta here."

"Not until I rescue your writing."

"My father thinks it's cute. Why do you even care?"

"I wouldn't be doing this if you were a shitty writer, Fran. People don't know how good it is. I won't let this happen. You're being a pissy little shit."

"Then I'll kill myself for real. My papa has a gun."

"Go ahead. As long as I get this thumb drive back."

I was now getting the spins something fierce. I thought of something clever to say just as the first taste of vomit hit the back of my throat.

Oranges

From a flatbed truck the guards distribute yellow mesh bags to workers lined up outside the blue portable where we get our labor assignments. From far away, in the frosty glow of the 10 p.m. lights, I seem to see bags of onions fall into their arms. Just our luck, I think, to be cast into this wasteland to be given raw onions.

But no. Huzzah! The bags are full of oranges.

The orange I get is tender and cool. It has an "outie" navel as though to prove it's a living thing with a mother. While other workers tear into their fruit like ravenous hyenas, I undress my orange slowly, pulling off sticky cheeks so as not to injure anything underneath.

The smoke of burning garbage drifts on the wind. A drone zips overhead and makes the birds scatter. At the pickup spot, standing between Xu Xuo and Brother Gao, Fang licks his fingers, rasping his dirty hands clean like a mother cat. He's managed to score a cheap pair of glasses.

"My sweetie loves oranges," he says, gazing up at the widening sky. "They're her favorite fruit, but she only eats them in winter." For a moment I think he's talking about his wife. Then I realize he means the woman behind the door.

Xu Xuo has eaten his orange from the inside out, crushing the wedges with his teeth, smashing his lips into the white underside of the peel.

"I told you he was an animal," says Fang.

Some men trade their oranges for sweet potatoes, batteries, a wooden flute. I spend half an hour picking off all the white stuff until I have a perfect, naked globe.

I am on the verge of eating the first wedge when I see a tall, pale man headed toward me carrying a baby-blue notebook with a face on the cover. He steps through a plume of smoke and comes to a stop in front of a flaming fifty-gallon drum. The face on the notebook is a Japanese anime boy with long lashes. I catch the man's attention and hold out my orange, already peeled, perfect. Some people go their entire lives without having an orange peeled for them. He seems to understand that I want to make a trade. His eyes look bloodshot and he has a sickle-shaped scar on his temple. I ask to inspect the notebook, finding all but three pages clean. A brown tea stain covers a chunk of warped pages, but otherwise the paper is in great shape: an open sea for my imagination.

"The orange for the notebook," I say.

The rusted drum stands burning behind him, and in the firelight the man appears both shadowy and glowing, as though he has some priestly importance.

The man laughs. His teeth are awful. He needs a shave. Fingernails black. He says, "The orange and tomorrow's meals, all three meals, for the notebook."

I hold out the orange.

He doesn't take it. "The orange and the next two days' meals."

"Okay," I say. "You get the orange and all my meals over the next two days."

He laughs again, showing red swollen tonsils. He wheels around and dunks the notebook into the flaming barrel. I lunge forward, too late, and burn my fingers.

But garbage is generous. For days I collect flyers, invoices, quarterly reports, anything with a clean white backside—I even ask other workers to gather scrap paper for me—and soon I have a sheaf of seventy-five pages. I sew the pages together with some thin copper wire I've taken from radios and call the finished product my "garbage folio." Good enough. I keep a ballpoint pen and a Faber-Castell pencil under my cot. The first night, while the others are sleeping, I write from midnight to 3 a.m., thanking God for putting me on the day shift again, as nighttime is best for me. On an old record player I listen at low volume to the Peking Opera circa 1942: "The General Secures the Village" and "The Final Butterfly." To stay awake, I drink lots of water so I'm in a constant state of needing to pee.

I write letters to Mac, letters to Vesuvius and Queena, to Rebekah, to my poor father who is possibly to blame for driving me away to China but nonetheless does not deserve this mystery, this nightmare of a lost son. I think of that American boy sent home in a coma from North Korea, the media images of the father wearing the son's sport coat, and wonder if my father has grown thin enough to fit into mine. How bad is the cancer? What's happening to his dick? How long did he put up with the burning sensation and the blood in his urine before he finally alerted the doctor? I've been so absorbed with my own suffering, I haven't thought of his.

Occasionally I go off on the Chinese government, trying to locate someone or something to blame for this injustice, then burn the paper.

I write fables and poems and one-act plays. I write in German, Yiddish, English, Chinese, and broken Spanish. I wish for a language as accurate as music. As if it could keep me sane, I draft assignments for my students. I write a letter to my old college roommate, to an old girlfriend from Wilmette. I read over the letter to my father and see all that is missing, so much unsaid. What good would it do? I'm much too tired to go there now.

As a result of these nights, I'm a zombie by day, but what do I care? I am trudging over garbage looking for bottles and cans. I'm so damn clumsy. My depth perception suffers, I feel a worsening state of health, my joints sore, chest aching. But when I fall down, and fall down again, nothing breaks. I have no illusions that my writing will survive this place. My work will be burned or buried. For this reason my writing may be as good as it's ever been. Raw, pure, honest, with no pandering to any audience or market. Burn everything for all I care. Just let me write. Let me stay here. Don't send me back to Kun Chong. There's so much good material here.

The bucket-wheel excavator, the largest strip-mining vehicle known to God, looks like a suspension bridge resting on a central base. Imagine a steel structure capable of rotating 360 degrees horizontally and with the ability to raise one arm up and down in the manner of a draw bridge. At one end you have the Miner, which is a giant whirling wheel pronged with giant shovels large enough to scoop up a small house. Of course these shovels have teeth. The Miner gets pulled up and down by steel pulleys eight to a side. Upon lowering, the spinning wheel gouges into the trash or the earth (what is the difference?) and sends the material rolling back on conveyer belts past the center base to the span on the other side, which of course serves as a counterweight to the improbably heavy gouging wheel at the other end, the Miner, which has already been described.

The bucket-wheel excavator is mobile but slow. It can only move on a level plain, which other land-sculpting machines are only too happy to provide by arduous gouging, raking, tamping. This is accomplished by bulldozers and rollers that by comparison look like toys. An army of toys sculpts the terrain until there is a great level area about the size of two baseball fields for the excavator to move upon. It is worth staying alive to witness the largest land vehicle on earth approach a mountain of trash, raise its arm like an angry god and then come down with harrowing blows upon soft things that once looked so hard. The dust kicked up by the action is thick enough to make the Miner disappear in a thick haze like a zeppelin slipping behind a storm cloud. The sound is orchestral chaos, a kind of thunderous percussion that makes the wildest heavy metal band sound like peeping mice. First there is the attack of one shovel hitting the mound, a kind of thunderclap, and then there is an ever-rushing crush of sound that is both constantly changing and always the same.

One evening as my crew and I are headed back to our barracks, we see an unshaven man chained to a cangue by the side of the muddy road. Because he can't reach up past the board to feed himself, he relies on other prisoners to give him food. His name, address, hometown, and crime are written on the planks of the cangue. His name is Liu Bing, he is from Wu Tian, and he has been convicted of money laundering.

Fang walks in the lead, hopping over a puddle and tugging on his loose pants. He's really losing muscle mass, particularly in the neck and shoulders. He looks back at me and says, "Practically everybody here has been tortured except you, the American."

I'm too tired to respond. I kick a tea tin out of the way.

Brother Gao says, "No. I think Francis, you were tortured, yes?"

"Well, fuck," says Fang. "What's the story, Boss? If you're so good at storytelling, tell us what happened."

We stop and have a look at the man in the cangue. He is a burn victim, his face badly scarred along the left side, lips bloated. Fang pats me on the shoulder in a very effeminate way, almost like an evil blessing if that makes any sense, and I'm ready, happy to tell a story— only I'm too distracted by the burnt man. I try to ignore him. The prisoner grunts and cranes, opens his mouth for food.

"Hey, friends," he bellows. "Just a little something to eat. Just one pork bun?"

"Give him some food," I tell the group, coughing, hacking. "And I'll tell you a story."

"A true story," says Fang. "Something real."

"With a wicked ending," laughs another man who has tagged along with us. I guess there are eight of us now, traveling through Area 44. A gang of eight is a lucky number in the Middle Kingdom, I suppose.

"Who among us has any food to spare?" says Brother Gao.

"I've got a sweet potato," says Fang. "I'm only a little hungry."

We give the man mashed sweet potato, water, and oranges. We have no pork buns. We feed him like an animal or an infant, hand to mouth. Scraps of food fall on the cangue, and he reaches for them with his tongue, to no avail. We pick chunks of sweet potato out of the dirt and put them back into his mouth. He says thank you so many times it almost ruins the moment. But it's good. No guards are here. We give mercy to one man doubly tortured. I pray that no drones pass overhead, given that I'm about to break one of the cardinal Kun Chong rules, which, in my defense, have only been hinted at in Area 44.

The sun sets behind the trash heaps. Cool spring air arrives. We build a fire and rest in the lee of the mountain, safe from the traffic on the dirt road. The trucks have stopped hauling for a time, and the crying of magpies hits the air. One man manages to produce a small bottle of moonshine and the men hurrah. Brother Gao smiles nefariously and shushes them like a mother. *Don't laugh too loud. Don't act drunk, or the guards'll hang us.* The bottle goes around and every man is good about sharing. I try to beg off but Fang insists, yet I pass again, suspecting I've got pneumonia or something nobody wants, knowing not what.

Xu Xuo hangs out on the periphery as usual, sitting in the passenger seat of an abandoned delivery truck. Perhaps he pretends that he is once again a driver.

"Shhh," says Brother Gao. "Begin."

All I do is tell the story of the night I was captured in Beijing and tortured in a basement. I figure it's what the men want—something of the spy thriller genre without any spies. No hero. Just one fool and a few evil men.

在战争中

The night Queena escaped, I was thrown into a sedan and hit with a tranquilizer. My last clear memory of that night was a KFC sign flashing past my window.

I felt the queasy drop of an elevator. By the time I came to and felt myself being pushed in a wheelchair, the dank odor of the air confirmed I was in a basement, perhaps somewhere deeper than a basement in the underworld of Beijing.

I then found myself in a bright windowless room of hard chairs, metal filing cabinets, and blue video screens. Two men with military-style haircuts, wearing black slacks and blue button-down shirts, stood across a wooden table from me. They began the interrogation by showing me every racy photo Lulu had texted me during our two-year relationship. Next they produced a video of a prostitute I had visited ages ago in Shanghai. They uploaded these images to a Gmail account, entered my mother's email address, and hit send. They showed me footage of a man who looked exactly like me fellating another man. The technology was no Photoshop hack-job but a masterful rendering of some lurid reality. They sent these images to my father. With the use of AI technology they had produced a recording of me saying awful things to my father in a voice that was exactly mine in timbre and inflection. They showed me a report of my suicide in the Jinan City newspaper. They showed an article written for the *China Daily*, outlining my money laundering and embezzlement schemes, my attempts to get over my gay self-hatred through mistresses and prostitutes. As far as the outside world knew, I had paid a fourteen-year-old boy for sex, given him drugs, and caused his suicide. I had climbed to the top of a bridge in Jinan and plunged thirty meters to my death.

Francis Kauffman, dead at thirty-nine, lost in the Yellow River.

In the next room, I could hear another man screaming in pain. He sounded like an animal gone to slaughter.

The strange nature of my torture, though disgusting, made me wonder if I'd be spared the worst forms of physical torture because I was American.

They told me to get undressed.

I expected to be raped.

I was slathered with lard and thrown into a pitch-black room full of hungry rats. I endured many bites. I fought back with my own teeth.

Then it was a white room at freezer temperature with a thick wooden chair in the center that looked exactly like an electric chair but without wires. I was strapped down. Needles were shoved under my fingernails, causing a pain so volleying and intense that I passed out from the screaming. I came to and said I would tell them anything, though I knew nothing. They forced me to drink vomit.

One of the torture artists had a large mole on the right side of his face, and I wondered about the first time his mother had noticed the mole, what she thought. That my interrogators had mothers seemed a necessary thought. I vomited the vomit on myself. They gave me donkey semen to drink.

I screamed that I would tell them anything.

"We aren't interested in your lies," they said, as this was not their first rodeo.

"I have the truth."

The guy with the mole said, "Do you think this is like some movie? We have no aim to get information out of you. You have nothing for us. You are a worthless piece of shit. No, my friend, this is pure punishment."

They let up for a time. I was conscious of my own breathing, the vomit drying on my skin. I heard the man in the other room wail again. I focused on the scuff marks on the blue vinyl loafers of the scrawnier interrogator of the two. I told myself that as much as I was suffering, this paled in comparison to a woman getting gang-raped, which happened a hundred times a day.

He had very skinny legs. I supposed his kneecaps were shaped just like mine. His heavy Beijing accent left little doubt where he was from. His wristwatch was gilded and cheap. He probably went home every night to his apartment and drank *baijiu* and watched violent movies. He probably had one child. The thing I would never get over was the level of actual pleasure the men seemed to experience. They weren't just doing their job. They had taught themselves to enjoy inflicting pain on others. No amount of art or imagination had prepared me for this wicked truth.

I was shivering now, noticing for the first time how cold I really was. Pain at the ends of my toes and fingers. Penis numb.

The guy with the blue shoes said to his mole-faced friend, "I think he's ready to get fucked," and I didn't believe them. In a small moment of clarity I realized that most of what they had done, save the needles under the fingernails, was perfectly legal even by my own country's standards, had in fact been approved by the President of the United States and his team of lawyers and generals. The emails might never be sent. The images of Lulu kept private. The story of my suicide never published. Perhaps the donkey semen was really fermented goat milk. Say the vomit was only pig slop flavored with acid. Say, on the other hand, it was all true, all legal, all a testament to the human imagination. Someone once wrote that war is a failure of the imagination. To that, I say bullshit. War and torture are animated by tremendous creative energy.

At long last, the men took a few pumps of hand sanitizer and left the room like physicians ready for their next patients. I heard the screaming man next door and knew it was a recording, as I'd heard the same three-note bray two hours earlier. I figured the worst was over.

Another crew of lower-level artists came into the room, unstrapped me, and took me to an empty room, where I was kept awake without food or water for twenty-four hours—a length of time I guessed by the number of shift changes and my own need to shit.

Then came my opportunity to meet with my so-called lawyer. He was a flaccid man with greasy hair, coke bottle glasses, and yellow teeth. He had soup crust on his tie. He looked drunk.

And here came the only spurt of laughter out of me that entire time, laughter, which at that moment had to be a kind of insanity, if not a gracious gift from God. For I thought of my father back in Green Heights complaining of Mister 400, his lawyer, and what I would have given for a high-stakes lawyer in that moment.

This man, this not-lawyer, picked a piece of dead skin off his lower lip and asked me why I was laughing. He seemed insulted somehow that his entrance prompted me to giggles.

"Pain," I said. "I'm not laughing. I've been tortured."

He seemed to buy the argument and took out a pale green legal pad. I could not figure out who had it out for me. Who wanted to spend so many resources on a harmless teacher of Business English, on a meager writer of outlier fiction?

"Your Chinese is very good," he said.

"What are the charges?" I asked.

"Multiple."

"Can I call my embassy?"

"No."

I thought I was Capone-like, hauled into custody on financial improprieties, but that was not so. I was charged with money laundering (two counts), embezzlement, harboring a fugitive, fomenting civil unrest, stealing state secrets, accepting bribes, and coercive intercourse with a student. To back up this ultimate lie, I found out from my lawyer that the secret police had "examined" Queena and interrogated her as to her sexual history. They claimed to have found my semen in her body, with what scientific method I can only imagine. Further, they blamed her for her father's suicide, citing evidence from workers in the textile market that Mr. Chen was deeply depressed about his daughter's counter-revolutionary involvement.

Of course I expected nothing out of my counsel. His legal pad was marred with all manner of phone numbers and doodles, and his notes on my case were scant. So when he pulled a sheaf of documents from his briefcase—photocopies of evidence to be submitted in a court of Chinese law—I was rather impressed. More surprised than anything else. Here was proof that I was head of a shell company in Panama, named, "Go English! LLC." Here were receipts showing that I had charged Mr. Li exorbitant rates for English lessons, and here was evidence that I had used the receipts to clean dirty money from a Columbian drug cartel. No sooner had I written this off as another fiction to go with my suicide and sexcapades than I saw my signature on two of the documents. These were the very papers my secretary had brought to me from time to time. Mr. Li wanted everything on the up-and-up, she had said. He could write off the expenses as professional training. Then I remembered all those times she had brought me documents to sign, how she never left the office until I was done signing, how she stood just inside the doorway, pretty Miss Mu, smoothing the front of her neat skirt, smiling bashfully. What felt awkward at first I chalked up to another cultural custom I simply had to get used to.

My counsel showed me receipts of every small deposit I had made at three different banks on behalf of Dean Chong.

He showed me photographs of Queena's hiding spot inside the bed in my apartment. He showed me a signed affidavit in Queena's handwriting—no mistaking her mechanical calligraphy—stating that I had forced myself on her. This was followed by a photo of my bed sheets with a pink stain nestled in the wrinkles—a shot that was most horrific in its artistic quality.

Finally, he showed me a photograph of a body hanging by a rope between two trees on a rubber plantation. This was a black-and-white photo that looked both old and timeless, the white trunks of the trees marching away into obscurity, the wheelbarrow gallows toppled on its side, the death grimace of the hanged man. Queena's father.

That was the last image I recall before they hit me with another tranquilizer and transported me to Kun Chong.

燃烧

"That's it," I say to my men. "That's the end."

I'm suddenly very thirsty, looking around for a jug of water. The men are rapt, mouths hung open, as silent as the hanged man at the end of my torture story. No one says anything for a long time. Far off, a dog is barking. The crushing of the bucket-wheel excavator can be heard in the distance.

"Nothing more?" says Fang. "That's how it ends?"

I nod, exhausted. My mouth is dry. I've never been so thirsty, yet I can't bring myself to sip the moonshine.

The men say, "*Hen hao, hen hao*," in sturdy voices. No other language I know compares with Chinese for the satisfaction of saying, "Well done," "Very good." It just feels better in Chinese than in English or German. The men look at each other and nod, smile, murmur *hen hao* again. They gaze into the purling fire with expressions that seem to say, *Yup, that's how it is. That's the world.* I love these men. They are my brothers.

They would drink again if they could, but there is no white liquor left. There is no food and no water. No ink stone or iPhone. Already the story is settling into their bones. A few strangers come up and shake my hand, bow, smiling. Fang is bragging that he knows me, this foreigner, his very excellent cell mate. He says I am a famous writer in America, a teacher at one of China's famous universities, and holder of two advanced degrees from a famous university. He adds that I was heavily involved in the Epicuria project to boot. He keeps saying, *My cellmate. The only American.* Sure, I seemed like a fag at first, but I turned out to be a great guy.

Fang stands right beside me, thinner than I've ever seen him but finally bearing a soul, and I do mean *bearing*. Smiling. His chunky glasses are taped at the left hinge. His facial hair is thin.

"Can I have some water?" I say.

"Hey, kid," he hollers to an ethnic boy at the edge of the gathering. "Go to the creek and get Fran-zuh some water. Make sure it's clean."

He pats me on the back and says, "My friend, the writer. The only man brave enough or stupid enough in all of Area 44 to attempt literature. *Hen hao. Hen hao*, my friend. We should do this every Friday night. We should have story night every Friday. What do you say?"

"My pleasure," I say. "Until they kill us."

I smell spicy food. I look across the rutted path and see one of the guards in a black jumpsuit eating noodles from a steaming container, eating as he walks, ordering us to disperse, telling us to get back to the barracks and report for work. Nobody really expects to start another shift tonight, but we do what the guard tells us. By now we know how to play along. His bowl of noodles is huge, enough for three men, and I must say it's a bold move to stroll alone into a covey of half-drunk prisoners, though it's also true that this guy is packed with muscle. He must be one of the body builders who works out in the old brick factory, lifting bricks and old engine blocks, anything fit for the purpose. He is easily the strongest guy at Area 44, his arms thick as hams. Still, most guards are smart enough to travel in groups of two or three.

"Back to the barracks, you little vermin! Giddy up!" he says, tossing another pallet onto the fire. He slurps some noodles, looks at the prisoner in the cangue, and says, "What do you want?"

Meantime, a swarthy kid has brought me a bucket of water. Without caring a wit about bacteria, I tip the container to my lips and guzzle until my stomach hurts. The water is cool and delicious and I drink until my belly's full. I start down the hill back to the barracks with ten or eleven men following closely behind, more or less surrounding me. They walk in step with me. They want to be close to my body. It is a lovely feeling to walk with men like this in the cool span of the floodlights. It is vain but lovely to hear them gush about my story, which was no great shakes, just an account of torture, though it's possible that because I was speaking in Chinese, I simplified things and made a more artful account than I could have done in English.

"Tell us, Teacher, how is it that we find ourselves in such a wicked world, and you can tell us such a wretched and disgusting story, and we like it?"

"It wasn't that good," I say.

"But we loved it. Especially the worst parts."

"Even a middling pork bun tastes like heaven after fourteen days of starvation."

"I was a mean son-of-a-bitch to you back at Kun Chong," says Fang. "I hope you can forget about it."

"Teacher Kauffman remembers everything," says Brother Gao.

"Don't worry, Fang," I say. "We're good."

"I was going through a lot. I felt bitter about everything."

I cough into my hand, stop, suddenly realizing I have left my mask back at the fire circle. I must have taken it off to tell my story. I have no choice but to go back. Xu Xuo keeps trudging down the hill ahead of us. The other men refuse to let me go alone. Brother Gao, Wu Kaiming, Fang, and some new friends—one Uyghur from out West and two Han guys from Xi'an—we all trail uphill together, though I know they are tired of walking. I trip on a two-by-four, and Fang keeps me from falling on my face.

"Careful, Teacher," he says.

We are coming around a heap of wooden pallets when we see the orange fire raging, and across the story circle, the guard with his pants down getting serviced by the man in the cangue. The moaning has started. Two dogs by the fire help themselves to the leftover noodles, but the guard is too lost in his sin to notice.

Work Will Set You Free

Now it is spring. I am working the day shift and feeling ever more sick, coughing up blood and phlegm. But the sky is blue. It rained last night, big rain, and the mosquitoes have hatched from puddles and the birds chitter. Sounds I have not heard for months. Sun glints off chrome and tinsel refuse. The bucket-wheel excavator grinds ceaselessly. All things considered, I don't feel as weak as yesterday or the day before. I have lost considerable weight, down to sixty kilos. In spite of the exercise of working in the mine, my muscles are thin and weak. Back hurts. Neck sore. The birds chatter and some even sing. The workers up on Woodscrap Hill banter, alive with morning energy and happy to laugh at almost anything. They're like day laborers anywhere in the world content to have a job and a few good guys to hang with. Something falls. A bundle of scrap metal? A car chassis? Yellow flowering weeds sprout from the complicated soil. The residents of Area 44 are awake and stirring in their shanties, getting ready for the day. I smell boiling corn, hard-boiled eggs, and fried cabbage.

Xu Xuo is down on his haunches in the dirt road, ass three inches from the ground in that position that is common among the poor. As he picks food out of his teeth, he watches a dog chase after a mouse in the garbage heap across the dirt path. He squints a lot and I know why. He has that gouged pupil that lets in too much light. He smiles at the scene with the dog, which is only a puppy, confused, perplexed by the actions of the mouse. Then the puppy sees itself for the first time in a mirror and jumps back into the road, trots away with that guilty expression common to curs. Xu Xuo takes from his pocket a chunk of salted meat and gets the dog's attention. He feeds the dog and brings it into his lap, tumbles back on the dirt as he scrubs the dog's ears.

I watch them for a time. The dog struggles out of Xu Xuo's grip. My former cellmate stands and smiles at me. "I like that dog."

"Let's go," I say, with no intention of killing him. "I want to show you the taxis. Yesterday I came upon a giant pit of hundreds of yellow taxis, like a graveyard for taxis. You have to see this. But we must go slow. I'm weak. It might take us forty minutes."

I point to the mountains and the sky. The rotating wheel of the bucket-wheel excavator bobs into view above the mountain, then down again. I'm thinking of a Moonraker sweeping in and out of view at an amusement park somewhere in my past, and the up-and-down path of a roller coaster which made the Moonraker seem to yaw like a ship on stormy seas.

"I'm interested," he says, squinting in the sun. "But what about our work?"

"What can they do to us?"

He steps closer and points out his gouged-out pupil. "Lets in more light. That's why I used to drive the night hours."

He comes along. We hike for half an hour up switchbacks, past piles of gathered metal and plastic, past men dousing junk piles with kerosene. They will ruin my blue sky with their black smoke. Here is a pine tree growing out of ravaged soil. Here is a crushed rickshaw. Here a soiled mattress soaked with rain. For a time we fall into step with each other and there is that together feel of climbing a mountain, but as with most hikes a space opens between us. I walk alone. I'm too weak and slow for Xu. He is excited to see the cars, and I begin to wonder if I haven't overhyped the scene. In my memory it was a sight to see, this great pile of yellow taxis in a gulch, all of the cars more or less intact.

I stop to catch my breath on a level spot near a little hamlet where some of the locals live. I smell bad food again, see a chicken scratching in a coop. I feel a cough coming and try to hold it, relax the chest muscles.

That's when I see my little girl crying by the chicken coop, precious Lina with shining cheeks. She wears a yellow dress and a lavender sweatshirt with a spider web on the front. The words "Funny Days" are written in spider silk. She is turning over the trash, muttering words I can't quite understand, either because she is distressed or speaks a local dialect.

"What's the matter?" I say, crouching low.

"I lost my doll."

"What is your doll's name?"

"Xiao Xiao."

"Does Xiao Xiao have black hair?"

Lina nods.

"About this big?"

Another nod.

"How was she dressed the last time you saw her?"

"She was wearing a silk dress for a party."

I get down on my haunches, eye-level with the beautiful child. "Yes, and do you know why she was dressed for a party? Because she wouldn't want to attend her very own wedding without wearing a pretty dress. This is what I've come to tell you. I've climbed this mountain to tell you the story of Xiao Xiao and the handsome horseman, a good man who was not especially rich and not especially poor, but just right, an expert horseman, and how this handsome man took Xiao Xiao for his wife. Would you like to hear the story?"

"I want my doll. Where is she?"

"The only way you can ever know the whereabouts of Xiao Xiao is to listen to the rest of the story. Do you have time? Can you run inside and tell your mother or father I'm here, and they can meet me if they like, because I'm a good man who only wants to tell you a story?"

"They're working," she says, indicating the dump beyond the ridge. "Do you have my doll?"

"I don't have your doll. She is very lucky. She went away to live with a fine husband as all young ladies must do at some point in their lives. Are you ready to hear the story?"

She nods. We find a place to sit, I on a beer crate, she on a yellow bucket.

Xu Xuo has come back to find me. He stands a good fifty meters away, watching the girl and me, too far away to hear my story.

I weave this thing whole cloth on the spot, in a zone of creativity that is surely one of the greatest joys in life, a satisfaction that's hard to match. I'm surprised by the coherency of the story for a first attempt. But of course, it isn't truly the first draft. Every story told is really some other story told again. Every new story is also every old story. Sometimes Lina laughs at something the horseman says. Sometimes she asks questions about the horse or the flavor of the moon cakes in the tale.

After I paint the scene of the horseman returning from battle and washing Xiao Xiao's feet and asking forgiveness for his killing ways in war, Lina knocks her knees together and asks if I have any food. She is fully convinced her doll is living in another world in a willowy garden with a handsome husband and three horses.

"Food," I say. "Yes, I'll bring you some food and the rest of the story tomorrow."

"I thought the story was over."

"I still haven't told you the really happy part," I lie, before taking my leave for the evening.

"What happens?"

"See you tomorrow, Lina. Goodbye."

I trudge off to join Xu Xuo.

We hike up to an outcropping where there is less and less trash as we go higher. At times, the path veers to the edge of the valley, only a foot or two from the precipice. Xu Xuo is nervous but feigns politeness, indicating I should go first. I ignore the offer. I have no idea if he designs to kill me to prevent me from killing him first. Of course he knows of my charge. Back at Kun Chong, the conversations were always open, cruelly so. He is not stupid. What he doesn't know is that I'm feeling merciful. If I kill him out of mercy, to free him from later suffering, that's a story I can live with. And now I wonder why Xu Xuo hasn't committed suicide. That would seem a logical choice and not hard to pull off in a place like this—which means he must consider himself worthy of living. Which means the following: If he wants to live, killing him cannot be considered an act of mercy; it is an act of murder. But perhaps killing him can be considered an act of mercy for Brother Gao, Kuku, Jack, Kaiming, and even Fang—for they would no longer carry the burden of having to commit murder. Nor would they carry the guilt of having done it. But maybe Fang would feel no guilt anyway. Just because he likes me now doesn't mean he likes everybody. Just because he's ball-less doesn't mean he's incapable of cruelty.

Perhaps it's the possibility that Fang will be the executioner that prevents me from shoving my hiking partner in the back. Over the precipice. But more than anything it feels repulsive, physically unnatural, like eating noodles while standing on your head, or drinking urine, or eating vomit.

The height at the spine of this mountain of garbage is impressive, the drop-offs on either side not only steep but precipitously murderous.

We stand for a time looking out over the pit with the old taxi cabs heaped in the center, glass shattered, tires flat, roofs crunched, but some fully intact. Like new. It makes no sense why some of them are in such good condition.

"I wonder how deep it is?" I say. "How many do you think there are?"

"A lot. It's just cars."

He's not impressed. And why should he be? He's an asshole who doesn't like art. I've known this all along. Or maybe I'm the asshole for seeing art in all this misery. He fingers some wax out of his ear and hawks a wad of spit into the valley below, not far enough to reach the pile of cars.

When I hover too close to the edge, I get butterflies. I could easily push Xu Xuo left into the taxi graveyard, where the symbolism is all too obvious, or push him over the right ledge and hope his body rolls into the rotating teeth of the Miner. The earth is level down at the bottom where the bucket-wheel excavator sits. If the operator in his cab presses the right buttons and pulls the necessary levers, the base could slide forward on its tracks and the boom holding the harrowing Miner could swing fifteen degrees counter-clockwise so as to tear apart the slope just beneath us, thus making it easier to throw a victim into the teeth.

But I am weak and Xu Xuo is strong. Of the few words he has spoken, the most resonant ones are, "I would rather die in a fight than at the executioner's wall." Unless everything lines up perfectly well and I have a chance to kick him in the rump, I fear that a struggle would describe my end, not his. So I leave him alone. On our way down the mountain, he finds a glass case with monkey fur figurines inside, the tiny guys playing badminton. Xu Xuo peers inside and giggles in a way I have not seen.

"Look, look!" he says. "The little critters are right in the heat of the game. This one is finely done, finely done. My uncle was a monkey fur artisan. He once gave me a box with chariots and warriors inside."

I say, "Well done," and we head down the mountain together.

That night, working from 10 p.m. to 2 a.m. by the floodlights in the window, I write the second half of Lina's story in Chinese. I add silly pictures that please me, but revisions are needed and the script is sloppy, so I recopy the story before finally collapsing into sleep.

For My Father
Born 1939 —

The nurse says I have fluid in my lungs. She indicates a chart on the wall, using a laser beam to point out the grape-like sacs in my chest where infection has caused scarring and knotting of tissue, though I'm only half certain she's used the word *knotting*. The nurse says it will be up to one of the doctors to go over the x-rays with me. She asks my name and I tell her.

"Fran-zuh," she says and I correct her. She says, "Fran-zuh" again and I say "Francis," but even after this she can only manage, "Fran-xi-zuh."

For nine hours I wait in a back room that smells of rubbing alcohol and moldy sheetrock. I am fully expecting to be put in the hands of some hack. Nine hours without food. At last they blindfold me, put me in a wheelchair, and scoot me down a long, inclined corridor that smells of new paint. Never one for skateboards or downhill speed of any kind, the ride terrifies me. Why so fast? I can feel the breath of the attendant on my neck as she strains to keep me from flying into a wall or colliding with another prisoner. Now we ride an elevator. Now backwards up a few stairs, the attendant grunting. She's a strong woman. She whirls me around and pushes me through flapping doors into a large drafty place full of voices and moans.

When she takes off the blindfold, I look up and see a chaos of murals on the ceiling. Newer works are painted over older works, except in cases where the older piece is so good that no artist can bring himself to defame it. I'm no art critic, but I can tell abstract art from realism. The smeary stuff in yellow, carmine, gold, indigo, and teal is painted over some of the old-school realism. The older stuff is less colorful and more detailed, as if chiseled out of rock, and in no time I realize that my view of the heavens is a depiction of the nine levels of Buddhist hell.

It bears noting that I'm in a large warehouse with hundreds of other patients. The place feels like an old brewery, with twenty-foot ceilings and sturdy steel posts and massive I-beams. Patients are quartered off by flimsy bamboo screens covered with graffiti: finger paintings in blood or bubbly taggings like on box cars. The whole infirmary is a binge of expression. No doubt, the prisoners who've been deprived of art have gone nuts with the opportunity.

I sit on an examining table waiting for a doctor. The sheets are paisley. Over my head looms a pastel of a bonneted French peasant girl pouring water into the mouth of a dragon. She could be the subject of any painting by Manet, only she has a cangue around her neck, and her foot is chopped off and bleeding. A dog licks at the open wound. To the left of the girl is a patch of crumbling paint extending to a beam of rusted steel. I think of the girl as my sister and the dragon as my father, though the analogy makes no sense. The planks of the cangue extend far enough that perhaps the girl cannot see that she is pouring water into a dragon's mouth, nor will she ever be able to raise the pitcher to her own mouth to drink the water. Nor eat. Is that the point of the cangue?

I haven't had much appetite lately. I haven't eaten in twelve hours, but suddenly I'm very hungry. Maybe the art has primed my appetite. I don't know. I look at the half moon of the girl's breast and feel another longing I haven't had in some time. Terribly exhausted, my hunger fades, and I fall back on the examining table.

After a time that is either long or short, a nurse pushes me awake.

A tall, stooping doctor in a white lab coat steps into the cubicle and takes up my chart. He introduces himself as Dr. Xia and at once I know him to be the famous bird doctor from Tsing Hua University, the man who concocted the vaccine against Avian Bird Flu.

"I'm not a pulmonary specialist," he says flatly, flipping through the pages of the chart.

I ask for a glass of water. He leans into the breach and snaps at a nurse, and in no time I am brought a lime-green thermos full of hot water.

"I'm not a pulmonary specialist," he says again, this time in English. "But I put in a few months in the countryside many years ago as a village doctor. It is a mining town. As you might imagine, I see a lot of chest ailments."

His expensive Italian loafers are badly scuffed. By the cinch marks in his belt, I can tell he's lost a good fifteen pounds. He is a dapper man but very tired, less kempt than he should be. He needs a haircut. He speaks excellent English, and for once I am too tired to want to impress anyone with my Chinese; it is a relief to speak as I think. I take a sip of water and almost burn my tongue. He knows who I am but not where I'm from. When I tell him I went to the University of Chicago, he nods as though impressed, then rattles off the names of our famous economists. He looks nothing like my father, yet he reminds me of Otto Kauffman in the way that he seems too-early defeated. Dr. Xia should have more gas in his tank, but the world has sucked him dry. I get the feeling he likes me. In spite of the hellish images on the ceiling, I feel a spurt of optimism that perhaps I'll be given special treatment and be spirited home.

I ask him how he ended up in a place like this.

"I was doing the best work of my life," he says. "And they tells me to retire. I mean, really ground-breaking work in the areas of viral mutations. And they says I have to stop working, all because of the mandatory retirement age. It is maddening. Perhaps I am naïve. I never been a member of the Party, but I thought they would make an exception for me, because of my status, because of the nature of my work."

He presses his fingers to my lymph nodes, neck, armpits, chest. "I got angry. I thought my stature put me above ze law. I say some rashful things about the wrong people and earn myself a two-year sentence."

"They make you care for prisoners," I said. "That makes no sense."

"From your perspective, it makes all the sense in the world. But I understand what you say. For the average Chinese, they will see the illogic of taking me out of the research field so as to adhere to an archaic national policy, while allowing me to patch up felons. In any case, I'm here to make you better. Remove your shirt."

He puts his cold stethoscope against my chest and listens to my breathing. "We need to test your sputum," he says. "We take a sample and test it for drug resistance. There's no use giving you antibiotics if they doesn't work on the bacteria theirselves."

"Why are they letting you take care of me?"

"Because it is a diplomatic embarrassment to let you die."

"But nobody knows I'm here. My parents think I committed suicide."

"Who knows what people outside know? Or in any case, I'm only giving you my best guess. I have stopped trying to interpret rationally the actions of the government. Please. On your back."

I look up at the peasant girl and then my eyes wander to the image of a man with an incredibly long tongue being yanked out of his mouth by a noose. I want to say the noose is attached to a water buffalo, but the scene gets cut off by my bamboo screen. Only in this prison can I look up to the Heavens and see Hell.

My shock is not lost on the doctor. He looks up at the panoply of color and says, "Apparently the warden enjoys paintings."

"Which means art is not totally against his policy."

"I can't speak for the warden. I'm told he isn't consider this art. He considers it reality."

"If you take propaganda for reality."

"No. That's not what I says. In the case of these murals, he considers them to be a more accurate representation of reality itself than, say, this table right here, or that jar of cotton balls. I'm sorry. My English is so bad, so bad. In fact, if I do not misunderstand him, he believes the penetrative quality of these murals is so great as to be more real than our thoughts theirselves. What is more real, Mr. Kauffman, this table right here, or your mental scheme of the table?"

"I don't know. We could discuss it for days, if I didn't feel so sick."

"If I am not pushed into immunology when I was a student, I might have studied psychology, especially neuropsychology. I would like to bridge the gap to philosophy. When people feel joy or suffering, I like to pull this stuff out of the brain and examine the substance. The warden would claim, I am sure, that the mural above is the most exact, suffering reality there is."

"That's crap," I say. "Men are getting tortured here. One guy in my cell got castrated. Another guy got raped by a guard in the vineyards."

This last image hangs in the air. The doctor presses his fingers to my elbows and knees, making pain where there was no pain. "Have you had the night sweats?"

"Yes."

"The x-rays suggest you once had tuberculosis in a long time ago. Did you have it as a child?"

"No."

"You are sure?"

"I know for a fact I never had tuberculosis."

He nods. "A sputum test will answer our most important question."

Dr. Xia lays his stethoscope on my chest and asks me to sing at the top of my lungs. I sing "Blank Space" for Queena, a song I hate for a girl I love. The doctor looks up at the ceiling and says, "The warden views these murals as ultimate reality. Do not question him on this. I happen to know for a fact that he is fond of you, all things considered, so it not out of the question that you meet him again and have a conversation over tea. A cup of tea."

"Or a bucket of vomit."

"One cannot rule out anything in Area 44."

"Is the Kun Chong warden also the warden here?"

"Yes. As a matter of fact, if you don't mind my asking, please put in a good word for me if you meet him again. He's not bad guy. Certainly not the worst. Please put in a good word for me." He swivels on his stool and says, "I've got to check this guy out next."

Only now do I realize that I'm sharing the cubicle with another patient. A man in a blue tunic lies across from me on an examining table. He moans like a cow, his foot trapped in a bloody bandage, waiting for his turn to be examined. I feel a prick of shame that I hadn't noticed him till now, though I suppose I can be forgiven considering my state of exhaustion and the distracting ceiling show.

Dr. Xia scoots back on his stool and says, "You must wear a mask and you must sleep alone. Their policy is very strange. If you are not very sick, you shall not be excused from the work crews. If you have a serious yet curable disease, you are allowed to recuperate and have a work schedule conducive to regaining your health. If you have an incurable disease, you cannot be excused from work crew."

"And in my case?"

"I am not ready to quarantine you. The infirmary will send someone to inform you of the results of the skin test and the sputum test. In the mean times, wear your mask."

I take a sip of hot water. The lining inside the thermos shimmers pretty as poison mercury.

"Most cases are curable," he says, "but you'll need to take four antibiotics over a six-month period. I'm afraid that in China we have some very bad strains. Many of thems are resistant to drugs. But until the test comes back, until the antibiotics fail, and even if they do, I won't have justification to take you off the lines. If you wish, Mr. K, I can add an addendum to my report suggesting you be given only Level 5 jobs that doesn't require a lot of lung capacity. But I can only make recommendations. Once you get out there in the hills, the foreman has absolute authority."

The man with the bloody foot starts moaning louder now. His bandage is stained a plum color. The poor guy is thin and dirty, with terrible teeth. The doctor turns toward him for a moment, purses his lips, checks his IV bag, and shouts into the breach, "Hey, nurse! Get this guy some morphine!"

She comes in and attaches a drip bag and in no time the man is moaning softer. Dr. Xia slumps down in a chair against the wall and says, "I'm too tired." He closes his eyes and listens to the din of the infirmary.

I look up at the cangue on the ceiling and start telling him my story.

在下午

My grandfather, Amschel Kauffman, was taken to Sachsenhausen Concentration Camp in 1938, the morning after Kristallnacht. He was a glassmaker and glazier who specialized in stained glass. He had his own shop in Berlin on Kurfurstendamm, and for him the Night of Broken Glass was an especially painful event.

By the time he arrived at Sachsenhausen, there were some five thousand prisoners housed there, including political prisoners, professional criminals, and Jews who had been brought in on bogus charges. SS boys of only sixteen or seventeen yelled at him, forcing him to do the Sachsen Salute on his knees, hands clasped behind his back, as they screamed, "Which whore shat you into the world?"

The camp was meticulously maintained, with triangular sections of grass and plots for roses and tulips. Not much growing in November but a few yew bushes and clumps of holly. They took him to the print shop and inked a number on his forearm.

He slept in a hut with thirty other prisoners in triple bunks. He bathed with close to three hundred men, the water scalding hot one moment, then ice cold the next. They ate cabbage soup for every meal, every now and again a bit of sausage or a bread ball. There were football matches and orchestra concerts on Sundays, regular shootings of prisoners who stepped out of line. Men were publicly flogged. The prisoner would be laid out on an instrument that looked like a gymnasium horse, given a piece of felt to chew on, and beaten with a tube of rubber.

The systematic transport of Jews began a year later.

Some were taken to the gas chambers at Lublin. Some were killed by carbon monoxide right there at Sachsenhausen, herded into vans and driven into special airtight chambers. A crematorium was built. Some Jews of special skill were spared, fifty watchmakers put to work repairing hundreds of thousands of watches stolen from the dead. Printmakers pressed counterfeit South African rands and U.S. dollars. Sculpture artists, painters, and photographers were put to use for the aesthetic pleasure of the SS officers. My grandfather worked in the laundry house for a total of two years, cleaning the zebra uniforms and sending them through the gassy de-lousing machines. It was better than working in the stone quarry, where men keeled over dead of exhaustion or got shot for loafing.

With each wave of new prisoners, Amschel would seek out the Berliners and ask if anyone knew the whereabouts his once-pregnant wife, Anna. Nobody knew a thing. Then one day a man with cabbage on his breath whispered that Anna K had gotten out of Germany with fake papers. Where to? He didn't know.

The news brought the cruelest kind of joy and nevertheless helped him get through the long days. Wake-up call was at 4:30. The men were counted. After the counting they would wait in the hut for the better part of an hour, then march to the parade ground to be counted again. One morning, the count came up short by one man, who was soon found hanged in the woods outside camp. No one was allowed to move from the parade ground until the corpse was brought in on a stretcher and at last counted.

His march from the laundry house to his block (on awful wooden shoes) involved a path that skirted close to the neutral zone, a gravel swath between the yard and the wall like the warning track on a baseball field. If he happened to be walking astride some Ukrainian who hated him, he could get shoved over the line. The guards in the watchtowers did not care how a man crossed the line, only if he crossed it. One afternoon, as the winter birds were singing in the fir forest beyond the fence, a prisoner got pushed into the neutral zone, and in the rain of bullets my grandfather felt a tug at his trousers. The prisoner fell dead on the black gravel. Amschel looked down and saw a bullet hole in his pant leg. Later, he was roundly excoriated for not taking care of his uniform, then forced to do a Sachsen Salute for forty minutes as punishment. He was reminded again that he had been shat into the world by a whore. He was told that his wife was just now in the brothel getting screwed by a Hauptsturmfurher. He hadn't known there was a brothel at the camp. He doubted the officers would choose a woman who was five months pregnant for their whore. Of course she would no longer be pregnant, but he couldn't help thinking of her any other way.

Thousands of prisoners were taken every week in transport to Lublin. Smoke rose from the crematorium twenty-four hours a day. That my grandfather, a lowly laundry worker, had been spared his life did not make any sense. He was burly like my father and by all rights should have been put to use constructing buildings or quarrying stone. One day while he was getting his hair shorn, an SS guard asked him if he was a stained-glass artisan. He said he was.

"Prove it," said the guard, a mere child of seventeen.

Amschel looked out the window at a crow alighting on a fence. He opened his mouth but couldn't speak. Then he said, "One of the ways to fix the color in the glass is with urine."

"Fine. Come with me."

He was put in the back of a navy blue car with three other men. This automobile was not one of the vans meant for killing. The driver took them through three gates to the officers' compound, past a tulip garden dressed in April glory, past a gymnasium and the officers' mess hall, to a large stucco villa with blackened windows.

The driver said, "The Kommandant lives there. Get out."

The villa was newly-built and in perfect order except for several large strips of tar paper covering the windows. At first glance, one assumed this to be some sort of protection against bombing raids (but the Allies were not to clobber Sachsenhausen until 1943 at the earliest). As the prisoners walked up the stone path toward the entrance, they admired sandstone fountains and marble urns planted with orange geraniums. They saw a blond boy tossing a boomerang on a manicured lawn. The prisoner on my grandfather's left, who looked gaunt and defeated, said, "I was the construction manager for this house." The other man, a sand-haired fellow named Mort, said he was an architect.

Kommandant Fritz Stark was waiting for them behind a large oak desk in his study. He was a man of medium build, with wavy black hair cropped short on the sides, a prominent nose, and penetrating black eyes. The room was dim because of the tarpaper, but a number of fancy lamps shed light on the parquet floor, the carved furniture, silk tapestries, and shelves of books.

Stark flicked his riding whip to his left, indicating the blackened windows.

"You can see what my problem is. The first shipment of windows was unfortunately destroyed by bombs whilst in transport. The French get lucky every now and again. The second attempt got short-circuited by one very stupid Jew who took it upon himself to spread rumors that I was a boondoggler. He has been taken away."

Stark then went on to explain their assignments, that Amschel would be in charge of fabricating windows for the existing villa, whilst the construction manager and architect would design a new wing to be used as a falconry. He wanted stained-glass windows in the study and the drawing room, possibly in the falconry, and lead-paned windows in the other rooms. He wanted images of mountains and streams and rutting stags, idyllic country scenery of men on the hunt, perhaps some pretty maidens milking cows, that sort of thing.

The prisoners took measurements. My grandfather asked the Kommandant if it would please him to have the window frames fashioned in the same shape as some of the great cathedrals of Germany, knowing already that he would make windows in the image and likeness of the Synagogue on Oranienburger Strasse. To the untrained eye, the style of windows was not so recognizable: a pair of arches with a circle at the top, the framing made of sandstone, the stained-glass pieces made by Amschel himself.

Was my Opa a hero or a fool to take such a risk?

Let us keep in mind that he had a wife who was pregnant at the time of his arrest, and while he can be forgiven for not knowing that she and baby Otto were already on a ship to Canada, he should be faulted for not exercising basic protocols of self-preservation. Ergo, my grandfather was an idiot and an ass, at best a very bold Jew. Let's not make him a hero for choosing his religion over his family, for choosing synagogue windows over a chance to be with his son. True, the Kommandant was not from Berlin and so wouldn't recognize the windows. In any case, it was a Moorish style common to many cathedrals and imperial buildings. And why didn't the Nazis despise Moorish arches? As with most things Nazi: no rational answer.

The three fortunate Jews were put to work in a shop prepared especially for them, with two drafting tables, good pencils, a work bench, and a cabinet stocked with chemical supplies. But no kiln. Any sense that their lot had improved—the work was much more interesting than doing laundry—got sapped by the fact that the crematorium stood next door. The men never got used to the smell.

Nobody said what all three were thinking: that the SS would probably make Amschel use one of the ovens in the crematorium as his kiln. Nevertheless, he drew up several large cartoons and requested a meeting with the Kommandant.

When Amschel entered the study, the Kommandant's wife and son were present, seated off to the side on a silk upholstered couch in the bay of the black windows. The wife was a pretty, somewhat plump redhead that Amschel glanced at only once. He saw sunburned cheeks, the shape of her body in a white dress and that's all. The son, a boy of about seven, also had wiry red hair.

Almost no natural light entered the villa from either the first or the second floor, and in the dimness the wine in Stark's glass looked dark as the blood drawn into a syringe. The Kommandant seemed a little drunk at this time. He spoke in a loose voice to his wife about wallpaper and lamp shades. He exhaled a heavy breath of manure-smelling wine as Amschel spread his cartoon drawings on the oak desk. The wine was surely French.

"The stag needs bigger antlers," said Stark, "but it's not bad."

"I will need some specialized tools of iron."

"The blacksmith will help you."

"And the colors will need to be fixed, so they are of the highest quality, pure and everlasting. For this, I will need vinegar or wine, though I can use urine if it would please your excellency. I am only asking because I don't want the guards to get the wrong impression, if, sir, they were to see me—"

Stark took a champagne flute from the sideboard, unzipped his trousers, and urinated into the flute.

"Use this," he said, handing over the warm glass.

Rather than zip up, the Kommandant loosened his belt and held his penis for all to see, saying, "Have you ever seen such a thing of glory? Sometimes I like to have a Jew wash it for me, as I am a very clean man."

The wife turned away.

"But you have much work to do. And in any case, I don't think you're worthy of cleaning my perfect phallus."

The mother and son sat quiet as moths on the silk couch.

Amschel stepped back, holding the warm glass in both hands. "If it would please the Kommandant, may I ask for a few more materials to complete the job?"

Stark, now put together, slammed his wine glass on the desk and unleashed a spit-showering tirade at my grandfather. "What more do you want? Do you know how lucky you are not to be at Lublin? Or the quarry? Why must you bother me with each petty detail? Such incompetence of your race is why I am on this side of the desk and you are on that side. What do you want?"

"I need lead, sir, to make the strips between the images. I need a kind of metal that is pliable."

"Lead we can get from bullets. But we have a war going on and must save as much ammunition as possible. Bullets will be harvested from the dead. Would you like to be in charge of this task, Amschel?"

"I would prefer it not, sir."

"Well, then, we'll have to pick out the lowest swine of Jew among you to take on this errand. One who is a Jew and a professional criminal would be best, or a Jew and a homosexual. Or one who is both a Jew and a murderer, the absolute lowest scoundrel you can think of, one who has been shat out of a whore's arse. The most abject scoundrel among you. Do you know any man in your block who fits this description?"

Amschel was aware of the soft body of the wife to his right, the innocence of the child beside her. He desperately wanted to look at them, but he kept his eyes on the oak desk.

To answer the Kommandant's question in the negative would be to contradict him. "I am sure such men exist here, sir, but I do not know of any in my block, not that I can immediately point out."

The presence of the child in the room was making him increasingly uncomfortable.

"Surely, you do. You are housed with the Jews and the German criminals. How can there not be a scoundrel among the swine? Either you finger a man or you yourself will be carving bullets out of the bodies, do you understand?"

"Yes, Sir Kommandant."

"Are you interested in surgery? Were your ancestors crude barbers?"

He thought of a man who occupied the top bunk in the corner of the hut, a certain Schub who had stolen food and cigarettes. He was not well-liked in the hut. He was a bully and a braggart. Truth be told, Amschel hated this man, but Schub also had three children, assuming they hadn't been gassed, and no one deserved the job.

The Kommandant slapped his riding whip on the desk and shouted, "Give me your answer!"

"Schub. Gerhard Schub."

"Very well. He would be well advised to search out those prisoners with multiple gunshot wounds. To be efficient, tell him to hang around that watchtower near the infirmary. Those boys seem to have itchy trigger fingers."

For weeks after that my father's father worked long hours in the shop. To his relief, the Hauptfurher in charge of the crematorium installed a separate kiln for glass-making. Amschel mixed ground copper and iron oxide with powdered glass to get just the right colors. The stag looked very good. The dividing iron the blacksmith had fabricated worked like a charm. He meticulously laid strips of lead between the forest scene and the Bavarian castle.

In time he finished two arched windows and a circular window to perch above them like a full moon over twin mountain peaks. Alternately, one could say the windows were shaped like the tablets Moses had brought down from Sinai. Mort the architect informed Amschel that the stone mason was almost done with the sandstone framing and that much retrofitting needed to be done to please the Kommandant.

Amschel and his co-workers triple-checked their measurements, lest some miscalculation lead to a flogging.

On the day they brought Amschel's colorful panes into the villa, the tarpaper now gone, sunlight streamed into the room along with a soft breeze of honeysuckle, almost as if light and smell were one in the same. The panes fit perfectly. Stark was pleased, but he showed not an ounce of glee, as one of his subordinate officers was in the room and it was necessary to act as though stained glass was not some lavish luxury but a necessary adornment in the battle for Europe, no different than medals on an officer's uniform. Rainbows of light bled through the glass in a manner that was both glorious and sad. Hallelujah in hell.

"Tomorrow is Sunday," said the Kommandant, standing on a bearskin rug in the center of the room. "You get one day of rest, and then you are back at it. Two more window frames to go!"

Those were the last words Amschel Kauffman heard from the Kommandant. The following Monday, as my grandfather was walking back from the shop for lunch, a young guard stationed in a watchtower decided to harass him for sport. It was a beautiful sunny day, with clear blue skies and a sweet sappy scent wafting from the fir forest beyond the fence. Shift change meant there were twice as many guards around the tower: an audience for the red-haired guard. The boy had a long white neck. He stood on the upper level of the brick tower at a distance of no less than ten meters from my grandfather, close enough that the dimple on his chin was discernible. The kid was too skinny for his hat. His hand looked starch-white against the trigger guard of the machine gun. The other guards were carrying on about the brothel, how even if you got to go there you'd likely get a whore who'd been pounded by ten officers. How it would still be worth it. How whoring was the only thing more fun than shooting Jews.

"You with the cap," shouted the red-haired boy to my grandfather. "Step into the neutral zone, or I'll shoot you."

My grandfather said he would prefer not to.

"If you don't follow orders, I will report you to the blockfurher and he will have you flogged in the courtyard. Don't you trust me, you swine? I'm telling you to cross the line. I promise I won't shoot."

The boy had freckles and chestnut eyes. He probably liked ice cream.

Amschel looked up and said, "Anyone who crosses into the neutral zone will be shot. It says right there."

The blood coursed in his ears. A breeze rushed out of the forest, tangy and sweet. The line of prisoners behind him had stopped to watch the spectacle. He saw the black eye of the boy's rifle, aimed straight for his chest. A flock of blackbirds coursed through the sky above the tower, stretching out and bending inward like a flag curling in the wind.

"Cross the line, or I'll shoot. Do what I say."

There wasn't time for the other guards to recognize Amschel Kauffman as the artisan who was doing special work for the Kommandant. There wasn't time to warn the boy. He fired a warning shot into the dirt.

Amschel stepped over the line, and the boy shot him.

The next day, the Kommandant marched the boy into the woods at gunpoint.

游泳

Dr. Xia gets up from his stool and looks at the murals on the ceiling. He lets out a sigh and says, "We are wicked animals. No other species compares."

I cough and cough, too exhausted to speak again.

"So you have told a tale of revenge," he says, his tone lightening. "A terrible story but well-told."

"I don't know if the Kommandant ever shot the boy," I say. "Maybe he only scared him."

"We'll never know. Why did you tell me this story, Mr. K?"

"Because I'll never see my mother and father again. I love them very much. My father, he was a real jerk sometimes, but I loved him all the same. He'd be happy with this story, I think, and would've liked that I told the story of his father, a man he never met. Sometimes I wonder, I wonder, I really wonder if it would be easier if one never met one's father."

"My father was a cruel, brutal man, but I'm glad I knew him." He tugs his pants and cinches his belt one notch tighter. "Do you want to know how he taught me to swim? He threw me into a lake and taunted me with a bamboo pole, holding it just out of reach. He figured if I could not drown, I could swim."

Dr. Xia looks a little less exhausted. I don't flatter myself to pretend my story has helped him. God knows he has his own methods of survival. He attends to patients sixteen hours a day, six days a week. He is a prisoner like all of us.

He grabs the thermos from my crotch and almost takes a drink, then thinks better of it. I'm not sure if he hasn't wiped tears from his eyes. Maybe it's just faulty tear ducts and fatigue. Maybe my story has got to him. He hands me the empty thermos, shrugs by way of apology, and sighs deeply.

The morphine has quieted the man with the bloody foot. He gets wheeled out of my cubicle, and moments later two female guards wearing red hats bring in a woman in chains. She is in labor, bellowing even louder than the man. I figure this has to be Fang's lover, but then I realize Fang's concern could not be this far along. Not enough time has passed. Dr. Xia gives her a look that is half sympathy, half annoyance, and asks me if my father is still alive.

Before I can answer, the baby starts to come. It smells bad. The doctor walks behind a screen and washes his hands.

Scrap Mountain

Another blue sky day. Warm. After a morning spent sorting computer parts, the foreman has left us alone. I go for a walk in the sun, up the road towards a copse of trees that stands behind one of the mobile sorting stations. I want to take off my overshirt—some of the workers digging a sewer line are naked to the waist—but I don't want to reveal my folio. I am on my way up the valley road when the foreman calls me back. "*Ka-Fu-Men*! Don't forget your basket."

I turn and see Xu Xuo by the row of wicker baskets. He gives me a basket, and with one of his doggy looks, says, "I go with you?"

I'm not in the mood to be chummy. I shoulder my basket and trudge off to work alone, feeling Xu Xuo's gaze on my back. Undeterred, he tags along through the trees and through a shitty field of corn. I keep an eye on him and manage to shake him by ducking into a portable toilet, where I snatch a bit of prisoner's sleep.

An hour later I spot Lina's lost doll Xiao Xiao sitting on an old rice cooker, her legs crossed, back arched, one arm twisted back ninety degrees in a painful-looking position. I'm not sure if millions of little girls name their dolls Xiao Xiao or if my young friend is brilliant. The name could mean "little fella" or "little laugh," or possibly "young for a short while." If I'm not mistaken, Xiao Xiao is the name of that cartoon stick figure known for his martial arts prowess, his vanquishing of villains. This Xiao Xiao is a Chinese doll with painted nails and pig tails, four freckles on each cheek.

In a Disney movie, Xiao Xiao might come to life with the sparkle of a butterfly, hop off the rice cooker, and scurry up the valley road like some loyal dog, "La la la," all the way back to Lina's shack. At first I am happy and wanting nothing more than to rush up the road in my weakened condition and surprise Lina with this resurrection. I want to please a child. Who doesn't want to please a child?

But she must never see this doll again. The doll would make my story a lie. It would teach her to believe some Disney falsity that heroes come back after death. Better to have a true story than a false reality.

I pop open the rice cooker, shove the silken-haired beauty into the pot, and snap the lid closed.

I am ready to find Lina and hand off my story when the foreman catches up with me again. He wears a very nice pair of blue rubber boots he must have rummaged from the piles.

He tells me that Scrap Mountain is dangerous today because the bucket-wheel excavator is tearing into the east bank and weakening the hillside, which, he reminds me, is built of landfill and therefore not the most stable of mountains. "Too dangerous," he says. "We're working the terraces today."

"Since when do you care about worker safety?"

This foreman is a compact man with a buzz cut and round spectacles. "It's not your place to ask questions."

"There's a family that lives up there. A little girl. At least let me hike up there and warn them about the situation. You say there could be a landslide?"

"I'm not responsible for the families up there. My only concern is my men, and in this respect I must deny your request."

Fine.

I play it cool. If I'm recalcitrant, he won't take his eyes off me all day. Resigned, ever the persecuted one, I join the other skinny workers in the terraces. We are supposed to dig an irrigation ditch for a rice paddy. The sun shines hard and I sweat through my undershirt. The folio rides sticky against my belly, threatening to slip out of my clothes every time I bend over to pluck something out of the refuse.

Fang looks weak. He's lost a lot of muscle mass. He wields the pick like a boy who's chosen a too-large tool to impress his father. I think of the public swimming pool when I was a boy, how I hated undressing in front of my father. He was so big and packed with muscle, and I was so scrawny. Here I am again, Papa, scrawny as ever. And even Fang, the "real man" who used to do pull-ups from the barred windows of our cell, would be no match for my old man.

For a time I work silently with Fang, removing anything of value that he turns over with his pick, moving out of the way, moving in a rhythm that isn't half bad. You can't say there isn't a great trust between a man swinging a pick and his partner.

I spit another gob of bloody phlegm on the dirt. I cough for five minutes, and the hard work of the chest makes me hot. I don't know exactly how tuberculosis kills a man. I make a mental note to ask Dr. Xia the next time I see him, if I see him. What vital function does consumption ultimately consume? I have never stopped to ask myself this simple question. If I were drowning, or suffering a heart attack, the answer would be obvious. If I had suffered a gunshot wound, stabbing, or blow to the head, I could explain my demise. I probably shouldn't be anywhere near these guys. I tighten the straps of my mask.

During a break, I wipe sweat from my temple and look around at the other workers. Brother Gao is tossing scraps of wood onto a bon fire. He asks me what the doctor said and I don't answer. Seagulls boomerang in the sky over one of the shipping containers. The ever-grinding sound of the bucket-wheel excavator plays in the distance.

Then with a shot to the heart, I say to Fang, "Where's Xu Xuo?"

He nods in the direction of the mountain. "I don't know. I saw him walking up the valley road a short time ago."

The rice cooker is empty.

I search for weapons. Nothing. I abandon my basket and start jogging up the rutted path. I'm in terrible shape. I wheeze. I cough. I keep dropping my folio and finally decide to hold it in my hand and risk confiscation. Four kilometers to go. The path winds among twisted shrubs, smoking pyres, and stacks of trash sorted according to type. Metal. Wood. Plastic. The air grows increasingly dusty as I climb. The ground quakes from the excavation. Still no sign of Xu Xuo. I realize that I've had nothing to drink all morning and am terribly dehydrated. In a pile of scrap lumber I find a two-by-four with a huge nail sticking out of the end. In my movie mind, I put the nail right through Xu Xuo's eye. Such a sick, sick man deserves blindness, so he can't see little girls, or so little girls can't see him seeing them. If only killing were easy. The wood feels like a cricket bat. My right hand feels strong. I have long fingers. I suspect my grip will remain firm until the end.

I gain the level area of the shanty town. Fifty meters ahead, trudging into a little dip in front of Lina's shanty, I see Xu Xuo with the doll, his brown hand ringed around the pale beauty. If I have been disgusted with my thoughts, I must have blacked out the feelings, or made them up in a story so the real is not so real but only some wicked fantasy. The evil. We kill what we can't stand. What infects us. We are all this evil, so we try to kill ourselves. Amputate. I charge forward with my folio in one hand and the two-by-four in the other, suddenly lacking conviction in my weapon.

And with the sweat stinging my eyes and the dust from the excavator hanging everywhere, with my dizzy mind, I realize that the man trudging by the shanty is not Xu Xuo, nor is he holding a doll. This is a different man. The doll is a cob of corn. Maybe he's a resident of the shanty town, a worker, or a prisoner. Without taking notice of me, thank God, he trudges over the ridge and out of sight.

The excavator takes another big chunk out of the mountain. Deafening sound. I've lost my folio. Fuck. It's no use.

I stop for a moment to catch my breath and check my bearings.

Is this Lina's shack?

I recognize the bamboo fence posts holding the chicken wire. I recognize the sweatpants with the blue horse icon hanging on the clothes line. The chickens cluck mildly when I tug open the gate.

I pass through a tight entryway where the family stores their eggs and chicken feed. Over the din of the excavator I hear Peking opera blaring from a radio inside. I duck under a swag of electrical wires and find myself breaking the fourth wall of a dark scene. I smell dish soap. The innermost room of the shanty is so gloomy, and my vision so spotty coming out of the bright day, it takes a moment to come to terms with what's going on. I see Xu Xuo sitting on a vinyl couch with his pants off, shirt on. Lina plays in a blue wash tub of sudsy water. The doll is naked. Lina is shirtless to the waist, wearing a pair of boys' red swim trunks.

Things rarely work as planned. If memories cannot be trusted to go backward accurately, and fantasies cannot be trusted to go forward accurately, who's to say the present is any more reliable? Xu Xuo's head is not in position for a clean blow to the eye, and as much as I want to blind him or gouge out his heart, I take what the world gives me, which is a clean shot to the ear. In his state of arousal, under the roar of the excavator, he doesn't hear me coming. Of course I can't hear the board meeting skull and the nail puncturing the ear, but it feels like sound, and if sound is only vibration, who's to question my mind? For it is done. It is already past. To say I have struck a nerve is to put it mildly. The death of us is quick. The head goes down, bringing the body with it. What better way to end this man than a spike through the brain. He has no soul.

Lina is crying.

Xu Xuo writhes on the ground, falters, spasms, up, then down.

"It's okay," I say. "This is only a story. That man is not real."

But she is mad, cowering in the makeshift kitchen by a hot plate. She thinks I might come after her next. She disagrees with me.

"No," I say. "You're wrong about me. I am the good man. I am the hero of the story. I will take the bad man away."

Later it will sink in what a terrible, selfish mistake I've made: that in my attempt to spare Lina a nightmare, I have given her a nightmare.

All is adrenaline. I have more than enough strength to pull Xu Xuo by his coiled pants out across the yard, chickens scurrying, across the path, and over to the edge of the pit. Brother Gao and Fang stand watching from the middle of the road. Turning him over once, twice, I see his still-engorged genitals and his bloody ear, and then he is lost in the tumble of debris and dust, down into the forward roll of the Miner.

Description of a Quarantine

What will I be when I was?

A son who disappeared, never married, never lived on in the family business or the family name; a memory erased; a prisoner, a murderer who died at forty of a disease which far from being eradicated from the planet eradicated him from the planet; obsessed by a weird kind of writing that never weathered the storms of time, as he was the author of only two great stories and two orphaned novels; never deeply in love with another woman to the extent that he would sacrifice himself for her; never strong enough to live in communion with others unless by brutal force; selfish and self-absorbed; without a soul; a Master of both Arts and Business who might have martyred himself for a political cause had he not lacked the guts.

And now I am sick to the point of dying. And now I have my own bed. My chest foams with blood, joints ache, body sweats profusely, and in this fevered state I want to give up, give in, give all, give nothing. What, then, is the point in remembering? I should ask Dr. Xia and Mac to destroy all my stories the moment I die, but they won't listen. If you are reading these words in Chinese, English, or German, if there is somewhere in the ghetto a Yiddish version, you know my memory has been preserved.

No one visits me in my quarantine. There is no final scene where Brother Gao and Fang Feng don hazmat suits, and throwing caution to the wind, pat me on the shoulder and warm my hand and thus risk contracting a deadly strain of tuberculosis. No sentimental good-byes. One must die alone as one has only ever been. Alone. The bed sores alone could kill me. Plastic tubes crawl out of me and I smell plastic. Plastic will last five hundred years. The stuff is dynastic. I watch a hairy spider crawling out of a rusty seam in the ceiling tiles. I know this about dying: You spend your whole life convinced there is no afterlife, sure as there is no Bigfoot, but when the terror of that final end creeps closer, you wonder what is out there. Why am I afraid? I am so very afraid and so very sad to go to nothing and therefore sad about nothing. The EKG blips like a video game. I think of the '80s in America. I sweat hot and am cold. I see a strange doctor behind a glass wall. I see a woman with her arm shoved into a fur. I smell dirt on my digging snout.

I dream I am liberated by an army of college students, youthful faces, the truly beautiful people with ivory teeth and full lips, shining eyes and quick breath, while I lean over coughing. These are my students, not in fact but in spirit. They are my beautiful, ambitious clever pupils, now stronger than me.

In the glare of the sun, I keep hoping to see Vesuvius clambering over the rubbish in a pair of flimsy boots, or Queena tip-toeing through the jagged refuse. But the sun is very white and hot, blinding to the eyes, and I know that Vesuvius and Queena are dead—know this not because of spiritual divination but because the world is a mean place effected by passion and chaos, and it stands to reason that one of those two monsters has taken my girls.

There are many things hidden to me. I know the time but not the date. I know there is action in the streets but not the extent. I know there is a new Chairman of the Communist Party to replace the assassinated one, but I don't know his name. I am going to die today and I want to know the date of my death as one is allowed to know the date of his birth. It is a silly thing to waste what little energy I have on mundane historical records. I want to know how old I am, how long I have lived within these walls of time.

When I fall back into another period of rest and slip out of consciousness, and yet still feel myself holding to some center of gravity, to this "I" at the core, I dream that I am out in the plastics mine again with Xu Xuo and Fang, some of the other prisoners, a boy named Max from my third grade class, a girl named Julia from a summer camp on Crooked Lake, and some guards carrying a pry bar and another carrying a tool which in America is called a Pulaski and in Germany is called something else. The guard is Chinese, but he keeps saying, "In English we call this a Pulaski. Pulaski. Say it!" but I cannot speak. I can only understand. I stand there in the burning air terrified that the guard will hack into my side, causing a brown liquid to trickle out of the folds of my stinking body. Xu Xuo in that moment is naked, playing with his erect penis. Fang is ordering him to put his clothes on.

Just as I am about to be killed, there comes an army of young people, not my students exactly but exactly like my students, youthful and fresh. They are strong and beautiful and dressed in colorful Western clothes, every one of them taller than their parents and with good teeth.

They come in such great numbers over the fields of trash that they don't need weapons. The awful guard with the boil on his chin drops his Pulaski. Another tries to bury his plastic assault rifle under a pile of ancient roof tiles.

They come to liberate me.

They don't say, "We have come to liberate you!" or "You are free!" They say, "You have been of use. You have been of use!"

I don't know what language they speak because I don't hear particular words of a particular language. More, it is a kind of music that isn't music or language exactly but is incredibly precise.

Towards a free place they carry me to my death in an airplane, which they tell me is the first aircraft to fly over Europe, and when I say this is impossible and suggest they might earn a higher mark if they "police their logic," a pretty girl from Class #2 puts her finger to her lips and says, "Shh, Francis, you need rest. Just admire upon the beautiful world," but I cannot do this because I want to correct her grammar, only I cannot speak; it is just the sort of dreaming when you cannot will your body to move but desperately want to roll out of bed but cannot move but want to move, you must, you can't, you must. She says, "Admire upon the world" and I let the bad grammar stand, and laughing uncontrollably, let it wash over me like clean water and ask her to speak again, only I can't speak and yet she understands, says, "Francis, it's your special day. All you have to do is admire upon the world. But if you want to do one more thing, you may let me kiss you good night."

"No. My body is repulsive. Don't touch me, I'm disgusting."

"I will kiss your mind then," and she pecks me on the forehead and I finish my time here by gazing out the window as the plane banks, and the wing dipping, so that I can see the jagged earth and the spiny back of The Long Wall marching over the mountains. I seem to be heading in the path of the sun. Going higher. The wall far beneath me grows fainter and fainter and the final sensation isn't so much that I am losing sight of the wall but losing sight itself. Everything white.

June 3, says the nurse. Today is June 3.

"You are free," said the officer to the condemned man in the native tongue. The man did not believe it at first.

—Franz Kafka

Author's Note

Dozens of people allowed me to pump them for details that helped with this book. Kind people, you know who you are. *The Buchenwald Report*, by David Hackett, and Odd Nansen's *From Day to Day* were especially helpful for details related to Sachsenhausen. The Mao Zedong quote at the front of the book comes by way of Bao Tong.

Acknowledgements

I want to thank the Ettner, Chatz, Sheridan, and Murphy families for their friendship and kindness to my mother. I want to thank my students in China and America for their laughter and willingness to change. *Xie xie* to my colleagues in the PRC. Thanks to Chuck Robinson and Alice Acheson for their professional guidance. Another round for the boys up on Prozac Mountain, for their music and wisdom: Larry, Keith, Andy, and John—y'all are forever my brothers. To my songbirds, Arielle and Lindsay, may you harvest well. For all the good folks at Skagit Valley College, keep teaching to your passions. A wee bit of shame for never properly thanking my writing teachers, especially Erin McGraw, Tom Chiarella, David Klooster, Tracy Daugherty, and the late Ehud Havazelet. Thanks to my writer friends Daniél Chacón, Ed Miles, March Crimes, Daniel Raeburn, Christina Chiu, and Adrianne Harun. Thanks to Marco the drunk Italian, who magically gave me a boost of faith one night in Beijing. To Garrett Hongo and all the good folks at the University of Oregon Program in Creative Writing, thank you for giving me a chance back in the day. Which brings me to the heroes that pulled this manuscript out of a heap of submissions—Andrew Gifford and his team at Santa Fe Writers Project: especially Monica, Melanie, and Wendy. For the TFs, Jimmy, Marc, and Jack—the night never has to end. Special thanks to the Sargent family: Madeleine, John, Anne, Melanie, and the late, great Poppos. To my brothers and sisters, John, Anne, Trish, and Pete, thank you for loving me and for loving each other. Thank you to my late father, Jerome David O'Connell, for his love of music, fly-fishing, and family. A final kiss of gratitude for my mother, my daughter Amelia, and my superhero Julie.

About the Author

Winner of the Tobias Wolff Award in Fiction, Ted O'Connell is a writer and musician whose creative products have been featured in literary magazines, taverns, and music halls throughout the country. He plays mandolin with the Prozac Mountain Boys and guitar with The Scarlet Locomotive and has twice served as a visiting professor in China. Originally from the Chicago area, Mr. O'Connell lives in Bellingham, Washington with his wife and daughter.

Find the author on Instagram @writertedoconnell

Also from Santa Fe Writers Project

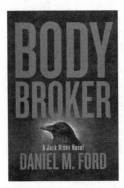

Body Broker *by Daniel M. Ford*

When a teenager disappears from an elite boarding school, local police throw the seemingly innocuous case to their neighborhood PI. Enter Jack Dixon: college dropout, ex-cop, and ex-cook. What should be a simple case quickly turns sour, pushing Jack into the path of Nordic biker cultists and vicious drug dealers. But the houseboat-dwelling PI is determined to find the truth—and the missing kid—even though his persistence leads him into a thorny tangle of drugs and violence that could rip his sleepy waterfront life apart.

Milk *by Simon Fruelund*

Conveyed without grandeur or pathos, the revelations in these minimalist stories demonstrate clearly and effectively Fruelund's gift of subtlety and nuance; like scenes from life, characters' dramas are played out in brief but brilliant flashes.

> *"This consistently beautiful book has a quietness that recalls the stark Danish countryside, the stories' primary setting."*
> — Publishers Weekly

Muscle Cars *by Stephen G. Eoannou*

A powerful journey through the humor, darkness, and neuroses of the modern American Everyman...

> *"Eoannou's debut collection is all—all—heart."*
> *—Brett Lott, author of* Jewel,
> *an Oprah Book Club Selection*

About Santa Fe Writers Project

SFWP is an independent press founded in 1998 that embraces a mission of artistic preservation, recognizing exciting new authors, and bringing out of print work back to the shelves.

Find us on Facebook, Twitter @sfwp, and at www.sfwp.com *sfwp)*